Thomas Seccombe

Lives of Twelve Bad Men

Thomas Seccombe

Lives of Twelve Bad Men

ISBN/EAN: 9783337412982

Printed in Europe, USA, Canada, Australia, Japan

Cover: Foto ©Andreas Hilbeck / pixelio.de

More available books at **www.hansebooks.com**

LIVES OF

TWELVE BAD MEN

ORIGINAL STUDIES OF EMINENT SCOUNDRELS BY VARIOUS HANDS EDITED BY THOMAS SECCOMBE

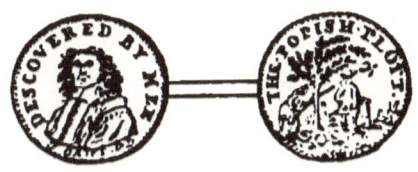

"Σοφοὶ μὲν πονηροὶ δέ."

London

T. FISHER UNWIN

PATERNOSTER SQUARE

MDCCCXCIV

TO THE MEMORY

OF

BARRY LYNDON, Esquire,

THESE MEMOIRS

ARE

PIOUSLY

DEDICATED

CONTENTS.

NOTES ON THE ILLUSTRATIONS.

PORTRAIT OF SIR EDWARD KELLEY   .   .   *to face* p. 38

This portrait is after a mezzotint by R. Cooper, and was originally executed for Baldwyn's edition of William Lilly's Autobiography, London, 1822. A note states that it was prefixed to Dr. Dee's "Book of Spirits," 1659, a work which it is not easy to identify. It certainly resembles the older portraits, one of which is given in Meric Casaubon's work. There is another portrait in the Museum Print-room, subscribed "Eduardvs Kellaevs celebrus Anglus et Chymiæ Peritissimus. Ex collectione Frederici Rothscholtzii."

PORTRAIT OF MATTHEW HOPKINS   .   .   *to face* p. 55

This curious woodcut forms the frontispiece to the witch-finder's "Discovery of Witches" (see p. 65). On one side sits Elizabeth Clark, who gives the names of her imps, and on the right is another witch, perhaps Helen Clark. It was reproduced in Caulfield's "Memoirs of Remarkable Persons," 1794, where it is described as "correctly copied from an extreme rare print in the collection of J. Bindley, Esq." It is similarly reproduced in the first volume of the *Anthologia Hibernica*. A rude portrait of Hopkins in a cuirass and a conical hat, as he is here represented, is prefixed to a reprint of his "Discovery" issued in 1838.

PORTRAIT OF JUDGE JEFFREYS   .   .   *to face* p. 67

There are two engravings in the British Museum from this fine portrait by Kneller—one by Isaac Oliver, the other by E. Cooper. Both, but especially the former, are extremely rare. It is uncertain whether the title was ever actually conferred (see p. 91). It has been seriously asserted that the titles "Earle of Flint," &c. (as reproduced at the foot of the portrait), were given satirically. Another fine portrait of the judge by Kneller was engraved by R. White, who executed our portrait of Titus Oates, in 1684.

JEFFREYS TAKEN AT WAPPING   .   .   *to face* p. 92

The original of this plate, dated December 12, 1688, and described as engraved for the "Devil's Broker," represents the Lord Chancellor surrounded by a crowd of persons, who are conducting him to a place of safe keeping, and, in the meantime, not sparing their reproaches. It is worth noting that his eyebrows are not shaved off, as Reresby states them to have been, as a means of disguise. On the right, above, is Father Petre, and at the foot is the devil issuing, amid flames, from the earth, and clawing a Jesuit's head. This print was very popular both in England and the Netherlands.

PORTRAIT OF TITUS OATES   .   .   *to face* p. 95

This portrait of the perjurer, drawn and engraved by R. White, was executed in 1679, when Titus was at the zenith of his popularity. The verses below are fitter for reproduction than the scurrilities appended to the uncomplimentary portraits of him "peeping through a two-inch board," or as "Oats well thresh't," which became the fashion in 1685 :—

> "Behold the Chief and Happy Instrument,
> Whom Providence for Britain's safety sent.
> Westminster (?) taught him, Cambridge bred him, then
> Left him instead of books to study Men.
> And these he studied with so true an Art,
> As deeply div'd into the very Heart
> Of Foul Conspiracy. . . . . "

This is the most authentic portrait, though it is perhaps surpassed in interest by another, entitled "Bob Ferguson ; or, the Raree Shew of Mamamouchee Mufty." This in reality represents Oates, his head-dress being half a Jesuit's cap, half a Turk's turban. He carries a Protestant flail in his right hand ; on his left side he wears a loose cloak. The title is a reference to the notorious plotter with whom Oates is compared. Mamamouchi (*homme habillé à la Turque*) Mufti are two cant words borrowed from the ballet in Molière's *Bourgeois Gentilhomme.* The lines below are rich in choice allusions to the more outlandish traits in Oates's character. Other portraits of him are numerous.

THE DEVIL, TITUS OATES, AND THE POPE . *to face* p. 117

This print, which was probably published in 1678, explains itself. The partnership between those two oft-quoted functionaries, the devil and the pope, forms the subject of numerous rhymes and pictures at this period. A woodcut of "The Plot first hatched at Rome by the Pope and the Cardinalls " forms the ace in the pack of playing-cards already alluded to. The devil is here represented crouching under a table at which the pope and cardinals are sitting. Another broadside, with a typical cut, was entitled, "London's Drollery ; or, the Love and Kindness between the Pope and the Devil " ; and in a similar vein were conceived "A Nest of Nunne's Eggs," "Rome's Hunting Match for Three Kingdoms," and "The Pope Haunted with Ghosts."

OATES, HIS DEGREES . . . . *to face* p. 142

This is one of a large number of satires upon Oates, examples of which are almost as numerous as the laudatory productions. The crushed eggs on the pillory are prophetic only of the artist's hopes, the mezzotint having been published two days before Oates's actual punishment. The devil perched upon the gallows behind looks wistfully at his pupil, and dangles a balter over his head.

THE BEAUTIFULL SIMONE . . . *to face* p. 155

This portrait of Lovat in female attire refers to the report current at the time that he was taken disguised as an old woman, and some added that he was found spinning and smoking a short pipe (see *Westminster Journal,* June 28, 1746). The foundation for the myth is confined to the fact that Simon's hiding-place in the hollow of a tree was discovered owing to the protrusion of a few of the many yards of flannel in which his body was swathed.

This admirable contemporary print is entitled, "A Perspective View of Westminster Hall with both Houses of Parliament Assembled on the Tryal of Simon, Lord Lovat." Subjoined is a key to the figures. A—Speaker, B—Members of House of Commons, C—Other members, D—Managers for the House of Commons, E—The Managers' Clerks, F—Lord Lovat, G—Witness giving evidence, H—Prisoner's counsel, K—King's box, L—Prince of Wales's box, M—Duke of Cumberland and other members of the Royal Family, N—The box where Princess Amelia sat during the trial, O—Foreign Ambassadors, P—Peeresses, T—Earl of Orford's gallery. The most important numbers are :—1—The King's Chair, 5—The Lord High Steward, 6—The two archbishops, 7—The bishops, 8, 9—Dukes and barons, 10—Earls and viscounts, 14—The judges, 15—Serjeant at the Mace, 16—Lord High Steward's Purse-bearer, 17—Clerks belonging to the House of Lords. The scaffoldings, we are particularly informed, were hung with red bays, except where the House of Commons sat, and that portion was covered with green bays.

This mezzotint of "Colonel Francisco," with his thumbs tied, which was executed in 1730, is fully described in the text (p. 213). Other portraits in the Print-room at the British Museum are, "To the glory of Colonel Don Francisco upon his delivery out of gaol," and "Colonel Charteris contemplating the Venus of Titian."

The rough woodcut from which this is taken is probably the only contemporary representation of the Thief-taker in existence.

This, which is by far the most elaborate of the portraits of Maclaine, is reproduced in Caulfield's "Memoirs of Remarkable Persons." The face bears a decided resemblance to that of the portraits prefixed to the "Contemporary Lives," which are mentioned in the Appendix of Authorities. The names of both the original artist and the engraver are unknown.

The number of these portraits and illustrations of the close of Maclaine's career testify to the extraordinary interest which was excited at the time by this very unattractive rogue. Another engraving in the Museum represents him in Newgate surrounded by members of the fair sex, who are making a liberal use of their pocket-handkerchiefs. It is entitled, "Newgate's Lamentation ; or, the Ladys last farewell of Maclean." Lady Caroline Petersham, afterwards Countess of Harrington, who is here depicted speaking on the outlaw's behalf, was satirised in some other engravings, of which we have not been able to find any trace. According to the advertisements in the contemporary papers, she was portrayed, with Miss Ashe, as one of Maclaine's "doxies," and also figured in "The presentation of the purse of gold to Maclean by the subscribers."

This likeness of Fitzgerald, which was originally engraved for the *Monthly Mirror*, has been said to exhibit great duplicity. Investigation has revealed the melancholy fact that the same block has done duty both for the duellist and for the actor, Stephen Kemble. As, however, no other portrait of Fitzgerald is known to exist, it would be rash to deny to this one the merit of resemblance.

For permission to use this illustration from Superintendent Hare's book, "The Last of the Bushrangers," we are indebted to the courtesy of Messrs. Hurst and Blackett. A full description of the armour depicted will be found in the text.

For information respecting the authorities used in the compilation of the Twelve Lives, the reader is referred to the Appendix of Authorities at the end of the volume.

PREFACE.

THE practice of whitewashing has proved as injurious to biography as the worst taint of bigotry or partisanship in the pages of history. Of course there are no really bad men extant in England at the present day, so that the process might naturally be expected to be but little in demand. But many picturesque figures of the past have undergone this philistine disfigurement. Richard III., Henry VIII., Bloody Mary, and Oliver Cromwell, have all been rehabilitated, and the last, at least, demonstrated to be much nearer akin to a saint than a sinner. The very pirates of romance, men such as Sir Henry Morgan and Captain Kyd, have been proved to be no worse than they need have been; and as for literary characters, any unamiable traits that might have been attributed to certain members of that saintly band have long since been shown to be misinterpreted virtues. The villain has been banished to the detective story, and every deviation from the path of mere collective morality is explained by either artistic temperament or psychological eccentricity. The tendency has gone so far that one is led to ask oneself, not without the gravest apprehension, " Is there, then, no evidence to be found of extreme depravity ? " For the wholesale elimination of the utter villain from history could hardly be regarded save in the light of an æsthetic calamity. Fortunately for lovers of the picturesque, as the result of careful inquiry, a few choice spirits have been found whose robust vices have defied the insidious influence of research : men whom it would certainly be premature to make any attempt at whitewashing. This work, then, avows as its serious object the rehabilitation of the bad man in his native badness.

Society is apt to flatter itself that exceptional talents are denied to persons who indulge in the worst forms of depravity. But it can hardly be denied that some of the individuals whose exploits we have recorded, from materials which have hitherto been often completely unexplored, were men of really great ability. All of them attained to eminence in ill-doing, and if they had devoted their energies to more legitimate pursuits, would doubtless have long since found authoritative biographers. "An honest man," as Schiller says, "may be formed of windle-straws, but to make a rogue you *must* have grist."

Our first principle being the exclusion of other than unmitigated miscreants, the process of selection, though far from easy, was much simplified. To turn, albeit regretfully, from palæontological evidences of villainy was imperative. History possesses a fine mammoth criminal in King John, but the deposits in which are to be found the records of his activity are unsavoury with age, difficult of exploration, and incapable of exact exposition. The bad men of modern Britain exhaust our scheme, and ample material has been found without extending the rake to any scandal older than Queen Elizabeth. So, too, the temptation to paradox has been sternly resisted, and the task of resolving such compound characters as those of Lord Verulam and John Churchill, Eugene Aram and Leonard Macnally, has been left to the perennial ingenuity of essayists less single-minded and less modest than ourselves.

A natural succession of precedents led us almost insensibly to fix upon twelve as the number of subjects; and if, as has been affirmed, "the phrase *a bad man* has rather degenerated in England," let it be our worthy endeavour, by associating it with such men as Titus Oates and Jonathan Wild and Thomas Griffiths Wainewright, to restore to a really expressive and comprehensive term as much as possible of its native vigour. As biography, like gossip, is rather apt to be spoiled by moralising, this corroding element has as far as possible been eliminated. Nevertheless, and in case any serious reader, after a perusal of the book, should entertain any doubts as to its precise ethical drift, we are free to maintain with the utmost sincerity that, since "George Barnwell" has been denied to the London prentices, no narratives of life and adventure have appeared more commendably moral in tendency than these; and they are frankly and freely suggested as a source whence earnest and improving divines may point their morals and enliven their pulpits. That their researches have led the writers of this volume into some exceedingly curious byways of social history is a fact which, it is trusted, will be patent to the general reader no less than to the advocates of social purity and to those specially interested in antiquarian matters.

Our contents will be found to exhibit a striking diversity in the manner of the crime as well as in the historic period and status of the criminal. Our unifying principle is pre-eminence in ill-doing. Our fit protagonist is Bothwell, a spacious villain of the bloody, bold, and resolute type. In piquant contrast figures the vulpine alchemist, Sir Edward Kelley, a rival to Galeotti in pretension, to Cagliostro in cunning, and to Casanova in profligacy. The reigns of the o'erwise author of "Dœmonologie . . . divided into Three Bookes" and his successor are appropriately represented by Matthew Hopkins, the witch-pricker; then comes a portrait of Judge Jeffreys, cramoisie from bullying witnesses adverse to the Crown, whose career (in spite of attempts to powder his visage to a semblance of refinement) remains a standing reproach to judicial history, and in its endowment with lethal properties is only approached by that of his monstrous contemporary, that upas-tree of his period, Titus Oates. The era of political vicissitudes and of the Vicar of Bray is represented by yet another historical personage, the double-faced old Jacobite fox, Simon Fraser, Lord Lovat. Him follows Colonel Francis Charteris, a valuable corrective to erroneous notions respecting the teacup times of Queen Anne, who possesses, moreover, the peculiar interest that attaches to vice-specialists. The professional rascality of the eighteenth century is represented by that weevil among criminals, Jonathan Wild, and by James Maclaine, a robber whose fame has become clouded, but in whom the absence of redeeming qualities is really noticeable. The possibility of another injustice to old Ireland has been obviated by the selection of Fighting Fitzgerald from among a mob of meritorious countrymen and contemporaries. England reasserts its supremacy with the pseudo-Italianate scoundrel, Thomas Griffiths Wainewright, poisoner and precioso; and the tale is suitably completed by that too enterprising colonial, Ned Kelly, the bushranger. The picturesque achievements of this last are worthy of the best traditions, and afford welcome refutation to the charge of nineteenth-century tameness or degeneracy.

Each criminal has been given in charge of a competent and responsible person, not so much for purposes of dissection as of description *ad vivum*. If any of their crime-stained stories prove entertaining, it is well. But poverty of crime has in no case been atoned for by a wealth of biographical imagination. The following memoirs are in every case the outcome of genuine research among contemporary records, combined with reference to the most authentic of subsequent sources. So the chief authorities are given for each memoir, though a pious profusion of sepulchral stumbling-blocks—such as are interpolated references—has been carefully avoided. It has been attempted, in fine, to dissociate accuracy from its frequent concomitant, deadness; and, in the words of the worthy Lawrence Eachard, to represent culpable lives and actions "with all simplicity and fidelity, as well as all freedom and decency."

163, HOLLAND ROAD, W.
    April 5, 1894.

EARL OF BOTHWELL.

(1536–1578.)

" A race of wicked acts
Shall flow out of my anger, and o'erspread
The world's wide face, which no posterity
Shall e'er approve, nor yet keep silent."
SEJANUS.

THE frenzies which issued from the Silver Casket still
show, at the remove of three centuries, a power for
havoc of the patriotic heart and critical brain which would
do credit to a second Pandora. We praise and damn Queen
Mary with the earnestness of a sixteenth-century Scot ; and
research is powerless to stay the eternal squabble of sentiment. An earnest Mariolater lately announced that his
beautiful quarto would "finally dispose" of the " calumnies
of hostile historians," but this confidence in an ending of the
matter was but part of the critical madness. One topic,
however, remains behind, about which we do not quarrel overmuch. The character of the man who shaped the destinies
of Mary, who raised the mystery we cannot solve, has passed
down to us and been accepted with an unanimity which is a
relief. Bothwell in all the fairy books of this thrilling period
is the bold bad man ; to dispel which pleasant fancy would
be unseemly. Though some have made him ugly, as others
have found Mary divinely fair, we may, for peace's sake, give
him the credit of goodly features: a well-favoured villain may
better the melodrama. Meanwhile, as the sanely generous

biographer has not yet found him out an honest man seeking some principle of good by strange paths, we can hurt no feelings, and may not be charged with fanaticism, if we retell in brief the story of his boldness and his badness.

I.

James Hepburn's father, Earl Patrick, gave him haughtiness and a mind for ambitious schemes. From his mother Agnes, daughter of Lord Henry Sinclair, the "fader of bookis and lare" of the poet Gawin Douglas, he might have drawn some gentler inspiration, but the roving nature of the Sinclairs, which drove them to seek honour in Norway and the East, sorted more readily with the spirit of the Hepburns. Thus fittingly endowed for his future lordship in wild Liddesdale he passed to Spynie Castle, probably before his father's divorce in 1543, to spend his early years with his kinsman Patrick, Bishop of Moray. But the discipline was easy,—a round of feasting and merry tales and of amours which were neither episcopal nor Platonic. Young Hepburn must have succumbed to the delights of Spynie had he not felt the stir of doing in his blood ; but the lessons of his reverend kinsman were not and could not be forgotten. There is reason to believe, from the evidence of some letters, that his intellectual education had been good. Some of his books, on mathematics and the art of war, have been preserved, but they prove little beyond his good taste in binding. He lived too rapidly to be a student, and the exploits and subtleties of his later years do not suggest the teaching of Valturin or Sextus Julius.

On his father's death in 1556 he became fourth Earl of Bothwell and succeeded by right to the offices of Lord High Admiral of the kingdom, Sheriff of Edinburgh, Haddington, and Berwick, Bailie of Lauderdale, and Keeper of the castles of Hailes and Crichton,—thereby winning a position in men's eyes and in actual power scarcely inferior to that of the royal house of Hamilton. Earl Patrick had been reconciled to Mary of Guise, the Regent, some years before his death; and his son gave early proof of his loyalty to her party of French sympathies by signing, on December 14, 1577, the act constituting commissioners for the betrothal of the young Queen to the Dauphin. Ere the year was out England was involved in the Franco-Spanish strife, and so Scotland, with a Guise for ruler, could not be idle. It was the old game of checkmate on the Borders, with moss-troopers for pawns and a castle or two to be taken. The Scottish nobility, hating the French aliens in their midst rather than dreading broken crowns, refused the Regent's bidding; but young Bothwell was eager to ride with his Liddesdale vassals into England. In after years he cherished the memory of his boyish zeal, not only for the 'irreparable damage' which he had done, but because it was the burgeon of his lifelong hatred of England and her Scottish partisans.

On the accession of Elizabeth and by the Treaty of Cateau-Cambresis Scottish politics seemed to become more placid, and Border troubles were settled by commissioners of both nations, among them being Bothwell, now Lieutenant-General of the Scots Marches, with " the haill charge alsweill to defend as to assayle." But it was only a cessation of wild soldiering in the borderlands, for Elizabeth, like her father, would not let pass opportunities given by the dissensions in the North, now more embittered in the name of religion. In her wisdom she saw more hope of havoc among the wretched Scots nobility from a Sadler and his gold than from a Belted Will and his rough-riders. Bothwell, though professing the Reformed doctrine with such earnestness as he could, kept by the Regent; but he longed for adventure in her cause, to assail rather than to defend, and he had not long to wait. Having got word that the Laird of Ormiston was riding from Berwick with a goodly bribe for the Lords of Congregation, he swooped down on him by the flank of Dunpender Law in East Lothian, and carried the poor man and his money-bags to his castle at Crichton by " the sluggish mazes of the Tyne." The Lords liked ill this unfriendly act, for Bothwell had sent but three days before for a safe-conduct, and had hinted, if not promised, that he would do their schemes no harm. Thereupon Lord James Stuart, afterwards Earl of Murray, and the Earl of

Arran hurried off with troops and artillery to Crichton, to find that the young scamp had fled, and, grievous to tell, had not forgotten the Dunpender booty. He laughed at their summons to surrender it, and, when he heard that in revenge they had played wantonly with his goodly halls, sent a cartel to Arran to meet him before French and Scots. "First," replied the angry Earl, "when ye may have won back the name of an honest man, which by your last exploit you have lost, I shall be ready to give you satisfaction which is meet; but not before Frenchmen, to whom you assign the precedence over Scotsmen, for there is no Frenchman in this kingdom with whose judgment I will have anything to do." Bothwell had no need of such jibes to increase his sympathy with French policy. If he had to flee from Linlithgow, he was willing to undertake the keeping of Stirling for the Regent. When, despite the French success at Leith, matters looked serious, he was chosen as an emissary to seek aid at the French Court. He fretted at Crichton till his departure, telling his liege-lady that he was desirous "to be at all tymis in the roum quhair service occurris", but as he lacked "the commoditi thairto" and had not "hasti aspirans thairof" he required her aid by "vrytings", which meant money credit as well as credentials to the French Court. The sweet recollection of the Ormiston pocket-money would not clear the Paris bills of an ambassador. The sudden death of Mary of Guise hastened his mission, and, after some uncertain movements north of the Forth, he effected his escape in the autumn of 1560, and landed in Denmark.

He journeyed to Paris in good style, part of the way under the friendly escort of the Danish King; not assuredly in breathless haste, for he found time to dally with one Ann Throndssön, a noble Norwegian with a dowry of 40,000 dollars. The lady, like her namesake of the ballad, had cause to make moan at his sugared words, for he left her in the Netherlands with no means of maintenance or return except the credit which her jewels brought. At Paris he could not effect anything for his party in Scotland, for the plot of Amboise had compelled Guise's thoughts homewards; but he received a welcome pension of 600 crowns, and, from the young Queen of Scots, the honour of a commission to summon a Scottish Parliament. To Throckmorton, the English ambassador, he appeared to be a "vainglorious, rash, and hazardous young man," on whom "it were meet for his adversaries to have an eye" and whom they must "keep short,"—an appreciation of the man which, if not exhaustive, was as true as it is interesting.

Bothwell arrived in Scotland, in February, 1561, with poor prospects of political stir. He may have been again in France for a time; at all events he was back in Edinburgh in that autumn when Mary, doubly widowed, returned with something of a sad heart to the land of her birth. Her earliest endeavour was for peace among her quarrelsome councillors and nobles. Bothwell and his old friends of Dunpender and Crichton were ordered to forget their rancour, or, at least, the shows of it. But she had not such ability to put down feuds as her son was to have in his Scotland, and circumstance was not so kindly. Privy Councillor Bothwell was among the first to disobey. There was some trouble at the house of a 'respectable' merchant, of the stuff of which city magistrates are made, about his buxom daughter-in-law Alison, who had the credit of an amour with Arran. Bothwell, with his boon companion the Marquis D'Albeuf and the Prior of Coldingham, had, in an access of rowdiness, endeavoured to woo the young lady by breaking down her guardian's doors at dead of night. It was a horrid scandal, the more so as the Assembly was in session. The wrath of the godly and peaceable found its expression in a protest by the 'Professors of Christ's Evangel.' The Hamiltons, with that love of justice which attacked noble houses with the waywardness and suddenness of some unknown distemper, saw fit to speak loudly of the offence, and managed matters so to their liking that a goodly riot was raised. The amorous French ambassador, whom "scarce ten men could hold," was with difficulty shut within the Abbey, and Bothwell was only stayed in his hurry from his lodging by the unambiguous threats of the Master of Maxwell and his following. It was possible to Mary to pardon the night-doings of an uncle from Paris, but Bothwell's offence could not be overlooked. So he was ordered to leave the capital, and that despite some endeavour to be reconciled by the help of John Knox. His peaceful intentions towards Arran and his friends were but short-lived, for one day he came across the Laird of Ormiston and his party a-hunting, and for a second time carried off a Cockburn to Crichton. Again was appeal made to Knox, and the preacher, sick of these unseemly bickerings among the men of Reform, did his best to make peace. The Earl went so far as to " lament his formare inordinate lyef," and was induced by Knox's politic argument to submit his differences with Cockburn to Arran, and thereafter to meet Arran himself. They met at the Hamilton Lodging by the Kirk-o'-Field, were lectured by the peacemaker, and then chopped hands and embraced. Next morning they were still friendly enough and pious enough to go together to hear a sermon. So ended the little farce at the Kirk-o'-Field ; the heavy tragedy was to follow.

Unfortunately for Bothwell's peaceful mood, Arran's mind became unhinged. The former had gone, shortly after the reconciliation, on a visit to Lord Hamilton at Kinneil, and his host's son, suddenly filled with wild imaginings as to its purport, rode off in a frenzy to the Court at Falkland, and told a pretty tale of treachery, of the threatened abduction of the Queen, and of the despatch of her hated step-brother James. When Bothwell arrived at Falkland he was put in durance, for, though the Lord James knew Arran to be mad, and could get little proof, if any, of Bothwell's guilt, it was an opportunity of personal revenge too good to lose. Bothwell was sent to St. Andrews, and, after six weeks, to Edinburgh Castle. But his foe had his troubles in plenty, none the fewer since Huntly had been advanced to the chancellorship. It required but another causey squabble to set parties by the ears and to raise a rebellion in the country of the Gordons. Bothwell heard from his prison window the sough of the shouting and the sword-clatter of the Ogilvie and Gordon retainers, and, like a chained dog, chafed at his enforced absence,—the more angrily, as greater encounters would surely follow. He succeeded in breaking ward, not improbably by a daring descent from his window, though some gossips had it that he got easy passage by the gates. He fled to his Border castle of the Hermitage. If, as Knox says, his common residence was in Lothian, he certainly showed that he was far from panic-stricken. But to little purpose, for all hope of resistance fell by the defeat and death of Huntly and the imprisonment of his son. Bothwell tells us in his autobiography, with a strange twist in the sequence of facts, how his horror of "that cruel murder" and his desire to know how he stood with the Queen prompted him to leave the Castle of Edinburgh. "Being free," he adds, "I resolved to go to France by sea,"—a laconic reference to his sorry plight before his escape in a small vessel from North Berwick.

His journey 'by sea' was somewhat tedious. A storm drove his little ship on the rocks of Holy Island, and the runaway, despite some "shows of friendship from Englishmen, such as he should not have expected,"—so runs the ingenuous story,—was soon after pulled ignominiously out of bed near Berwick, and lodged in Tynemouth Castle. There he remained till the triumphant Murray convinced Elizabeth that such an unruly thwarter of English policy should be put in safer ward. Strange fears distracted the mind of the unfriendly Randolph, the English agent, when he heard of this proposal. "I beseech your Grace," he writes to Cecil, "send him where you will, only not to Dover Castle, not so much for fear of my aged mother, but my sister is young and has many daughters." The anxious Englishman had perhaps just heard that poor Ann Throndssön had turned up in Scotland to make plaint about her absent lover, and had received but the courtesy of a passport to her native land. Early in 1564 Mary, urged, it is said, by his mother, the Lady of Morham, but perhaps by the politic friendliness of Lethington, requested that he should have liberty to pass whither he pleased. So Bothwell, as he himself says, "continued his design of making journey to France," and did it with such courteous despatch that Randolph relapsed into serenity about the dovecot at the ferry.

Bothwell was well received by the Most Christian King, and, as before, enjoyed his bounty,—though there is reason to doubt his marginal boast that he was made Captain of the Scottish Guard. Exile and inaction, however, were truly to his quick bosom a hell: he was tired of breathing hatred of his enemies across the Channel : intrigue, even in Paris, unless a helpmate to ambition, was poor pleasure. Thus pressed, he returned secretly to Scotland in the spring of 1565. It was a bit of dare-devilry, for Murray was stronger than ever. He found his way to his Border castle, and was resolved to enjoy as long as he might the recreation of defiant lordship amid his unruly retainers. His arrival gave new life to the broken men of Lidlesdale. There was still no lack of opportunity for wild adventure, for harrying and burning, nor would there be for fifty years to come ; but there was now no longer any hope of professional recognition by rival chancellors. The calling had reached a painful state of disrepute. There was no romance about the doings of Hab-o'-the-Shaws and his friends ; and a rhyming sexagenarian wrote of them as " the thievis of Liddisdail." On Bothwell's appearance in 1561 these ruffians had taken encouragement, and had defied a Warden's endeavour to get redress at the Hermitage ; on his arrest in 1563 the Borders were threatened with their revenge but now, with their high-born desperado in their midst, the good old times seemed to return. He irritated more than Murray, for the number of the vassals which he kept about him was large, and, as he was ever impecunious, he must reward them at the expense of honest folks. Randolph, in bitterness of spirit, foresaw great disorders from this mischief-maker, and the English Warden, Lord Bedford, though well accompanied, was afraid to move about " because Bothwell was with such a rout of thieves and lawless people so near." Murray could not afford to be unheedful, and importuned the Queen for his overthrow; but Mary told him that she could not hate one who had done her service. In the end Murray succeeded in obtaining a summons for his appearance on the old charges of conspiracy at Kinneil and breaking of ward. This, it appears, was done by Mary's advice, though there were suspicions in the minds of some that she favoured his misrule as an antidote to the hateful ascendancy of her step-brother. Bothwell promised to appear, but, when the day came, and with it rumours of the arrival of Murray and Argyll with a large retinue, he pondered on his prospects before this armed assize, and, pondering, sent the Laird of Riccarton to protest his innocence. His absence was, after the manner of the law-courts, construed as proof of guilt; but nothing further was done, Mary herself forbidding the sentence of outlawry which his rivals had demanded. Meanwhile Bothwell had again found his way to North Berwick, and was on the high seas towards France when the Court was sitting. Once more to fret in exile; but opportunity was at hand.

The story of Mary's correspondence with Elizabeth, and of her resolve to marry Darnley; the consummation of her desire; the trouble which ensued from Knox and his friends on the score of religion, and from Murray because of thwarted ambition; Mary's energetic suppression of the rising,—these are matters of common knowledge. Her position had, however, to be strengthened and secured, and she was astute enough to recall the man who had already done her service, and who would thwart her kinsman with all the thoroughness of unexpected power and personal hatred. Her husband was a pretty thing, but Bothwell was better when storms had to be stilled, or stirred. Elizabeth felt this when she wrote to Cecil: " Yt is wyshed if theie (Bothwell and Seton) do arryve in Englande that theie myghte be putt in good suerty for a tyme to passe their tyme ther." But Bothwell had no mind for another holiday in England, as Captain Wilson, Elizabeth's agent, found to his chagrin at Flushing. This worthy had done his best to intercept him, but, by a daring dash under sail and oars, Bothwell's two small vessels escaped the shots of the English craft, and sped without further impediment till they reached, on September 17, 1565, the Scottish coast at Eyemouth. His breaking of ward was forgiven, his honours restored, and he was off with Mary to the South in the wake of the fugitive Murray. " I was ordered," he says, " to pursue the said Earl of Murray out of the kingdom of Scotland into England ; which I did." Quickly done, and briefly told. Fortune's wheel had gone round. Murray was in exile, and the lawless Lord of Liddesdale, now Warden of the Marches, watched the highways and fords with the Queen's horse and foot.

II.

During the lull which followed on his acquisition of power, Bothwell, now in his thirtieth year, found time to marry. It was not the commonplace ' settling down ' of the tired reveller. He had, like all first-water villains, his fits of horror at his past " inordinat lyf ", but he was too restless and had too much on hand to uphold the doctrine of orthodox sobriety. His marriage with Jean Gordon, sister of his party-friend, the Earl of Huntly, was primarily to strengthen his political position. The union was by the express counsel of the Queen ; and Huntly was a good ally to keep. As yet there is no evidence whatever that he was meditating a more ambitious move, and no proof that it was suggested to him. He still humoured the Reformers by refusing, contrary to the Queen's wish, to be married during mass ; but whether he posed as Protestant by conviction, or by policy, or by obstructive indifference, it would indeed be hard to say.

The marriage took place in the Abbey Kirk of Holyrood on February 24, 1565-6, and the royal household honoured the occasion by holding high festivity for several days.

> " Lord Love went Maying,
> Where Time was playing,
> In light hands weighing
> Light hearts with sad."

Light hearts mostly then ; but in little less than a week confusion and horror, and a miserable Italian foully done to death. It was an ominous day for Bothwell, the early shadow of his darker future, and at a time when his heart was freest from guile. Darnley's insane fit of jealousy, his Judas kiss, and then Ruthven's cold steel aroused, perhaps completed, that Queen's hatred from which sprang the darker evil of our tale.

> "You have taught me worthier wisdom than words ;
> And I will lay it up against my heart."

Bothwell's first impulse in that bloody hour was to arms and to his Queen, but the sight of superior numbers and the threats of Morton cooled his ardour. He resolved on immediate flight, and with one or two companions escaped with difficulty by a back window. He did not rest till he found shelter in his castle at Crichton. "Had we not escaped," he moralises, "we should not have been better treated than Riccio." Now that he had a free hand, his chief thought was to deliver her Majesty from her rough keepers, and to this end he schemed with Huntly. They were prepared to try the hazard of ropes over the palace walls, but Darnley's flighty spirit and lack of nerve made such endeavour unnecessary. After interviews with the rebel lords, including Murray who had well timed his return from exile, the wretched pair left Holyrood about midnight, with poor accompaniment, and arrived in the early morning, after a stiff canter, at the Castle of Dunbar. Safety brought revived spirits, and the call to arms went forth. The first to arrive was Bothwell at the head of a goodly troop of vassals.

Mary had ever found Bothwell loyal, even in her greatest straits. She had liked him for his dash and spirit. What wonder that she came to like him more, under the constant fret of a worthless consort growing daily more petulant and unsympathetic !

> "How fairer is this warrior face, and eyes
> With the iron light of battle in them left
> As the after-fire of sunset left in heaven
> When the sun sinks, than any fool's face made
> Of smiles and courtly colour."

And what wonder, too, that Bothwell, though loyal, yet

ambitious, cunning, and daring, would seek to better the opportunities which might turn liking into loving! From the hour of Mary's triumphant return to her capital his influence grew. In worldly wealth he had his reward,—the rich benefices of Melrose, Haddington, and Newbattle, a goodly slice of the patrimony of the Earl of March, but, chief of all, the Castle of Dunbar, so comfortably near his own Lothian towers. The torment of an empty purse was at last removed. He boasts not a little of the favour and access which he enjoyed at Court, and tells with conscious pride that he determined to live peaceably with his neighbours, and not to think of "vengeance or quarrel" on account of the imprisonment and exile which he had endured. He was wise enough to assume the manner of the dove, and to help Knox to put to rights the untoward confusion which had begun to vex the party of Reform; so amiable indeed as to befriend the Laird of Ormiston. Small punishment was eked out by Mary; and even Murray was pardoned. After a month's easy exile in Argyll, the hated step-brother banquetted in the castle with the Queen and Bothwell and Huntly. Nothing embarrasses and weakens opponents so much as the show of unexpected lenity. There were courtesies to spare, even for them, so long as Darnley played the fool.

In the autumn of 1566 Bothwell retired from Edinburgh to his wardenry in the South, to lay by the heels some of his erst friends of Liddesdale for Mary's coming justice-eyre at Jedburgh. During one of his sallies from the Hermitage he strayed from his men and fell in the way of the renowned freebooter John-o'-the-Park. Bothwell, with that severe official manner which was proper, refused a private understanding; which not pleasing outlaw Elliot, there resulted a vigorous give-and-take with pistol, sword, and dagger. Law had a narrow triumph. John dragged himself off to an early death on a knoll near by; Bothwell, perilously wounded, lay till his men came up. He was carried to his castle gate, but entrance was refused by some unruly prisoners, who had made themselves masters, till the Warden had promised to make suit for their lives. On the eighth

day of his sickness, when his wounds were healing, he was
visited by Mary. She had ridden all the way from Jedburgh,
a good twenty miles and a rough road. Folks talked much
of this tender courtesy. Was it regard for the serviceable
Warden, or the pleasing young man? She had ridden hard,—
the morrow's fever told how hard: was it to escape the
roving moss-troopers, or to hurry to "give him comfort,"
to talk of the hanging of Armstrongs and Elliots, or to
know how it really fared with her friend? Answer it as we
may, and infer from it as little as we can, it remains a
pretty episode. Of its effect on Bothwell we need not
have a doubt. Ambition, ever willing to be prompted,
would readily build a future on past success. If the
"mass of writings" which came from Jedburgh were
but political confidences or assize-reports, he could at
least read between the lines. He had opportunity, ere
long, at his castle of Dunbar, to test the truth of his interpretation.

At Craigmillar we hear the first whisperings of wishes and
schemes. Mary appeared to Du Croc to be ill at ease. "I
do assure you," he wrote, "she is not at all well; and I do
believe the principal part of her disease to consist of a deep
grief and sorrow; nor does it seem possible to make her
forget the same. Still she repeats these words, 'I could
wish to be dead.' We know very well that the injury she
received is exceeding great, and her Majesty will never
forget it." Lethington guided the counsels of the fretful
lords about her, and in the end spoke for them to her about
her consort. He did not hesitate to suggest divorce. Mary
flinched, lest thereby her infant's future might be imperilled;
but Bothwell, pleased for once with the drift of the Chame-
leon's argument, joined in with the pretty story how he, the
son of divorced parents, had not lost his heritage nor his
sovereign's favour. They reasoned on, and Lethington
waxed bolder; his friends would "find the means", and
Murray would "look through his fingers" at their doings.
"Madam," by way of peroration, "let us guide the
matter amongst us, and your Grace shall see nothing
but good, and approved by Parliament." If as yet it was

but of divorce that they had thought, in a few days they had made up their minds that the "young fool" should be "put off by one way or another," and more, that "whosoever suld tak the deid in hand, or do it, they suld defend and fortify it as themselves." Thereafter Bothwell had communication with the exiled lords. On Christmas Eve Mary yielded to the importunities, first urged at Craigmillar, and bade them return. In three weeks' time Bothwell, after a brief visit to the South for some practice of authority among the brawling Borderers, met the returned Morton at Whittinghame, and urged prompt action. His mysterious statement that the Queen "would have it to be done" was perhaps begotten of his own eagerness; at any rate, Morton would not be joint conspirator till he had written proof. Preparations went on, and Bothwell a second time (February 7th) sought Morton's aid. Again a cautious refusal. Bothwell had resolved "to tak the deid in hand." For the rest, his laconic "which I did" is the epitome; but how he did it he left history to say.

In the evening of the last day of January, 1567, Darnley and Mary were met by Bothwell beyond the western gates of the capital. The Queen had gone to Crookston, near Glasgow, to visit her husband in his convalescence,—a show of reconciliation which caused wonder to many who had heard of his conduct at Stirling. The sick man was not taken to Holyrood, "through fear," says our auto-biographer, "of endangering the health of Queen and infant." There was a subtle inconsistency in sending him, on the plea of infection, to the house near the Kirk-o'-Field, and fitting up a bed for the Queen in an adjoining room, as there was in putting him, on the plea of "helsumnes of air", in a botched-up ruin in a slum of beggars' cottages and rank-grown graves. The separation, which was necessary to Mary alone, might have been easily obtained in the palace, but the house at Kirk-o'-Field could be better spared for the practice of Bothwell's dark magic. From Holyrood came silk cushions and tapestries which had been plundered at Corrichie; the sick-bed was hung with violet velvet and covered with blue taffeta,—kindly courtesies, like our favours and gift of blessings on the mornings of our acts of justice.

For ten days life at Holyrood held on in its wonted gaiety, with no serious suspicions of the dark councils in Bothwell's chamber. On Sunday, February 9th, the household were to be specially merry over the marriage of one Pagez, a popular master of ceremonies. The Queen's promise to grace the masked ball in the evening was not unwelcome news to the conspirators, and probably hastened their decision. Bothwell hied from a conference with his minions to join the Queen at a farewell banquet in the town in honour of the ambassador of Savoy. At the parting of the guests he slipped out and rejoined them in the neighbourhood of Darnley's lodging. As there was time to spare before the masquerade, Mary with a few nobles followed thither to visit the sick-chamber,—a favour surely the prettiest or the most fiendish which Scottish history has recorded.

At nine they entered, passed upstairs by the chamber where Mary had slept on previous nights, and entered Darnley's room. There was some semblance of early courtship in the meeting,—kisses and the gift of a ring. The noble attendants sat aloof, eager at dice. Bothwell could not yet join his charitable mistress. About ten o'clock two horse-loads of Dunbar powder had been brought round outside the city walls to the postern of the dwelling, and the sacks had been placed in a large barrel to save time and labour in carrying them within. But the doorway was too narrow, and Hay of Talla, John Hepburn, and the Ormistons had to scurry to and fro with their little loads till all was deposited in the Queen's room, Bothwell the while bidding them hasten in their work. This done, Hay and Hepburn were locked in to put the train in order, and the Earl mounted the stair. At eleven came the farewells, and royalty descended, tripping by the closed door unheeding, and, with torch-bearers before, passed through the quiet wynds to Monsieur Pagez's merry-making. Bothwell joined in the fun, the better to mask suspicion when questions came to be asked ; but at twelve he retired privily to his chamber. Off went his velvet and silver finery, on plain hat and doublet and a long black cloak.

What else but a first-murderer this dark figure wandering forth in the blackness of a winter midnight: who could mistake it, whether it paced the streets of old Edinburgh or the boards of Drury? The second and third murderers hurried on behind. The palace sentinels stopped them, but the words "My Lord Bothwell's friends" gave them passage towards the town. The Canongate Port was shut, but the same phrase pulled John Galloway out of bed and opened the gates. When they had reached the garden wall of Darnley's lodging, Bothwell, though his hand was still weak from a sword-cut from John-o'-the-Park, climbed over with Mary's servitor Hubert. In half-an-hour they returned with the two men who had been arranging the train and had fired it. The powder was slow of action, and Bothwell, grown impatient and "angry", would have returned to the house to see "if the lint were burning enough", had not his kinsman restrained him with a confident "Ye need not." And just in time, for

> " Came the wind and thunder of the blast
> That blew the fool forth who took wing for death."

The murderers' first impulse was to climb the city wall, but its height baffled Bothwell's wrist and Hubert's quaking knees. So back to the Canongate Port. The pass-word given, "What crash was that?" asked John Galloway. "We know not", they said, and hurried on to the palace. Bothwell quaffed off some wine, and then to bed, to be roused in half an hour from his feigned slumber by a messenger black with fright and scarce able to speak. "What is the matter, man?" quoth the anxious bed-clothes; and thereafter "Fie, treason!" He rose, donned his velvet and silver, and went straightway to the chamber of the Queen. Later he met Sir James Melvil, and told him it was "the strangest accident that ever chancit," for "the powder come out of the luft (sky) and had burnt the King's house." But in the true story of his life he speaks of the putting of powder beneath the bed and of the setting of it on fire by some foul traitors rather than by a reckless Heaven. He does not tell us that his accomplices that morning received gifts and promises of lasting favour should they hold their tongues. He revisited the scene in style becoming the Sheriff of Edinburgh, with a troop of men-at-arms to search for the traitors, and gave orders for the removal of the body from the garden, where it had been found undressed and unharmed,—which distant position, nakedness, and lack of scars and burns caused shaking of heads, and a suspicion of that half-hour when he was within the garden wall. The Queen's surgeons said nay to the suggestion that Darnley had been strangled, and the murderer's accomplices in their most earnest moments of confession denied the charge. Bothwell may stand free of this imputation, though the proneness of the popular mind to think nothing too horrible for the villain is a fact of some interest.

We must not be distracted by the nice questions which have arisen from Mary's subsequent conduct and utterances, both weighty and trivial,—whether it was chance or God "that put it in her head" to pass the powder room, or neither; whether she had no knowledge or suspicion of the traitor for whose arrest she had offered a large reward. Her guilt, her indifference, or her innocence can neither diminish the tragic interest of the story nor yet mar Bothwell's villainy by extenuation. Mistrust of Bothwell grew faster than doubt of the Queen. Placards were posted on the church doors and at the street corners, showing his portrait in rough with the superscription, " Here is the murtherer of the King." As yet Bothwell paid little heed. Though charged to guard the young Prince at Holyrood, he would ride out to Seton for an afternoon with the Queen at the butts. But when dark hints were made about her Majesty and the market-women began to cry out against her, and when the victim's father made complaint against Bothwell and others and demanded their trial, something had to be done. " I begged the Queen and Council," his good conscience writes, " to allow my being called to justice." Lennox and his friends were requested by Mary to appear and make the indictment. Bothwell had not forgotten the lesson that armed retainers were the best advocates.

3

He had been ordered to have no more than six of a body-guard; he obeyed by presenting himself for trial with nigh four thousand at his heels. Lennox, like Bothwell himself in days gone by, saw the hopelessness of his cause at such an assize and endeavoured to have the trial post-poned. Queen Elizabeth sent a letter to Mary in his behalf, but Lethington stayed its delivery. The legal farce was acted over again; there was no pursuer, as there had been no defender; the luckless fifteen thanked their stars, and readily gave " Not guilty." Four thousand men might have given Bothwell a cheery countenance in court, but Laird Ormiston noted his pallor and concern. " Fye, my lord, what devill is this ye ar doand? Your face schawis what ye ar: hald up your face, for Godis sake, and luik blythlie. Ye might luike swa and ye wer gangand to the deid. Allace, and wo worth them that evir devysit it. I trow it sall garr us all murne." " Had your tongue," said Both-well, " I wald not yet it wer to doe. I have an outgait fra it, cum as it may, and that ye will knaw belyve." It was remarked that on many occasions when he spoke with men his hand was on his dagger. The miscarriage of the popu-larity which he had expected from the Protestant lords had darkened the issue of his plot, but had made him almost nervously alert. Legal formalities over, he proclaimed by placards on the places where his dishonour had been written his challenge to all, gentle or simple, rich or poor, who dared to call him traitor. Two days later (April 14th) Parliament met, and in willing spirit confirmed the act of court and his titles and possessions and added the gift of lands round his castle of Dunbar. By his influence Huntly was restored to his forfeited estates. A safe Dunbar and a grateful Huntly would mean something in a few weeks.

III.

After the meeting of Parliament Bothwell was not so reticent about his matrimonial schemes, nor so careful in suppressing the pleasing rumours. As early as the 30th of March the Englishman Drury had drawn attention to the unusually steady pointing of the Palace weathercock. It had veered so much of late, and the times were so gusty, that men had grown tired of straining their necks. On the very night when the Estates had dissolved we have the first authoritative evidence of Bothwell's intentions. "After I had won my case," he proceeds, "there came to my lodging eight-and-twenty of the Parliament, of their own free-will, without my asking, and did me the honour of offering me their assistance and friendship." This meeting at Ainslie's Tavern was, says a sometimes face-tious historian, like a present-day State dinner,—but with this minor difference, that hagbutters more bland of mien and rosier of hue take charge of the free-will of the guests. Bothwell thought the supper passed off well,—thanks, doubtless, to the presence of his men-at-arms. Here is his pleasant account of the toast of the evening. "First, they acknowledged that I had done my duty in defending my honour in all things of which I had been accused, and for that reason would give their lives, goods, kin, friends, and all whom they could control to support me against all who would, in whatever manner, pursue me for the foresaid crime. Moreover, each one heartily thanked me that I had borne myself so friendly towards them. (Cheers for the hagbutters.) They said that they saw that the Queen was a widow and might have children ; that she had yet but one young Prince ; that they did not wish her to marry a stranger ; and that it seemed to them I was the worthiest in the realm. (Cheers for the Lord High Admiral.) To this end they had resolved to do what they could till the marriage was accomplished, and to oppose all who should put obstacles in the way. At the same time they consulted how I might legitimately repudiate my princess, according to the laws of God and the Church and the custom of the country." Bothwell's words are a not unfair summary of the bond which the wretched twenty-seven,—Eglintoun had slipped out,—had to subscribe. To clinch the matter, he produced a false writing from the Queen testifying her wish for such a desirable match. This was a half lie, the con-

fusion by the confident villain of the early future with
the present. He could not, however, have ventured on
this wile had there not been already some hint of acquies-
cence on the part of Mary. Even if the liaison, which
some papers have hinted, were a libel, Bothwell had reason
to be confident in his power to bully; if it were a fact,
it proved a subservience, which to a blusterer was but an
incentive to seek the glory which would come with legal
recognition.

On 21st April Mary rode to Stirling to see her infant son,
who had been removed thither for security. Bothwell, on
the pretext of Wardenry duties, gathered together a large
troop of spearmen and marched southwards, but after a
short ride he thought better of his Borderers' insolence,
wheeled to the right, and advanced towards the highway
between the capital and Linlithgow. Mary's visit to Stirling
had been brief, for she is found at Linlithgow on the 24th.
Next day her company was overtaken by Bothwell at the
Foul-brigs (fitting place!) at the river Almond. The Earl
had some story of dangers which threatened her Majesty,
and how he had come to take her to a place of safety. Her
retinue was dismissed, but Huntly, Lethington, and Melvil
were compelled to gallop with their mistress and her keeper
to his castle of Dunbar. Some wise-heads afterwards said
that Mary had made the tryst by the Almond, and that she
was not honestly frightened or indignant when Bothwell laid
hand on her bridle.

Bothwell's mood was not what it had been at Mary's last
visit to his fortress. He astonished poor Melvil with loud
boasts "that he would marry the Queen, who would or who
would not, yea, whether she would herself or not." Mary
was certainly at a disadvantage. Later she admitted as
much in her instructions to the Bishop of Dunblane when
he set off for Paris to explain how she had come to
give her hand to Bothwell. The letter is a poor piece of
excuse-making, suggestive, after the manner of such
epistles, of wilful misconstruction and deceit; but, though
it may prompt us to doubt her motives, it may be accepted sa a fair exposition of Bothwell's aggressive con-

duct since the death of her husband. The "visage" which she gave him may have been "ane ordinarie countenance" for a nobleman who had done loyal service, or it may have been something else; but of the interpretation of the royal favour which would suggest itself to Bothwell there is no room for doubt. He began his wooing with gentle words, and asked pardon for his frowardness, explaining it by love for her and fear for his own life; "and thair began," writes Mary, "to mak ws a discours of his haill lyff, how unfortunate he had bene to find men his unfreindis quhome he had never offendit; how thair malice had nevir ceasit to assault him at all occasionis, albeit onjustlie; quhat calumpnyis had thai spred upoun him twiching the odious violence perpetrated on the persoun of the King oure lait husband; how unabill he was to safe himself from conspiraceis of his innemeis, quhome he might not knaw, be ressoun everie man professed him outwartlie to be his friend; and yit he had sic malice, that he could not find himself in suirtie, without he wer assurit of oure favour to indure without alteratioun; and other assurance thairof could he not lippin in (trust), without it wald pleis ws to do him that honour to tak him to husband; protesting alwayis that he wald seik na uther soveraintie bot as of befoir, to serve and obey ws all dayis of oure lyff; joyning thairunto all the honest language that could be usit in sic a cais." There can be no fiction here. It calls to mind the meeting at Ainslie's Tavern, the poor soul's craving for friendly support. But the arguments now, as then, had to be supported by threats; he must rely again upon his hagbutters. "In the end he schowed ws how far he was procedit with our haill nobilitie and principallis of oure Estaittis, and quhat thai had promeist him undir thair handwrittis. . . . And yit gaif he ws lytill space to meditate with oure self, evir pressing ws with continewall and importune sute." Then, when by pointed reference to state difficulties he had "brocht ws agaitward to his intent", he "partlie extorted and partlie obtenit our promeis to tak him to our husband." To press for an immediate marriage was an easy bit of dragooning, and so "as be a bravade in the begyinning he had win the fyrst point, sa ceased he nevir till be persuasionis and importune sute, accumpaneit notheles with force, he hes finalie drevin ws to end the work begun at sic tyme and in sic forme as he thocht mycht best serve his turne." It does Bothwell no small credit as a professional hector to have overmatched the spirit which had led troops towards Corrichie and had faced the murderers of Riccio. Must not the perplexed analyst suggest that that spirit may have been broken since then, and, further, ask, was it by political worry or by passion?

Bothwell had one little piece of business to attend to before the banns could be published. Jean Gordon was still his wife. It required some manœuvring to get this respectable lady out of the way; but she was good enough to set up no obstacles. Her collusion may have been the result of ennui, or of the hopelessness of thwarting him; perhaps, rather, of the expressed desire of her brother Huntly. A double process was instituted, so that the Queen's marriage might not be troubled in future with the quibbles of Protestant or Catholic divines. In the Reformed Commissary Court the wife made complaint of some early infidelity, and obtained a verdict against her spouse. The husband, on the other hand, pled in the Catholic Consistorial Court the old plea of forbidden degrees, and, as no papal dispensation, the dearest care of fathers-in-law in doubtful cases, was forthcoming, likewise obtained decree against their continued union. So exit Jean, to appear later on in the minor parts of Countess of Sutherland and Lady of Boyne. This "vertuous and comelie lady" lived on till 1629, with the added reputation of having "great understanding above the capacite of her sex": which appears to have been true, now that we have found out that she took the dispensation for her marriage with Bothwell with her to Dunrobin and buried it in the charter-room there. Another Jean might not have been able to keep the precious paper in her pocket. Disclosure, however, would have availed little, for the Catholic divines would have remembered that the mass had been omitted at the ceremony. The divorce was not a serious affair. "Ma femme repudiée," writes the Earl in his marginal, and only, note of the proceedings.

On the 3rd of May the Queen and Bothwell journeyed to Edinburgh. They marched in by the West Port, a seeming peaceful company, with spears hid, and Bothwell, like a good courtier, leading the Queen's jennet. They stayed for a few days in the Castle, and ordered publication of the banns, which caused no small grumbling by Master John Craig, minister of St. Giles. On the 12th they passed down to the palace of Holyrood, the Queen dropping by the way a word of commendation of Bothwell to the judges in the Court of Session. In the evening, as fitting preparation for the morrow, she made her lover Duke of Orkney and Shetland, and knighted a few, including the Laird of Ormiston. The marriage was celebrated the next day by the Bishop of Orkney according to the Reformed rites, just as Bothwell had ordered at his previous wedding. The ceremony was not brilliant, neither in the *personnel* nor in heartiness; the sullen dislike of the streets seemed to have infected the palace. Not so Bothwell. He had reached the goal of his ambition. Thrice had a Hepburn aspired to the hand of a widowed Queen of Scots; his father had had promise; he alone had put on the ring. He was in right good humour. He would pledge healths and chaff Sir James Melvil, not forgetting to hint how well he was going to play the ruler. But, as the evening grew, and wine untrussed his kingly points, he "fell in discourse of gentlewomen, using sic filthy language" that even Sir James had to retire,—a good omen for Mary's May marriage, and not less auspicious than his early fits of temper and jealousy!

Bothwell was resolved to make good his jolly boast about his fitness for princely duties. His letters to potentates were courteous enough, but were not lacking in kingly pride. Elizabeth was honoured with one in his best style. He said he knew she did not like him, but made bold to tell her that her ill-will was unjust. Men of nobler birth might have secured his place, but to none would he yield in the desire to preserve her friendship. This swagger did not, however, last long, for Bothwell had to reckon with discontent at home. The hatred of the nobles had grown at his undue elevation and his insolent bearing, and in the fear of

French ascendency and all that that would mean. They were willing, too, to magnify Mary's unhappiness, and to pose as guardians of the young Prince's interests. Bothwell's liking for hagbutters and military levies for baiting his Borderers gave them excuse for action. Mary and he had set out for the Marches on the 7th of June, and were resting at Borthwick on the 10th, when news came that Morton was approaching the castle with twelve hundred horse. It was useless to offer resistance with their small force, and Bothwell therefore fled to Haddington. Mary was free to escape from the thraldom in which the lords said she was pining. She took her liberty by riding, about midnight, dressed as a page, to the keep of Cakemuir, where Bothwell was in waiting. On the morning of the 11th, ere the summer sun was up, they arrived once more at the castle of Dunbar. Morton and his friends had meanwhile returned to Edinburgh, and, having made easy entrance, issued their pithy manifesto for the doing of justice and the purging of the realm " of the infamy and slander wherewith it yet remained bruited among all nations." On the 14th the Court moved from Dunbar towards Edinburgh with a poor following of two hundred hagbutters, sixty horse, and a culverin or two, hoping to gather strength as it straggled through Bothwell's domains. That night the confederates got word of the advance, and set out in better circumstance to meet the Queen. Bothwell, after a night halt at Seton, took up his position on Carberry Hill among the old trenches which had done service for the English twenty years before. The Lords made menace from the lower ground beyond a small stream which skirted the hill. It was a battle of threats and parleys. First came Du Croc, the French Ambassador, after serious but bootless argument with the Lords, bearing a message from them that, if her Majesty would leave the cative in whose power she was, they would show their loyalty on their knees; otherwise Bothwell must answer for his crimes by single combat in sight of the levies. Mary told him she took ill their rebel acts against the man whom they had given her in marriage : if they asked forgiveness, she, too, would forgive. Whereupon my lord, who had just joined the Queen, demanded "in a loud voice", that his lines might hear and be nerved by his defiance, whether it was with him that they wished to pick a quarrel, and, if so, for what offence. He had no other desire than to be friendly with all; they were envious of his honours. He would meet his peer in single combat, if only to save the Queen from her miserable plight and her lieges from a bloody field. Mary, however, intervened, and forbade Du Croc to take the message of her dear Bayard. Meanwhile there had been a movement of some of the confederate forces over the stream, and Bothwell, in the afterglow of his grandiloquence, asked him to stay on the hill, as did Scipio of old, to see the goodly scrimmage. But Du Croc very properly said that it was too painful a sight for ambassadorial countenance, and departed, leaving the Queen in tears. As his story did not pacify the Lords, he continued his journey to Edinburgh in sadness. No battle ensued. After the change of position there was a parley between the lines, and single combat was again proposed, this time by Bothwell's own captains. First, young James Murray offered to fight; but the man who had stuck up libellous placards against him was too unworthy. Then his brother Tullibardine; but his rank was little better. Bothwell would have Morton take his glove, but the Lords thought they could better spare Lord Lindsay, who was eager to fight with the braggart as a reward for past services, and especially for helping the despatch of Signor Riccio. These wordy delays raised suspicion in the minds of the Lords that the Queen's party were playing with them till reinforcements came from the Hamiltons, and they accordingly made a flank movement under Kirkaldy of Grange, to make sure of Bothwell should he wish to flee. This action had its effect on the Queen's band. In the late afternoon it had so dwindled away that Mary saw no hope in resistance. She summoned Kirkaldy, heard his plain tale how she must leave her husband if she would remain their honoured sovereign, and, restraining Bothwell's hagbutter, who had been bidden to fire, accepted the inevitable. As the laird rode down to his friends, Bothwell entreated her—these are his words—"to retire to Dunbar and to leave us to fight her just quarrel, according to our desire to honour and serve her and for the regard which we had to the public good and the peace of our country." He found it "impossible to move her from her purpose, or to make her hear any remonstrance"—her, who would have gone with him to the world's end in a white petticoat, and had ridden to him at midnight in a page's dress. He had better go to Dunbar alone this time, and as fast as he might. Doubtless there was some emotion at the parting with her dear ruffian : the Captain of Inchkeith said she looked sorely grieved. When Kirkaldy returned she kept him in conversation till the Duke was well on his way, and then delivered herself up. So they parted, and for ever. Three days later the runaway sent for a small box which he had left in Edinburgh Castle, but the messenger was waylaid, and the silver casket was sent to my Lord Morton. Had George Dalgleish had better luck there had been a difference in the making of history and the books thereon. In their parting they had sought each other's safety; they had but vowed an eternal misery.

Bothwell was safe enough in his sea-fortress; all the heralds' trumpets in the market-place could not have blown down his walls had he chosen to stay. But there was little good to be had from defiant inaction ; and there was hope that the Hamiltons and other friends might be stirred in his cause, and in that of his wife, now completely at the mercy of the Lords of Congregation. So, on the 27th of June, within sight of the spot whence he had twice taken secret passage to France, he set sail with two ships for the North. He found his way to the seat of the Earl of Huntly and endeavoured to raise the men of Strathbogie. Failing in this, he departed hurriedly for the familiar rooftree at Spynie, and found shelter and solace with his merry kinsman. An English prisoner at the castle devised a plan for taking or killing the bishop's guest, but it came to naught, for Lethington thought it better for the peace of Scotland that the uncanny Duke should escape. There were stories circulated of Bothwell's slaughter of one of the prelate's youngsters, and of the drowning of a page who was too weak of will to be trusted with the Duke's secrets.

But the evidence is far from convincing: *de odio facilius creditur.* After a sojourn of some weeks,—for which the bishop had soon to answer,—Bothwell re-embarked and sailed out of the Moray Forth towards his dukedom. When he arrived at Orkney, the bailiff and keeper of his castle of Kirkwall showed such scant respect that in two days he found it necessary to set out for his more northern domains. Olaf Sinclair and his men welcomed him to Shetland and tendered the ancient due of an ox and sheep. This island loyalty prompted the Lord High Admiral to take courage. He cast covetous eyes on two large well-armed Hanse vessels lying off the coasts. Arrangements were made with the captains, and the ships joined his Scottish craft. What did he intend to do with his four vessels? Was he but safeguarding himself against possible attack from the South, or was he meditating some frolic with the merchant-men on the high seas? There was but the difference of a hat between a Liddesdale freebooter and a North Sea corsair. He had not long to wait to show his prowess, for, on August 25th, four Scots ships, sent by Murray, now Regent, arrived off Bressay Sound. They were under the command of his Carberry friends, Kirkaldy and Tullibardine, and they carried the person and blessing of the bishop who had married him at Holyrood. The Admiral's ships, on the approach of the enemy, cut cables and sailed out by the northern end of the Sound. It was a hot chase, but the *Pelican* and her companions were not to be caught. The *Unicorn*, with the headstrong Kirkaldy on board, pursued the last of Bothwell's ships, but she came to grief on a sunken rock, and left her captain, bishop, and merry men to be rescued by the rest of the fleet. Bothwell, who was on land at dinner with Foud Olaf when the Regent's ships arrived, escaped over island and ferry to the far north Unst, and there rejoined his fleet. As some of his men had been left on shore in the scurry at Bressay, he sent one of his vessels for them round by the west side of the islands, with instructions to follow the *Pelican* into the North Sea. He had, however, little time for new plans, for, on a sudden, Kirkaldy bore down on him and hard pressed him for three hours in a running fight. Bothwell lost a mast by a cannon ball, and was in danger of defeat, had not a wild breeze risen and lashed his own vessel and another out into the ocean. The Regent's ships gave up the chase, and the dark spirit which had troubled Scotland so sorely passed away for ever, out into the mist and storm, amid the fitting discord of wind and cannon and the curses of disappointed foes.

IV.

The skelter of the night and following day ended off the Norse island of Karm. Bothwell's pilots were out of their reckoning until the chance courtesy of a Rostock vessel offered to guide them into the calmer waters behind. But by ill-luck his Danish Majesty's warship the *Bear* encountered the weather-beaten crafts as they crept havenwards, and Captain Christiern Aalborg thought fit to ask some explanation of their presence. "We are Scots gentlemen," replied Bothwell's master-mariner, "who wish to go to Denmark to serve his Majesty." This excellent desire was not considered equivalent to letters of safeconduct, the more especially as Bothwell protested that those who should have given him a passport were under guard. By a clever ruse, Aalborg divided the Scots sailors, some to his own vessel, on the plea of supplying them with fresh provisions, others to the mainland to the kindly care of the Karm folks, whom he had roused against the "freebooters." This done,—a sore vexation to Bothwell, who could easily have "demonstrated" (his own word!) his superior strength, —there followed the announcement that they would all to Bergen in merry company. Whereupon Bothwell, as in genuine melodrama, proclaimed his nobility to the meddlesome Dane. In all approved instances the hero discloses a trig and modish garb beneath his foul disguise. Unfortunately for Bothwell his silver-laced doublets were in the vessel which he had ordered back from Shetland, and the princeliness of a boatswain's dress, patched and bespattered, was too obvious a joke to a first-class official, who could not have heard of the strange ways of Caliphs or of the Philosophy of Clothes. And straightway they all set sail for Bergen.

Eric Rosenkrands, governor of the castle of Bergen, sent on board a commission of twenty-four eminent pier-masters and commission - agents to examine Aalborg's prisoner. They so bothered him about his passport that he had to startle them with the query, " From whom should he get a passport, being himself the supreme ruler in the country?" His bourgeois censors could not treat him very harshly after that ; so he was allowed to stay at an inn " at his own expense "—whatever that might mean. He tells that he had invitations to dine at the castle ; and we know from local records that Eric did feast him in his hall, perhaps for curiosity, perhaps for those post-prandial romances which might not have travelled from Spynie or Holyrood. He could walk about the town as he pleased. " I thank the good Eric," says the memoir, " for the confidence which he placed in me"; and it tells no more of Bergen, except that one day Bothwell was told to go to Denmark. But why? First, nasty suspicions about his ownership of the ship *Pelican*, erst of Bremen. Then, the awkward ignorance of his own hirelings as to his identity, for both policy and hurry had made him conceal it from them in Shetland. To hear them say that he was a David Woth,— and the Bergen folks tell that the said David had been recently doing a little privateering on his own account,—was poor support of his claims to respectability. Further,— would the most gullible of men accept the situation if Mr. Sims, and not History, had written it?—Ann Throndssön was living in Bergen, and, of course, confronted her dear scoundrel in court. All this looks very like the fifth act, but Ann was paid off with the promise of money from Scotland and the gift of his smaller vessel. He had been endeavouring to get a passport from the unwilling Eric, when yet another disclosure made the good people of Bergen determine to send him to Copenhagen. For, when things looked ill, Bothwell had sent for a casket which was hidden among the ballast, though at his examination he had said there was nothing in his ships for which he cared. It was opened in the castle with full legal ceremony, and found to contain, among other papers, a copy of his impeachment as a murderer, robber, and traitor, with the offer of the Scottish Lords for his person, and a letter of lament from Queen Mary. There was a strange fatality for him in caskets, even in Norway. This was enough, by way of testimonial as to previous character, for commandant Eric and the burgomasters of Bergen. His strange requests, one day to go to Scotland, another to France, another to Holland, his endeavour to get a boat to take him to hostile Sweden, his "several mocking expressions" against them, especially that he would be quits with them in time to come, made them anxious to be delivered of the uncanny man who had drifted to their shores. On the 30th of September Captain Aalborg set sail for Copenhagen, and Bothwell, with but four or five of his companions, went also in the *Bear*.

Frederick II. was not at his capital when the ship arrived, but the fussy High Steward, Peter Oxe, received him, and, because of a letter which he had received from the Earl of Murray, detained him in gentle ward in the royal castle. There was some correspondence between Frederick and Oxe on the subject, in which the former showed himself inclined to look leniently on the case of his royal cousin's spouse, despite the warning of his slave that Bothwell was "very cunning and inventive", could no longer be kept with safety in the said castle, and should be despatched to another castle, say, in Jutland. These arguments were the more unavailing by reason of a letter from Bothwell to Frederick, which the honest Oxe had sent on with his own, and the king seemed likely to let his guest remain in easy captivity till his return to his capital. But it chanced that with provoking impropriety there arrived a Scottish herald, who had been storm-tossed for two months, with a letter in the name of James VI., containing the inevitable demand for Bothwell's surrender. Frederick could not choose between the Scottish story and that of his prisoner, who pleaded he had been acquitted of the charge of murder, and was the husband of the Queen, herself an unwilling recluse in the islet of Lochleven. So he resolved that the disputants might, if they would, hammer out the truth on Danish soil, and Bothwell might write for witnesses and papers; but, for better security, the latter should go to the arched chamber in Malmoe Castle, where a former High Steward of Denmark had been lodged. "And we command you," wrote Frederick to Constable Kaas, "that you wall up the secret closet in the same chamber, and, if the windows with the iron trellis be not strong and quite secure, that you see to that." Danish High Stewards, whether in prison or at large, had not been equal to Bothwell in "cunning and invention."

Bothwell carried with him to Malmoe the true story of his life and misfortunes, from which we have already culled not a few of his most studied veracities; and there he added a shorter petition, craving liberty and aid for the rescue of Mary from Lochleven, and promising, with assumed authority from Mary and her Council, to hand over the Orkneys by way of recompense. This offer was most politic, for the Danes were still hankering after their old possessions, and it came all the better from the man whose patent of earldom of these islands was among the arrested papers. This may, as one biographer has hinted, have been the reason why Bothwell, though still a prisoner, was guarded by Frederick from all the heralds, ambassadors, and agents who demanded his hateful person.

Into all the intrigue which is associated with the names of Captain John Clerk and Thomas Buchanan; into the prayer for Bothwell's execution in Denmark, the handing over of his servants Murray and Paris, whom we last met at the Kirk-o'-Field; into events connected with the death of Murray and the fiercer persecution by the next Regent, Lennox, father of the murdered Darnley,—into these we cannot be expected to enter. They are the topics of our larger histories and the pet labour of Professor Schiern. There the reader will find how well Bothwell kept his wits in the crisis, how astutely he completed the discrediting of

Clerk, how comfortable he managed to make his durance in Malmoe, so comfortable, indeed, that we are led to expect that he is on the eve of liberty. Strangely enough it was but the prelude to the last and saddest episode of the tragedy, for suddenly, on June 16, 1573, for some reason which record does not name, he was hurried off to a foul dungeon in the lonely castle of Dragsholm. What it was that had thus compassed his exile Bothwell probably did not know, though he may have seen how his prospects with Frederick would darken as news came and re-came of the growing strength of his foes in Scotland, and, worst of all, of the bloody deeds on the Eve of St. Bartholomew by the French partisans and blood-relations of his Queen.

The governor of Dragsholm had seen well to his outer trellises, for Bothwell's friends and foes for long knew naught of how he fared within the grim walls. Then came those rumours which ever cling to such mysteries,—that he had died, that he " was greatly swollen, not dead", then, at last, with the persistence almost of fact, that he had succumbed to slow disease. We know, at least, that in 1578 he was buried by the sea in the lonely church of Faareveile. If poetic justice be not requited by the cruel durance of his later years, or the artistic soul be not satisfied by the weird ceremony amid the screaming of the wild sea-birds on that restless shore, let those who will fill in with what colour they may the horror of his dying madness. "Ad sordes aliasque miserias accedente amentia, vita turpiter acta dignum habuit exitum." So the ideal villain is complete, and that world, which, confident of endless deliria and an everlasting dungeon, yet likes, for Art and the Preacher's sake, to see a little meted out before a spirit passes from their midst, smiled complacently at this bitter foretaste of his woe. But Bothwell can never be a mere George Barnwell, the scoundrel of the virtuous tale, who is punished and dies, as surely as the goodly youth finds his princess and is for ever happy. The measure of his magnificent iniquity is the unending fascination of his life. Not a hundred history books, sober and fantastic, not twice

as many reams of Swinburnian verse can drive him, or his
lovely Duessa, into that limbo to which all flabby villainy
does inevitably go. His mischief made, he vanished from
the world weirdly and in shadow, as Mephisto does : like
him he is perennially interesting.

SIR EDWARD KELLEY.

(1555-1595.)

> " He bears
> The visible mark of the Beast on his forehead ;
> And for his *stone*, it is a work of darkness,
> And with *philosophy* blinds the eyes of man."
>
> *THE ALCHEMIST.*

IN the year of grace fifteen hundred and fifty-five, at the hour of four o'clock p.m., in the town of Worcester, there was born an infant who subsequently bore the name of Edward. There would have been something wanting to the fitness of things if the name of so doubtful a character had been above doubt ; and if a man of such duplicity had not also possessed a double designation. Accordingly, although Edward's original name was Talbot, he appears to have found it convenient occasionally to dub himself Kelley, and by that appellation he is known to fame. The stars had marked him out to be a man of " clear understanding, quick apprehension, and excellent wit, with a great propensity to philosophical studies and the mysteries of nature," but the days of his youth and apprenticeship to an apothecary at Worcester gave few signs of the future that awaited him. At the age of seventeen Kelley proceeded to Gloucester Hall, Oxford, but his academic career was cut short after a residence of twelve months ; perhaps he did not consider the university a suitable arena for the exhibition of his peculiar talents, or it may be that a premature display of them prejudiced the authorities against allowing him proper scope for their further development ; at all events Kelley never graduated in anything but deception, or became master of any

KELLEY AND DR. DEE INVOKING THE SPIRIT OF A DEAD PERSON.

art but that of lying. He seems to have adopted a manifold calling; he became, either in turn or all at once, a lettered rogue and vagrant, a roving astrologer, a London attorney, and a deft forger.

The pursuit of one or other of these professions brought him into Lancashire, where he attained notoriety by digging up the body of a man who had been buried the previous day, and by means of incantations making it answer questions which he put concerning a certain young gentleman of quality: Kelley was his guardian, and naturally felt some anxiety to learn the exact manner and time of his death. Accordingly, with friendly solicitude and the help of an accomplice named Paul Waring, he performed the orthodox black ceremonies (as shown in the accompanying picture), and proceeded to extract the desired information. Either he found some difficulty in fulfilling the dead man's prophecies, or their accomplishment was not attended by the needful pecuniary gains, for immediately afterwards Kelley found it necessary to practise as a forger; his was as yet a 'prentice hand, and the lack of artistic finish exhibited by this performance, "together with certain other foul matters," led to the loss of his ears in the pillory at Lancaster. This was a serious blow for one who coveted the reputation of a philosopher, but Kelley's ingenuity devised a skull-cap which not only concealed his loss but gave him a sage and sober look which deceived even his most intimate enemies. He found it convenient, however, to retire to Wales, where he adopted the name Kelley, and spent some time wandering about as an itinerant astrologer, eking out a hand-to-mouth existence. His travels were not altogether fruitless. A certain innkeeper, with whom he stayed, had become possessed of an old and curious manuscript, which had been discovered in the tomb of a bishop in a neighbouring church; some fanatics or thieves had sacrilegiously opened up his grave in the hope of securing the treasures said to be concealed within it. They found nothing but the aforesaid manuscript and two small ivory bottles, containing respectively a ponderous white and red powder. These pearls beyond price were

rejected by the "pigs of apostasy"; one of the bottles was
shattered on the spot and its contents for the most part lost.
The remnant with the other bottle and the manuscript were
disposed of to the innkeeper, who, in his turn, sold them to
Kelley for one pound sterling. With this treasure Kelley
made his way to Dr. John Dee, whose fame as a hermetical
philosopher had probably reached his ears; and thus began
a partnership pregnant with instruction and interest.

Dee and Kelley were excellent types of the two classes into
which mankind is divided by those who consider themselves
exceptions to the rule. Dee was a fool and Kelley was a knave.
When such conjunctions occur they are generally happy for
the knave, and Kelley succeeded in making out of Dee what
must then have been the comfortable income of £50 a year,
besides board and lodging. Dee was a man of parts; educated at Cambridge, he devoted himself assiduously to the
study of mathematics and astrology; he made a practice of
working eighteen hours a day, so that his subsequent mental
aberrations need not excite much surprise. He was now in
his fifty-fourth year and had published many learned works,
but his astrological studies had once, at least, nearly proved
fatal to him. He had been consulted by some of Elizabeth's
servants as to the date of Queen Mary's death, for which
offence he and two others were thrown into prison. Dee was
charged with heresy as well, and when the former accusation
was dismissed he was left to the tender mercies of Bonner;
he combined, however, a certain amount of cunning with his
folly and succeeded in proving his innocence to the satisfaction of his judge. The accession of Elizabeth brought him
into royal favour; his mathematical and astronomical
learning gained him the friendship of mariners bent on the
discovery of a north-west passage and other adventurers
such as Gilbert, Hawkins, and Frobisher; he knew Burleigh
and Walsingham; even Elizabeth herself used to call at his
house at Mortlake, and when Dee was ill sent her own
physician to attend him. But social advancement did not
divert Dee from his search after the secrets of life, and his
practice of astrology seems to have added considerably to his
income. One evening he was pursuing this mysterious

occupation when he was dazzled by a sudden blaze of light and a being appeared at his window who professed to be the angel Gabriel and presented him with "the philosopher's stone." It was a round piece of polished cannel coal, but is always referred to as the crystal, and after passing through various adventures and hands, including those of Horace Walpole, it is now said to repose in the British Museum. Other crystals have, however, claimed the honour of being Dee's; one such belonged to Richard James Morison, better known as Zadkiel, who made use of it to interview Christ and His disciples. A distinguished admiral who charged Zadkiel with "gulling the nobility" by its means, was in 1863 sued for libel and cast in damages to the extent of twenty shillings.

For some time Dee found but little use for this supernatural gift; he was unable to distinguish clearly what the spirits who appeared in it said, and forgot their communications before he could write them down. He had already employed several skryers, or seers, with varying degrees of ill-success, and the last, whose name, Barnabas Saul, should have been a guarantee of permanent grace, began to suffer from loss of spiritual insight about October, 1581, and by the following March the well of his imagination had completely dried up. Kelley's appearance was therefore like that of an angel—perhaps a little in disguise. He received the story of the crystal with rapturous delight and unhesitating credulity. To his eye of faith the spirits appeared in no stinted measure, and immediately he was constituted Dee's "skryer." It was he who looked into the crystal and heard the communications of the spirits while Dee took them down at his dictation. In Butler's words—

> "Kelley did all his deeds upon
> The devil's looking-glass, a stone."

This alchemical neophyte was now fairly embarked on his career: more fortunate than modern mediums he escaped exposure, and made a living out of his profession. Various opinions have been held as to his good faith; he may have been more sinned against than sinning, and diabolical

ingenuity is said to have been merely the guise which his
childlike simplicity assumed. But reality or disguise, no
manner of doubt as to its astounding nature remains after
an impartial study of his adventurous career. He devoted
himself energetically to the practice of his art, and, indeed,
to interpret the sayings of his spiritual interviewers was no
easy task; their utterances, according to another famous
magician, "were very indistinct, and they spoke like the
Irish, very thick in the throat." As a rule their prophecies
were not given vocally, but they signified by "forms, shapes,
and creatures what was demanded." Dee, moreover, had
an unreasonable habit of expecting the spirits to be able to
answer questions on all subjects, and this necessitated hard
work on Kelley's part to acquire sufficient knowledge to
meet these demands. But all this did not satisfy his restless energy; he broke out into lucubrations in Latin verse
on the philosopher's stone which pass all understanding
save that of an alchemist. These have been frequently
republished, and a translation has even recently appeared.
Kelley also wrote numerous recipes for transmuting
baser metals into gold, but he appears to have found
precept in this respect more practicable than example.
His position does not, however, seem to have met all his
ambitious requirements, and he made an attempt to leave
Dee, taking every precaution to ensure discovery in time
for Dee to prevent his departure by the offer of a fixed salary
of £50 a year besides board and lodging. Probably on the
strength of this, Kelley married; his master had just taken
a second wife, and the two families lived together with
almost apostolic community of goods. Kelley was introduced into the fashionable society which occasionally called
at Dee's house, and the credulous interest of these visitors
in astrology suggested the idea that the crystal might become an invaluable aid towards the realisation of certain
ambitious schemes that he had conceived.

In the year 1582 there came to England a Polish noble
named Albert Laski or à Lasco; his father had been one
of the pioneers of the Reformation in Poland, but Albert
followed the fashion and returned to the Roman Catholic

ingenuity is said to have been merely the gu... ... ...
childlike simplicity assumed. But reality or ... ...
manner of doubt as to its astounding nature r... ...
an impartial study of his adventurous career. He ...
himself energetically to the practice of his art, a... ...
to interpret the sayings of his spiritual interview... ...
easy task; their utterances, according to anoth... ...
magician, "were very indistinct, and they spoke like
Irish, very thick in the throat." As a rule their ...
were not given vocally, but they signified by "...
and gestures what was demanded." Dee, more ...
ar a reasonable habit of expecting the spirits to be ...
answer questions on all subjects, and this necessit... ...
work on Kelley's part to acquire sufficient kn... ...
meet these demands. But all this did not sati... ...
less energy; he broke out into lucubrations in I... ...
on the philosopher's stone which pass all und... ...
... that of an alchemist. These have been ...
... and a translation has even recently ...
Kelley also wrote numerous recipes for tra...
base metals into gold, but he appears to ha... ...
precept in this respect more practicable th... ...
His position does not, however, seem to have n... ...
ambitious requirements, and he made an attempt ...
Dee, taking every precaution to ensure discover... ...
... ... to prevent his departure by the order of a fixed ...
... ... a year besides board and lodging. Prob...
... ... this, Kelley married; his master had g...
... ... wife, and the two families lived tog... ...
... ... ostolic community of goods. Kelley ...
... ... the fashionable society which occasional...
... ... house, and the credulous interest of th... ...
in astrology suggested the idea that the crystal ...
... ... an invaluable aid towards the realisation of ...
... ... schemes that he had conceived. ...

In the year 158... there came to England a Poli... ...
named Albert Laski or à Lasco; his father had be...
... pioneers of the Reformation in Poland, but A...
... ... the fashion and returned to the Roman C...

SIR EDWARD KELLEY.

fold. Attracted to England by the fame of Elizabeth, he was made much of at the Court and taken, among other places, to Oxford, where he was much disappointed not to find Dr. Dee, whose hermetical fame had excited his curiosity. An interview was easily arranged between the two in London, and Laski became an enthusiastic devotee of the spirits; Dee and Kelley were nothing loth to admit him to their séances, but not their secrets, for Laski was a bird as ripe for plucking as they could wish. His ambition and vanity were only surpassed by his credulity. The spirits, charmed with his childlike faith, responded liberally to his desire for revelations, and their disclosures were as flattering as they were extraordinary. At their first attempt, there appeared in the crystal " a pretty girl of seven or nine years of age, with her hair rolled up before and hanging down very long behind, with a gown of sey, changeable green and red, with a train that seemed to play up and down like and seemed to go in and out between the books lying in heaps." Madimi— for such was her name—was a bright, attractive creature, exceedingly willing to give all the assistance in her power, even to the length of learning Greek, Latin, and Syriac, if that would be of any use, but it usually happened that when very inconvenient questions were asked by Dee to which Kelley's knowledge or inventive faculty did not supply him with an answer, she was called away by her mother, an ill-natured person, to look after her young brothers and sisters. On this occasion, however, she found time to intimate that Laski was fated to become the ruler of two kingdoms, and to promise him as great a future as Kelley thought his vanity or credulity would stomach. " His name," said she, " is in the book of life. The sun shall not pass his course before he be a king, his counsel shall breed alteration in his state, yea, of the whole world." The one thing needful to secure entrance into his earthly kingdom was apparently to provide sustenance for Dee and Kelley; at least this was Kelley's interpretation of Madimi's behest. Laski's vanity proved equal to the task, and he became more and more dependent upon the oracular utterances of the spirits.

In the whole story there is nothing more touching than the consideration of the spirits for Kelley's welfare and comfort; they even condescended to such minutiæ as to bid him sit down during their interviews because they knew it was troublesome to him to stand. Curiously enough it seems to have come to their ears that a warrant was out against Kelley for coining false money, and with prompt solicitude they commanded Laski to take Dee and Kelley with their families and return to his estates in Poland. The order was no sooner given than obeyed, and this embryo church of the spirits embarked with all its goods and chattels on a trading vessel a little below Greenwich. But the winds and waves have a grudge against fugitive prophets; their departure was signalised by the commencement of a storm which caused their speedy disembarkation on the Isle of Sheppey, as neither Dee nor Kelley aspired to the *rôle* of a second Jonah. There they waited three days; their second attempt proved that the most spiritual exaltation is no proof against physical prostration, but at length they landed at Brill on July 30, 1583; proceeding through Holland, Friesland, and Germany by way of Embden and Bremen, they arrived at Lubeck where they remained during November and part of December. On Christmas Day they reached Stettin, and it was not till February, 1584, that they found a haven of refuge in Laski's broad estates near Cracow.

Here was a veritable promised land flowing with milk and honey. Laski's pockets were well lined, and supplied all their wants; the communications of the spirits were nicely adjusted to his liberality. Each act of generosity on Laski's part was rewarded with a new and more generous promise from Kelley's ghostly friends, whose skill in explaining delays in their fulfilment might well be called superhuman, while any suspicions as to their genuineness were banished for the time by the gradual approach to success made by the experiments in transmuting baser metals into gold. This formed the main occupation of the little leisure which Kelley's angelical visitors permitted him. The powder procured from the Welsh innkeeper was prolific of expectations, and Kelley showed great industry in the consumption of materials provided at Laski's expense; at length a piece of metal cut out of a frying-pan was transmuted into pure gold, and sent with the pan to Queen Elizabeth as conclusive proof of Kelley's alchemistic talents. Meanwhile Laski's means grew small by degrees and beautifully less; his estates were mortgaged almost to their full value, and as Kelley's experiments in alchemy cost more than the gold produced was worth, they were not a very valuable source of income. An introduction to Stephen Batory, King of Poland, did not increase the resources of this band of philosophers, as that redoubtable monarch was wary in his dealings with the unseen world, and hesitated to part with his money before he got its value. The goose appeared to have laid its last golden egg, and the spirits, accommodating as usual, began to suggest that perhaps after all Laski was not the chosen instrument for the redemption of the world by means of universal monarchy, and to hint that Kelley's presence was required elsewhere.

There was no lack of aspirants for the honour of his society; two emperors—Ivan of Russia and Rudolf of Austria—sent invitations to their respective Courts, but the friendship of a private individual with fewer calls upon his purse and less power of vengeance in case of disappointment was preferred to the fickle favour of princes; Dee and Kelley with their families removed to Cracow in March, 1586, and after various wanderings took up their residence at Trebona with a Bohemian noble named Rosenberg. Here their "actions" were resumed with renewed vigour and expense; and the result was an ounce and a quarter of gold. But the manipulation of spirits is easier than the manufacture of gold, and practice had perfected Kelley's imagination, ventriloquism, or clairvoyance; he no longer saw them as in a glass, darkly; his visitors came thick and fast to the crystal, and were of all sorts and conditions, from "angelical creatures and spiritual beings down to a divel of Hell," with whom Kelley, drawn it may be by the force of mutual attraction, seems to have been peculiarly intimate. Gabriel, Raphael, Uriel, and Michael all appeared at Kelley's call, while humanity was represented by a galaxy of strange

women in stranger costumes. Their revelations were
catholic, and ranged from paradise and the kingdom of
heaven to hell and the kingdoms of earth; the mysteries
of the future no less than the secrets of the present were
disclosed, though, unlike Cassandra's, their prophecies were
always believed and never came true. On one occasion
Kelley came to Dee in a state of righteous indignation; he had
discovered that a description of some countries given by the
spirits had come straight out of Ptolemy, and declared them
to be a mere snare and a delusion. Dee rose up in defence
of his angelical creatures, and his belief was only strengthened
by Kelley's doubts.

Similar occurrences were frequent, and it would seem
that Kelley treated Dee in the most approved method of
dealing with women; he always asked for what he did
not want and said what he did not mean. Whenever
he particularly wished Dee to believe the sayings of the
spirits, he expressed disbelief himself, and his master invariably rose to the bait. But artifice was rarely necessary, and only when it was more than usually evident
that the sphere of the spirits' communications was strictly
limited by the range of Kelley's knowledge. These were
always made in Biblical language, a knowledge of which
was the only virtue to which Kelley pleaded guilty; and it
was a virtue eminently qualified to impose upon a pious fool
like Dee. But the "sermon-like stuff" served up by the
spirits was not all that Kelley heard in the crystal. Sometimes it thundered in the stone; once he says, "I have heard
a voice about the shew-stone very great, as though men were
beating down of mud walls—the thumping and shussing and
cluttering is such." Bountiful converse with angels like this
was reserved for the faithful few, and could only be the
reward of scrupulous observance of all spiritual requirements. These are said by a famous astrologer of the next
century to be "neatness and cleanliness of apparel, a strict
diet, upright life, and frequent prayers to God"; another
wizard is said "to have been much given to debauchery, so
that at times the demons would not appear to the speculator;
he would then suffumigate; sometimes to vex the spirits he

would curse them and fumigate with contraries." It would seem that the demons, like gods and other mortals, take pleasure in incense offered at their shrine; or the fumigation may have been by way of a personal disinfectant. The same authority states that the reason why Kelley "had not more plain resolutions and more to the purpose was because he was very vicious unto whom the angels were not obedient or willingly did declare the questions propounded." But these charges might with equal justice be brought against most astrologers and might be attributed to professional jealousy, for Kelley certainly saw much more in his crystal than any one else did.

The usual interleaving of astrology with alchemy now received a fresh impetus from Kelley's acquisition of a new elixir; the story is told by William Lilly, the famous astrologer already quoted, " who had it related from an ancient minister who knew the certainty thereof from an old English merchant, resident in Germany at what time both Dee and Kelley were there." According to this unimpeachable and conclusive authority, while the two philosophers were at Trebona a certain friar called on them; as he knocked Dee peeped down the stairs and instructed Kelley to give the polite answer that he was not at home. The friar replied that he would take another time to wait upon him, and some few days after came again. Dee required Kelley to return the same answer if it were the same man. Kelley did so. This was too much for the friar's patience; he broke out into angry reproaches. " Tell thy master I came to speak with him and to do him good, because he is a great scholar and famous; but now tell him, he put forth a book and dedicated it to the Emperor: it is called ' Monas Hieroglyphicus.' He understands it not; I wrote it myself. I came to instruct him therein, and in some other profound things. Do thou, Kelley, come along with me; I will make thee more famous than thy master Dee." Kelley hesitated, but finally joined the friar and obtained from him the elixir. There is a Mephistophelian air about this story, and some have been so irreverent as to suggest (on insufficient evidence) that the reverend friar was none other than his Satanic majesty, who demanded Kelley's soul in exchange for the elixir; in that case neither could be congratulated on the bargain. Kelley, however, was more fortunate than Faust, and this event was followed by unusual liberality on his part; at the wedding of one of his maidservants he gave away £4,000 worth of gold rings. The unlucky friar's existence was now of course superfluous, and was conveniently cut short; perhaps the spirits who showed such unfailing consideration for their votary did not stick at a trifle like murder where he was concerned, but Kelley's enemies have taken a mean advantage of the evidence being against him, and attributed the friar's death to poison administered by his pupil.

This was one of the many occasions on which Dee and Kelley quarrelled and had temporary separations. In the course of these Kelley appears to have visited Antwerp where, according to Dee, he fought valiantly against the Spaniards during the siege in 1585. Both found lucrative occupation in transmitting to Burleigh such news as they could pick up from abroad, and Dee had a permanent salary as Queen's intelligencer. They always, however, came to an agreement again, and continued their alchemistic and other labours. On one occasion, at the instigation of the Papal nuncio, they were expelled from the Emperor's dominions, but Rosenberg's intercession procured their return to Prague. Their dubious occupation gained them many enemies, and they lived in constant dread of spies. One of these was a certain Francis Pucci who had insinuated himself into their confidence, and accompanied them from Cracow to Prague; he was a tool of the Papal nuncio in Prague, and informed him of all that passed between Dee and Kelley, and when they were expelled tried to persuade them to go to Rome, where they would assuredly have had a very warm reception from the Inquisition. Rudolf still hesitated between his belief that Kelley could make gold and his deference to the nuncio; at one time Dee and Kelley are conspicuous marks of his favour, at another they are fleeing from his resentment. But in spite of all interruptions the conferences with the spirits and experiments in transmuting metals proceeded merrily at Rosenberg's expense. Once, after a more than usually serious squabble between the two philosophers, Dee appointed his son Arthur his skryer, but the uninventive boy could see nothing in the crystal, and Kelley's success in interpreting things that had been invisible to Arthur made Dee more convinced than ever of his indispensability. He was restored to his position with a firmer hold than ever on Dee's weak mind, and the spirits continued to give vent to unending prophecies of ruin and success in terms that rendered their application sufficiently easy to any one whom they might subsequently seem to suit.

At length the iteration of such abracadabra became a trifle wearisome, and either Kelley or one of the spirits was responsible for a variety of the entertainment. Evil communications are popularly supposed to corrupt good manners, and before long Kelley's devotion to spiritualism degenerated in appearance into a cult of carnalism. It were, however, unwise to inquire too curiously whether Kelley corrupted the spirits or the spirits Kelley; it is, moreover, the privilege of the holy to stand unspotted in equivocal situations, for to the pure all things are pure, and Kelley, with a conscience void of offence, did not shrink from disclosing to Dee revelations of the angelical beings, which in the case of a less irreproachable character might have been attributed to a prurient imagination. Madimi, who first appeared on the scene as an innocent and attractive maiden, began to evince an acquaintance with carnal affections which ill became her tender years and spiritual character. Some of the spirits adopt a garb gradually more scanty and meretricious, and at last Madimi is seen clothed only in her native modesty, itself a garment only too threadbare and transparent, while her language might suggest that she had been revelling in Milesian novels or the Decameron; other spirits again, anti-types of Chaumette's goddess of reason, proclaim new doctrines of moral degeneration in the language of prophets and the garb of prostitutes. One of these Corinthian ladies was the herald of a departure in the direction of the doctrine of which Brigham Young has become the high priest, and Utah the headquarters.

Matrimonial felicity was not among the blessings vouch-safed to Kelley. His wife was as ill-favoured as Dee's was comely, and he does not appear to have been equal to the taming of the shrew; but with the evidence as to Kelley's morality before him, the unprejudiced observer will no more connect this fact with the circumstances that followed than he will impute to so profound a philosopher a weakness so mundane as an eye for beauty. Still less will he charge so pious a believer with wilful infraction of the seventh commandment. Such innuendoes need only be mentioned to be dismissed as unfounded and malicious, leaving the reader free for an unprejudiced consideration of the facts.

On Friday, April 18, 1587, after the usual prayers, the spirits, with equivocal gestures and "provocations to sin," gave Kelley to understand that a Divine command required him and Dee to live in such manner as to have their wives in common. With what feelings of horror such an injunction would be received by a man of Kelley's morality and honour may be more easily imagined than described, and he at once took refuge in the assumption that spiritual love and charity was all that was meant. But the unconventional detail into which Madimi entered at the next séance left no room for doubt as to her meaning. A less conscientious medium might have been tempted to conceal such unpalatable revelations, but no such idea crossed Kelley's mind, or, if it did, it was at once dismissed as unworthy of his character and reputation. Only one course remained to a sensitive and honourable man, and that was a counsel of despair; he roundly declared that these angelical beings were the servants of Satan and the children of darkness because they manifestly urged and commanded in the name of God a doctrine damnable to the laws of God and His commandments; for his part he would have nothing more to do with them, and sacrificing his salary to his honour he left his master.

This new doctrine was no less a stumbling-block to Dee than to Kelley, but his faith was more robust and proof against all the insidious assaults of the devil, reason, or scepticism; Kelley's language shocked him and defeated its own object. What more conclusive proof could he have than Kelley's disgust, that this was a genuine command of the spirits? and what more terrible catastrophe could happen to him than by Kelley's departure to be cut off from intercourse with those spirits who had become his guides, philosophers, and friends? At length, actuated, no doubt, solely by consideration for his master, Kelley yielded to his entreaties and consented to resume his position and salary. Had this unhappy victim to spiritualism and friend-ship been an unprincipled debauchee bent on securing his neighbour's wife, the most diabolical ingenuity could not have devised surer methods of attaining the consummation he devoutly wished for, than the communication of the angelical beings. "What is sin?" asked Madimi at their next séance. "To break the commandment of God," answered Dee. "If the self-same God," was the rejoinder, "give you a new commandment, taking away the former form of sin which he limited by law, what remaineth then?" "Then must the same God be obeyed," confessed Dee, and the injunction about having their wives in common was repeated with a threat of terrible punish-ment in case of disobedience—"Behold, evil shall enter into your senses, and abomination shall dwell before your eyes as a recompense, and your wives and your children shall be carried away before your face." Dee trembled and obeyed; his wife consented "for God His sake, and His secret purposes," and a solemn agreement was drawn up and signed by the four parties concerned, to give effect to this new commandment.

But even this heroic measure did not bring a millennium to this singular community, and quarrels, strange in a fraternity so completely guided by the spirits, broke out between the two pious philosophers. At length they agreed to part. Dee handed over to Kelley his powder, books, and instruments, and departed through Germany to England, where he arrived on December 2, 1589; he subsequently became warden of Manchester, and lived to the ripe age of eighty-four. Kelley remained behind at Prague, where he enjoyed the unabated confidence of Rosenberg and the

Emperor. Even Dee apparently had as high an opinion of him as ever, for, though he occasionally complains in his diary of Kelley's behaviour, he recommended him to Burleigh as a man of the keenest intelligence and utmost value for gathering information respecting the secret counsels of foreign states, as well as thorough master of Hebrew, Greek, Latin, French, and Italian—a testimonial not more credible than most panegyrics, in face of a later statement of Dee's that Kelley was quite innocent of Greek. Kelley, however, in spite of his honours, did not feel secure; the Emperor's goodwill was dependent upon the alchemist's ability to provide a sufficient quantity of gold, while the Papal nuncio was constantly urging the imprisonment of a heretic and wizard. There were, besides, numerous other aspirants to favour and a philosopher's fame, who were not sparing of insinuations as to Kelley's honesty and ability. These were ominous symptoms. Kelley, a competent reader of the signs of the times, began to look around him with a view to feathering a nest in a new quarter. Whether or not " his patriot soul within him burned, his footsteps home once more to turn, and tread his native strand," Kelley, after mature reflection, fixed upon England. There were, however, initial difficulties. The suspicion of being a forger and conjurer is not a good introduction anywhere, least of all for a prophet returning to his own country; and Kelley's first object was to create as favourable an impression as possible in the minds of Queen Elizabeth and the Court. He had never quite abandoned the idea of returning to England, and his gift of that remarkable piece of gold cut out of a frying-pan, accompanied with the insinuation that he who had done such a feat once could do it again with obvious advantage to a penurious and parsimonious princess, was doubtless intended as an incentive to an invitation.

In 1589 a fresh means of ingratiating himself presented itself to his mind. It was an age of plots and poison, when every Protestant prince was supposed to be the mark of Jesuit weapon; but a few years had passed since the silent William had fallen a victim to a Jesuit's dagger,

and England was still ringing with the discovery of a
similar attempt upon the Virgin Queen. What better
title to gratitude than the disclosure of such machinations?
Patriotism, according to Johnson, is the last refuge of
scoundrels; and Kelley felt himself compelled, by the
interests of his country and himself, to discover another
Jesuit intrigue; he had himself before had dealings with
the Jesuits who were said to be his friends and ghostly
fathers, but no right-minded man would hesitate to throw
over his friends at the call of duty. The device might
be a little stale, but a generation that has seen Pigott
needs no persuading that people, even grave and reverend
seigniors, when in the mood, possess unbounded credulity;
and the association of the term Jesuit with the conspiracy
was sufficient testimonial to its genuineness. Kelley, then,
had his theory; the next step was to make facts fit the
theory or invent them. It is an easy task, even for
German scholars; it is a trifle to the average imagination, and Kelley was to the manner bred, if not born.
A victim was soon forthcoming in the person of Dr.
Christopher Parkins.

This worthy person was an Englishman, and had been
a Jesuit in Rome. Some years previously Burleigh's son
visited the Eternal City, where a somewhat indiscreet
expression of Protestant opinions brought down on him
the fury of the mob; he owed his life to Parkins's intervention. In gratitude he brought the quondam Jesuit back
to England; his father made Parkins Dean of Carlisle,
and he was frequently employed in missions abroad. One
of these journeys took him to Prague, and there he seems to
have had intercourse with some Jesuits, probably to learn
their secrets with a view to informing Burleigh. This came
to Kelley's ears, and gave him his opportunity. Rapidly
concocting a story with enough detail to give artistic
versimilitude to his invention, he despatched a couple of
servants to London with the following important disclosures, through Divine Providence, made to him in confidence by " one Parkyns, a Jesuit come from Rome to Prague
in Bohemia." The Pope and his confederates had evolved

5

seven methods "of murthering her Majesty Queen Eliza-beth, so that if the first, second, third, fourth and fifth failed, the sixth or seventh should take effect, though all the devils in hell said nay." Parkins was the instrument chosen to proceed to Dantzic, and thence, in the habit of a merchant, to England, as "he was the King of Spain's right-hand man in all his treacherous enterprises against England."

Parkins wrote in great trepidation to Walsingham, hoping that Burleigh would lend his assistance to deliver the innocent from the malicious practice of enemies. He obtained a testimonial from the King of Poland, and the continuation of his embassy proved that confidence was still reposed in him. But Kelley's patriotism met with a reward which must ever encourage the cultivation of similar virtues in others. Burleigh wrote urging him to return to England, and explaining to him of what inestimable use he might be by his admirable art in rescuing his native country from the mighty preparations of the King of Spain. There were indeed, he continued, "some that spake against him as pretending to do a thing impossible; and others had said, that some such there had been, that pretended to that skill, that proved but cheats. But that they at the Court had a more honourable opinion of him." This letter is not without a suspicion of irony, and it concluded with a request that Kelley would send a small portion of his powder to make a demonstration with before her Majesty, or at least enough to defray her charges that summer for the navy. Kelley found the sting of the letter in its tail, and the invitation does not seem to have met with a very eager response. At any rate he remained in Bohemia.

The cloud that threatened him had for the time rolled by; and once more he basked in the sunshine of Imperial favour. His fortunes were now at their zenith. Burleigh wrote two letters more effusive than the last, full of compliments and regrets at his non-arrival in England. The Emperor offered substantial inducements for him to remain, and Kelley was created a Baron of the Empire and Marshal of Bohemia. Agents travelled all the way from England to

consult with him on the north-west passage, and returned
crest-fallen when he declined to sanction the scheme. But
even these marks of honour could not silence the murmur-
ings of the people, and with them Kelley was in no good
odour. Report said that he was deeply in debt. He had
been indiscreet in some of his references to the Emperor and
his Court, and laboured under the suspicion of an attempt to
poison him, of which the following account is given. Rudolf
was reported to be suffering from a throbbing of the heart ;
" Sir Edward Kelley distilled an oyl for it ; which being sent
unto the Emperor, and Sir Edward's enemies being by,
persuaded his Majesty that it was appointed to poison him.
Proof was made of the force of it ; and it wrought the effect
of poison. Some said the throbbing of the heart was given
forth for a colour to hide a more infamous disease ; which
I leave in doubt. The circumstances beat shrewdly about
it. For the oyl is said to have had the vertue of effecting
in favour or otherwise, according to the quantity. Which
for an inward disease soundeth somewhat improbably."
Kelley had, moreover, shown a distressing modesty which
was much misunderstood. A certain Italian named Scoto
had got an introduction at the Court, and challenged Kelley
to an exhibition of his art, which the latter, too generous to
publicly convict a rival of imposture, chivalrously declined
on the plea of sickness. Rudolf was too opaque to appre-
ciate such motives of self-abnegation, and his suspicions
were not allayed by a letter of the Duke of Bavaria,
informing the Emperor that a Venetian alchemist, whom
he had executed at Munich, had confessed to being in sworn
league with Kelley. Rudolf was accordingly not inclined to
allow this retiring alchemist to escape scot-free, and the
intelligence that Kelley had received an invitation from
Queen Elizabeth, and was preparing to depart, convinced
him that a prison was the most efficacious means of preventing that undesirable consummation.

So far Kelley had flourished like a bay-tree on his one
peculiar talent. But accidents will happen even to the
biggest scoundrels. His preparations were progressing
favourably, and by the 29th of April all was ready for

his departure on the morrow. Shortly after dark, however, a friendly hint was sent him that it would be well not to stand upon the order of his going, but go at once. Kelley was not slow to act; he gave no sign, not even to his family, but procuring a horse set out alone for Sobislaus, a town twelve miles from Prague, belonging to Rosenberg. On the next day at noon an unwonted crowd of visitors gathered round his door; it consisted of a portion of the Emperor's guard, the captain and lieutenant of the castle, the provost of the town and a secretary of state, accompanied by the usual mob of urchins and idlers eager for anything new. They had chosen that hour, expecting to find Kelley at dinner; but the bird had flown, and all they could do was to seize his property and seal up the doors; his servants were bound and carried off to prison, and every means was taken to extract his whereabouts from his brother without much success, as his ignorance was as great as their own.

The Emperor's rage knew no bounds; he swore like a trooper, or, as the chronicler has it, "in Dutch fashion"; orders were immediately issued to have the highways watched; every possible hiding-place in Prague was searched, and a post despatched to Rosenberg commanding him forthwith to deliver up Kelley if he took refuge with him. On the 2nd of May he was overtaken at Sobislaus. He had shown his usual cunning in his choice of a retreat, and when charged with his flight, with an air of injured innocence exclaimed that nothing was further from his intentions—he was merely on a visit to his dear friend and patron the Earl of Rosenberg. He protested against being arrested, and said he was a Bohemian (which was true), and councillor of state; but Rudolf was inexorable, and a courier returned with an order for his imprisonment in the castle of Pirglitz, three miles from Prague.

Kelley's first attempt at escape was thus frustrated. But this insult offered to so eminent a man was not allowed to pass unnoticed by the English Court; the Queen despatched an agent named Webb with letters to the Emperor on his behalf; diligent inquiry was made into the cause of his arrest, and Webb's representations seem to have produced some effect upon the Emperor. At all events Kelley was once more set at liberty in October, 1593. But his freedom was short lived. Elizabeth sent a Captain Peter Gwynne to induce him to return to England, and Kelley, having gained sufficient experience of Rudolf, was by no means loth; but a report about this plan, or a fresh access of piety and submission to Rome on the Emperor's part led to the necromancer's re-imprisonment in 1595. This was too much for the patience even of a philosopher: he murdered one of his guards in a moment of exasperation, and thus rendered his position desperate. Perpetual imprisonment stared him in the face. Kelley was not a man to submit calmly to such a fate; he determined once more to escape. His place of confinement was on the city wall; some friends procured horses to be under his window at two o'clock in the morning. Kelley tore up his sheets, and, tying them together, made a rope which reached nearly to the ground. On hearing the appointed sign he began his descent, but alas! he had been no believer in the doctrine that neither eating nor drinking is necessary to man, and corpulency had been the consequence of living not wisely but too well. His descent was scarcely begun when the sheets gave way, and Kelley's fall resulted in the fracture of two legs and a rib. His injuries proved fatal, and after lingering two days in a cottage close by, this sixteenth-century Cagliostro went to join the angelical beings or devils of hell with whom he had enjoyed such entertaining and edifying converse during life.

He left behind him one request. " I venture to hope," he writes in his treatise "De Lapide Philosophorum," "that my name and character will so become known to posterity that I may be counted among those who have suffered much for the sake of truth." The foregoing sketch, biassed though it may be by a pardonable *lues biographica*, is a humble and pious endeavour to meet this pathetic appeal, and show forth a martyr to alchemy and truth in the light he deserves; it is, perhaps, not too much to hope that as such it may afford some comfort, solace, and gratification to Kelley's troubled spirit and to those of the noble army of his imitators and apologists who yet tarry among us, to whom it is, with confidence and affectionate esteem, submitted for approval.

MATTHEW HOPKINS INTERROGATING TWO WITCHES.

MATTHEW HOPKINS.

(DIED, 1647.)

" By the pricking of my thumbs
Something wicked this way comes."
Macbeth (Act iv. sc. i.).

AFTER having been comfortably ignored by the majority
for many centuries, a minute knowledge of witches,
their nature, institutions, and homicidal habits, evolved
amid the forests and mountains, the legends and myths of
Germany, seems to have reached England and become
general during Tudor times. With a curious mental rapidity
the dullest of mankind assimilated the theory and practice
of witchcraft. Men of all ranks became greatly exercised as
to this new department of the universe, much alarmed at
the increasing number of witches and the appalling extension
of their powers. Before the middle of the seventeenth
century the subject had already been solemnly expounded
and carefully systematised by the learned. John Gaule,
in his " Select Cases of Conscience touching Witches
and Witchcraft " (1646), expresses the views of a conscientious believer at this period. From Deuteronomy xviii.
and other Biblical sources he deduces not only the fact
of witchcraft, but principles of witch-classification, " the
nature, the signes, and the markes of witches."

The first law directed against witchcraft proper, making it
a felony, was passed in 1541, and was renewed by Elizabeth
in 1562. Jewell, preaching before the Queen, piously prayed
that " the witches and sorcerers, who in these last four years
are marvellously increased, may never practise further than

upon the subject." But with the advent of James I. the real mania began. The King, who had written a work on Demonology, was a firm believer and had presided in person at several trials in Scotland. One poor woman told him that Satan, with a tremendous oath, had declared " he was the greatest enemy he ever had." This delighted the King, who bragged about it till the end of his life, but did not spare the witch. Another performed before him the very dance she had danced for the pleasure of Satan. The King encored the dance, but burned the poor girl, who had thus lied in vain. Some of the stories were, however, too much even for the credulity of James, who stigmatised many witches as " extreme lyars."

As soon as James came to England, the Parliament, to please him, passed a stringent law against witchcraft, which was responsible for much that followed. Fashion and interest now combined with an already sufficiently strong belief to spread the mania. The delusion became epidemic and penetrated to all parts of the kingdom.

Even the greatest men are not able wholly to escape from their environment. Alone of the Elizabethan dramatists, Ben Jonson, whose strong common sense was worthy of his great intellect, and who was intimately acquainted with occult literature, speaks with no uncertain voice. In his masterpiece, " Volpone," and in his admirable comedy, " The Devil is an Ass," he ridicules fearlessly and unsparingly not only witch-finders, but witchcraft itself. What James thought of his Poet Laureate is not recorded. It is difficult to say what Shakespeare's opinion was on almost any subject, and witchcraft is certainly not one of the few exceptions. His witches, at once grotesque and terrible, embody one phase of the popular belief. They raise storms, they sail through the air, they kill swine, cats and toads are their familiars. But what their creator thought of their reality cannot be known. It is even doubtful whether the great mind of Bacon was free from this delusion. In his " Advancement of Learning," he seems to credit the accounts of witches, but as he was a courtier, and his work was dedicated to the greatest enemy the devil ever had, it is perhaps permissible to doubt his sincerity in this matter. Later, Selden took up the doubtful position that witches, whether real or not, should be executed for their evil wishes, though they might have no power to realise them. Still later, Sir Thomas Browne, the author of "Vulgar Errors Exposed," aided and abetted Sir Matthew Hale in the trial and condemnation of two wretched old women upon evidence which it would be complimentary to call ridiculous.

The witch panic reached its climax during the reign of saints in this country. Multitudes were destroyed between the accession of James I. and the triumph of the Puritans. At least three thousand were hanged or burned during the Long Parliament and the Commonwealth. The time was ripe, and Matthew Hopkins, "Witch-finder General," the Sprenger of England, sprang into being, "new hatched to the woeful time."

Matthew Hopkins was born in Suffolk, early in the seven-teenth century. He was the son of James Hopkins, of Wenham, Suffolk, a "minister." Scarcely anything is known of his early life, but it appears that he practised the law, first at Ipswich, and afterwards at Manningtree in Essex. In 1644 his career as a witch-seeker—a trade never before formally taken up in England—began. His attention appears to have been first called to the subject in March, 1644, when seven or eight witches met in his neighbourhood and offered sacrifices to the devil. Four witches were hanged for sending the devil, in the shape of a bear, to kill him in his garden, a proceeding which naturally incensed him. About this time his success in discovering the devil's works caused the execution of twenty-nine witches in a batch, and made him abandon the law for the calling of a "Witch-finder General."

In this capacity he journeyed on horseback through Essex, Suffolk, Norfolk, and Huntingdonshire, with an assistant named John Stern, and a female searcher. His charges were twenty shillings a town, besides expenses thither and back, and twenty shillings for each witch convicted. Supposed witches were urged to confess, and on the strength of their own confession were hanged. If they refused to confess, they were searched. The "searching" was a process that was hideous in its cruelty: nevertheless Hopkins asseverates that divers witches "have come ten or twelve miles to be searched, of their own accord, and hanged for their labour."

Hopkins was the first to reduce the practice of witch-finding to a science and to systematise the methods in vogue, besides adding novelties of his own invention. He had four principal tests, those of "pricking" and "swimming" being, as he said, the most satisfactory.

A suspected witch, then, was subjected to one or more of the following tests :—

1. She was stripped naked, shaved, and searched for the devil's mark, of which a third teat on any part of the body was the most decisive of guilt; but any mark which was insensible to pain, and which refused to bleed when pricked, was sufficient for the witch-finder's purpose. This method, though a favourite one with Hopkins, was not so widely adopted in England as in Scotland, where the "prickers" formed a separate trade.

2. The witch was placed on a stool, bound if she resisted, and closely watched for at least twenty-four hours, during which time she was kept without meat or drink. If a fly, wasp, or other insect entered the room the watchers endeavoured to kill it; if it escaped, nothing could be clearer than that it was the witch's imp come to suck her blood.[1]

---

[1] This part of the procedure is described with more minuteness by Gaule, who had it on the authority of a witch-finder, confirmed both by a witch and by a witness of the proceedings : "Having taken the suspected witch, she is placed in the middle of a room, upon a stool or table, cross-legged, or in some other uneasy posture; to which, if she submits not, she is then bound with cords; there is she watched and kept without meat for the space of four-and-twenty hours (for they say that within that time they shall see her imp come and suck). A little hole is likewise made in the door, for the imps to come in at; and lest it should come in some less discernable shape, they that watch are taught to be ever anon sweeping the room, and if they see any spiders or flies, to kill them. And if they cannot kill them, then they may be sure they are her imps."

This test, which was the invention of Hopkins himself, was applied to an old woman who confessed that four flies who appeared in her room were her imps, named " Ile-mauzar," " Pye-wackett," " Pecke in the Crowne," and " Griezzell Greedigutt," names which Hopkins declared "no mortal man could invent."

This test was also applied in the case of Elizabeth Clark. With this woman Hopkins watched for three nights, assisted by his confederate Stern, and on the third night she confessed that the devil had appeared to her in the shape of a " proper gentleman." Also that he had three imps, a little dog—white with sandy spots—named " Jar-mara," a greyhound called " Vinegar Tom," and a third, like a polecat, whose name the conscientious Hopkins could not remember at the trial. All these imps were seen by Hopkins himself, and, in addition, a black cat, three times as big as an ordinary cat. This, on being pursued by the greyhound, vanished, and the latter returned to Hopkins "shaking and trembling exceedingly." Stern added the valuable testimony that the third imp's name was " Sacke and Sugar."

3. The third method was to make the suspected witch walk incessantly for many hours till, her feet being blistered, and herself exhausted, she was ready to confess anything to avoid further torture. This was the plan adopted with John Lowes, for fifty years Vicar of Brandeston, in Suffolk. He was nearer eighty than seventy years of age, described by Baxter as a " reading " parson, a strong Loyalist, and no doubt obnoxious to the Parliament on that account. Under the torture described he confessed that he had two imps, and that he commissioned one of them, when he was walking on the shore near Landguard Fort, to sink a ship. This ship, which belonged to Ipswich, was picked out by Mr. Lowes from amongst a number of others, and sank immediately. Fourteen widows were made in a quarter of an hour, and the other ships sailed unconcernedly on. It is worthy of note that, though nothing could have been easier than to verify this remarkable statement, no inquiries were made, and the whole thing was taken for granted. Mr. Lowes

confessed and gloried in many other mischiefs, and declared that he had a charm to keep him out of gaol. In this he was, however, mistaken, for he was hanged at Framling-ham shortly after. He died declaring his innocence, and reciting from memory the Burial Service of the Church of England. This horrible murder was committed in the year of grace 1645.

4. The witch was swum. This was the favourite test of Hopkins, and was applied by tying the right hand to the left foot, and *vice versâ*, and then placing the victim, wrapped in a sheet or blanket, carefully upon the water. If she sank, she was drowned, but without loss of character; if she floated she was found guilty and burned, the idea being that the sacred element used in baptism refused to receive into its bosom an accursed witch.

The career which Hopkins hewed out for himself was fortunately not a long one. It only lasted some three years, but during that time, according to his confederate, Stern, he procured the execution of more than two hundred women. All this time he had the complete approval of Parliament, who sent a committee to support him, and assist, or in other words intimidate, the judges.

At Bury St. Edmunds in 1645 Hopkins procured the execution of eighteen witches in one day, and one hundred and twenty more were left for trial. But the appearance of the King's troops caused an adjournment, and probably saved many lives. At Yarmouth in the same year, sixteen women, all of whom confessed, were hanged.[1] One of these, whose imp took the rather un-common form of a blackbird, made a waxen image of a child, and buried it. She pointed out the spot, but as no image came to light it was quite clear that the devil had removed it—the more so, though the logic of this is not quite obvious, as the child, who had suffered grievous torments, recovered immediately. Another victim had two children by the devil, but as soon as they were born they ran away in "most horrid, strange, ugly shapes."

[1] "Collection of Modern Relations." London, 1693.

At Ipswich Hopkins was also very successful.[1] Many were hanged or burned, notably one "very religious woman" who had three imps—a mole and two dogs—and who had bewitched her husband to death, and also a person who refused to lend her a needle.

At Faversham also, in 1645, which, on the whole, was perhaps Hopkins' best year, though as the records of many of his cases are lost this is not certain, three witches were put to death.[2] In these cases, as in many others, the devil provided his victims but very sparingly with money. In no case did he give more than one shilling at a time, and more frequently sixpence, or even threepence. For this moderate largess, and the promise of an imp, these foolish women had signed away their salvation, had lived in contempt and abject poverty, and had finally been burned alive. But it never seems to have struck any what wretched bargains the witches made for themselves.

In 1646 we find Hopkins at Huntingdon, where he procured the condemnation and murder of numerous unhappy women.[3] Their imps were mostly mice. One Joan Willis was specially favoured by Satan, who visited her in his famous character of "Blackman," and accommodated her with two familiars named "Grissell" and "Greedigut"— dogs with hog's bristles on their backs. To another he appeared as a bear, in which disguise, it will be remembered, he first attempted the virtue of Hopkins himself. One Elizabeth Churcher had two imps named "Beelzebub" and "Trullibub," which to the ordinary eye seemed to be merely walking sticks. But Hopkins said they were imps, and Hopkins being, like Brutus, an honourable man, *convicta et combusta* was the only possible result. Another woman met with the same fate on the evidence of her little seven-year-old daughter, who deposed that her mother rode on a bedstaff. Another had an imp named "Pretty," whose

[1] "Lawes against Witches." London, 1645.
[2] "Witches at Feversham." London, 1645. It is uncertain whether Hopkins took part in the Faversham trials.
[3] "The Witches of Huntingdon" (seven trials). London, 1646, 4to.

speciality was the slaughter of capons. This comparative harmlessness did not, however, save its mistress from the extreme penalty. All these women, and many more, were indiscriminately burned or hanged on the evidence of Hopkins and his confederates, with such outside assistance as could be obtained from children and other foolish or wicked persons, and with the full sanction of the committee of Parliament.

In 1647 he was active at Worcester. There is a great similarity in the witch trials. But in one of the Worcester cases the devil wished to enter into the honourable state of matrimony, from which it may be inferred that the Worcester witches were younger and more attractive than the ordinary witch, who was old, decrepit, and miserable. One of them on being asked what Satan was like replied enigmatically that he was a " properer " man than Hopkins. This is not necessarily a compliment to the Prince of Darkness if we may judge from an extant portrait of the other worthy.

Hopkins was not, however, allowed to proceed long without serious opposition. The first to enter the field against him was John Gaule, the Vicar of Great Staughton, in Huntingdonshire, already alluded to, who in a pamphlet published in 1646 denounced Hopkins as a common nuisance. Gaule, who was a firm believer in witches, states early in his work, " He that will needs persuade himself that there are no witches would as fain be persuaded that there is no devil, and he that can already believe that there is no devil will ere long believe that there is no God." [1] He declares that many popes, friars, nuns, and priests have been notorious witches, and denies the difference between good and bad witches, but divides them into two classes—active witches who act with the devil, and passive witches who are acted upon by him, such as demoniacs. But notwithstanding the orthodoxy of his belief, he denounces the witch-finding trade, and particularly Hopkins, declaring that he would have witches detected by the power of the magistracy and the ministry.

[1] An argument repeated by John Wesley as late as 1768.

"Every old woman," he writes, "with a wrinkled face, a furr'd brow, a hairy lip, a gobber tooth, a squint eye, a squeaking voyce, or a scolding tongue, having a rugged coate on her back, a skull-cap on her head, a spindle in her hand, and a dog or cat by her side, is not only suspected but pronounced for a witch." As for Hopkins's signs, he added, they discover no witch but the user of them.

This pamphlet draws from Hopkins an insolent letter addressed to the authorities at Staughton, in which he stated his intentions to visit their town, provided they showed their due sense of the honour intended them by entertaining him with all respect, and provided they were not, like their pastor, supporters of witches and "such cattle." In case the answer to this should not prove satisfactory he stated that he would waive this shire altogether and betake himself to such places where he might do and punish not only without control, but with thanks and recompense. No answer was returned to this precious communication, and the terrible threat to strike the place out of his visiting list was duly carried out.

This was the beginning of the end, and from Gaule's attack Hopkins never recovered. Several other clergymen, much to their credit, raised their voices against him. Gaule's hint was taken up in certain "queries" presented to the judges at the Norfolk assize, in which the theory that Hopkins was himself an arch-wizard, or something worse, was not obscurely propounded. The calumniated "Discoverer" found it necessary in May, 1647, to publish a pamphlet (so quaint and naïf in its seventeenth-century phrasing that it has been deemed worthy of fuller description at the end of this paper) in answer to the queries and in defence of his methods.

On his return to Essex in 1647 Hopkins, who in three years had made himself more dreaded than any witches, was attacked on all sides. He was accused of sorcery, and it was asserted that he was acquainted with Satan, whom he had cheated out of a memorandum book containing a list of witches. On one occasion he was set upon by a mob, and escaped with difficulty. And it is much to be regretted,

for the sake of poetic justice, that there is no sure
foundation for the story that this canting scoundrel, who
committed his cruelties with a mask of piety, was himself
swum. The statement was long believed that his own
favourite test was applied to him, that he floated, was
taken out, tried, and executed. Hutchinson, in his
" Historical Essay Concerning Witchcraft," written in
1718, certainly states that his thumbs and toes were tied,
that he swam, and was hanged. But there appears to
be no record of this trial, and another account says that
he sank and was drowned, while a third avers that he
swam and escaped from the hands of the mob. There are
some lines in " Hudibras " (Canto III., 139–154), which are
probably responsible for the continuance of this belief.

> " Hath not this present Parliament
> A Ledger to the Devil sent,
> Fully impower'd to treat about
> Finding revolted witches out ?
> And has he not, within a year,
> Hang'd three score of 'em in one shire ?
> Some only for not being drown'd,
> And some for sitting above ground,
> Whole days and nights, upon their breeches,
> And feeling pain, were hang'd for witches.
> And some for putting knavish tricks
> Upon green geese or turkey-chicks ;
> Or pigs that suddenly deceas'd
> Of griefs unnat'ral as he guest ;
> Who after prov'd himself a witch,
> And made a rod for his own breech."

There is no doubt, however, that he gave up the ghost
in 1647, for the register of Mistley, near Manningtree,
contains an entry to the effect that Matthew Hopkins,
son of James Hopkins, Minister of Wenham, was buried
on the 12th of August, 1647, at Mistley. After his
death his confederate, Stern, published in his defence a
" Confirmation and Discovery of Witches," in which he
boasts of the destruction of two hundred women, and
describes Hopkins as a model of virtue and holiness.

The justificatory pamphlet previously mentioned, and laboriously written by Hopkins himself, is not to be overlooked. It bears the title, " The Discovery of Witches : in Answer to severall Queries lately delivered to the judges of assize for the County of Norfolk," and was printed in 1647 with the well-worn text from Exodus (xxii. 18), " Thou shalt not suffer a witch to live." It takes the form of answers to queries which had been, and were likely to be, objected against Matthew in the exercise of his vocation.

To the first insinuation that he " must needs be the greatest witch sorcerer and wizzard himselfe else hee could not doe it," he replied simply, " If Satan's kingdom be divided against itselfe, how shall it stande ? " To the fourth query his answer is so particular as to deserve quotation. " I pray where was this experience " (in matters diabolic) " gained, and why gained by him and not by others ? "

" The discoverer never travelled far for it, but in March, 1644, he had some seven or eight of that horrible sect of witches living in the towne where he lived, a towne in Essex called Maningtree, with divers other adjacent witches of other towns, who every six weeks in the night (being alwayes on the Friday night) had their meeting close by his house, and had their severall solemne sacrifices there offered to the Devill, one of which this Discoverer heard speaking to her imps one night, and bid them goe to another witch, who was thereupon apprehended, and searched by women who had for many yeares knowne the Devill's marks, and found to have three teats about her, which honest women have not : so upon command from the Justice, they were to keep her from sleep two or three nights, expecting in that time to see her familiars, which the fourth night she called in by their severall names and told them what shapes, a quarter of an houre before they came in, there being ten of us in the roome. The first she called was—

" 1. Holt, who came in like a white kitling.

" 2. Jarmara, who came in like a fat spaniel without any legs at all. She said she kept him fat, for she clapt her hand on her belly and said he suckt good blood from her body.

6

" 3. Vinegar Tom, who was like a long-legged greyhound, with an head like an oxe, with a long tail and broad eyes, who, when this Discoverer spoke to and bade him goe to the place provided for him and his angels, immediately transformed himself into the shape of a childe of four yeeres old without a head and gave halfe a dozen turnes about the house, and vanished at the doore.

" 4. Sacke and Sugar, like a black rabbet.

" 5. Newes, like a polcat.

" Immediately after this witch confessed several other witches . . . and upon their searches the same markes were found, the same number, and in the same place, and the like confessions from them of the same imps, and so peached one another thereabouts that joyned together in the like damnable practice, that in our Hundred in Essex, 29 were condemned at once, 4 brought 25 miles to be hanged, where this Discoverer lives for sending the Devill like a Beare to kill him in his garden. So by seeing diverse of the men's Papps and trying wayes with hundreds of them, he gained this experience, and *for ought he knowes any man else may find them as well as he and his company, if they had the same skill and experience.*"

He concludes by indignantly rebutting the charge that his main object was to fleece the country. " Judge," he says, " how he fleeceth the country, and inriches himselfe, by considering the vast summe (of 20s.) he takes of every towne."

Judicet ullus.

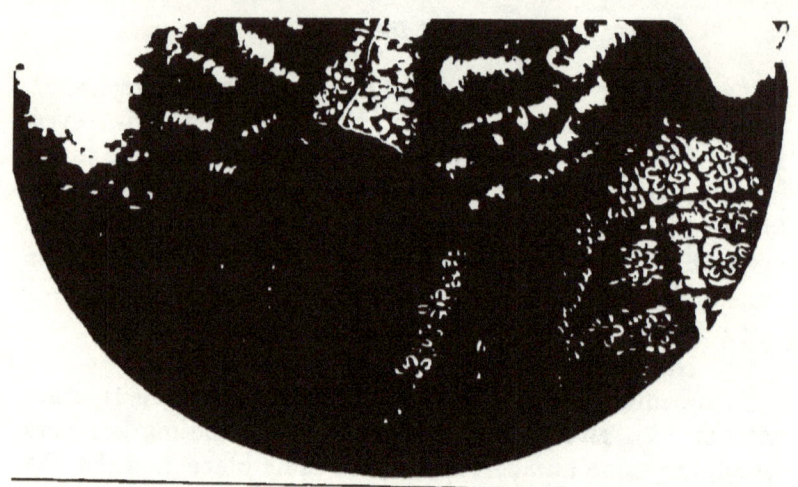

The Right Hon.ble *George* Earle of Flint Viscount Weikham Bar.tt
of Weim L.d High Chancelour of England one of his Ma.ties most hon.ble
Privy Councell

G Kneller pinx: E Cooper sc.

JUDGE JEFFREYS.

JUDGE JEFFREYS.

(1648–1689.)

"In praise your lordship, but ye've had your share
Of that before, if not too much by far;
And new a nobler field for curses are:
Yet I'll not curse, but leave it to the Croud,
Who never talk their rage, but speak aloud.
In all the labyrinths of your crimes they'll track ye,
And with ten thousand furies they'll attack ye.'

— *Life and Death of George, Lord Jeffreys,* 1703.

I.

What worse was Jeffreys a bad man? Not one vice ye
distinguish him from quite a crowd of respectable people of his
day. It was rather the greater field which he had for his
actions, the domineering power of his personality and the
rare affairs which he managed, that gave him an evil reputation in his own age and a worse one in ours. When reading
speeches in court one feels at once that Jeffrey was a
great bully, and as this personal power quickly drove him
and a crowd of unscrupulous rivals to the head of his
session, so it distinguished him from them as a villain
of common order. His father, John Jeffreys, survived
him and was a Welshman of Acton, in Denbighshire. He
was respectable, and brought up a large family with credit—
that is to say, so far as he had anything to do with it.
Afterwards when his son came into Wales he refused
to him. One brother of the Judge went as consul into
——, and another became a successful clergyman. George,
the son, tried various schools, ending with West-
and from Busby, as he wished, in spite of his

The Right Hon.ble GEORGE Earle of Flint Viscount _____
of _____ L.d High Chancellour of England one of his Ma.ties
Privy Counsell

: Posthas pinx

GEO: JEFFRYS.

JUDGE JEFFREYS.

(1648–1689.)

"I'd praise your Lordship, but you've had your share
Of that before, if not too much by far ;
And now a nobler field for curses are :
Yet I'll not curse, but leave you to the Croud,
Who never baulk their rage, but speak aloud :
In all the lab'rinths of your crimes they'll track ye,
Worse than ten thousand furies they'll attack ye."

Life and Death of George, Lord Jeffreys, 1705.

I.

IN what sense was Jeffreys a bad man ? Not one vice will
distinguish him from quite a crowd of respectable people of
his day.   It was rather the greater field which he had for his
actions, the domineering power of his personality, and the
great affairs which he managed, that gave him an evil reputation in his own age and a worse one in ours.   When reading
his speeches in court one feels at once that Jeffreys was a
man of ability, and as this personal power quickly drove him
through a crowd of unscrupulous rivals to the head of his
profession, so it distinguished him from them as a villain
of no common order.   His father, John Jeffreys, survived
him, and was a Welshman of Acton, in Denbighshire.   He
was respectable, and brought up a large family with credit—
that is to say, so far as he had anything to do with it.
Long afterwards when his son came into Wales he refused
to see him.   One brother of the Judge went as consul into
Spain, and another became a successful clergyman.   George,
the sixth son, tried various schools, ending with West-
ninster, and from Busby, as he wished, in spite of his

father, to go to the Bar, he passed to Trinity College, Cambridge, leaving, however, before graduation. In London he was a haunter of taprooms, but very attentive none the less to the little arts of getting on in the world in which he was afterwards so proficient. His biographer records that he was poor, and probably sought the tavern because he had no better place to go to, or no other place at all. For his wit, or what passed for wit, he could get a free dinner, and after all he was not yet twenty. So passed his student days. During the Plague, a tradition, which Woolrych half believes, says that he once pleaded at the Kingston Assizes. Two years after the plague he was called to the Bar. There is said to have been a great deal of legal business at the time of the Restoration, and it is suggested by one writer that the main set of it lay towards the Guildhall and Clerkenwell. At Hicks's Hall, then, in the City, and probably on the home circuit, Jeffreys first made his mark. He cannot have known much law, but he had just what was wanted in the smaller courts—a knowledge of the world picked up from studying the weaknesses of men in pothouses, and a quick, ready, rough sort of wit which, as Macaulay says, went straight to the point. No sensible person will believe that a man ever became Lord Chancellor of England without something in which he was better than his neighbours, and that something not of the worst. Jeffreys had a good voice, audible at a considerable distance, as a witness confessed in the trial of Sir Patience Ward for perjury, and he soon became what we would now call the leading junior. Woolrych records a few anecdotes of this time which well illustrate the style of cross-examination then in vogue. A countryman was giving evidence in a leathern doublet, and when Jeffreys came to cross-examine he bawled out, "You fellow in the leather doublet, pray what have you for swearing?" The man looked steadily at him, and said, "Truly, sir, if you have no more for lying than I have for swearing, you might wear a leather doublet as well as I." Such was the practice at Hicks's Hall.

Jeffreys now designed to advance his fortunes by a rich marriage, and paid his addresses to the daughter of a wealthy merchant in the City. As the way then was, he worked by deputy, having secured the good graces of a companion to the lady. Unfortunately the intrigue was discovered and the companion dismissed. A marriage, nevertheless, took place in May, 1667, when Jeffreys married, not the lady, but the companion, whose name was Sarah Neesham; she was the daughter of a clergyman.

The City connection, which his successful practice at Hicks's Hall was enlarging, was now to prove valuable to Jeffreys. A namesake, John Jeffreys, an alderman of London, known as "The Great Smoaker," took a fancy to him, and by his influence he became, in March, 1671, Common Sergeant of London in succession to Sir Richard Browne. One of his earliest services to the City was his appearance before the Council at Whitehall on behalf of the Worshipful Company of Stationers who had suffered damage by the printing of a psalter which the piratical publisher had skilfully named the King's Psalter. It was on this occasion that Jeffreys is reported to have commenced his speech in the following remarkable fashion. Speaking of the opposing publishers: " They have teem'd with a spurious brat, which, being clandestinely midwiv'd into the world, the better to cover the imposture they lay it at your Majesty's door," &c. Of this kind of eloquence all one can say is that it was successful : Charles was amused, and the case went in favour of the Stationers.

It was rumoured that Sir John Howel (before whom Penn had appeared for street preaching) was about to retire from the Recordership, and Jeffreys saw that if further advancement was to come it must come from the Court party and not from the City. He was a boon companion of Chiffinch, the celebrated page of the back stairs, and, though his loyalty in the City seems to have been questionable, Chiffinch probably reported him as a suitable man for the King's shifty business. The Duchess of Portsmouth may have aided him, as he was of her party ; in any case he became Recorder in succession to Sir William Dolben, who had followed Howel for a short time and who proved in the King's Bench subsequently that he had remembered what

Jeffreys had forgotten—his City principles. This in 1678 ; he had become Sir George Jeffreys in 1677. Just before he became Recorder his wife died, and he lost no time in marrying the widow of a Mr. Jones, who was daughter of Sir Thomas Bludworth, a former Lord Mayor. There were reasons not very honourable to Jeffreys for this speedy re-marriage, and his wife was afterwards noted as a " dame of most slippery courses."

Sir George now presided at the Guildhall and frequently acted as Crown prosecutor. In the hurricane of excitement about the Popish Plot he found it hard work to steer a steady course towards advancement. He was evidently perplexed by " the wild tacking of the Court." At first, accordingly, he professed to be an upholder of the Protestant religion, whether sincerely or not may be left to others to decide ; but he certainly was little worse than his contemporaries ; Wool-rych discovers a number of instances in which he seems to have been more lenient. But his reward soon came, for he " scrupled so little, and did so much " ; he was made a Sergeant-at-Law in 1680, a Welsh Judge, and Chief Justice of Chester, and in 1681 became a baronet. All this before he was forty.

His intimacy with the Court was now established. As Solicitor-General to the Duke of York he was no exclusionist and indeed seems to have tried to influence the Corpora-tion in the duke's favour. He grew very arrogant as he rose so rapidly, and experienced the checks to which such men are liable. At the Kingston Assizes in 1679 he mono-polised the conduct of a case and was ordered by Baron Weston to hold his tongue. He foolishly complained that he was not being well treated. The Judge retorted, " Ha, since the King has thrust his favours upon you in making you Chief Justice of Chester, you think to run down every-body ; if you find yourself aggrieved, make your complaint; here's nobody cares for it." After another attempt to speak Jeffreys burst into tears. The best description of his life at this time is that furnished by Henry Booth, the member for Cheshire, and afterwards Lord Delamere (in the course of a speech, however, be it remembered upon the Corruption of

Judges): " But I cannot be silent as to our Chief Judge, and I will name him because what I have to say will appear more probable : his name is Sir George Jeffreys, who, I must say, behaved himself more like a Jack-pudding than with that gravity which beseems a Judge: he was mighty witty upon the prisoners at the bar ; he was very full of his jokes upon people that came to give evidence, not suffering them to declare what they had to say in their own way and method, but would interrupt them, because they behaved themselves with more gravity than he ; and in truth, the people were strangely perplexed when they were to give in their evidence; but I do not insist upon this, nor upon the late hours he kept up and down our City: it's said he was every night drinking till two o'clock, or beyond that time, and that he went to his chamber drunk ; but this I have only by common fame, for I was not in his company ; . . . but in the mornings he appeared with the symptoms of a man that overnight had taken a large cup." The speaker further showed what in those times was a more serious cause of complaint than these irregular habits—the neglect of the assize business.

Jeffreys had now taken the Court side and must stand by his masters. The Popish plot had not produced the effects which some had hoped, and the attempt to convert it into a means for removing the Duke of York from the succession in favour of the Duke of Monmouth had hitherto failed. In the conflict between the Petitioners and the Abhorrers Jeffreys was forced to take a side, and as an abhorrer he naturally displeased his old friends in the City. His conduct in obstructing the presentation of petitions in Parliament was referred to a select committee, and that committee, through Mr. Trenchard, reported very unfavourably of him in 1680. He seems to have been cowed, and weakly surrendered his Recordership to Sir George Treby. Charles, who had a stouter heart, does not seem to have wished him to give way, but observing "that he was not Parliament-proof," he allowed him to retire. Jeffreys was on this occasion, at all events, as North says, " none of the intrepids." The mob burnt him in effigy.

It is somewhat strange to notice that after these difficulties Jeffreys still possessed considerable interest in the City. The Court could do nothing for him for the present, but his wife's relations had influence; the City was not very united. Jeffreys, being appointed Chairman of the Middlesex Sessions, which were held at his old haunt Hicks's Hall, attempted to prevent Dissenters from serving on the jury. He thus came into conflict, as he had hoped, with one party in the Corporation, as the Under Sheriff had the returning of the panel. The dispute ended in the Sheriff's reforming the panel; but Jeffreys was soon far too busily employed in other affairs to take much thought of what was doing at Hicks's Hall.

In the year 1681 he amply vindicated the Court's choice of him as an instrument. He secured the conviction of Fitzharris by a speech of great force and vigour which fairly carried the jury with him; at the trial of the titular Archbishop Plunket he forgot himself in the violence of his rhetoric and had to be checked by Sawyer, the Attorney-General. But any one who wishes to get a good notion of the judicial ferocity of the time must read the accounts of the trial of Stephen College. College was clearly a villain, though a good many people of his acquaintance seem to have thought otherwise; but he was fighting for his life, and in the sultry courthouse, through the long August days, had to keep up a hand-to-hand fight with Jeffreys. The Attorney-General and the Solicitor seem to have kept fairly quiet, but Jeffreys thundered and swore and bandied jokes with the witnesses— in fact did exactly what he was paid to do. He had a nasty rap or two, however, having not overclean a record. Two witnesses reminded him of his troubles in Parliament, and it cannot have been pleasant to have had the reminiscence suggested by Oates.

In attacking the privileges of the City in 1682 and 1683 Jeffreys gratifies at once his hatred of the aldermen and of the Dissenters. His subsequent exertions against the northern towns were dictated by a love of power and a desire of pleasing his master. Charles, not being very exacting, not even requiring the " little probity " demanded of

Dubois, Jeffreys became Lord Chief Justice of England in 1683, and was at once called on to preside at one of the most memorable trials of the time—that of Algernon Sidney. " Let us have no remarks, but a fair trial, in God's name," he began. This sounds well enough, being occasioned by the whispering to the jury which went on in court. But even if the whole of the villainy of the trial be not true, he had a very odd notion of fairness. " I must," said the unfortunate Sidney just before judgment, " appeal to God and the world, I am not heard." Of Jeffreys, however, one said, " So as he rode on horseback he cared not whom he rode over." A few days after the trial he was noted by Evelyn at a wedding and reported to be very merry—though Evelyn was somewhat hard to please in the matter of gravity, as Pepys has borne witness.

Before James became King, Jeffreys had a great opportunity for proving his attachment to the Throne. He was admitted to the Cabinet. He was the King's instrument in freeing the Romish recusants. He never seems to have been a Roman Catholic, though he may have " hesitated, repented, trembled," as it was said at the time. His horror of Dissent continued through life. A minister called Rosewell fell in his path at this time, and after being imprisoned with some severity, owing to the temper of the Chief Justice, only escaped by an accident. Much, no doubt, of the severity he exercised was due to his opposition to Lord Guilford, whose place of Lord Keeper Jeffreys coveted, and who, moreover, headed the moderate party at Court just as Jeffreys headed the advanced one. Jeffreys secured the advancement of Sir Robert Wright in spite of Guilford's opposition, and if he be said to have pushed the fortunes of a worthless lawyer, Guilford is not without blame in yielding to the King's wishes.

In running foul of Baxter, under King James, Jeffreys, in gratifying his hatred of a Dissenter, employed language which fully justified Charles II.'s description of him as possessing " more impudence than ten carted street-walkers." The blame of the conviction, however, rests rather with the law than with the Judge; and of instruments Sir Roger

L'Estrange must come in for condemnation as well as
Jeffreys. Let us follow the trial in the authorised account.
Baxter was committed, by Jeffreys' warrant, to the King's
Bench prison on February 28, 1685, for printing and pub-
lishing, " Quemdam falsum seditiosum libellosum, factiosum
et irreligiosum librum, called a Paraphrase on the Testament
with notes, doctrinal and Practical." So runs the indictment.
On the 15th of May, having pleaded not guilty, he moved for
more time, being ill. This brought out Jeffreys in his most
dreadful mood. He roared out, " I will not give him a
minute's time more, to save his life. We have had to do with
other sort of persons, but now we have a saint to deal with ;
and I know how to deal with saints as well as sinners.
Yonder stands Oates in the pillory, and he says he suffers for
the truth, and so says Baxter, but if Baxter did but stand on
the other side of the pillory with him, I would say two of the
greatest rogues and rascals in the kingdom stood there."
This language is doubtless vigorous, but it is hardly calculated to secure a man a fair trial. Baxter had little worldly
prudence. He stood forward as a representative man, and
on the 30th of May, when he was formally tried at the
Guildhall, he was represented by Wallop, amongst other
counsel, a lawyer peculiarly objectionable to Jeffreys. The
passages reflecting on the bishops marked by Sir Roger,
having been read out, Wallop proceeded to argue that they
were rather matters for the Bishops' Court, and in any case
were not libellous. " Mr. Wallop," says the Lord Chief
Justice, " I observe that you are in all these dirty causes!
and were it not for you, gentlemen of the long robe, who
should have more wit and honesty than to support and hold
up these factious knaves by the chin, we should not be at
the pass we are at." " My Lord," says Mr. Wallop, " I
humbly conceive that the passages accused are natural
deductions from the text." " You humbly conceive," says
Jeffreys, "and I humbly conceive. Swear him—swear him!"
" My Lord, under favour, I am counsel for the defendant ;
and if I understand either Latin or English, the information
now brought against Mr. Baxter upon so slight a ground
is a greater reflection upon the Church of England than

anything contained in the book he is accused for." Said
Jeffreys to him, "Sometimes you humbly conceive, and
sometimes you are very positive; you talk of your skill in
Church history, and of your understanding Latin and
English; I think I understand something of them as well as
you; but in short must tell you that if you do not understand your duty better, I shall teach it you." Upon which
Mr. Wallop very wisely sat down, and Rotheram urged, with
small success, Baxter's well-known moderation in dealing
with the Church of England in his writings and practice.
Baxter himself added that he had incurred the censure of
some of his own party for his attitude. "Baxter for
bishops," said Jeffreys, roused in a moment; "that is a merry
conceit indeed! Turn to it! turn to it!" Upon this Rotheram
read a passage from the Paraphrase to the effect that great
respect was due to those truly called to be bishops. "Ay,"
says Jeffreys, "this is your Presbyterian cant—'Truly called
to be bishops'; that is himself, and such rascals called to be
bishops of Kidderminster (an allusion to Baxter's request to
be allowed to continue preaching there) and other such-like
places; bishops set apart by such factious snivelling Presbyterians as himself; a Kidderminster bishop he means,
according to the saying of a late learned author; and every
parish shall maintain a Tithe-pig Metropolitan." Baxter
beginning again, Jeffreys: "Richard, Richard, dost thou
think we will hear thee poison the court? Richard, thou art
an old fellow—an old knave; thou hast written books enough
to load a cart; every one is as full of sedition (I might say
treason) as an egg is full of meat; hadst thou been whipt
out of thy writing trade forty years ago, it had been happy.
Thou pretendest to be a preacher of the gospel of peace, and
thou hast one foot in the grave; it is time for thee to begin
to think what account thou intendest to give; but leave thee
to thyself, and I see thou wilt go on as thou hast began; but
by the grace of God I'll look after thee. I know thou hast
a mighty party, and I see a great many of the brotherhood
in corners, waiting to see what will become of their mighty
Don; and a doctor of the party (looking at Doctor Bates) at
your elbow; but, by the grace of Almighty God, I will crush

you all." This celebrated harangue cannot properly be understood without Jeffreys' summing up, but the vigour of the
language is unmistakable; the speech was reported by friends
of Baxter, who had good reasons for not forgetting it.

The whole case of course turned on the construction of the
selected passages. Atwood took the natural course of reading some of the context which would throw light on their
meaning, but to this Jeffreys, probably a little wearied,
objected at once. "You sha'n't draw me into a conventicle
with your annotations, nor your snivelling parson neither."
"My Lord" replied Atwood, "I conceive this to be expressly
within Rosewell's case lately before your Lordship." "You
conceive," said Jeffreys—"you conceive amiss; it is not."
"My Lord, that I may use the best authority, permit me to
repeat your Lordship's own words in that case." "No, you
sha'n't; you need not speak, for you are an author already,
though you speak and write impertinently." Jeffreys proceeded to attack what Atwood had published, and Atwood to
defend it. Jeffreys often ordered him to sit down, but he
stuck to his argument on the construction of the passages,
and in the main, as Jeffreys confessed, he had his say. Poor
Baxter had no say, as Jeffreys wished to clear the way for his
summing up. "'Tis notoriously known" he began, "there
has been a design to ruin the King and nation; the old game
has been renewed, and this has been the main incendiary.
He is as modest now as can be; but time was when no man
was so ready at, 'Bind your kings in chains, and your nobles
in fetters of iron,' and 'To your tents, O Israel.' Gentlemen,
for God's sake do not let us be gulled twice," and so forth.
This gives the strength of Jeffreys' position in all these
matters, and to some extent affords an excuse for his violence.
The opposition were traitors, just as they had been in Henry
VIII.'s time. A criminal lawyer will tell you that it is hard
enough to get free out of the dock at the present day, no
matter how you got there in the first instance, and the
presumption of guilt was in the time of the Stuarts, and
later too, very strong against any who were caught. The
criticism frequently raised against the Tudor and Stuart
trials that they proceeded so cruelly on such slender evidence

does not properly meet the case. The real evidence was generally the whole life of the man on his trial. The Government judged that he ought to be killed, and ordinary men knew that as a main thing the Government ought to be supported, and, finding the verdict, left the court to set out the legal reasons, with which they had little to do. It is obvious that in a period when such principles ruled the instruments of Government must not be judged too harshly, being in a large measure the instruments of the people. The jury who found Baxter guilty were doubtless ordinary citizens, and it won't do to say too often that these seventeenth-century juries were bullied into their verdicts. They cannot all have been. A far more probable solution would regard them as caring very little about the matter at all, only perhaps thinking Baxter a nuisance. Nuisance or not, his trial illustrates the stormy atmosphere of a Restoration Court of Justice.

When James came to the throne he already knew the value of Jeffreys, previously his Attorney-General. He became a peer as Baron Jeffreys of Wem, and had a chance of distinguishing himself in the trial of Oates, which is elsewhere related in this book.

II.

If Jeffreys had died in June, 1685, he would have been hardly heard of, or would have been known only as Shower, Wilkins, Hawles, or Wright are known. He might have been remembered by a few persons as the persecutor of Baxter; but he probably would not have been notorious.

But the Western Assize was at hand. In his Somersetshire progress, which Mr. Ewald has carefully traced, we see a striking instance of the degeneration which comes of opportunity. Monmouth landed in June, 1685, and all was over in July, but Jeffreys was not sent out till August, when the country was quiet. As his Elegy says:—

" 'Twas him the Popish party wisely chose
To splutter Law, and the dinned Rabble pose."

Not for the reason given, but because he had a cruel, determined heart, and, when he had chosen the stronger side, stuck at nothing. On the circuit he was known as " The Lord General Judge" because, as one of his biographers says, " he went not only Judge, but had a Breviate under King James's hand, to command what Troops he pleased to attend his commands from place to place. And was Lieutenant-General as well as Judge, and he gave daily the word, and orders for going the rounds, &c., and ordered what party of Troops he pleased to attend him." A curious incident is recorded of this military progress, which well illustrates the terror which was inspired : " 'Tis to be remembered that the fellow called Tory Tom, at Wells, for his dirty sauciness was sent to the guard by this Major (in command) ; when presently this Tory Tom petitioned some persons to intercede with the Major and sent the Major a letter, desiring his liberty ; for that if he or any one should give Tory Tom an ill word to Judge Jeffreys, the Judge would hang him right or wrong with the rest of the prisoners." Such was the spirit in which the gloomy cavalcade set out for Winchester. With Jeffreys in the commission were William Montague, a man of integrity, who was afterwards turned out for standing too stiff in the matter of the dispensing power, and three puisne judges, one of whom was Sir Robert Wright, a true butcher-bird, as Woolrych says, and one who had been advanced by Jeffreys. The trial of Alice Lisle was the only case at Winchester. Jeffreys had now impaired his constitution by overworking and overdrinking, his originally handsome features were becoming bloated and savage, and, as his nerves were shattered, he required constant stimulant. He was probably hard pushed in purse as well as body, and seems to have regarded the assizes as a good opportunity of repairing his fortunes. It is difficult to say, of course, what bribery is nowadays, but at the close of the seventeenth century, when judges were in the habit of taking presents, it meant certainly less than it does now.

Lady Lisle was the widow of that John Lisle, of the Council of State, who, after taking part in the Government of the Commonwealth, fled to Switzerland at the Restoration. He was, on the 10th of August, 1664, shot down at Lausanne, as he was going to church, by two men in disguise, carrying musquetoons. Lady Lisle had only afforded common hospitality to two refugees from the insurrection; "both ill men enough indeed, and one in a proclamation." Hicks, one of these two, was a Dissenting divine, and was said to be brother to the Dean of Worcester, who, if the story be true of his refusing to plead for his brother, was not fond of the connection. The tale may have been fabricated. It was very easy to prove that the men were traitors, but in doing so it is noteworthy that almost all the questions were put by Jeffreys in person; some notable passages took place. Pollexfen, who strangely figured as counsel for the Crown, swore one James Dunne as a witness, and warned Jeffreys at the time that he was unwilling. Hence, in the course of examination, the following remarkable address was delivered by the Lord Chief Justice: "Now mark what I say to you, friend: I would not by any means in the world endeavour to fright you into anything, or any ways tempt you to tell an untruth, but provoke you to tell the truth, and nothing but the truth—that is the business we come about here. Know, friend, there is no religion that any man can pretend to, can give a countenance to lying, or can dispense with telling the truth; thou hast a precious immortal soul, and there is nothing in the world equal to it in value. There is no relation to thy mistress, if she be so; no relation to thy friend; nay, to thy father and thy child; nay, not all the temporal relations in the world can be equal to thy precious immortal soul. Consider that the great God of heaven and earth, before whose tribunal thou, and we, and all persons, are to stand at the last day, will call thee to an account for the rescinding His truth, and take vengeance of thee for every falsehood thou tellest. I charge thee, therefore, as thou wilt answer it to the great God, the Judge of all the earth, that thou do not dare to waver one tittle from the truth, upon any account or pretence whatsoever; for though it were to save thy life, yet the value of thy precious and immortal soul is much greater, than that thou shouldst forfeit it for the saving of any the most precious outward blessing thou dost enjoy ; for that God of heaven may justly strike thee into eternal flames, and make thee drop into the bottomless lake of fire and brimstone, if thou offer to deviate the least from the truth, and nothing but the truth. . . . For I tell thee God is not to be mocked, and thou canst not deceive Him, though thou mayst us. But I assure you, if I catch you prevaricating in any the least tittle (and perhaps I know more than you think I do ; no, none of your saints can save your soul, nor shall they save your body neither) I will be sure to punish every variation from the truth that you are guilty of." Dunne was a man favourable to the rebels, and had given them assistance, hence it was difficult to get much out of him, and a long examination ensued. At one point he contradicted himself. Jeffreys was down on him at once. " How came you to be so impudent, then, as to tell me such a lie ?" " I beg your pardon, my Lord." " You beg my pardon ! That is not because you told me a lie, but because I have found you in a lie." The Judge, of course, laboured hard to show the connection between Lady Lisle and the rebels, and hence the evidence of Dunne was of some importance, as he had brought Hicks and Nelthorp to the house on the night in question. As the examination continued, and Dunne prevaricated more and more, Jeffreys became more and more furious. His appeals to Heaven and suggestions of future punishment grew more frequent. At one time he turned almost in despair to the jury and said : " What pains is a man at to get the truth out of these fellows ! And it is with a great deal of labour, that we can squeeze one drop out of them ! A Turk has more title to an eternity of bliss than these pretenders to Christianity, for he has more morality and honour in him." Later in the same vein : " O blessed God ! was there ever such a villain upon the face of the earth ?" and again " I hope, gentlemen of the jury, you take notice of the strange and horrible carriage of this fellow ; and withal you cannot but observe the spirit of that sort of people, what a villainous and devilish one it is. Good God ! that ever the thing called religion (a word that people have so much abused) should ever wind up persons to such a height of impiety, that it should make them lose the belief that there is a God of truth in heaven. . . . It may well make the rest of mankind, that have any sort of faith in a Deity and a future life, abhor and detest both the men and their religion, if such abominable principles may be called so. A Turk is a saint to such a fellow as this; nay, a Pagan would be ashamed to be thought to have no more truth in him. O blessed Jesus! what an age do we live in, and what a generation of vipers do we live among!" and so forth.

In all this Jeffreys was carried away by passion, and over-shot the mark. As Dunne said, he was "cluttered" out of his senses. But in method Jeffreys was acting on an instinct of his own, which seldom failed to effect its purpose. He was talking the language of the man—the language of Non-conformity. Dunne was made use of to prove the harbouring of rebels, and, with the aid of Colonel Penruddock, who had made the arrest, a case was made out to go to the jury. The poor prisoner had small chance of explaining, and, as she did not produce any relevant evidence, the summing up was dead against her. A juryman asked the very pertinent question whether she could be convicted of harbouring traitors before they had been judicially decided to be such, received the answer, undoubtedly a wrong answer, that such was possible. It was on this technical ground that the subsequent reversal of the sentence was based. The jury retired, and after some explanations by Jeffreys, found the prisoner guilty, the Judge remarking when the sentence was recorded that he considered the evidence as full and plain as could be, and that had he been among them, and the prisoner his own mother, he should have found her guilty. What Jeffreys meant when he advised her to use her pen and paper well is not quite clear. It can hardly have been an invitation to bribery, or it would have been given less publicly. It more probably was meant to suggest that the prisoner would gain by betraying others, and this view seems most in accord with Jeffreys' often repeated assertion that the Western Rebellion was throughout a plot of the Dissenters.

The King's business settled at Winchester, Jeffreys passed on to Salisbury, but no one was executed there. Thence to

7

Dorchester, where he was observed to laugh ominously when the preacher alluded to mercy in the assize sermon. A violent charge to the jury succeeded, "so passionately expressed as seemed rather the language of a Romish Inquisitor than a Protestant Judge," after which the jury found true bills against thirty prisoners for high treason committed in aiding and abetting the Duke of Monmouth. It did not matter much perhaps what the prisoners did, but they made death certain by putting themselves on their trial, Jeffreys having fairly warned them that "if the country found them guilty they should have but little time to live." Twenty-nine were condemned, sentence was pronounced, and the warrant issued for their execution. This drastic method was employed to save the trouble of trying the hundreds who remained. Jeffreys may well have been anxious for haste. He was tortured by the stone; the court sat late as it was, and if all had been fairly heard the trials would have taken months. Thus he hoped that by trying on Saturday and hanging on Monday a wholesome terror would be infused throughout the West. It is to be feared also that direct inducement was given to confession by agents of the Judge, promises being made to the prisoners that in that direction lay the only hope of mercy. The culprits were now either intimidated or deceived, and business proceeded more rapidly. Nearly three hundred were condemned to death, but of them only seventy-four seem to have been executed. The rest were punished in various ways, some being transported, some fined, and others flogged. Jeffreys knew how to be severe in the arrangement of the whippings; but such was the general terror that little notice was taken of anything short of death. One Wiseman was ordered to be flogged in every market-town in Dorset.

The whole countryside was now gloomy with men's quarters swinging on the gibbets, and there was fear of much more before the assizes were concluded. Jeffreys moved with his cavalcade towards Exeter, and was everywhere surrounded with suppliants, who begged mercy for their relatives waiting the coming of the Lord Chief Justice in the gaols of Exeter and Taunton. These he very rightly repulsed, but his method of treating them seems to have been rough. At a gentleman's house where he was resting for the night a broil arose among the Judge's servants, in the course of which pistols were fired, giving him ground for supposing that an assault upon his life had been intended. Probably he was in pain also, but he had no excuse for promising the people of the place that not a man from their district, if convicted, should escape.

The Devonshire element in the rebellion was not large, and, as one says, "here there was a little sparing." As a matter of fact, the King's mercy was very generously exercised at Exeter, if the "Western Martyrology" is to be believed, as there were 243 prisoners and only 12 executions. There was heavier work waiting in Somersetshire. Taunton was crowded with prisoners who had been slowly hunted down by bands of soldiers or captured on the field of battle. Moreover, it was considered necessary to make an example of the town which had been so eager to receive the ass in the lion's skin. One hundred and thirty-four prisoners were executed, 198 transported, and others of the 400 waiting trial variously dealt with. So Mr. Ewald's careful statement. The almost contemporary account which has come down to us, though a little wild in its figures, is not without a certain severity of language which suits the subject. "Amongst these at Taunton were divers eminent persons that had been taken in the West and carried to London, and brought down there to compleat the bloody tragedy in those Parts : Mr. Parrot, Mr. Hewling the Elder, Mr. Lisle, Mr. Jenkins, Mr. Hucker, and divers others were very eminent. To take notice of every particular in this matter will alter our Design, and swell the Book to too great a bulk, being only designed for a pocket companion, and useful it may be to see the cruelty of men when in their Power, and how the Devil stirreth up his Instruments, to pursue those that adventure for the Cause of God and Religion. Here were in this country executed 239. The rest that were condemned were transported, except such as were able to furnish coin, and that not a little ; for an account was taken of men's abilities, according to which the purchase for life must be managed by two of his (Jeffreys') favourites, who had a small share, the rest went into his Lordship's pocket; according to the actions of Rome where sins of any kind may be pardoned for money. This indeed was a glorious design in the eye of Mother Church, to root out heresies by executions and transportations, to make room for a pack; here expedition must be made to conclude at Wells; For that a great man being fallen, our great Judge designing his chair, which in short he had, as the reward of so eminent and extraordinary a piece of service as he did for the advancement of the Roman Catholic interest which is cruel always where it prevails." The story of the girl's death from fright of Jeffreys may or may not be true, but she died at Taunton, and was one of those who had helped to work Monmouth's banner.

Dreadful scenes were enacted at Wells, where Ken did his best for the prisoners. The total number of deaths was not great, however, for a great rebellion. It was rather the suddenness of the thing—the fact of its being confined to so small an area—that produced such an impression. Jeffreys once asked an officer how many the soldiers had killed, and was told a thousand. "I believe," he reflected, "I have condemned as many as that myself." The real reason for the move to Wells lay in the fact that the accommodation for prisoners at Taunton would not allow of any further addition to the number of those waiting punishment. Many were accordingly taken to Wells in carts, and ninety-five suffered there the extreme penalty of the law.

At Bristol there were many who sympathised with the rebellion, but who had been kept in check by those of the King's party. Hence very few were executed. The fame of the Judge General had gone out before him, and he was received with great state and ceremony by the magistrates, in spite of the fact that he had slighted them by putting his name before that of the mayor in the commission, and that he viewed the corporation with anything but favour. When he saw the preparations which had been made he merely said, "Lord, we have been used to these things," and proceeded with his charge to the grand jury. Beginning with an allusion to the excitement of the townspeople, he said,

"Gentlemen, I find here are a great many auditors, who are very intent as if they expected some formal or prepared speech, but assure your selves, we come not neither to make set speeches, nor formal Declamations, nor follow a couple of puffing Trumpeters; for Lord we have seen those things Twenty times before: No, we come to do the King's Business. But," he went on, "I find a Special Commission is an unusual Thing here and relishes very ill; nay the very women storm at it, for fear we should take the upper hand with them too; for by the by, gentlemen, I hear it is much in fashion in this city for the women to govern and bear sway." He then turned to subjects which made every heart beat faster. Speaking, as he said, not "in so smooth language as you may expect," owing "partly to the pain of the stone under which I labour, and partly to the unevenness of this day's journey." Who cannot see the prematurely old man with savage and bloodshot eyes, pulling himself together to do his best for his employers, his mouth twitching with pain, and pouring out a rough, ferocious eloquence of which the trembling audience felt every word? "Good God! O Jesu! That we should live in such an age." "Had we not the Rye Conspiracy wherein they not only designed to have murthered that most blessed (for so now we may conclude him to be with God Almighty) prince?" "Had we not the Bill of Exclusion?" "Had we not the cursed Counsel of Achitophel? Great God of Heaven and Earth! what reason have men to rebel? but as I told you, Rebellion is like the sin of Witchcraft; Fear God, and, Honour the King, is rejected by people for no other reason, as I can find, but that it is written in St. Peter. Gentlemen, I must tell you, I am afraid that this city hath too many of these people in it. And it is your duty to search them out: For this City added much to that ship's Loading; there was your Tylys, your Roes and your Wades, men started up like mushrooms, scoundrel fellows, mere sons of Dunghills: these men must forsooth set up for liberty and property. A fellow that carries the sword before Mr. Mayor, must be very careful of his property, and turn Politician, as if he had as much property as the person before whom he bears the sword; though perchance not worth a grote. Gentlemen, I must tell you, you have still here the Tylys, the Roes, and the Wades: I have brought a brush in my pocket, and I shall be sure to rub the dirt wherever it lies, or on whomsoever it sticks. Gentlemen, I shall not stand complimenting with you, I shall talk with some of you before you and I part: I tell you—I tell you, I have brought a besom and I will sweep every man's door, whether great or small." The King's cause was well served in Bristol, but there must have been a party there for the enemy, as a signal had been made to them from the river. There were too many trimmers in the city. "These men stink worse than the worst dirt you have in your city; these men have so little religion, that they forget that he that is not for us is against us. Gentlemen, I tell you, I have the Calendar of this City here in my hand; I have heard of those that have searched into the very sink of a conventicle to find out some sneaking rascal to hide their money by night. Come, come, gentlemen, to be plain with you, I find the dirt of the ditch is in your nostrils. Good God! Where am I? In Bristol? This City, it seems, claims the privilege of hanging and drawing amongst themselves: I find you have more need of a commission once a month at least." And more to the same purpose, reading oddly enough now, but pregnant with meaning enough then. If some of the corporation could have been caught it would have been a valuable take, but this was impossible, and only three persons were executed.

Jeffreys now returned homewards, and as part of his reward received the right to ransom Pridaux, who had to pay £15,000. With this and other moneys similarly collected he began to buy land. The bloody assize was over, and he had little time to take stock of his gains, both in Court credit and current coin. He was destined without delay to achieve the single step that severed him from the summit of his profession. A new sphere of activity opened out before him.

III.

Jeffreys became Lord Chancellor in September, 1685,

being then only thirty-seven years of age. One of his first offices was to meddle in the affair of Francis, the murderer of Dangerfield. In securing his hanging, from whatever motive it may have been done, he certainly avenged a most brutal and cowardly outrage; so that we need have no quarrel with Jeffreys for hanging Francis. The contemporary account says of this curious incident that, after Dangerfield had been flogged, "in his return home, one Francis stabbed him into the eye with a sort of a tuck in the end of his cane, which touching his brain, he was hardly ever sensible after, but died of the wound in a few hours, not without great suspicion of poison, his body being swoln and black and full of great blains all over. The murderer fled, but was pursued by the rabble, who had torn him to pieces, had not the officers rescued him. He defended and justified the fact whilst in Newgate, saying, He had the greatest men in the kingdom to stand by him; to whom after his trial, and being found guilty upon clear evidence, great applications were made, which had been successful for his pardon had not Jeffreys himself gone to Whitehall, and told the King he must die, for the rabble were now thoroughly heated. Attempts were made to bribe Mr. Dangerfield's wife, that she might consent to the pardon of her husband's murderer; but she too well deserved to be related to him, to sell his blood." All of which surely redounds to the credit of the Chancellor: the attempt of a friend to narrate the events in verse cannot be said to be altogether successful :—

" Such marks he wore, as Scythians ne'er invent,
 At which all but a Francis would relent.
 He Hell and his great Master does invoke,
 Then with a generous fury gives the stroke.
 Wretch well thou aimdst, too well thoust struck his head,
 Thoust pierced his eye, or else he'd looked thee dead."

It took the Chancellor some time to accustom himself to his new position. He was very powerful, and used his power carelessly. At one time he was able to snub Sir Thomas Jones, who had incurred his hatred by getting the

headship of the Court of Common Pleas which Jeffreys
would have preferred himself. In the King's Speech at the
ensuing opening of Parliament there were many unconstitu-
tional admissions, and on the consideration of them Jeffreys
adopted the fashions of Hicks's Hall for the moment; he
was, however, humiliated and his proposals neglected.
This may have taught him caution. In the trial of Henry
Booth, Lord Delamere (who had once called Jeffreys a Jack-
pudding), for high treason, Jeffreys was nominated High
Steward and behaved quietly enough.

Jeffreys was at first willing to go the whole hog with his
master, and accordingly was placed upon the Ecclesiastical
Commission. He became necessary to its sittings indeed,
and soon was busy enough in the affair of Dr. Sharp,
rector of St. Giles, known as the railing parson. Sharp
was very hot against the Papists, and in August, 1686,
the King sent to his bishop, Compton, to request him
to suspend the rector on account of one of his contro-
versial sermons. This the bishop very reasonably declined
to do, and was himself in consequence suspended. In this
matter Jeffreys went straight to the point: " Why did you
not obey the King ? " Compton remained suspended until,
as was said, " all the great rough riders were unhorsed," but
his temporalities were not interfered with.

As an Equity Judge Jeffreys held his court at Dr. Shep-
herd's Chapel, in Duke Street, Westminster. He had a
house looking into St. James's Park, and one Pitt, an unfortunate bookseller of a speculative turn, put up a new
court for him and enlarged his house on the promise of a
grant of land which he never obtained. The house was
afterwards inhabited by the Dutch ambassadors who came
to congratulate William on his accession, and later became
the Admiralty office.

Some personal notes of Jeffreys flow from the pen of one
who, as Johnson would say, was no careless observer of the
passages of those times. " His friendship and conversation
lay much among the good fellows and humorists; and his
delights were accordingly drinking, laughing, singing, kissing,
and all the extravagances of the bottle. He had a set of

banterers, for the most part, near him ; as in old time great men kept fools to make them merry. And these fellows abusing one another and their betters, were a regale to him. And no friendship or dearness could be so great in private which he would not use ill, and to an extravagant degree in public. No one that had any expectations from him was safe from his public contempt and derision which some of his minions at the Bar bitterly felt. Those above, or that could hurt or benefit him, and none else, might depend on fair quarter at his hands. When he was in temper and matters indifferent came before him, he became his seat of justice better than any other I ever saw in his place. He took a pleasure in mortifying fraudulent attorneys, and would deal forth his severities with a sort of majesty. He had extraordinary natural abilities, but little acquired beyond what practice in affairs had supplied. He talked fluently and with spirit ; and his weakness was that he could not reprehend without scolding ; and in such Billingsgate language as should not come out of the mouth of any man. He called it 'giving a lick with the rough side of his tongue.' It was ordinary to hear him say, 'Go ; you are a filthy, lousy, knitty rascal !' with much more of like elegance. Scarce a day passed that he did not chide some one or other of the Bar when he sat in the Chancery ; and it was commonly a lecture of a quarter of an hour long. And they used to say, 'This is yours ; my turn will be to-morrow.' He seemed to lay nothing of his business to heart, nor care what he did or left undone ; and spent in the Chancery Court what time he thought fit to spare. Many times on days of causes at his house, the company have waited five hours in a morning, and after eleven he hath come out inflamed and staring like one distracted. And that visage he put on when he animadverted on such as he took offence at, which made him a terror to real offenders ; whom also he terrified, with his face and voice, as if the thunder of the day of judgment broke over their heads ; and nothing ever made men tremble like his vocal inflic-ions. He loved to insult, and was bold without check ; but that only when his place was uppermost. To give an instance. A City attorney was petitioned against for some abuse; and affidavit was made that when he was told of my Lord Chancellor, 'My Lord Chancellor,' said he, 'I made him;' meaning his being a means to bring him early into City business. When this affidavit was read, 'Well,' said the Lord Chancellor, 'then I will lay my maker by the heels.' And with that conceipt one of his best old friends went to goal. . . . But this Lord Jeffreys came to the seal without any concern at the weight of duty incumbent upon him; for at the first being merry over a bottle with some of his old friends, one of them told him that he would find the business heavy. 'No,' said he, I'll make it light.' But, to conclude with a strange inconsistency, he would drink and be merry, kin and slaver, with these boon companions overnight, as the way of such is, and the next day fall upon them ranting and scolding with a virulence insufferable."

So he continued during James's short reign, doing his best for the King's own foolish projects, persuading the judges in 1687 to agree to support the dispensing power and acting as chief agent, though no Papist himself, in coercing the Universities. At Cambridge James strove to free the Roman Catholics from disability in the person of one Alban Francis, a Benedictine monk. On February 7, 1687, a royal letter commanded the University to admit him to the degree of M.A. without any oath being administered, any statute to the contrary notwithstanding. The King, in fact, dispensed with the opposing Acts of Parliament in Francis's favour. The University stuck by their oaths, though the vice-chancellor, Dr. Peachell, was but a timid man, and they wisely wrote to Albemarle, their chancellor, on the whole matter. The next step of importance was the appearance of the vice-chancellor and representatives from the senate before the Ecclesiastical Commission; amongst those who came up from Cambridge being Newton. Jeffreys was just the man for Peachell, and caught him tripping in no time. " The Lords took notice that you allege an oath; that oath, it seems, hindered you from obeying the King's mandate. Pray what was the oath?" " My Lord, this is a new question . . . and I beg leave and time to answer it.'

"Why, Mr. Vice-Chancellor, this requires no time," &c. Dr. Cook, one of the civilians, wished to help the bewildered Peachell, but was kept out of the discussion; good-humouredly, however. But when the vice-chancellor recovered a little, he had the best of the argument, for the Court case of one Lightfoot would not hold water when examined. The end of the business was that Peachell was suspended.

At Oxford there was more at stake, and the contest was more severe. The presidentship of Magdalen was vacant, and would have been an influential position secured, if James could have carried his man, Anthony Farmer. The fellows, however, would have none of him, his life being scandalous and he otherwise deficient, and decided on Hough. Farmer, when examined closely, would not bear the light, and hence the Court party did not insist further on him, but they deprived Hough in favour of Parker, a Papist, who was put in possession by force. In all this Jeffreys bore a main part, noisily inveighing against the fellows whom he somewhat roughly treated. In the course of his dispute with them he called Henry Fairfax a madman, and said that he ought to be kept in a dark room. Osmond, the chancellor, dying, Jeffreys would undoubtedly have been put in his place but for the celerity of the University in preferring another. There were, it seems, designs at the time on other foundations in favour of the Papists, notably the Charterhouse, where on an election Jeffreys received such a rebuff that he "flung away" in a rage and the place was left in peace.

Had James lasted longer Jeffreys would have been pushed out by his cousin, Sir John Trevor, a man of quite as much natural ability and quite as little heart as the Chancellor, but a man of much more self-control. Just before the fall of the Stuarts James seems to have designed an earldom for Jeffreys. He is called Earl of Flint on the engraved portrait by Cooper, after Sir G. Kneller, a reproduction of which appears in this volume. But it is very doubtful whether the earldom was ever given; doubtful in itself the more, because, at the end of the reign, Jeffreys did all he could to check the Romish policy of his master. He objected to the embassy of Castlemaine, but was temporarily restored to favour on the quarrel between Rome and France. His part became more and more difficult to play. He had to bring pressure to bear on the seven bishops whilst really disapproving of the whole business. A story that he favoured Lord Pembroke's heiress in a lawsuit and that she afterwards married his son belongs to this period.

> " Old Tyburn must groan
> For Jeffreys is known
> To have perjured his conscience to marry his son."

But it seems that no blame attached to Jeffreys at all, and that he decided quite justly on the points of law raised. It is notable, as his biographer confesses, to remember how little of what Jeffreys established was afterwards upset.

We find the Chancellor as a witness at the birth of the Old Pretender. He now knew how serious things were becoming, and urged the calling of a Parliament. He also advised the restoration of the City charter, but when he went in state to deliver it to the aldermen he met with a very ill reception.

James now vanishes, weakly reviling the man to whom he owed so much. Just before the king's flight the seal was taken from Jeffreys, and his life was not safe for an instant. He had made a very true jest at his own expense when the Prince of Orange's Declaration was issued ; being asked what were its heads he answered that " he was sure his was one." Such was the general hatred which his name inspired that James got a good deal of credit for leaving him behind.

He was living in Father Petre's lodgings at Whitehall. Hurrying thence he disguised himself as a sailor, and hoped to pass by a coal ship to Hamburg. The mate giving information, a warrant was applied for, and on its refusal the mob hurried back to the ship. Jeffreys had, however, changed into another ship, and in the morning had gone on shore to drink ale at the " Red Cow," in Anchor and Hope Alley, near King Edward's stairs. Here he was discovered under singular circumstances. Long before, " there was a scrivener of Wapping brought to hearing for relief

JEFFREYS TAKEN DISGUISED AT WAPPING.

... metime ... ... temporarily, restored ... ... Parliament was and ... ... He ... ... the acted Irish question ... ... senses. ... way ... ... in a law suit and the ... ... this ... d.

... m man ... man
... keys is known
... prepared discon ... ...

... that no claims attach ... ...
... ... he justly on the ... ...
is ... ... he graph ... confesses, to ...
... ... established was ... ...
... ... meelior as ... ... at ... ...
Planned ... ... knew now serious this ... we ... ...
a large ... ... g of a loc... ... . He also adv...
restoration ... City charter, but when he went ... s
... ... men he met with a very ill recept ...
... ... des, we adv ... ... the man to ...
... ... Just before the ... ... 's flight the ...
... ... keys, and his ... ... was not safe for an ...
He ... ... a very true ... at his own expense with ...
Prince of ... ... 's Declaration ... ... h being asked
... his ... ... answered that "he was sure his w...
... ... would have ... which ... ... inspired
... ... deal of credit for leaving his ... ...
... he was ... ... in Father ... ... 's lodgings at ...
Harrying t ... ... down ... as a ... ...
to pass ... ... to Hamburg. ... ...
... ... a warrant ... ... ked for, and on ...
me ... ... ships. Jeffreys had...
the ... ... on the morning ...
sh... ... ... at the "Red Cow," in Ann ...
Alley near King Edward's ... stairs. Here he was ...
under ... ... circum ... ... ces. Long before "th...
a ... ... of Wapping brought to Leaving her

JEFFREYS TAKEN DISGUISED AT WAPPING.

against a bummery bond; the contingency of losing all being shewed, the bill was going to be dismissed. But one of the plaintiff's counsel said that he was a strange fellow, and sometimes went to church, sometimes to conventicles; and none could tell what to make of him; and 'it was thought he was a trimmer.' At that the Chancellor fired; and 'A trimmer!' said he; 'I have heard much of that monster, but never saw one. Come forth, Mr. Trimmer, turn you round and let us see your shape,' and at that rate talked so long that the poor fellow was ready to drop under him; but at last, the bill was dismissed with costs, and he went his way. In the hall one of his friends asked him how he came off? 'Came off?' said he; 'I am escaped from the terrors of that man's face, which I would scarce undergo again to save my life; and I shall certainly have the frightful impression of it as long as I live.'"

This scrivener happened to come into the cellar at the "Red Cow" on the morning of the 12th of December, 1688, in quest of some of his clients; his eyes caught that face which made him start; and the Chancellor, seeing himself eyed, feigned a cough, and turned to the wall with his pot in his hand. But Mr. Trimmer went out and gave notice that he was there; whereupon the mob flowed in and he was in extreme hazard of his life; the Lord Mayor, however, saved him and lost himself. For the Chancellor "being hurried with such crowd and noise before him, and appearing now so dismally not only disguised but disordered, and there having been an amity betwixt them, as also a veneration on the Lord Mayor's part, he had not spirits to sustain the shock but fell down in a swoon; and, in not many hours after, died." It was indeed a strange sight—

> "He took a collier's coat to sea to go;
> Was ever Chancellor arrayed so?"

To get safe into gaol Jeffreys had to assist the trembling Mayor in drawing up the warrant for his own commitment. At his own request he was taken to the Tower in charge of two regiments of train bands. He was refused bail, and examined by a Commission of Lords; but there was little to be done with or to him. Unused to confinement, "his chronical indispositions, the stone, &c., increased very fast upon him. The ingenious Dr. Lower was his physician." Dr. Scott, who visited him, could get no confession from him of severity on the Western assize, he stoutly asserting what was doubtless true enough, that he had come far short of what James wished.

The last days of Jeffreys, long drawn out by Macaulay, are rich in melodramatic material. The visit of his old victim, Tutchin, the present of the oyster barrel containing a halter, the visitations of the Dean of Norwich and Dr. Scott, Prebendary of St. Paul's, the curses of the mob, and the prisoner's exclusive devotion to the brandy bottle have been rendered familiar. The state of popular feeling precluded all hope, though Jeffreys approached William diplomatically with an acknowledgment that "his crimes were as numerous as his enemies," and a promise to discover secrets. The street poets had computed with "cannibal ferocity" how many steaks might be cut from his well-fattened carcass, but under the combined influence of spirits, disease, and prison walls, the ex-Lord Chancellor became almost a skeleton. A little more than four months after his capture, on April 18, 1689, he died in prison in the forty-first year of his age. The French Jacobites asserted with conviction that he had been poisoned by William. His corpse was laid next that of Monmouth in the chapel of the Tower.

Few will be left to dispute Jeffreys' claim to a place in this collection, though many might agree with Mr. Leslie Stephen when in his judicious essay on "The State Trials," he writes: "If ever I were to try my hand at the historical amusement of whitewashing, I should be tempted to take for my hero the infamous Jeffreys. He was, I daresay, as bad as he is painted; so perhaps were Nero and Richard III., and other much-abused persons; but no miscreant of them all could be more amusing. With all his inexpressible brutality, his buffoonery, his baseness, we can see that he was a man of remarkable talent. Wherever the name of Jeffreys appears we may be certain of good sport."

TITUS OATES.
Anagramma
TESTIS OVAT.

This is the true Originall taken from the life
done for Mrs Brook and here answerd All others are counterfeit

TITUS OATES.

TITUS OATES.

(1649-1705.)

W... ... ... given or done unto thee, th... ... ... ?
... ... sharp arrows, with hot burning ... ...

Psa... ...

I.

I ... ... a native of the county to have ...
that ... ... was of Norfolk origin. His fath...
... ... state of the almost universally current ...
... ... ignorant fantastic ribbon-weaver
... ... have been a son of the rector of ... ...
... ... Samuel was born at Marsham on Novem... ... ...
9... ... ...ted a sizar of Corpus Christi College, Ca... ... ...
... 1657, was created Master of Arts in 16... ...
... ... by Bishop of Norwich on September 29th, 16 5.
...ara...risti... the Oates family was the case with which
... ... revolved upon well-oiled pivots. With the ad...
... ... Puritan frenzy Samuel appears to have simul...
...ly contemplated matrimony and turned Anabaptist.
...idence must be left for psychology to work out.
... to have married about 1645, but the mother ...
...retains her incognito. Dr. Jessopp feels ...
... express a hope that the poor woman died early.
... however, was not the case. During the year 1660,
... was at the zenith of his glory, we are assured

TITUS OATES

Anagramma

TESTIS OVAT.

This is the true Originall taken from the ...
done for HEN. BROME and RIC. CHISWELL ...

TITUS OATES.

TITUS OATES.

(1649–1705.)

"What reward shall be given or done unto thee, thou false tongue ?
Even mighty and sharp arrows, with hot burning coals."

Psalm cxx. 3.

I.

IT is painful for a native of the county to have to record
that Oates was of Norfolk origin. His father, Samuel
Oates, in spite of the almost universally current belief that he
was "a poor ignorant fantastic ribbon-weaver," seems in
reality to have been a son of the rector of Marsham, in
Norfolk. Samuel was born at Marsham on November 18th,
1610, admitted a sizar of Corpus Christi College, Cambridge,
on July 1st, 1627, was created Master of Arts in 1634, and
ordained by the Bishop of Norwich on September 24th, 1635.
A characteristic of the Oates family was the ease with which
its members revolved upon well-oiled pivots. With the advance of the Puritan frenzy Samuel appears to have simultaneously contemplated matrimony and turned Anabaptist.
The coincidence must be left for psychology to work out.
He seems to have married about 1645, but the mother of
Titus still retains her incognito. Dr. Jessopp feels constrained to express a hope that the poor woman died early.
This, however, was not the case. During the year 1680,
when Titus was at the zenith of his glory, we are assured

by Roger North in his "Examen" that the liar's mother came to him and related to him a dream that had tormented her. The dream, or rather nightmare, was to the effect that she was with child of the devil, and was agonised by the pangs of birth. And, having told her story, the good woman shook her head sadly, and remarked with significance that she did not like the way her son was in. Beside the fact that, as late as 1697, Titus spoke of his "aged mother" as still existing, this is all we know concerning Mrs. Oates—the subject of numerous jests not more pleasing than indelicate.

With the liar's other parent it is otherwise. Having turned Anabaptist, he was sent out as "a Dipper" into the shires, then into Surrey and Sussex, and in 1646 into Essex, and, more particularly, the parts about Bocking and Braintree. Edwards describes him and his doings in his Gangraena. "This is a young and lusty fellow, and hath traded chiefly with young women and young maids, dipping many of them (and using them in private more familiar), though all is fish that comes to his net. . . . A goodly minister of Essex coming out of those parts related he hath baptized a great number of women, and that they were called out of their beds to go a-dipping in rivers—many of them in the night—so that their husbands and masters could not keep them in their houses: for these offices he got ten shillings a-piece." In March, 1646, a young woman named Anne Martin, actually succumbed to this regenerating zeal, with the result that the Dipper was bound over to the Sessions at Chelmsford, to be held in April, 1646, and committed to Colchester gaol.

The Dipper's chief doctrine appears to have been that the saints were a free people. This he made manifest by the solemn warning to the Parliament which he launched from his prison. They had better be careful, he threatened with characteristic assurance, not to "cart the ark" nor otherwise meddle with the saints, himself and followers. The latter, according to Edwards, were mainly composed of avowed drunkards and whoremongers. Yet so great was the fellow's vogue, that, while in Colchester gaol, "there was great and mightie resorte to him, many coming down in coaçhes from London to visit him." He was finally acquitted, and next appeared at Dunmow in Essex. Here, however, the Dipper's fame had preceded him, and his expected victims, reversing the usual order of proceedings, threw him without ceremony into the Chelmer; nor was he permitted to emerge from the baptismal stream until effectually encrusted with Chelmer ooze and mud, to the peculiarly adhesive character of which the present writer can testify. Surfeited with dipping, Samuel turned his attention to education. He served usher for abbreviated periods at a succession of schools, and was still occupied in fathoming the possibilities of the profession when Titus was born at Oakham in 1649. As chaplain to Colonel Pride and his regiment—a post which he obtained probably in the course of the next year—Samuel became a man of no little importance, and doubtless added largely to his already curious store of experience. Here again, however, his theory and practice with reference to that immunity of the saints, of which he was so firmly convinced, led him into conflict with the authorities, and, in December, 1654, he was arrested by Monck while in Scotland for 'stirring up sedition in the army." He seems to have adopted a vagrant life until the Restoration, when he promptly saw the error of his ways, returned to the bosom of the Established Church and was, in 1666, presented by Sir Richard Barker to the Rectory of All Saints, Hastings. Here he was a party to some most disgraceful proceedings, in which, however, his son Titus had the principal share; and he was in consequence outed from his living, drifted to London and lived "sculking about Bloomsbury." It is only right to mention here that Crosby in his "History of the Baptists" credits him with a conscience (which smote him at this juncture), stating that he left his living and returned to the Baptists of his own accord. If so, his senile predilection for the Baptist Communion offers a curious analogy to that professed by his son in his later days. Fond and frolicsome memories may have clustered round the old dipping days, from which the lapse of years had effaced

8

all recollection of Dunmow. That the old rascal was in
need of a new birth is only too apparent. But here we
must leave him.[1]

The king of liars was born at Oakham, as has been
mentioned, in 1649. Though he is stated by more than
one writer to have had a brother, William, who achieved
some distinction as a horse-stealer, it is more probable
that he was an only as he was an unique child. His
anxious parent procured his admission as a free scholar
to Merchant Taylors' School in June, 1665.

Of the many distinguished alumni of Merchant Taylors,
few, if any, have shown earlier promise. In his very first
term he is alleged to have cheated the authorities of his
entrance money. In the school register a contemporary
MS. note describes him as " The Saviour of the Nation,
first discoverer of that damnable hellish plot in 1678."
But so frail was Titus's tenure of good report, that a slightly
later addition is to the effect, " Perjured upon record and
a scoundrel fellow." He "had to leave" Merchant
Taylors in about a year and went to Sedlescombe
School, near Hastings, whence he passed as a "poor
scholar" to Gonville and Caius College, Cambridge, on the
29th of June, 1667. Here is an example curiously overlooked
by Macaulay, in which the advantage is, as usual, on the
side of the less ancient and less splendid foundation
Oxford cannot boast of a Titus Oates among her alumni
" By the same token," says Adam Elliot, "the plague and
he visited Cambridge at the same time."

It can hardly have been misfortune which rendered Titus
such a constant bird of passage. Early in 1669 he passed once
more to St. John's College, where his father, now in full
flush of Anglican zeal, most carefully sought out an Arminian
tutor for him. This tutor was Dr. Thomas Watson, who had
been fellow of St. John's since 1660. In 1687 Dr. Watson

---

[1] He died on February 6, 1683. See Wood's "Life and Times
1894, vol. iii. p. 36; *cf.* Additional Manuscript, No. 5860, f.
288, in the British Museum (a paper on this worthy subject by the
learned Dr. Zachary Grey).

was consecrated Bishop of St. Davids, but in 1696 (significant fact), he was deprived for simony. Having been already "spewed out" of Caius, Oates's "malignant spirit of railing and scandal was no less obnoxious to the society of St. John's." From St. John's College (admirable for its archives) we have the following report of him: "He was a liar from the beginning. He stole from and cheated his taylor of a gown, which he denied with horrid imprecations; and afterwards at a communion, being admonished and advised by his tutor, confessed the fact. . . . Dr. T. W. does not charge him with much immorality, but says he was a great dunce, that he ran into debt, and, being sent away for want of money, never took a degree."[1] Yet he seems to have made some friends, and, after one or more failures, contrived to "slip into orders" in the Established Church, being instituted to the vicarage of Bobbing, in Kent, on March 7, 1672-3, on the presentation of George Moore.[2]

In appearance the liar had grown up plausibly solid. His face was large, flat, and oval, with a portentous chin, his mouth "standing exactly in the middle of his face like the white in the centre of a target." In none of the contemporary, or nearly contemporary, portraits is this feature less pronounced than in the one which, on general grounds, we have selected for reproduction. "He has the largest chin of any gentleman in Europe," says Tom Brown, who called on him one day in Axe Yard; "by the same token they tell a merry story how he cheated a twopenny barber, by hiding it under his cloak." His nose was long and peaked; his periwig he wore fair and woolly. "Pray, what is the reason," said Charles II. one afternoon at the theatre, "that we never see a rogue in a play, but odds fish! they always clap him on a black periwig, when it is well known that one of the greatest rogues in England always wears a fair one?" Macaulay's picturesque description of Oates's hideous features, "his short neck, his legs uneven, the vulgar

---

[1] Baker MSS.   [2] Reg. Sheldon, Archiep. Cantuar. f. 534.

said, as those of a badger, his forehead low as that o
a baboon, his purple cheeks, and his monstrous length o
chin," is well known.　More picturesque still is the portrai
given in the pamphlet entitled, "A Hue and Cry after Di
Oates" which was published in 1681, and must be give
in its proper place.　It is sufficiently manifest both froc
what has been said and what left unsaid, that much c
the savage and still more of the beast lurked in Titu:
He was coarse and gross in his animal constitution; thoug
short of stature he yet had the chest and neck of a ta
man, and doubtless enjoyed that powerful circulation whic
is conducive to rapid action but not to sustained thoughi
So well was his demeanour suited to the part he had t
play, that to men not deficient in observation he appeare
choleric, impetuous, and even rashly confiding.　He affecte
to be open in manner and genial in converse.　He mad
friends as well as dupes among the unwary, and drew t
himself kindred spirits.

The possessor of these graces of manner and person di
not remain long at Bobbing, in Kent.　Before the end ι
1674 he obtained a license for non-residence, and shortl
afterwards left the place.　He went on a visit to his parer
in the adjoining county of Sussex, and seems to have of
ciated for a short period at the parish church at Hasting
A settled life did not suit him; he had to leave Hastings i
company with his father, in a very hurried manner and i
the worst possible odour.　What occurred was, very brief;
as follows: William Parker, son of the governer of the por
and keeper of a school in the little town of Hastings, ha
prudently denied to Titus all access to the youth confide
to his care.　His suspicions were very properly resente
by the liar, who proceeded to bring the most infamoi
charges against the usher.　His evidence was of such
character as will scarce bear reproduction, save in tl
"Proceedings" of a very learned society,[1] but it shows ev
thus early the master hand of Titus, punctuating his li
with startling and irrelevant detail.　Oates's prestige as ι

[1] See Anthony à Wood's "Life and Times" in the Oxford Historic
Society's Publications (vol. ii. p. 417); *cf.* MS. Ballard LXX. fol. ;

accuser, however, had yet to be established; Parker was found not guilty, and forthwith caused "Tytus" to be arrested in an action for £1,000 damages. And the liar, not finding bail, was thrown without ceremony into the lock-up at Hastings, pending his removal to Dover gaol. The Dover people weakly allowed him to escape, and he found his way to London and hid in one of the burrows about Gunpowder Alley—a famous hiding-place for diffident people—Jesuits, debtors, spies, informers, and others. He is said now to have taken his first trip across the water. It is certain that, after these events, he for a short time took up his permanent abode upon it. He managed, it seems, to get nominated chaplain on board a King's ship, a post which in those days was a base and dishonoured one. Until well on in the eighteenth century, the idea that its occupants should claim the title of gentlemen was held to be little less than monstrous. The hedge parsons, who filled it, were ordinarily men of ill repute, who brought no testimonials and were asked no questions.

That Titus should not have attained to the "damnably low" standard of morals and manners exacted by his new profession is curious: contemporary writers are agreed that he was expelled the navy; and once more Titus roamed like a hungry wolf through the quaint purlieus and labyrinthine lanes of Caroline London.

In his abject need he hit upon the notion of turning Papist. A proselyte in gown and bands could surely command a price! The fathers at Somerset House, where Catherine, Queen Consort, had her Roman Catholic chapel, were the best-abused men in London, but they would not let a poor convert want for the merest necessaries of life. So he fawned upon Whitebread and Pickering, two of the black-frocked gentry who flitted furtively about the capital, harmlessly enough, yet eyed and execrated by the people as harbingers of deadly evil, invested with the malignity of fiends and the potency of wizards. From these two men, who saved him from starvation, and were afterwards brought by him to the gallows, he boasted subsequently how, on occasion, he stole a box of consecrated wafers, which he styled in derision "a box

of gods." With these wafers he assured his audience many
a time, he used "to seal his letters for above a year and a
half."

By good fortune and the assistance of his new friends he
obtained, during the year 1676, some menial post in the
service of the Duke of Norfolk. While in his household,
according to the account given by his adherents in his
period of power, Oates overheard some whisperings
among the priests, who haunted Arundel, to the effect that
there was some grand design on foot, but could not learn
what it was in particular. "He had heard from his
Protestant friends and read in Sir Hamon L'Estrange's
'History of King Charles I.,' and other judicious authors,
that the Papists had for many years carried on a design
to introduce Popery again into these nations ; which created
in him a longing desire to sound the depth of it, and, i
possible, to *countermine* it. To this end he entered freely
into conversation with the priests, who, greedy of a proselyte
failed not to press him with arguments." To these arguments did Titus seriously incline, and having already become
reconciled to the Church of Rome, he now sought admis
sion to the Order of Jesuits. He found that the Jesuits
were the men "for his turn, because they were the cunning
politic men, and the men that could satisfy him." By then
he was formally reconciled to the Romish Church on Ash
Wednesday, 1677. Far from letting this little incident serv
for a reproach on the tongues of the Protestants, who adore
him in the days of his pride, Titus would lay his hand upo
his breast and impressively yet peremptorily call upon th
Almighty and His holy angels to bear witness that he ha
never changed his religion, but that he had gone amon
them on purpose to betray them. What his real intentior
were when he took the step is far from plain. That h
had any such design as he pretended is the least likel
hypothesis. The most simple is that England was rapid!
getting too hot to hold him. He conceived the life of
Jesuit emissary to be a merry and a roving one. The ne
cloth might serve as a better cloak for his criminal fanci
than the old. He doubtless foresaw many knavish pos

bilities, and snatched eagerly at the notion of a new sphere of credit; but definite project he had none. The Jesuits on their part were not scrupulous in their choice of instruments. They are not the villains of this story, but they are the villains of some others. Coarse weapons were needed for some of their projects, and Oates's brass may well have appeared to them an exceptional metal.

Under the auspices of his new friends Oates took shipping in May, 1677, and went to Valladolid, in Spain. He probably entered the Colegio de los Ingleses—a college specially privileged by Philip II., who had first seen the light in the old capital of Castile. Titus struggled on here among ncvel surroundings for about five months, but his conception of his new part did not tally with that formed by his superiors. Too soon he sought those relaxations which were, he had been told, the *casuel* of every self-respecting Romish ecclesiastic; and he supported his peculiar views of the situation's propriety with a precipitancy which was more generally felt to be out of place during his novitiate in a Jesuit college. Titus had to go, and, anxious to get rid of him at any price, the Jesuits willingly incurred the expense of shipping such a cargo from Santander to London. Thus briefly and ignominiously ended the liar's sojourn in sunny Spain. He subsequently styled himself a Doctor of Divinity— a degree which he stated he obtained from the University of Salamanca. But this was a lie. He was never at Salamanca, and he was never a D.D. None but priests were admitted to this degree by the Catholic Church and Oates was never a priest. He once applied in the course of the next year to the Archbishop of Tuam for orders, but was refused on the ground of insufficient character as to life and manners. The matter of the degree is well touched by Dryden in the epilogue to his " Mithridates " :—

> "Shall we take orders? that will parts require:
> Our colleges give no degrees for hire—
> Would Salamanca were a little nigher."

Whether Titus had made the acquaintance of that curious

and sinister being, Doctor Israel Tonge previous to his Spanish
voyage is not quite certain.   Tonge had once held the living
of Pluckley, in Kent, where reports of his neighbour, the
incumbent of Bobbing, may well have reached his ears.
He subsequently lived at Fox Hall (Vauxhall) in the house
of Sir Richard Barker, Samuel Oates's old patron, and there
doubtless Titus met him, probably at this juncture. A
London minister, whom Wood describes as " cynical and
hirsute, shiftless but free from covetousness," Israel was at
the same time three parts a monomaniac. He was a mean
divine, and his rectory of St. Mary Stayning being worth
barely £20 per annum, it is little to be wondered at if by way
of solatium, he should have relinquished theology for a form
of imaginative literature, less hackneyed and more (immediately) remunerative.

Scarce ever without a pen in his hand and a plot in his
skull-capped head, Tonge spent the time he could spare from
the hardly more chimerical pursuit of alchemy, in brooding
over the insidious growth of Papistry in these islands ; dressing lists of Jesuit assassins and devising imbecile anagrams.
Two examples will suffice : Edward Coleman—*Lo a damned
crew*, and Sir Edmondbury Godfrey—*Dyed by Rome's reveng'd
fury*. His rooms were a kind of literary factory and warehouse, whence he issued periodical diatribes against the
Society of Jesus ; and he was at this moment busy upon an
" Index to the Jesuits' Morals," which was intended to
quicken the sale of previous books and pamphlets without
number, unmasking the enemies' designs. He now came
forward, gave Titus clothes, lodging, and diet, and told him
" he would put him in a way."   For a time Titus shared his
literary labours. He began in 1678 " The Cabinet of Jesuits'
Secrets Opened," a colourless work, said to be translated
from the Italian, and completed by " a person of quality," in
1679. It is largely concerned with methods said to be
employed by the society for conciliating wealthy widows and
augmenting their revenues out of their estates. But Tonge
soon found more profitable work for his henchman. He had
for some time been suffering from a dearth of material. Of
literary material, indeed, he had enough and to spare, but

for local colouring and personal matter, and recondite detail of every kind, he was in somewhat the same position as a studious Cockney who should set himself to expound the private habits of the Chinese from knowledge acquired exclusively at the British Museum. Now a man who had lived among the Jesuits might surely be supposed to have obtained an insight into their little ways—as well as their vast schemes for the expurgation of Protestantism in England.

Titus was a voluble liar, but Tonge was not satisfied with his information; there was a want of actuality about it, as the French divine said when the grace of God was proposed to him as a subject for his discourse. By Tonge's advice, therefore, Titus now made a second application for admission into the Society of Jesus. His tears and promises subdued the reluctance of the provincial and in spite of his gross ignorance and his former backslidings he was, in December 1677, though near thirty years of age, entered among the "younger students" of the famous English seminary at St. Omer. Of his doings there we have some account in the "Florus Anglo-Bavaricus," a Latin account of the plot, published by the Jesuits of Liége in 1685. He seems to have played the *pion* over the younger students, to their no little discomfort; he stirred up endless dissension by his lies, and, when reproved, invoked the Deity, quoted the maledictory psalms, or at need rained tears, which he had *ad nutum;* was alternately brazenly impudent and fulsomely humble and cringing. A stranger of distinction who passed a night in the college asked, in the words used by Gregory Nazianzenus, "Quale monstrum sibi nutrit Societas." About eight months after a reluctantly granted admission, the fathers resolved to expel him at all hazards. Titus, in a moment of desperation, "knowing no place by land or sea where his past crimes would permit him to beg his bread," is said to have declared that his only alternative was to become Jesuit or Judas. On the 23rd of June, 1678, he was turned loose upon the world. The previous night he had been discovered by one of the fathers in the college chapel, sprawling over the altar. When asked what he meant by such a posture and proceeding, the noisome brag-gart ("arrogantiam redolens") declared he was having a last word with Jesus Christ.

Titus had hitherto ranged with equal relish but indifferent success over the whole scale of recondite roguery. He was now to anticipate in action the maxim of Swift, that since vice cannot be eradicated it should be specialised. He took up his permanent abode in the atelier of his old crony Tonge, whence in a few months emanated that prodigious pyramid of falsehood which has rendered its constructor little less famous than Cheops.

An unexpected ally and associate of the pair was Christopher Kirkby, a gentleman of a good Lancashire family, whose interest in the plot is unexplained but important. He was a man of crucibles and gases, who contributed to Charles II.'s morning's amusement in his laboratory, as Bap May and Will Chiffinch ministered to his nocturnal diversions. Titus soon convinced his docile pedagogue, the worthy Israel, that the right way to engineer a Popish plot was at all hazards to implicate and if possible interest the King in it. The possession of a pliant instrument in Kirkby lent itself admirably to this conception. The piece was accordingly primed and set by Titus, who was careful to keep his own energies and valuable person in masterly reserve.

The field of action was now prepared. Tonge was full of joyous anticipations. To him the plot was probably a reality. He felt as Cicero might have felt on the eve of communicating the conspiracy of Catilina to the Roman Senate. As for Oates, he had the plot and its anfractu-osities at his finger-ends; he had moreover the materials for the embellishments, which Tonge himself had never the spirit to invent or nerve to employ. Tonge was reconciled to the fabrication of such details as were necessary to carry conviction to a sceptical (save the mark!) generation. He thought, it is quite probable, that no ingenuity could devise plots more diabolic than those with which he had always credited the Jesuits. If a gigantic Roman Catholic conspiracy was not in existence, then was life to him less substantial than a dream. Oates, on his part, reflected that, if he knew little about the internal organisation of the Jesuits, and no more about their recent doings, the public of London knew infinitely less. And, little as he knew, there was not the slightest probability now of his ever knowing more. A bold stroke must be attempted now or he must let ambition for ever alone. The accession of Kirkby was most fortunate. The properties and *personæ* for the first act of the drama were all in readiness. For the rest Titus could trust to his skill in improvisation. It was high time then for the curtain to rise.

II.

On a fine sunny morning in August, 1678—the 12th of the month—Charles II. was taking his accustomed stroll in St. James's Park, aimlessly enough. The park was still the natural outlet to Whitehall, and the King was fond of exercising his spaniels there. There also he was in the habit of playing Mall, feeding his ducks at the decoy, and, on occasion, gossiping with Mistress Nell Gwynne, who looked down on him from one of the mounds at the back of her house in Pall Mall. His morning's walk was destined on this occasion to an unpleasant interruption. He had not strolled very far before he became conscious that somebody—probably a tiresome suitor—was lying in wait for him. The individual was Kirkby, who, at Oates's instigation, had taken up his station in the park, in order to give the King the first hint of the Popish plot—"that monstrous growth, with its root in hell and its branches in the clouds."

No monarch was easier of access than Charles, who no sooner witnessed his scientific acquaintance's manifest desire to waylay him, than he lent himself readily to his design. Kirkby then stepping mysteriously up to the King's side, uttered in a stage whisper, "Sire, keep within the company; your enemies have a design upon your life, and you may be shot in this very walk." The communication evoked less alarm than curiosity in Charles's mind. He calmly continued his walk, but appointed Kirkby to meet him privately at Chiffinch's that afternoon, so that he might hear more.

At Chiffinch's Kirkby unfolded the gist and nucleus of the plot. Two Jesuit knaves, Grove and Pickering, had undertaken to shoot the King with a "silver bullet" from "a screw-gun"; and further, one Wakeman, the Queen's physician, was at present taking steps to poison him.

Where had Kirkby got this *novella* from ? His friend Dr. Tonge had a lot of papers giving details. Tonge was accordingly, brought secretly to Whitehall and admitted to a conference in the "Red Room" that very evening. But Charles had no sooner looked at the mazy screed which Tonge called his "original narrative" than he felt the infinite boredom and absurdity of the whole thing. He was impatient to start for Windsor, and would not attend to the matter. He referred the entire incident to Danby, who had preserved a grave countenance during the interview. Unsympathetic influence having been removed, Tonge commenced that lurid *crescendo* of lying confidences which was to cost so many innocent persons their lives. He informed Danby that the documents in question had been thrust under the door of his chamber, that he did not know by whom this liberty had been taken, but could form a shrewd guess. Subsequently he confessed he had met the man who had submitted the papers, and that this man had owned to their authorship. Even thus crude was Oates's device for investing the "plot" with an appropriate air of mystery. The King was at once communicated with, and requested to order warrants for the apprehension of the would-be assassins, named in the paper, and to communicate the whole affair to the Council. Charles said no to both requests; the matter must be kept dark; "he would be very careful of himself." Tonge next stated that William [Grove] and Pickering had set out to Windsor to effect their fell purpose. On hearing this the King changed his mind and gave orders for their arrest. They never turned up, however, and for a good reason. Charles grew more incredulous than ever. To mention such an absurdity to the Council would only be to alarm all England, and "put thoughts of killing him into people's heads who had no such thoughts

before." The impression of fraud was only strengthened by
Tonge's next move. He told Danby that a packet of letters
addressed to certain Jesuits, and treating of matters connected with the plot, had been sent to Bedingfield, the
Duke of York's confessor, at Windsor. Shortly before
Tonge gave the information, the Duke had brought the
letters which Bedingfield had given him to the King, saying
that (although purporting to be from persons in Bedingfield's
acquaintance) they were written in a hand of which he was
ignorant, and that he could make nothing of them beyond
the fact that they seemed to contain certain treasonable
matter. They were, in fact, crude and transparent forgeries,
prepared in Israel's workshop. So far the whole affair
seemed a delusion, and would, in the ordinary course of
events, have died a natural death. Tonge and his
colleague were much cast down and perplexed at the
contemptuous neglect to which their bantling was subjected. They repaired, for concealment and security, to the
lodging of their poor dupe, Kirkby, at Vauxhall. Kirkby
himself repeatedly attended at Court, but Charles had already
formed his opinion of the plot, and invariably passed him by
without recognition. The plot seemed in desperate danger
of asphyxiation.

Unfortunately, at this juncture the Duke of York, with
his usual ineptitude, took a most unwise step. He thought
it an admirable opportunity to inflict a blow upon his an-
tagonists; he felt confident of convicting them of fabricating
false plots, and so he demanded an inquiry into the whole
matter by the Privy Council.

Simultaneously the liar played his master-stroke. On the
6th of September, 1678, he dragged off Tonge to Sir
Edmund Berry Godfrey, a well-known justice of the peace,
of strong Protestant principles. He was apprehensive,
needlessly as the event proved, of finding the Council
unsympathetic, if not distrustful. Godfrey received the
wildest flights of his fancy with mingled fear and
amazement, exactly the state of mind Oates wished to
induce. Three weeks later he returned, and decorated
the bald patches of his original narrative, making affidavit

to the truth of thirty-eight articles, in addition to the forty-three to which he had previously sworn.

Oates's disclosure was very briefly to the following effect: The Jesuits had been appointed by Pope Innocent XI. to the supreme power in this realm. The "Black Bastard," as they called the King, was a condemned heretic, and was to be put to death. If at any rate he did not become R.C., he could not continue C.R. The Duke of York was to be sounded on the subject, and, if he did not answer expectation, was to be despatched after his brother. Father Le Shee (Père La Chaise) had lodged ten thousand pounds in London for any one who would do the deed, and this had been augmented by ten thousand pounds promised by the Jesuits in Spain, and six thousand pounds by the Prior of the Benedictines at the Savoy. Sir George Wakeman had been offered ten thousand pounds to doctor the King's posset, but he haggled for fifteen thousand pounds; this was not withheld; he was promised the full sum, and eight thousand pounds had already been paid on account. Four Irish "ruffians" had been hired to stab the King at Windsor. Grove ("honest William") and Pickering had been further retained at fifteen hundred pounds apiece to shoot the King with silver bullets. Oates himself had been urged to undertake this task, but had pleaded his terror at the idea of letting off a gun. To make assurance doubly sure—in the unlikely event of a doctor, two silver bullets, and four Irishmen failing to take effect—a Jesuit, named Conyers, bought for ten shillings a consecrated knife "not dear for the work it had to do" to stick the "heretic pig" withal. All these little matters, and some others, had been snugly arranged at a "general consult" of Jesuits, which had taken place on the 24th of April, 1678, at the White Horse in Fleet Street. The business of the general consult having been transacted with harmonious brevity, that body divided into several smaller or departmental consults, each of which undertook the supervision of a given part of the scheme—one the poisoning, another the stabbing, and so on. Proceeding to generalities, the attestation described how the Jesuits had brought about the fire of London, and what a good thing they had made out of it.

They spent seven hundred pounds in fireballs, and made by plunder fourteen thousand pounds; they had made another fire on St. Margaret's Hill, and stolen two thousand pounds' worth of goods; they had also recently fired Southwark, and were now determined to burn all the towns in England. A paper model was made for the firing of London, and an "architectonical scheme" showing where to begin and go on as the wind should serve. Oates himself was assigned an important place among the incendiaries. "Natural feeling" prompted him to exhibit repugnance for such a task. As a proper penalty for such an ebullition, he was destined to horrible torture—as soon as he should have fulfilled his part; so he had *overheard*. Finally, a general rebellion was to be raised, and a massacre to take place, in which Charles, if he still survived, was to be slaughtered, and the Duke of York offered the crown on certain conditions; if he failed to accept the situation, then, in the Jesuits' own words, as reported by Titus, "to pot James must go."

Such was, almost to the letter, though it will hardly be believed, the monstrous tissue of unabashed ignorance and grotesque falsehood which Oates proffered to the credulity of a nation. That Charles had not already been "done for" was attributed to a series of accidents. The flint of Pickering's pistol had got loose, or later, Grove caught a severe cold which precluded his going to Windsor; on another occasion one of the conspirator's horses was "slipt in the shoulder." Pickering [1] had received severe "backside castigation" for his repeated failures. Grove had been threatened and coaxed; the reward had been constantly increased. Surely here were spurs to expedite the two "screwed gunners" who "as the devil and the doctor would have it, had been for years at the King's very throat." One may well ask, "Where, in the name of dulness, were our wits, when all this hideous piece of apocrypha was current gospel among us?"

[1] A quaint portrait of Pickering crouching behind a bush with the screw-gun at the charge is given on the knave of diamonds in a contemporary pack of cards; it is figured in *The Gentleman's Magazine*, 1849, pt. ii. p. 269. And see the coin on the title-page of this work.

As Oates had calculated, the Government could hardly allow his inflammatory disclosures to percolate London through private agency without taking any active steps in the matter.   On the 28th of September the Council summoned the redoubtable Titus before them, and they were soon fully occupied.   Twice a day they sat, and with every sitting grew more muddled and alarmed.   The liar surpassed himself. He appeared in a smart clerical gown and a new suit, specially borrowed for the occasion, on the excellent security of the plot, and, having once passed the Rubicon, threw away every shred of caution and reserve.   His volubility was extraordinary, and he swore himself hoarse over his continual embellishments of the forty-three articles of the original Tonge-Oates narrative.   The fatigue which he experienced afterwards served as a plausible pretext for the defects of his memory.   To any cool, impartial person of intelligence Oates's declarations were a complete exposure.   The only cool person of intelligence was Charles himself.   "What sort of man," asked the King of Oates during his examination, "is Don John?" (Don John being Johannes Paulus de Oliva, the general of the Society of Jesus, and chief director of the plot).   "A tall, lean man," replied the liar.   The King smiled, knowing the general to be a little swarthy, podgy fellow. Yet again, the King asked him where it was that he had seen La Chaise pay down his ten thousand pounds.   In the Jesuits' house just by the King's house at the Louvre, was the answer.   " Man," said Charles, "the Jesuits have no house within a mile of the Louvre."   The whole of Oates's story rested upon the monstrous supposition that Titus (whose actual career among the Catholics has been briefly narrated), was not only a chosen emissary and carrier of all the Jesuits' most important despatches, but that the contents of all the papers with which he was entrusted, were communicated to him by the deep contrivers of a secret and supremely dangerous plot.   He had no documentary evidence; yet he had had all the strings of the conspiracy in his hands.   So great had been the confidence reposed in his faith and honesty that the Jesuits were never tired of unbosoming to him the minutest details of their plan; he went about with open papers getting signatures, travelled on diplomatic missions in France and Spain, yet was allowed to overhear a conference in which he was threatened with torture for lack of zeal. As the accredited go-between among the Jesuits, Oates had obviously to acknowledge intimacy with the chief instruments in their hellish designs, such as Coleman and Wakeman, yet when he was confronted with them he did not know them. When they were introduced to the Council, in company with a few other persons, he was utterly unable to identify them. Could the fabric of a dream be more baseless than a story resting on a foundation like this? So great, however, was the fatuity of the Privy Council that to a majority of its members this galimatias appeared to be "above invention."

The King regarded the whole matter as too foolish. Greatly to the distress of his Council he at this juncture (October 2nd) left abruptly for Newmarket. He estimated that the performances of his "topping horse," Blew Cap, would amuse him even more than the folly of his councillors. Before he left, however, the Council had assigned Oates and Tonge lodgings in Whitehall, with a guard for their security and a weekly salary. Moreover, a large number of the persons denounced by Oates had been committed to Newgate and other prisons. Rife as was already the spirit of delusion, they could hardly have failed to be discharged, as the absurdity of Oates's allegations was made apparent, but for a concatenation of circumstances as sinister and mysterious as it was pregnant with misery and shame.

Among the large number of Catholics whom Titus had accused at a complete venture was one Edward Coleman, a man of some little notoriety and no little conceit. He was a convert from Protestantism, and full, as converts are, of foolish emphasis and indiscretion. His "sad, sunken eyes and his lean, withered countenance, shewing more ghastly pale while surrounded by his black peruke," fitted the part of a popish *intrigant* to perfection. His half-starved, emaciated look probably suggested him to Titus. And Coleman's looks did not altogether belie him; in the first flush of convert zeal he had carried on dangerous correspondence with La Ferrier and La Chaise. The Papists had a mighty work on hand in England, such was the high-falutin tenor of his not too serious communications — no less than the conversion of the three kingdoms and the exter-mination of a most pestilent heresy. There were never such hopes of success since the days of Queen Mary as now " in our day." He spoke, in fact, of the eternal crusade of Roman Catholicism against all governments and religions other than its own. The *modus operandi* was roughly indicated. To France was proffered the privilege of supplying gold to conciliate the English Parliament. The English Catholics, with the Duke of York at their head, were to work to-gether with France to bring about the conversion of England at the expense, if necessary, of political subservience to Louis XIV.

When Coleman's house was searched a deal box, con-taining letters to the effect above related, was found in a receptacle behind the chimney, and some packets of letters were discovered in a drawer under his table. He had plenty of time to escape, but felt a misplaced confidence in the speedy discrediting of Oates's *extravaganza;* so that he stayed at home and leisurely destroyed his letters, but by a fatal oversight overlooked those in the table drawer and in the chimney. Had he withdrawn all his papers nothing had appeared; had he left all it might have been concluded that the whole secret lay in them. These letters from an influential and well-informed papist were, in fact, the best possible evidence that Oates's tale of a conspiracy was the merest fabrication, but at the time they were re-garded as a confirmation of the substantial truth of Oates's story. The vague designs of Coleman were taken to be an outlying portion of the gigantic conspiracy so darkly adumbrated by Oates. The discovery made as much noise in and about London as if the very cabinet of hell had been laid open. "One might now," says North, "have deny'd Christ with less contest than the plot."

Great, however, as was the ferment caused by the dis-covery of Coleman's letters, it was insignificant by com-parison with that occasioned by the ominous event that followed and almost effaced it from the public mind,—another piece of undesigned evidence (as it was considered) of Oates's patriotism and veracity.

Oates had commenced his revelations to Godfrey on September 6, 1678. On Saturday, October 12th, the " best justice of the peace in England " left home at nine o'clock in the morning on a magisterial round ; he had to call upon a churchwarden and to transact business of various kinds for the then extensive and undivided parish of St. Martin's-in-the-Fields. He did not return that night, nor was he ever seen alive again. His servants grew uneasy and instituted a search ; the public soon shared their anxiety. Mysterious rumours supervened. At midday on Thursday an unknown man stated in a bookseller's shop that Godfrey's body had been found pierced through with a sword. That evening his body was discovered in a ditch on the south side of Primrose Hill, near Hampstead. He lay face downwards, with his sword through his body, his cane and gloves by him, rings upon his fingers, and in his pocket seven guineas, four broad pieces, two small pieces of gold, and a quantity of silver. His pocket-book and a lace cravat alone were missing. At first it was suggested that he had committed suicide, but this was negatived by the fact that his neck was broken, that his chest was much bruised, and that, as the medical evidence showed, the sword had been run through him after death. On the instant the wildest conjectures were rife as to the perpetrators of the deed, but opinion soon settled steadily in one current. A secret poison had long been at work in this poor Protestant land. Those hellish Jesuits, surely they must have had a hand in this ! " It was obvious that the Papists might do it in revenge for Godfrey's swearing Oates to his narrative." If it were objected that such a crude method of revenge squared ill with the Machiavellian subtlety with which the Jesuits were credited, had not Dr. Burnet seen with his own eyes " many drops of white wax lights, such as Roman Catholic priests use, upon Godfrey's clothes." Could one doubt one instant longer into whose hands the murdered justice had fallen ?

The credulous state of public opinion on the subject of the connection between Catholicism and crime had given Oates an excellent market for his lies. The Coleman disclosures gave things a desirable fillip. The Godfrey murder converted Oates into the hero and saviour of his country— a Protestant Cicero, outmanœuvring the Jesuitical Catilina. For a few weeks or months he may almost be said to have dictated the destinies of the kingdom. The dictatorship was naturally based upon terror. The state of panic which followed in the metropolis upon Godfrey's assassination, was in fact without parallel in our annals. Its keynote is struck at once by Sir Thomas Player's affirmation that all the Protestant citizens might rise the next morning with their throats cut. None doubted that the crisis was at hand. The " Book of Martyrs " was everywhere found upon the same table with the Family Bible, and was the more read of the two. The smoke of Smithfield fires was in the nostrils of every staunch Protestant. " To see the posts and chains put up in all parts of the City," writes the unexcessive Calamy, " and the train bands drawn up night after night, well armed and watching with as much care as if a considerable insurrection was expected before morning, and to be entertained from day to day with talk of massacre designed, and a number of bloody assassins ready to serve such purposes, and recruits from abroad to support and assist them was—*very surprising.*" The murder of Godfrey, with the black Sunday that followed soon after it when it grew so dark on a sudden about eleven in the morning that ministers could not read their notes in their pulpits without the help of candles, together with the frequent execution of traitors that ensued, and the many dismal stories handed about, continually made the hearts not only of younger but of elder persons to quake for fear. Not so much as a house was at that time to be found but was provided with firearms; nor did any go to rest at night without apprehensions of somewhat that was very tragical that might happen before morning. The shopkeepers complained of their loss of custom, for none would buy to-day what the Papists might burn to-morrow. The book trade languished in all branches but one—that of polemic

See here the Dauils Darling, plotting still
With Blood & Treasons all y. world to fill.
His Romish stratagems, Loe, Non can tell
Who cānot fathom to y. Depth of Hell.
Nothing but Murder'd Kings can him suffice
And flaming Citys as a Sacrifice

Yet see behind his chaire Whom Heavn̄ y hath Sent,
Whom God hath made a timely Instrument
Englands intended ruine to prevent
That which, y. Devil & y. Pope combin'd
Against our King and Protestants design'd
Disclos'd and frustrated by him we find.

Pope

Oates

The Emblem Explayn'd

A.A · the Popes Cabbinett
B   the Pope writing to the I esuites to
     be diligent in the carrying on the Plot
     but who so soever labors may be
C   beholden a son all his Contrivance
D   the Popes Crown who cries behind
     Oates is behind you.
E   the Popes tale of Supremacie falling
     downe confirmedly dissolute
F   a line which his forces might make him
     fall uppon y. word Romaine his Law
G   a crown w. Oates gives, bids my fie
     for his flesh, thrice former.

OATES, THE DEVIL, AND THE POPE.

... clearly tracts and broadsi... ... ... against ...
... ... In October, almost imm... ... ... after ... ...
... ...eared 'England's Grand M... ...rial "—a broad-
... ...stations of a most pr... ... ... dedicated
...rd S...esbury. The ...dication was ... en... ...h if it
... ... Shaftesbury had a...ady ...re...' that all
...pa...i ...med the credit of the Pro...t...t witnesses
... ...t ...pon as public e...mies. ... Dr...len's

... ...rse than pl...ting ... suspect the plot "

... ...ted broad...ide, which we have ...p...
... ... represented sitting at a table incit...g
...der ... ... extirpation of heresy. Oates sm...s
...at ... ... but is cra...ing his big head ... ... to
... ...'; an imp of Satan warns the p...st ...
p... ... ... on intruder, and the embarrass...t of
...isco... ... ... the Pope's tiara to topple off h... ...d
...frey's ... ...on October 31st was naturally ... ...
...t a ...r...t...nt demonstration. On Queen ... ...s
... ...ed with unusual solemnity on ... ...t
... ...ed ... an effigy of the Pope with the d... ... ...er-
...is e..., ...dels of Godfrey's dead body a...d of ...mish
... and ... ... in mitres and copes were carried through
... ...D...ie' Defoe, then a mere b..., ...k...d with
... ...at passed before him, and in after-ye...rs told
... ...y blunderbusses were burnished a...y, how
...an...l ...t...s and shoulder-belts and oth...r m...litary ge...
... ...t... ...on again, and soldiers once more disturbed
... ...e... ...quiet citizens.

... r...arded the havoc with interest and con...u...ed h...s
... ... A complacent feeling of *e...gi m...* ... ...
... ...h his sluggish veins and smothered ...y... ...
...t...t ...r alarm. A few short months ...go, d...t...d
... ...rd, he had been relegated, always ... s...i... ...
...ss' class at St. Omer; thence he ha... ... ...
...d starving, upon an unappreciative w...
...y, a stroke or two of luck, a deft a...

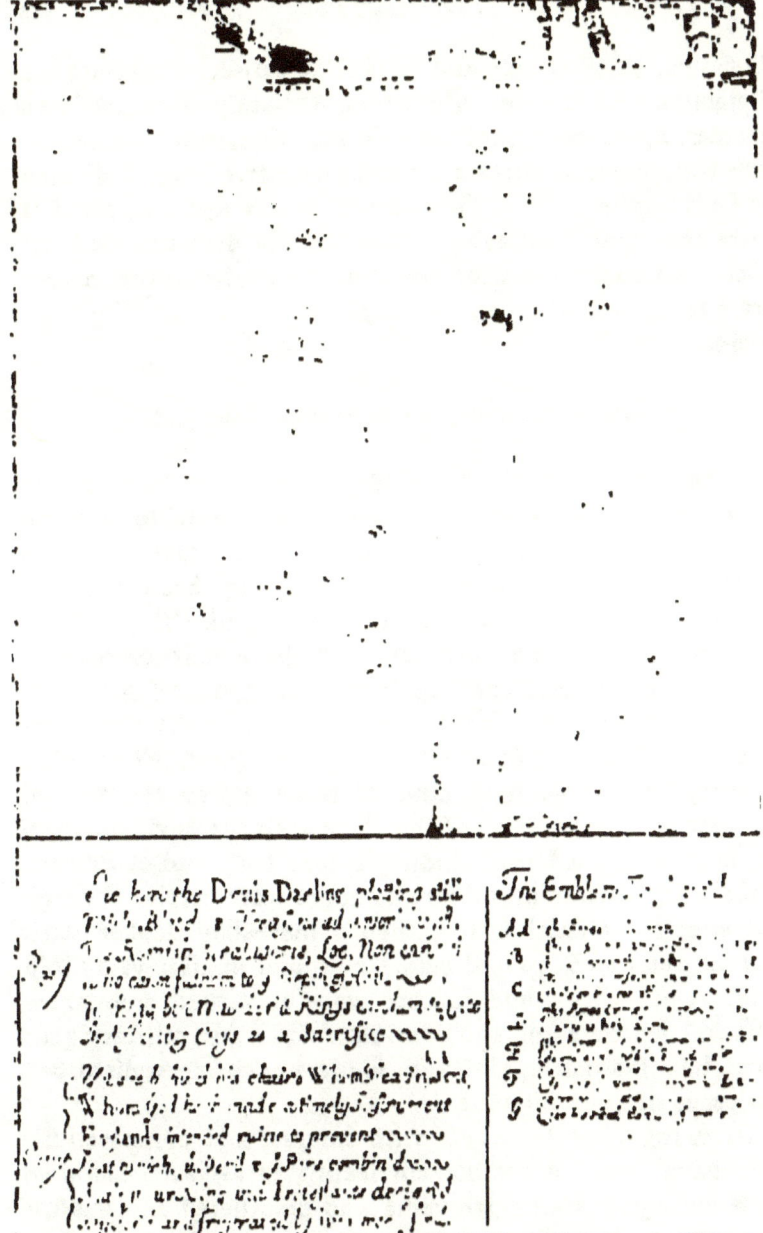

See here the Devils Darling p...... still
With Blood & Treasons ad...... ......
The Romish ......, Loe, Non can ...
who can ...... to y Papist sh......
I....... bee ...... Kings and ....
In offering Cro.... as a Sacrifice ....

Yet each his o his chaire Whom'........ .....
Whom god hev...... made at nely......ment
E..... land... intend... ruine to prevent ......
Iesuit... with... Devil & JP...... combin'd ....
Yet ...... working und Intelli...... design'd
.... and frustrated by him more ....

literature, chiefly tracts and broadsides, directed against the Catholics. In October, almost immediately after Godfrey's murder, appeared "England's Grand Memorial"—a broadside with illustrations of a most provocative kind, dedicated to Lord Shaftesbury. The dedication was apt enough if it were true that Shaftesbury had already declared that all those who undermined the credit of the Protestant witnesses were to be looked upon as public enemies. In Dryden's words:—

" 'Twas worse than plotting to suspect the plot."

In another illustrated broadside, which we have reproduced, the Pope is represented sitting at a table inditing an order for the extirpation of heresy. Oates stands stealthily behind, but is craning his big head over to decipher the screed; an imp of Satan warns the pontiff of the proximity of an intruder, and the embarrassment of the discovery causes the Pope's tiara to topple off his head. Godfrey's funeral on October 31st was naturally the occasion of a Protestant demonstration. On Queen Elizabeth's birthday, celebrated with unusual solemnity on the 19th of the next month, an effigy of the Pope with the devil whispering in his ear, models of Godfrey's dead body and of Romish bishops and priests in mitres and copes were carried through the streets. Daniel Defoe, then a mere boy, looked with wonder upon what passed before him, and in after-years told how the old City blunderbusses were burnished anew, how hats and feathers and shoulder-belts and other military gear came into fashion again, and soldiers once more disturbed the peace of quiet citizens.

Oates regarded the havoc with interest and composed his expressive face. A complacent feeling of *exegi monumentum* stole through his sluggish veins and smothered any qualms of amazement or alarm. A few short months ago, despised for a dullard, he had been relegated, always on sufferance, to the boys' class at St. Omer; thence he had been thrust, naked and starving, upon an unappreciative world. Sublime mendacity, a stroke or two of luck, a deft and well-timed

murder, and all was changed.   Now he was described as the
saviour of society, fawned on, caressed, not merely unex-
pectedly fed, but copiously feed.   The very Gallios of the
Court could not refuse him credence.   As for the Parliament,
all the terrors of the town were fully reflected there.   When
the Houses met on October 21st, the King hoped to keep
the business out of their itching fingers.   In the speech
from the throne the plot was barely alluded to.   A plot there
was no doubt, but the Government would surely unravel it.
The establishment of proofs and punishment of offenders
could be safely left to the normal agency of the law.   Let
the gentlemen of the Commons turn their attention to the
graver matter of supply.   But the King's Speech was no
sooner proposed for consideration than a general cry of
" The plot ! the plot ! " drowned the hall.   Far from ignoring
it, the Houses sat upon and incubated the plot, and nothing
but the plot from morning to night, and before three days
had elapsed petitioned the King to appoint a fast, sure prelude of national disgrace !   They required, moreover, the
removal of all Popish recusants, and implored the King to
exclude unknown persons from the presence.   One of the
Lords expressed the general sentiment in an exquisite tirade :
" I would not have," said he, " so much as a Popish man or
a Popish woman remain here, not so much as a Popish dog
or a Popish bitch, not so much as a Popish cat to purr or
mew about the King."   These elevated expressions were
warmly applauded, and a bill was rapidly passed for raising
all the militia and keeping it under arms for six weeks.

Gaping for more revelations, the House of Commons
instinctively sent for Oates.   So well did he ply them, and
so apt were they in assisting him out of inconsistencies that
Scroggs was sent for straight away, and twenty-six warrants
sealed for the apprehension of as many persons, including
the five Catholic Lords, Powis, Stafford, Petre, Arundel, and
Bellasis.   Oates had previously named Arundel and Bellasis
to the Council, but on the King's remarking significantly
that those two Lords had served him faithfully, recoiled with
an unctuous " God forbid that I should accuse any unjustly ;
I did not say they knew it, but only that they were to be

acquainted with it." The Whigs, in the meantime, used their opportunity to try and deprive the King of his control of the militia, and to carry through the impeachment of Danby. The King thereupon impatiently dissolved the Parliament. The country was left in a state of helpless panic, the precursor of dark and evil deeds.

To understand the virulence of the panic that needed to vent itself in a series of judicial murders, which are unique in the history of our country, a careful study of the temper of the populace and the exact political conditions is essential. But the universal prevalence of the epidemic of fear and hatred is worth noting here. Once rife, it cannot be said to have made any distinction of party. The Court party, horrified at the attack upon the royal person, joined to their former hatred of Popery a new and more lively horror of it as the faith of rebels. The country party saw in it the development of a conspiracy they had long dreaded. On no section of the community did the plot bacillus commit direr ravages than on the clergy. Protestant pulpits surged with scurrilities and lies directed against the Catholics. The most respectable of their order, men such as Sancroft, Tillotson, Stillingfleet, Barlow, and Sharp, did their utmost to magnify popular apprehension and to confirm the popular persuasion of the reality of the plot; as for Burnet, he could only express his astonishment at the moderation and forbearance of a Protestant people.

One of the most sensible men of his time thus summed up the general view which sensible men took of the situation. "The Parliament and the whole nation alarm'd about a conspiracy of some eminent Papists for the destruction of the King and introduction of Popery, discovered by one Oates and Dr. Tongue, which last I knew, being the translator of the 'Jesuites' Morals.' I went to see and converse with him at White Hall, with Mr. Oates, one that was lately an apostate to the Church of Rome, and now return'd againe with this discovery. He seem'd to be a bold man, and in my thoughts furiously indiscreete; but everybody believ'd what he said; and it quite chang'd the genius and motions of the Parliament, growing now corrupt and

interested with long sitting and court practices; but with all
this Poperie would not go downe. This discoverie turn'd
them all as one man against it, and nothing was done but to
find out the depth of this. Oates was encouraged, and everything he affirm'd taken for gospel; the truth is the Roman
Catholics were exceeding bold and busy everywhere, since
the Duke [of York] forbore to go any longer to the Chap-
pell." [1]

There was only one circumstance which now embarrassed
the patrons of the plot. Its credit depended entirely upon
the evidence of one witness. Until another could be found
an outraged Protestant populace might demand victims in
vain. If justice was to be travestied it was to be done
according to good old Anglo-Saxon formulæ. So several
weeks passed. Early in November, 1679, the difficulty was
surmounted. A man named Bedloe, self-styled captain and
full-blown villain, whose career had rivalled in infamy
that of Oates himself, deposed before the magistrates at
Bristol (October 28th) that Godfrey had been murdered by
Roman Catholics in revenge for his having taken Oates's
evidence. As with Oates, his memory was constantly im-
proved and operated in *crescendo* curves of audacity. The last
version of his story was that Godfrey was inveigled into the
court of Somerset House about five in the evening of the
12th of October, that he was strangled with a linen cravat;
that his body was deposited in an upper room which he
pointed out to the Duke of Monmouth; that he saw standing
round the corpse the four murderers and one Atkins, clerk to
Mr. Pepys [of the Admiralty; and that it was removed
about eleven of the clock on the Monday night. This
testimony was confirmed in a curious, though completely
inconclusive manner, by Miles Prance, goldsmith and maker
of religious emblems for the Queen's chapel in Somerset
House. He was drawn into the case by a strange and
untoward coincidence. Suspected on account of his connection and employment, Prance was arrested, and was being

---

[1] *I.e.*, since the Duke, afterwards James II., publicly acknowledged himself a Roman Catholic. Evelyn's Diary, October 1,
1678.

taken in custody to Westminster Hall, when he was recognised by Bedloe, who was passing along the Strand, as one of the four concerned in Godfrey's murder. Threats and a dark prison extracted from this unfortunate man a corroboration of Bedloe's story.

Three innocent men—two of them Roman Catholics—were executed for Godfrey's murder in February, 1679. By the public the murder was taken as a proof of the plot, while the plot appeared an equally plain proof of the murder. With regard to the latter—was it a sign of defiance or of guilty terror on the part of the Catholics? This could only be a matter for surmise until the conspirators, indicated by Oates, were convicted and the full hellishness of their designs exposed. It therefore became a nation's object to bring the accused persons to trial with as little delay as possible. But before any trial could be held the conviction was general that Titus had rather under than overstated the fiendish character of their machinations.

The next eighteen months of Oates's career are a matter of history and the facts, narrated by Macaulay, are doubtless in the possession of the peculiarly constituted schoolboy of his allusions. For the benefit of others they must be briefly summarised here. The trials began in November, 1678. On the 27th of that month Coleman was indicted before Lord Chief Justice Scroggs, and Justices Wilde, Dolben, and Jones, for compassing the death of the King. Recorder Jeffreys, Serjeant Maynard, and the Attorney-General Sir William Jones, opened the case for the Crown. Oates's probity was insisted upon; he was a veritable St. George fighting almost single-handed against this monster of a conspiracy. The damnable murder of Godfrey, so hellishly contrived, was feelingly alluded to. As to Coleman, his association with the triple design against the King's life was admitted to depend entirely upon Oates's evidence. Titus was at length triumphantly produced. "We desire," said Jeffreys, "that Mr. Oates be not interrupted." "He shall not be," said Scroggs. He began by describing his experiences as a letter-carrier. He had carried letters from Coleman and certain Jesuits to the rector of St. Omer. Included in

the packet were letters to Père La Chaise about the
ten thousand pounds paid down for the destruction of the
King. He also carried back the answer. Then he described
the "consult" at White Horse Tavern, which subsequently
split up into smaller groups. He received, he stated, a
patent from the Society of Jesus to be of the consult.
There the Grove and Pickering scheme was approved and
the rewards settled: Grove to have fifteen hundred pounds
down, Pickering, a religious man, thirty thousand masses.
The plot was communicated to Coleman, who warmly applauded it, and further wished to trepan the Duke of York
into the murder. "Gentlemen of the jury," said Scroggs
at this juncture, "do you hear what he says?" The jury:
"Yes." Coleman was also a party to sending forty thousand black bills to Ireland and to the design of chartering
"four Irish ruffians," nameless, but selected by Fogarthy,
to "settle the King's hash cheap." Finally, he was hand
and glove with Ashby, rector of St. Omer, in a project
for poisoning the King through the agency of Wakeman, the
Queen's physician. Coleman was to be Secretary of State
under the new dispensation, to date from the King's demise.
As the trial progressed an awkward point came up. At
the examination before the Council Oates did not know
Coleman, and told the King he had never seen him before,
yet now he spoke as if a long intimacy had existed between
himself and his victim. With some readiness Titus affirmed
that the examination before the Council occurred late in the
evening, when the candles flickered and the light was dim
and he was tired out with his exertions in arresting public
enemies. He failed for these reasons, so he said, to recognise Coleman on the instant, but directly he heard his voice
he was ready to swear to him. It was then shown that
Coleman had given his evidence *before* Oates was asked
whether he recognised him. In this dilemma Titus again
took refuge in the fatigue which had benumbed his senses.
But he was not long left in peace. "How came you, Mr.
Oates," he was asked, "Mr. Coleman being so desperate a
man that he was endeavouring to kill the King, to omit your
information of it to the King at that time? Why, with this

dreadful secret on your mind, did you not speak out then as well as now ? Coleman might have escaped."[1] These and other disagreeable, pertinent questions asked Scroggs of the brazen one. The marvel is that Oates was not entirely discredited. Unfortunately, his readiness and audacity augmented, the lucid intervals of the court became rarer, and the current of Protestant mania grew stronger. On this occasion Scroggs ventured to give the "saviour" a caution, and in summing up dwelt but lightly upon the evidence of Titus, and his precious ally, Bedloe. He relied entirely upon the letters for a conviction. Coleman trusted to his *alibi*, which broke down ; and he received sentence of death. On the 3rd of December his barbarous sentence was carried out.

At the next trial, that of Ireland, together with Grove and Pickering, on December 17th, 1678, Oates had the effrontery to swear that he had taken round the instrument embodying the resolve to assassinate the King, together with details about the reward, to the minor consults into which the major consult at the White Horse had resolved itself ; and further, that he had with his own eyes seen it signed by Whitebread, Fenwick, and Ireland, one after the other. He now said, moreover, that he had been sent over from St.

[1] Throughout the whole of the trial epoch Oates claimed and appropriated to himself the extraordinary privilege of doling out just as much " information " as suited him—in other words, as he invented it. He never made a full authentic statement, but kept back important " facts " in reserve. This peculiarity of the liar's evidence is well illustrated in " Peveril of the Peak," where, in answer to a judicial remonstrance, Scott makes Titus observe, " Maay laard, I will tell you a pretty fable." " I hope," answered the judge, " it may be the first and last which you shall tell in this place." " Maay laard," continued Oates, " there was once a faux, who having to caarry a goose aver a frozen river, and being afraid the aice would not bear him and his booty, did caarry aver a stoane, maay laard, in the first instance to prove the strength of the aice. . . . It was not to be thought that I should have brought out all the story at aance." This is a capital illustration of Oates's infernal impudence, nauseous style of pronunciation (see p. 134), and actual practice during these trials.

Omer to murder Tonge. During the whole of the time he swore he was so employed Oates was in reality at St. Omer, as was afterwards amply proved. Further details of the most preposterous kind flowed from this black tongue which wagged the more vigorously as its activity grew more fatal. He described the continual " stalking " of the King in the park by Grove and Pickering, who " champed " their bullets so as to cause a more jagged and dangerous wound. His embellishments were sought still further afield. Grove and his companions, he alleged, " turned into burlesque all that was done at the Council, or at the Parliament, or at the Courts in Westminster Hall, and sent it to the French King for him to laugh at." In fine, the old family of lies were all trotted out with some sensible additions, and the result that Grove, Ireland, and Pickering were all sentenced to death. Scroggs summed up with gross but universal prejudice against religionists, who in the Chief Justice's words " eat their god, kill their King, and saint the murderer." In things of this nature, he said, referring to the evidence of Oates and Bedloe on which everything rested, you cannot expect the witnesses to be absolutely spotless. The question of credibility he left to the jury, and the jury, consisting not of ignorant or, at least, not of uneducated men, but of baronets and squires, showed their shocking credulity by convicting. The perjury in the case of Ireland was singularly flagrant. Oates and Bedloe both swore to his presence in London during the latter half of August. Now Ireland accounted for his absence from London on every day between August 3rd and September 14th, and his statements were corroborated by a whole host of Catholic witnesses. Oates's allegations, on the other hand, were supported by the evidence of a single woman, called Sarah Pain, who swore to having seen Ireland at a scrivener's in Fetter Lane on August 20th. The unfortunate man was, nevertheless, convicted and sentenced to death, in vain pleading his relationship to the Penderells of Boscobel, and the death of his uncle, Francis Ireland, in the King's service. Four Popish plotters had now travelled the path to dusty death, but public opinion was not appeased. Five Jesuits, Whitebread, Harcourt, Fenwick, Gavan, and Turner, were tried and executed with appalling expedition during the month of June. Nor did the very next month lack its victim. The tenth martyr, the eminently respectable Catholic lawyer, Richard Langhorne, was executed on July 17th. He had been reprieved for a month in order that information might be extracted from him concerning the estates in the hands of Jesuits. When he was buried " his back was found to be full of stripes, which were thought to be a penance for the discoveries he had made."

Thus terminated the first phase of the plot. Hitherto an indictment for the plot had been synonymous with a conviction. Oates had been implicitly believed by the London juries. There seemed no reason to apprehend any alteration in the state of public feeling. Oates was accordingly emboldened to accuse the Queen on oath before the Privy Council of being privy to the plot, and of the design to kill the King. This was the accusation which in reality lay behind the next trial, that of Sir George Wakeman, the Queen's physician. And this trial proved most important — because the test case of the plot. It began upon Friday, July 18, 1679, at the Sessions House at the Old Bailey. Titus had three acolytes upon this occasion —Bedloe, Jennison, and Dugdale.[1] The main charge against Wakeman, that he received fifteen thousand pounds to poison the King's possett, has already been mentioned. Oates swore that he had heard the proposal made and after some haggling

[1] Dugdale—a wretch who swore to "general evidence" against Langhorne and Stafford, as well as on this occasion, but subsequently changed sides and confronted his old associates at the trial of Stephen College. His evidence either way was by that time quite discredited. He was not quite so proof against remorse as his fellows, it appears, for he began to "see spectres" as early as 1681, and died miserably of *delirium tremens* in March, 1683.

Both he, Bedloe and Dangerfield, were men of the worst possible character and of infamous careers almost from their cradles. Either of them, as well as William Fuller (hereinafter noticed), would deserve a place in this collection upon their proper merits, were it not that their stories come too much into collision with those of their great exemplar, Titus, chief among the perjured.

accepted.   But the chief witness had some very disagreeable moments during the trial.   He was asked by the
prisoner, " Have you not said before the King and Council
that you never saw me in your life, and that you did not
know me (Oates had just sworn to having seen the physician twice before his appearance at the Council) ?   Oates,
loq. : " My Lord, you may be pleased to know, when I saw
Sir George Wakeman at the Council, I had been up two
nights together, and the King was willing to excuse me
from any further examination being so ill and indisposed
for want of rest, in respect both of my intellectuals and everything else, I might not charge him so home ; but now I have
a proper light, whereby I may see a man's face, I can say
more to him."   Sir George : " This is just Coleman's case—
the light was in your eyes."   Yet Oates asseverated that he
had seen the other twice before the Council meeting—once,
when Wakeman had written a prescription in a hand subsequently identified as that in which an order to an apothecary
for poison had been indited ; secondly, when the definite
proposal to poison Charles had been made.   "And," said
Wakeman, " you knew all these things at that time I was
examined before the King and Council, and yet said
nothing.   Turn this way and answer me."

Oates : " I am not bound to answer that question."

Lord Chief Justice : " But you must answer his questions, if they be lawful."

After these aggravations Oates asked leave to retire
because, said he, " I am not well."

Lord Chief Justice : " You must stay, Dr. Oates, until
after their defence be over."   Here, however, Jeffreys
tenderly interposed, " If you desire to have any refreshment,
you shall have it got for you."   But all the slights put upon
the " saviour" during this trial could not extinguish his
passion for corroborative detail.   He described with lifelike
irrelevance a little scene, which he averred he had witnessed
at Somerset House.   A number of Jesuits were present, and
one after another, amid boisterous mirth, laid wagers as to
whether " the King should eat any more Christmas pies or
no."   A Benedictine monk, Conyers, laid he would not,

and another gentleman laid he would. Marshall, who was tried along with Wakeman, "went halves with Conyers he would not." This is a good sample of Oates's evidence. His memory was not good enough to save him from self-contradiction. At the same time his dulness of perception hid from him the full extent of his danger. So he trusted without undue confidence to his unrivalled impudence, and when in difficulty cast about for the first new lie that would serve his turn for the moment. When hard pressed he would shuffle and double and leave no stone unturned in his efforts to divert attention from the main point.

Scroggs summed up the case in a manner very disparaging to the evidence. "Look you, gentlemen, . . . we would not to prevent all their plots (let them be as big as they can make them), shed one drop of innocent blood, therefore I would have you, in all these gentlemen's cases, consider seriously, and weigh truly the circumstances and the probability of the things charged upon them." At the end of the summing up Bedloe remonstrated, "My Lord, my evidence is not right summed up." Lord Chief Justice Scroggs: "I know not by what authority this man speaks." The jury then, after asking if they might find the prisoners guilty of misprision of treason, and being told they could not, found all the prisoners "Not guilty." This case demolished the plot as Ireland's had established it. All the regular witnesses gave evidence here and all were disbelieved. If the other prisoners had been rightly convicted, these men should also have been convicted. But the question in this case was rather the guilt of the Queen than that of the actual prisoners. The day after the trial the Portuguese ambassador, on behalf of Catherine, called on Scroggs and thanked him for his services. Sir George Wakeman went beyond the sea. Scroggs was charged with bribery. Oates commenced further disclosures with a view to keeping up the excitement and fanning into renewed fervency the heat against the Catholics. But the plot had received a blow from which it never recovered. The acquittal ought to have been a warning to Oates: it was a sign that a reaction had commenced. In spite of certain appearances the King was

even at this time the most potent factor in the direction of
events.   He had witnessed, unmoved, the execution of
innocent men, but this attack upon the Queen was not to
Charles's taste.   " They think," he said, " I have a mind to
a new wife, but *for all that* I will not see an innocent woman
abused."

In spite of the waning prestige of the plot, another
life had to be sacrificed.   But the final situation was due
to some rather special causes, and not so exclusively to
that " heap of infamy" called Oates.   With a consistency
in crime that is at least extraordinary, Bedloe gave a death-
bed corroboration to the lies he had sworn to in the witness-
box.   And the fact that he was a Protestant gained a credit
for his declaration which all the protestations of the Roman
Catholics on the scaffold had failed to obtain.   Since the
time of Garnet, in fact, notions of Catholic equivocation
had gained acceptance, which caused the unsupported oath
of a Catholic to be considered a trifle light as air.   The
inveteracy of Shaftesbury, who was anxious to turn the plot
to political account, to score victims of mark and raise the
proscription to a higher plane, co-operated with this dying
devil's asseveration to make the trial of at least one Catholic
Lord inevitable.   The five Catholic Lords had been arrested
in October, 1678, and on the 3rd of December following the
grand jury of Middlesex had found a true bill of high treason
against them.   Notwithstanding these facts, the trial of the
first of them, William Howard, Viscount Stafford, was
delayed until November 30, 1680.   Stafford, who was only
allowed to consult his counsel when points of law arose,
defended himself with greater ability than was anticipated.
Dugdale and Turberville, as well as Oates, bore false witness
against him, and their support was material, for the star of
Titus had already passed its apogee.   Nevertheless Oates
swore that he had delivered a commission to Stafford from
the Pope as paymaster-general of the army which was to be
raised by the Catholics in this country.   This was an overt
act of treason, but this part of the evidence was unsupported,
and Stafford objected that two witnesses were necessary to
prove such an act ; his plea was, however, overruled and the

sequel is well known. The unhappy man was beheaded by the King's special grace on December 29, 1680.[1]

These trials are to be read in the History of England, but he that runs may not read the personal history of Titus during this period. His varying fortunes are indeed difficult to unravel, notwithstanding his activity and his efforts to keep himself well before the public gaze. He began 1679 well, by preaching at Wood Street Church, and during the next two years continued in great request in metropolitan pulpits. Attempts were, it was alleged, made to kidnap him, and, for the better security of his valuable person, he was, by the King's special command, "gated" or confined during the month of February to Whitehall and St. James's Park. Various "infamous" Papists and others who attempted to invalidate his testimony were arrested. One bright spot, amid the universal gloom of sheepish infatuation, was the refusal of Oxford University to grant him the D.D. degree. The manner of the refusal was on this wise. In October, 1679, Lord Lovelace, the most headstrong young peer of the country party until the notorious Lord Mohun took upon himself the office of Whig bully and assassin, brought Oates to Woodstock for a horse race, and procured him an invitation to the town pulpit. His sermon over and the race done, Oates had the effrontery to send word to the vice-chancellor, with half-jocular familiarity, that "he would come and wait on him, not surprise him for his degree"; but, in spite of this insolence, and the menaces of the mob,

---

[1] In addition to those mentioned in the text, the following persons owed their premature death primarily to Oates: Hill, Green, and Berry, executed for Godfrey's murder; Edward Mico, S.J., arrested by Oates while down with fever, and died in prison December 3, 1678; Thomas Mumford, *alias* Downes, *alias* Bedingfield, S.J., died in the Gatehouse dungeon, December 21, 1678; Francis Cotton, *alias* Neville, S.J., killed by being thrown downstairs by the pursuivants who arrested him, in February, 1679; Thomas Jennison, S.J., died in Newgate on September 25, 1679. Nine Jesuits were also executed and four died in prison, in the provinces. Like his prototype, Judas, Oates led in person the pursuivants, or others, who effected the arrests. These were usually made in the dead of night and by torchlight.

who shouted "Papists!" round their houses, the vice-
chancellor, Timothy Halton, Provost of Queen's College, and
Dr. Fell, took upon themselves, with memorable decency, to
utterly refuse to entertain the mock doctor's request. The
act was solitary. Apart from it Titus might have with
perfect truth uttered the words that were subsequently sung
in the streets of London :—

> " No man durst thwart me : with desire of pelf
> I rag'd and grew to such a peevish elf
> Had the King vext me, I had peach't himself."

Amid all his new and multifarious "duties" Titus was
perfectly happy—he thoroughly enjoyed the bustle, the stir,
the hectoring in court, and the flight of " sweaty nightcaps "
afterwards.

Nor, amidst his other activities, was his pen idle. He
had gained literary experience during his apprenticeship in
Tonge's workshop, and he now wrote with more confidence,
greater ingenuity, and an infinitely better acquaintance with
his market. So, in 1679, besides official accounts of "the
damnable, &c., . . . Popish plot," Titus followed up his
previous colourless work on the " Mystery of Iniquity" by
his much more spicy " Pope's Warehouse ; or the Merchandise of the Whore of Rome": a catalogue of Romish
Cheats published for the confusion of the Romish Beast.
Among the reliques enumerated, he reflects with scurrilous
gusto upon " Our Lady's Milk," " The towel with which
Christ washed His disciples' feet," the " dice with which
the soldiers cast lots for His garment," one of " St.
Stephen's boots," and one of the Virgin Mary's slippers. He
concludes by congratulating the English public that as long
as the plot kept them alert they would be safe from the
cheats of the Pope and his Popelings.

In October of this year, his great reputation having sustained without apparent injury the vexatious incident of
Wakeman's acquittal, he boldly accused by name to the
King a number of the Court officials ; on the other hand,
two ill-advised zealots, named Knox and Lane, were com-

mitted to the King's Bench Prison as "scandalisers" for having dared to breathe a doubt upon his unimpeachable integrity in the witness-box. He was evidently approaching the zenith of his fortunes—the condition in which North in his "Examen" quaintly styles "his trine exultation." "His plot was now in full force, efficacy, and virtue; he walked about with his guards, assigned for fear of the Papists murdering him. He had lodgings in Whitehall, and £1,200 per annum pension; and no wonder, after he had the impudence to say to the House of Lords that if they would not help him to more money he must be forced to help himself. He put on an episcopal garb (except the lawn sleeves), silk gown and cassock, great hat, satin hatband and rose, long scarf, and was called, or blasphemously called himself, the saviour of the nation. Whoever he pointed at was taken up and committed; so many people got out of his way as from a blast, and glad they could prove their last two years' conversation. The very breath of him was pestilential."

His audacity is well illustrated by an incident which Anthony à Wood relates. On October 21, 1679, as the Duke of York was returning from the Lord Mayor's banquet, Titus and Bedloe were stationed in a balcony, a sight for all Protestant beholders, in the house of "a blink-eyed bookseller named Cockeril, in Cheapside." A great rabble was in the street below them, and, as the Duke passed by, Titus led off a cry of "A pope! A pope!" Upon this one of the Duke's guard cocked his pistol and rode back, exclaiming fiercely, "What factious rogues are these?" The fickle mob vociferated "No pope! No pope! God bless his Highness." As for Oates and his ally, when their admirers looked up to the balcony, they had already vanished.

A little incident in the trial of Stafford is hardly less illustrative of the pitch of Titus's pretensions. The Lieutenant of the Tower had called upon Oates to curb the excesses of his satellites, who were mobbing the unfortunate nobleman in the precincts of Westminster Hall. They were witnesses, bawled Titus. "Not half of them are witnesses," said the Lieutenant; "keep the curs down!" "You're only a gaoler," impudently volleyed Oates, "but you're a rascal to boot." The other retorted, "But for your cloth I'd break your head." Serjeant Maynard felt constrained to take the saviour's part. It did not become the Lieutenant for a word to tell Mr. Oates he would break his head. "I should not deserve to be the King's lieutenant," responded the undaunted officer, stoutly, "if a man in another habit called me rascal, and I *not* break his head."

But the climax was, perhaps, reached in January, 1680, when Oates and Bedloe exhibited thirteen articles against Scroggs before the King and his Council, for misdemeanours in Court, browbeating evidence, and general dereliction of duty. The Lord Chief Justice, he gravely alleged, was very much addicted to swearing and cursing in his common discourse; he not only drank to excess, but got drunk on *prohibited* wines. Oates even told the Lords of the Council "y' he woud not positively say it, but he beleeved he shou'd be able to prove that my lord Ch. Justice danced naked"! When, however, the time came for a final hearing of these charges Titus found his audience not oversympathetic. Scroggs met the charges with skill and temper, and turned upon his assailants with so much blended wit and severity that they were glad to slink from his presence confuted, and for once thoroughly abashed. It is not surprising to hear that from this time the Chief Justice frowned upon them, spoke frowardly, and reflected much upon them.

The turning-point in their fortunes was at hand. In June, 1680, in spite of Oates's and Dangerfield's evidence, Lord Castlemaine was declared not guilty and discharged. In the following month the saviour's pension was reduced from ten pounds to forty shillings a week. But his decline and fall was not quite so rapid as this reduction might seem to indicate. The pension was raised again to sixty shillings weekly, and in September Simpson Tonge, the "unnatural son" of Israel of that ilk, was committed to Newgate for endeavouring to defame Oates, "his guilt being very plain." Titus was compensated for the annoyance of such litigation by a commission to search a Roman Catholic nunnery and boarding school at Hammersmith.[1] His effrontery was still unabated. Dining with the Bishop of Ely and Reresby in December of this year, he reflected upon the Duke of York and upon the Queen Dowager in such an outrageous manner as to disgust the most extreme partisan present. Yet "no one dared to contradict him for fear of being made party to the plot," and, when Reresby himself finally ventured to intervene, Oates "left the room in some heat," to the dismay of several present. The last of the perjurer's victims, a priest named Atwood, was convicted in February, 1681, but was reprieved by the King. In April, 1682, Oates's pension was again reduced to two pounds a week, and in August his enemies were strong enough to forbid him to come to Court and to abolish his pension altogether. He took refuge in the City amid the taunts of the Court poets. Safe in Broad Street he disregarded the horrible accusations made against him. The City dames were specially warned against an individual whose appearance is minutely set forth in Sir Roger L'Estrange's " Hue and Cry after Dr. O.: O yes! O yes! . . . A Salamanca Doctor, lost, stolen, stray'd, banish'd, or kidnapp'd out of Whitehall on Tuesday last. His marks are: The off leg behind something shorter than the other, and cloven foot on the nether side ; his face rainbow colour, and the rest of his body black. Two slouching ears ready to be cropped the next spring if they do not drop off before, . . . a short neck, which makes him defie the pillory, and thin chin and somewhat sharp, bending up to his nose ; he hath few or no teeth in the upper jaw, but bites with his tongue. His voice something resembles that of the Guinney pigs. His eyes are very small and sunk, and he is supposed to be either thick ey'd or moon blind, by reason that he did not know Coleman by candle light, though he had before sworn treason against him. . . . His food is the intrals and bloud of Loyalists ; he drinks the tears of widows and orphans. . . . His usual haunts are Dick's Coffee-house in Aldersgate Street. . . ." Let us break off in time, however, and collate this cameo of Dryden :—

[1] Lyson's " Environs of London," vol. ii. p. 420, under Fulham.

> " Sunk were his eyes, his voice was harsh and loud,
> Sure signs he neither cholerick was nor proud,
> His long chin proved his wit ; his saint-like grace
> A church vermilion and a Moses face."

The allusions to the exaggerated breadth of his speech are numerous, and not without good cause, if, as we are assured, he habitually spoke after this fashion : " Maay Laaid Chaife Jaistaice, whaay thais baisness of Baidlaw (Bedloe) caims to naithaing."

In the City Titus found abundance of sympathy and support, but it was by this time fairly plain that the plot, as a source of revenue, was utterly played out. The liar began casting about, accordingly, for new victims, and his first choice was not a happy one. The purposed victim was a certain parson named Adam Elliot, who had been a slave in Barbary. Titus alleged, his allegation being based upon information acquired " at Salamanca," that Elliot had turned Mahommedan during his captivity, and having thus obtained the relaxation of his bonds, had murdered his master and effected his escape. This wayward excursion from the beaten path of his perjuries was, by a singular coincidence, confuted by the testimony of the very " murdered " master under whom Elliot had served. This worthy follower of the Prophet happened to be in London in the train of the Emperor of Morocco's ambassador at the time of Oates's accusation. He strenuously denied that Elliot had ever turned Mahommedan, and as strenuously asserted his indefeasible right to carry him back as his slave to Morocco. Elliot retorted with a charge of slander against Titus, and claimed five hundred pounds damages, without, however, finding a jury to convict.[1] This was in

---

[1] Elliot subsequently got £20 damages of Oates for defamation of character. Oates's deposition against him, and his exhaustive and well-seasoned answer to the charges therein contained, are well worth reading. They are fully set out in Elliot's " Modest Vindication of Titus Oates, the Salamanca Doctor, from Perjury; or, an Essay to demonstrate him only forsworn in several instances." London, fol. 1682. For the Morocco Embassy, see some details in the Hatton Correspondence (Camden Society).

January, 1682. An infallible sign of the disrepute into
which the liar felt himself to be falling was given in the
following June, when he did not venture to put in an appearance as evidence against Kearney (one of the "four Irish
ruffians" who were to have beaten the King to death), who
was in consequence released for want of evidence.

The year 1683 is almost a blank as far as personal details
of Oates are concerned, save for several unsuccessful attempts
to indict him for a penal offence, and the appearance of a
pamphlet for the instruction of confessing plotters, entitled,
"The Auricular Confession of Titus Oates to the Salamanca
doctor, his confessor." Titus is here depicted confessing
freely to apostasy, perjury, "as natural to me as milk
to a calf," atheism, "to know and not to know a man at
the same time," *cum multis aliis*, including treason, rape,
"with numerous peccadilloes unbecoming the grandeur of so
culminate a delinquent." As Charles II. approached his
end the tide ran more unmistakably in favour of the
Roman Catholics. In May, 1684, the Duke of York felt
justified in instituting a civil suit against Oates for defa-
matory language. Witness after witness appeared to testify
to the use of the words complained of, and Jeffreys, who
had now assumed the ermine, interposed remarks anent the
moral character of the defendant, which contrast strangely
with his demeanour towards him when, as Recorder, he had
appeared for the Crown against Coleman and the rest. The
jury gave damages to the enormous extent of a hundred
thousand pounds, and Titus was thrown into a debtor's
prison pending the full payment of that amount. His
imprisonment may well have been solaced by the expectation of favours to come. His passion for public display
was yet to receive striking satisfaction. It was probably
by order from the court that, although he was only technically a prisoner for debt, the authorities of the King's
Bench prison loaded him with heavy irons. Nor were
these precautions unnecessary. His devotees were still
numerous and undismayed. The mastiff that guarded his
door was poisoned, and on the very night preceding his final
trial a ladder of ropes was introduced into the cell.

James II. had not been long upon the throne before his trial for perjury was proceeded with. There were two indictments—the charges being divided under two heads. First, that Titus had falsely sworn to a consult of Jesuits held at the White Horse Tavern on April 24, 1678, at which the King's murder was resolved upon. Secondly, that he had falsely sworn that William Ireland was in London between the 8th and 12th of August in the same year.

The first trial commenced at the King's Bench on the 8th of May, 1685. Oates never appeared to such advantage as when defending himself against overwhelming odds. Neither pluck nor consistency had been required of him before, but he now gave evidence of both qualities. His long frequentation of Westminster Hall gave him a familiarity with every portion of procedure, of which he took ample advantage. He challenged nearly every juror; he interrupted Jeffreys, insisted upon being heard, and showed himself in his treatment of witnesses an apt pupil of the then Chief Justice and his predecessor. He gave Jeffreys back every bit as good as he received. It was, if ever, a case of *arcades ambo*: either might have taken the other's place with perfect propriety.

The second trial took place on the following day. Oates's energy sensibly declined, but he nevertheless questioned all the numerous witnesses as to their religious opinions, and tried to convict them of inconsistency and error with regard to dates. Jeffreys was bubbling over with vivacity. Speaking of Ireland's movements, the Attorney-General remarked, " We shall prove that he [Ireland] went to Mr. Gerrard's at Hildersham ; there he was on August the 31st and 32nd." Lord Chief Justice : " How, Mr. Attorney, the 32nd ! I doubt you will hardly be able to tell us where he was then." The Attorney spoke of September 1st, when Oates had sworn that Ireland was in town. A whole cloud of witnesses now gave evidence to the contrary. Similar evidence had as conclusively proved alibis in the former trials, but in 1679 London juries believed that Catholic statements proved their opposites. Oates's defence was full and fluent in the extreme. He spoke of the hardship involved in his being hauled over the coals, after an interval of six years, for minute inaccuracies as to dates; he laid great stress upon the injury done to his cause by the refusal of the judges to allow him to call as witnesses certain of his old cronies, who were in Newgate. He quoted Scroggs's former animadversions upon the credibility of Catholic evidence with very considerable effect. At times he rose to a pitch of eloquence. With regard to the Papists, they had all, he said, been parties to the plot, and their evidence should not be admitted. "For," he went on, "there is a turn to be served by them against me, and a revenge they are resolved to take upon me; for they have hopes now of bringing in their religion, and are to welcome it with my ruin; and this is the cause of this prosecution. Their eyes do see now what their hearts so long desired, that is, the death of a great man who died but lately [Shaftesbury], and against whose life they had conspired so often and so long. My lord, if this had been the first conspiracy that ever the Papists were guilty of, there might have been some more scruple and objection in the case; but if you cast your eyes upon Campion and others in Queen Elizabeth's time; of Garnet and the powder-Jesuits in King James's time; and the designs of the Popish party in the time of the late King Charles the first, discovered to the Archbishop of Canterbury; if these things do pass for truth and there is no averment against so many records as we have of these conspiracies, then my discovery is no such improbable a thing: and I hope then the gentlemen of the jury will take it into their considerations, who they are that are witnesses in this case; men whose very religion is rebellion, and whose principles and practices are pernicious to the Government, and thereby they are to be looked upon as dangerous persons in Church and State."[1]

But all this eloquence availed him nothing. Jeffreys summed up with tremendous force against the prisoner— not forgetting to give occasional vent to the passionate fury he knew so well how to simulate. "Is it not a shame to this land," he burst out, "that it should be remembered

[1] Cobbett's "State Trials," vol. x. p. 1290.

what one of the witnesses this day testifieth—that when
Oates came to appear at the Council Table to attest a
matter of fact, before this innocent blood was spilt (for so
I must call it, if that which has been sworn this day is
true), the rabble should be so boisterous as to cry out,
'Where is that villain that dares come to give evidence
against Oates, the saviour of the nation?' Oh, horrid
blasphemy! that no less an epithet should be given to such
a profligate wretch as Oates, than that which is only proper
to our Blessed Head. As though Oates had merited more
than all mankind! and so indeed he has, if we take it in a
true sense. He has deserved much more punishment than
the laws of this land can inflict!" Thus were juries
charged in the good old times of the Stuarts.

With regard to the credibility of the Catholic evidence,
the Chief Justice asserted, with a vehemence which exceeded the present occasion, though seven years back it
would have been praiseworthy enough, "This I am sure
of, lying is as much the talent and inclination of a Presbyterian as ever it can be of a Papist: nay more, for it is as
inseparably incident in a Presbyterian (and such sniveling,
whining, canting knaves) to lie as to speak. They can
no more forbear lying than they can forbear speaking; for
generally as often as they do the one they do the other."
He, moreover, adjured the court, with the utmost solemnity, to take this opportunity of effacing the unenviable
stigma of a partial and sectarian justice. "Gentlemen,
I hope all eyes are opened (I wish they had been so long
since); let us lay the burden, the infamy and reproach of
those things, upon them that deserve it; for we cannot but
know, we are reckoned as a byword to all our neighbours,
and shall remain monuments of ignomiy to all succeeding
ages and times if we do not endeavour to discharge ourselves
and our religion and the justice of our nation from these
scandals."

The jury returned to the bar after half an hour's recess,
and delivered a verdict of "Guilty." The prisoner was
allowed eight days to move in arrest of judgment. The
defendant's exceptions to judgment as prepared by his

counsel, Mr. Wallop, were then read, and answered in due course by the Attorney-General. Jeffreys once more summed up, and after some consultation with his brothers, deputed Sir Francis Withins to pronounce the sentence, which was as follows :—

"First, The Court does order for a fine that you pay 1,000 marks upon each Indictment.

"Secondly, that you be stript of all your Canonical Habits.

"Thirdly, The Court does award, That you do stand upon the Pillory and in the Pillory, here before Westminster-hall-gate, upon Monday next for an hour's time between the hours of 10 and 12; with a paper over your head (which you must first walk with round about to all the courts in Westminster Hall) declaring your crime. And that is upon the first Indictment.

"Fourthly, (in the second Indictment) upon Tuesday you shall stand upon and in the Pillory, at the Royal Exchange in London, for the space of an hour, between the hours of 12 and 2; with the same inscription.

"You shall upon the next Wednesday be whipped from Aldgate to Newgate. Upon Friday you shall be whipped from Newgate to Tyburn, by the hands of the common hangman.

"But Mr. Oates we cannot but remember, there were several particular times you swore false about: and therefore as annual commemorations, that it may be known to all people as long as you live, we have taken special care of you for an annual punishment.

"Upon the 24th of April every year as long as you live, you are to stand upon the Pillory and in the Pillory at Tyburn just opposite the gallows for the space of an hour between the hours of 10 and 12.

"You are to stand upon and in the Pillory here at Westminster Hall Gate, every 9th of August so long as you live. And that it may be known what we mean by it, 'tis to remember what he swore about Mr. Ireland's being in town between the 8th and 12th of August.

"You are to stand upon and in the Pillory at Charing Cross on the 10th of August every year during your life, for

an hour between 10 and 12.   The like over against Temple
Gate on the 11th.

"And upon the 2nd of September (which is another
notorious time which you cannot but be remembered of)
you are to stand upon and in the Pillory, for the space of
one hour, between twelve and two, at the Royal Exchange :
and all this you are to do every year during your life ; and
to be committed close prisoner as long as you live.

"This I pronounce to be the judgment of the Court upon
you for your offences.   And I must tell you plainly, if it
had been in my power to have carried it further, I should
not have been unwilling to have given judgment of death
upon you ; for I am sure you deserve it."

Then the prisoner was taken away.

III.

Every beast, says Villon, clings bitterly to a whole skin.
As late as May 19th Titus was fairly confident, yet on the
20th dawned the day of his memorable laceration.   His
enemies trembled lest he should swallow poison, and every
precaution was taken.   Death would have seemed to all but
the mob a preferable penalty, but Oates's offences technically
only amounted to misdemeanour, and Jeffreys, with the best
intentions in the world, was unable to punish him as a felon.
The anomaly had been noted with a view to coming events
by an ingenious pamphleteer, who reflected in 1685 upon the
"Inconveniences attending wilful and malicious perjury;
with some reason why such crimes ought to be made felony."
Before Coke's time " Taitus " would have been summarily
strung up as an approver, *i.e.*, a King's evidence who, confessing his own guilt, has accused an accomplice who has
been proved guiltless.   The times were now more *lenient*,
and Tyburn in a " Courteous Invitation to the Salamanca
Doctor," deplored the loss of a monster

" For whom my triple Arms extended were
(To hug with close embraces) many a year."

The accounts given of Oates's punishment are various and conflicting, but the task of equating the discrepancies, such as they are, is a simple one. There was no real doctor provided to take the sham one's temperature or feel his pulse at periods during the course; still less a reporter to accompany the procession with a kodak, and give his successive impressions, or an accommodating interviewer to ask the victim precisely how he felt as he adjusted his gabardine over his dripping shoulders. Crowds of people turned out to see him, but some witnessed the show at its commencement near Aldgate, others at the conclusion near Newgate, and the demeanour of the patient changed sensibly as he proceeded. Abraham de la Pryme in his diary narrates how, at his father's house in Yorkshire, in 1686, from the lips of one Nat Reading, newly come from London, he heard that Oates was whipt most miserably. "As he was haild up the streets the multitude would pitty him and w^d cry to the hangman, 'Enough, enough! Strike easily enough!' To whom Mr. Oats reply'd, turning his head cheerfully behind him, ' Not enough good people for the truth, not enough.'"

This is sublime, but it was merely the *lever de rideau* of what was perhaps the cruellest bit of torture ever inflicted in these islands—one which we are expressly told was of an extreme severity, such as was unknown to the English nation. So exceptional, in fact, was the exhibition that a man of such humanity and good taste as John Evelyn himself could not forbear the temptation of a glimpse at it, and "chanc'd to pass just as execution was doing on him." The executioner was the notorious Ketch, the wretch who gave chop after chop with lingering gusto before he could bring himself to despatch Russell or Monmouth. He was readily accessible to bribes, it is true, and at the execution of Stephen College, "the Protestant joiner," in 1681, he is described as "most civil—thanks to the 5 guennies his [College's] relations gave him—permitting him to hang until in *most* men's opinion he was quite dead, before he cut him down, quartered him and burnt his bowels." From an executioner so scrupulously considerate, Oates might have anticipated similar courtesy, but unfortunately, on this particular occasion, he had been approached, not by Oates's own friends, but by those of his victims. So after a few hundred of this conjuror's strokes, Titus began to bound about behind the cart, and then to plunge despairingly. His shrieks descended the scale until his "hideous bellowings" resembled those of a bull, and he "swounded several times with the greatness of the anguish." The blood ran down in rivulets, but the scourge still continued to descend. The barbarity of such a flogging far transcended the military scourgings in Ireland, or those in the navy in its worst days; it approached much more nearly the barbarous executions under the Russian knout or the old Roman flagellum.[1] The fact that Oates's frame proved capable of standing such "inexpressible torments," as he afterwards described them, is a marvel, and was regarded as providential by his remaining partisans. . It seemed impossible that he should survive the second part of his sentence. James was entreated to remit the supplementary flogging; but he was as obdurate as he showed himself a few months later to the miserable Monmouth, as, tied with the silken cord, he writhed and crawled before him. He shall go through with it, protested James, if he has breath in his body. On May the 22nd the mangled frame of Oates was hoisted out of his dungeon. He was quite unable to stand, and seemed insensible; it was believed that he had stupefied himself with spirit. The carcass was attached to a tumbrel and dragged along a sullen and unresisting prey to the merciless Ketch. The worthy Edmund Calamy saw the second whipping, when the victim's back, "miserably swelled with his first whipping, looked as if it had been flayed." An assiduous spectator counted seventeen hundred stripes. In all he received not less than three thousand lashes. "Such a thing was never inflicted by any Jew, Turk, or Heathen, but Jeffries." The doors of Newgate at last closed upon him. His subsequent sufferings are thus by himself described : He lay ten weeks under the surgeon's hands, and after, by God's mercy (and the extraordinary

[1] Partridge's Almanack for 1692 states incidentally that Oates "was whip't with a whip of six thongs."

OATES—HIS DEGREES.

OATES—HIS DEGREES.

skill of a judicious chirurgeon), he had outlived their bloody usage, his enemies, still inveterate, penetrated his prison, attempted to pull off the plasters applied to cure his back, and threatened to destroy him; then they procured him to be loaded with irons of excessive weight for a whole year without any intermission, even when his legs were swollen with the gout, and to be shut up in the dungeon or hole of the prison, whereby he became impaired in his limbs and con-tracted convulsions, fits, and other distempers. It was said that in his cell he gave himself up to melancholy, and sate whole days uttering deep groans, his arms folded, and his hat pulled over his eyes. In 1688 the plausible rumour that he was dead gained a wide circulation. Yet the second part of his sentence was not forgotten, and notices appeared in the newspapers from time to time that Oates stood in the pillory by the Royal Exchange and elsewhere in accordance with the terms of his sentence.

Oates's prison amusements seem to have taken the form of a little pamphlet entitled, " Sound Advice to Roman Catho-lics, Especially the Residue of Poor, Seduced, and Deluded Papists in England, who obstinately shut both eyes and ears against the clearest Light of the Gospel of Christ." His apprenticeship under Tonge made this kind of work easy to Titus, and he probably regarded such productions as one of the minor obligations of his vocation. The work mainly consists of an enumeration of what are called " Popish Pranks," and contains a variety of novel information. Here are details respecting Pope Joan; how Adrian IV. fell out with the Emperor of Germany for holding his wrong stirrup; how Celestine III. crowned the Emperor and Empress with his feet, kicking off their crowns again with his toe; how Nicolas III. begot a bastard son with claws and hair like a bear—with other details, more or less edifying.

The London mob was far too Protestant to hold Oates in any very rooted abhorrence. Before the revolution was so much as dreamt of the multitude received him on the plat-form " with shouts in favour of the sorry fellow, and against the Catholics."[1] And more than this, on the days when he

[1] See Sarotti's Letter quoted in *Nat. Observer*, December 31, 1892.

suffers, writes Sarotti, the Venetian ambassador, to the Signory, the people neither inflict, nor permit any to inflict upon him the least hurt either by word or deed, as is done to others who undergo this punishment.[1]   On the contrary he is consoled by numerous and devoted sympathisers with the title of martyr and the gift of hundreds of five-shilling pieces; and other presents are sent to him in prison (he had been removed from Newgate to the King's Bench in South-wark), where he spends his days joyfully and comfortably in the company of the gaolers and his own friends.

This account, so conflicting with the liar's own pitiful tale, is doubtless somewhat coloured by the facile pen of a Roman Catholic alarmist, but it may be regarded as certain that very considerable relaxations had been made in the treatment to which Oates was subjected before the actual downfall of the Stuart *régime.*   The feeling which prompted the universal joy at the acquittal of the seven bishops may be safely taken to have included his gaolers, who would be readily disposed to regard Oates somewhat in the light of a Protestant martyr.   That such an one should sigh for a Protestant wind was only natural, and here again the liar doubtless met with sympathy from the staunch Protestantism of his environment.   In August, 1688, this feeling took a concrete form in the shape of an illegitimate son borne of a Protestant bed-maker in the King's Bench Prison.   The fact was, by Wood's account, the common report in London.   There is little doubt that, from a period anterior to the fall of 1688, Oates had begun to look forward to a career of renewed usefulness and prosperity.   The Prince of Orange reached London in De-cember, 1688, and before many weeks had elapsed the liar, who had promptly emerged from prison, was presented to William III., who received him " very kindly."   On March 31,

---

[1] Cases of death resulting from injuries inflicted upon persons in the pillory were by no means rare.   A notorious case was that of "Mother Needham," the simpering procuress of the first plate of Hogarth's Harlot's Progress, who, in spite of the strenuous efforts made by certain persons to protect her, was so pelted by the mob, in 1731, that she died before her sentence could be completed.

1689, he addressed to the House of Lords a long and effusive petition for redress, a comprehensive request in which the reversal of his sentence was evidently regarded as merely an item. Early in April the matter of the judgment in Oates's case came up for debate in the Upper House. Sir Robert Holloway and Sir Francis Withins, who had shared Jeffreys' bench, attended at the bar of the House of Lords to defend their sentence. Recondite precedents were proffered by them. If Coke and Bracton savoured insufficiently of the antique, there was a tongue-tearing law of Edward the Confessor against perjury. Had not Nabal, moreover, lost his life for a false oath? Lord Chief Justice Holt reserved his counterblast. It came, however, on May 31st, weighted with learning and wealth of precedent. Unreasonable whipping or torture of any kind, he argued, was inhuman, and, surprising corollary, unjust. Augustus, being invited to sup with Pollio, set a wretch free whom Pollio had ordered to be put into a pond of lampreys, to be gnawed to death for breaking some glasses. This whipping had been exorbitant; it was also "erroneous" put in Lechmere, and "never practised before in the lower part of Westminster Hall." "No gentleman was to be whipt," so the Lords had decided in Flood's case. As to the whipping, interpolated Eyre, it is plainly a villainous judgment, let Bracton say what he please. St. Paul redeemed himself by saying he was a free citizen; Oates had asserted that it was contrary to Magna Carta and against the liberty of a freeman of this kingdom. That Oates was not a saint, much less a gentleman, seemed immaterial. Then as to other parts of the sentence. Imprisonment for life was of doubtful validity. The unfrocking could not be inflicted by a temporal court, therefore the whole sentence is void. Tumbrels were for common bawds, Titus was not a common bawd, argal the sentence ought to be reversed. So argued these learned ermined casuists, and described the sentence to Parliament as erroneous, cruel, and illegal.

But all this legal incubation took time, and Oates was getting impatient. Consequently, while the case was yet being debated in the Lords, he unadvisedly sent in a petition for a bill to reverse his sentence to the Commons. So querulous and snappish were the two Houses at this period in their mutual relations that for a time it seemed highly probable that the ever-egregious Oates would be the occasion of a very pretty little quarrel between them. The Lords had qualms about the rehabilitation of such a reptile, which the Commons were utterly unable to understand. The Commons were for passing a bill of reversal forthwith. The feeling in the Lords was adequately expressed by the Duke of Leeds. A perjured scoundrel demanded the reversal of his sentence. Well, he had already been whipped from Newgate to Tyburn. Let their Lordships literally reverse his sentence by ordering him to be whipped from Tyburn to Newgate. Meanwhile the Upper House committed the liar to prison for breach of privilege.

On May 30th he petitioned the Lords to pardon any offence committed by inadvertence or ignorance, but was informed that exception was taken to his signing himself D.D. He answered that he was a D.D. of Salamanca. The explanation (which must have sounded something like a stale joke) was regarded by the Lords in the light of an impertinence. He was told to withdraw, and on appearing again was ordered to strike out D.D., which he said he could not do out of conscience, and was therefore remanded to prison. Affairs were complicated by the intervention of the King, who seems to have granted Oates a pardon in June; but this did not affect his recent misdemeanour, and Titus remained in the Marshalsea deriving what comfort he could from a donation of fifty pounds sent him in August by the Duke of Bolton.

The Reversal of Sentence Bill was all the while under discussion; the Commons pressing for its completion, the Lords bent on diverting it by means of amendments. The matter occasioned a heated conference between the Houses on the 13th of August, 1689, when the Commons dissented from all the amendments to which the Upper House resolved to adhere. The *pourparlers* proving abortive, the Commons anxiously demanded a fresh conference, to which the Lords diplomatically responded by appointing a committee to search after precedents for a conference after a resolution to adhere to amendments. The search appears to have been fruitless. But the Commons returned to the subject with unabated ardour a few days later, and a serious difference might have ensued but for the prorogation of Parliament on the 20th of the month. The Lords had creditably and successfully obstructed the passage of an ugly and superfluous bill, rendered still uglier by its precious preamble to the effect that the sentence was "of evil example to all future ages." The prorogation had the effect of setting the liar free. Scowling, cursing and abusing all parties, but particularly his friends, for their ingratitude, he once more defiled the earth, was once more seen in the presence chamber, and obtained from the King, at the earnest request of his faithful Commons, a pension of five pounds a week. So were the Lords spited and the liar paid for the dirtiest work ever yet done for a party.

IV.

Titus Oates was once more at large, but he felt that his individuality was gone, and that his life must henceforth be maimed and incomplete. An act of grace had restored him his freedom, but his sentence was still legally in force, and, as a convicted perjurer, his testimony remained invalid in a court of law. His extraordinary talents were in no wise impaired, but rather the reverse, from a period of disuse, yet by a refinement of cruelty he was wholly debarred from exercising them.

Titus was, in short, by way of falling a prey to a form of melancholy, to which even Burton was a stranger, when his interest in life was all at once revived by a prospect of vicarious perjury, and a finger in a new plot, conceived on a scale worthy of the liar's own inventiveness and ambition. Popish plots were now quite out of date; Whigs' plots paid no longer; but for Jacobite plots might there not be a glorious future yet in store? One William Fuller, who had from his youth been brought up to regard Oates as the cleverest and greatest of created beings, was at least

resolved to test their capabilities. For a brief description
of this neophyte's intimate obligations to the patriarch and
patron saint of perjurers, it were futile to attempt to super-
sede the classical passage in Macaulay, based as it is upon
the autobiography of William Fuller himself.

" In 1691, Titus, in order to be near the focal point of
political intrigue and faction, had taken a house within the
precinct of Whitehall. To this house Fuller, who lived
hard by, found admission. . . . A friendship, if that word
may be so used, sprang up between the pair. Oates opened
his house, and even his purse, to Fuller. The veteran
sinner, both directly and through the agency of his de-
pendents, intimated to the novice that nothing made a
man so important as the discovery of a plot, and that these
were times when a young fellow who would stick at nothing
and fear nobody might do wonders. The revolution—such
was the language constantly held by Titus and his parasites
—had done little good. The brisk boys of Shaftesbury had
not been recompensed according to their merits. Even
the Doctor—such was the ingratitude of men—was looked
coldly on at the new Court. Tory rogues sate at the Council
board, and were admitted to the royal closet. It would
be a noble feat to bring their necks to the block." Then
Oates, with the authority which experience and success
entitle a preceptor to assume, read his pupil a lecture on
the art of bearing false witness. " You ought," he said,
with many oaths and curses, " to have made more, much
more, out of what you heard and saw at St. Germains.
Never was there a finer foundation for a plot. But you
are a fool: you are a coxcomb: I could beat you: I would
not have done so. I used to go to Charles and tell him
his own. I called Lauderdale names to his face. I made
King, Ministers, Lords, Commons afraid of me. But you
young men have no spirit." Fuller was greatly edified by
these exhortations, but after a time he felt it inexpedient
for him to be seen in company with Titus Oates. And eventually his plot missed fire—and he himself was exposed.

Titus was again reduced to chew the cud of bitter fancy.
His jawbone was powerless, and the impenitent perjurer

"mourned like a turtle" over the dreariness of existence. The sense of unrequited services was intolerable, and he continued to rail against the faithlessness of princes and the ingratitude of ministers, until a check was administered to him by the reduction of his pension. Titus was summoned before the Council in May, 1693, and the lid of the secret service coffer rapped sharply down over his avaricious fingers.

It may safely be assumed that it was "chest" trouble which caused him at this precise conjuncture to cast about for a "doe," and, though passing strange, it is true that, in spite of the notorious infamy of his past, a lady with the required means was actually forthcoming. "On the 18th of August, 1693, Dr. Otes was married to Mrs. Margaret Wells of Bread Street (whose former husband was a Muggletonian, and she continu'd of the same persuasion)." She possessed £2,000 in money, and mighty little in the way of looks—a source of gratification, it is said, to the doctor, who was, however, greatly impressed "by the gravity and goodness of her person." The marriage caused the utmost astonishment at Garraway's and the coffee-houses generally, where nothing else was talked about for a whole day, and unspeakable pleasantries were circulated. A plate depicting the wedding is given in the fourth volume of Tom Brown's collected works. The bridegroom stands in the foreground, attired as a monk, and a grinning satyr is knotting a cord round him and the fair Wells, while, in the background, a fresco of the burning of Sodom is conspicuous. "The Salamanca Wedding," Brown's pamphlet celebrating the event, was so exceptionally scandalous that the author was arrested and imprisoned by order of the council.

Having now exhausted the occupations of every other circle of the Rogue's Inferno to which his terrestrial activities were confined, Oates still felt an unsatisfied corner of ambition in the direction of nasal psalmody. The same sort of mental, or ventral, twist which precipitates a wellsteeped cynic into Papistry of ultramontane variety, caused in Titus a hankering after utterance from the pulpit of a Baptist conventicle. He appears to have been finally

restored to the bosom of the sect towards the end of
1698.   The bounded Baptists had some scruples about
admitting so "notour and evil" a monster into their
midst, but his reputation as a swearer and a man of
passion affected them much more than his little propensity to perjury.   They were obviously worthy descendants of the fanatics who objected to bear baiting, not
because of the cruelty to the bear but on account of the
pleasure afforded the spectators.   Above all, his parson's
habit offended their sectarian niceness.   The liar protested
in a letter to a brother Baptist, dated October 13, 1696,
"I never swore in my life—unless it were before a magistrate
(significant proviso) ; For the talking obscenely, I protest in
the presence of God, it is a lye. . . . With regard to the
Habit, though it may give great offence, yet it will neither
be safe for me, nor of any advantage to the Church of
Christ to leave it off."   It was, perhaps, with a view to
conciliating the opinion of his new friends that Oates made
himself conspicuous in 1695 by striking a Mr. Green, the
archbishop's chaplain, in a spiritual court, though the exact
circumstances of this outbreak do not appear to be known.
The negotiations lasted in all about two years, and the
brethren might have proved inexorable had not the liar
been able to convince them of a satisfactory balance in his
goldsmith's books, if not in those of a higher authority.
The passage in one of his letters referring to this important
subject is sufficiently autobiographical to deserve quotation.
"You know, Brother," he writes, "that God hath made
use of wicked men to be Rods to correct those who belong
to him. . . . I bless his name for the Rod"—thus by the
way; then follows, "You may remember, dear Brother,
what an Objection you have made, in relation to my worldly
concerns.   That my unsettled state in the world, and my
Debts were in some measure a hindrance to my walking
with you, lest by the means of them some advantage might
be taken against me, and the way of God might be Evil
spoken of ; it being Scandalous with some for a Man of my
Figure in the world to be in Debt.   If that be still an
Objection, Oh praised be the name of the Lord for ever, that

Objection now will cease; for God hath inclined the King's Heart to me to Establish my Livelyhood in the World; so that I think and hope through his grace and mercy to me, and as a return of my humble, patient faithfull seeking his face, the King is wrought upon and hath granted by his Letters Patents under the Great Seal of England the sum of £300 per annum for me and my poor wife, for the term of 99 years if we both or either of us so long shall live, and I have also a grant of £500 to pay my debts. . . . Be therefore no longer severe against me by keeping me upon the Rack, but take compassion on my Soul," and he subscribes himself, blethering piously to the end, "Thy Ever Loving brother in the Faith and Order of the Gospel of our Dearest Redeemer, Jesus Christ the Righteous, Titus Oates."

A reference to the Treasury Papers corroborates the fiscal details given above. At the beginning of 1697 the liar memorialised the King for five hundred pounds to pay his debts, affirming that, unless this little sum were promptly paid over, he must perish, to the eternal disgrace of the Government. He had no clothes worthy to appear before the King, or he would have preferred his request (which was curtly refused), in person. Later in this same year the petitioner was still more urgent and explicit. He had received forty pounds a month from 1689 to 1692, in which year his annuity was cruelly retrenched. In the meantime, seduced by the King's promises, he had run deeply into debt. He was now in profound distress, and had a "poor aged mother" to maintain.

Titus seems to have multiplied the amount he had received by two, and the aged mother was, too probably, a fiction. Nevertheless, on the 15th of July, 1698, he was called into the Treasury, and was told that his modest requests had in substance been complied with, such was the paternal solicitude of the Government. He was to have five hundred pounds to pay his debts, and three hundred pounds per annum, to date from Lady Day, 1698, during his own and his wife's life, out of the Post Office revenues; and finally, it was gently intimated, he was "to expect noe more out of secret service money." The "cruel retrenchment" alluded to was due to the torrents of obscene scurrility with which Oates sought to drench his old persecutor, James II. With these queer productions of his fancy he regaled the coffee-houses which he honoured with his custom, to the scandal of the town and the intense annoyance of his butt's daughter, Queen Mary. His materials were subsequently utilised by Titus in two pamphlets, or " Pictures of King James . . . drawn to life." But no one durst publish them until after Mary's death.

Returning to the fulfilment of Oates's pious expectations, it is needless to state that he had other motives in verting from Conformist to Nonconformist (he had previously been both, as well as Papist), besides the pleasure, refined though it was, of rolling religious platitudes off his tongue, of writing unctuous letters and subscribing himself " your affectionate brother in our dearest Redeemer." He was in reality pursuing into the preserve a rich old lady, who was at loggerheads with most of her relatives, but above all with her husband, and upon whose testamentary dispositions he hoped to bring his benign influence to bear. On the old lady's death, in 1699, he was sadly disconcerted to find that she had left her money—a cool fifteen hundred pounds—else-where. His exasperation led him to interrupt the funeral in an unseemly fashion, and a few days after to demand back a pulpit cloth and cushion, which he had previously presented to the church. Four months later he sent them back to the church with this apology—that it was his wife, not he, who sent for them, and that he would have sent them back again the next day had it not rained. He had an ulterior object in renewing cordial relations with the Baptists, by whom he was warmly welcomed back, not-withstanding the leaky nature of his apologies. His ab-stention was attributed not to pique but to qualms of unworthiness ; once more he thumped the Wapping con-venticle cushions, and his persuasive plenitude won all hearts. His object was to revenge himself on the designing executor, who had contrived to get named chief legatee. He meant to recoup himself by going halves with the widower, who readily entered into the scheme, in whatever he could recover from the executors. So well did he manage to gull one and all of the parties, that before the end of the year, by the influence of the church elders and the unanimous consent of those interested, he got himself appointed arbitrator between the executors and the widower. Better refer the matter to a man who combined so much holiness and experience, than go to law. With a circumspect pomposity and display of legal legerdemain, worthy of the Lord Chancellor himself, Titus delivered his award— to the effect that the objectionable executor was to pay the husband fifteen hundred pounds. But, notwithstanding the plotter's modesty in limiting his share of the plunder to seven hundred and fifty pounds, and despite the histrionic talent which he had displayed, his ingenuous award was arbitrarily and peremptorily set aside by a decree in Chancery, dated November, 1702, in which the said award was plainly described as "revengeful and partial." Before this untoward termination to his career as arbitrator Titus had been expelled from the fellowship of the Baptists "as a disorderly person and a hypocrite."

The remainder of the liar's career can be very briefly summed up. Ejected by the Anabaptists at Wapping for his " scandalous behaviour," he went and lived privately in Axe Yard, Westminster, the place where Pepys had lived with his wife and servant Jane, and where he commenced writing his evergreen diary. Old age was powerless to confer the gifts of sobriety or decency upon him. So strongly addicted was the liar to the taste biblically ascribed to the dog, that he seems to have found his chief pleasure in haunting the purlieus of Westminster Hall, listening to the pleadings, occasionally brawling, and, doubtless, doing his best to still further corrupt the discreditable tribe of mercenary witnesses, whose infamy was so long a rank offence in England. The monotony of this kind of existence was broken by an assault which he committed in the summer of 1702 upon the eccentric Mrs. Eleanor James. Mrs. James was a person who presumed upon her notoriety to interview no less than five successive sovereigns upon their prospects of eternal welfare.   Meeting the informer in the Court of Requests one morning, she felt it to be her duty to put to him a few modest questions, such as why, being an Anabaptist, he presumed to wear the robes of the Church, of which she was at all times an enthusiastic and intolerant champion.   Whereupon the liar grew on a sudden so enraged that, in a violent and riotous manner, he struck her on the head with a cane.   As of old, we may be sure he felt the full weight of the preacher's injunction, " Whatever thy hand findeth to do, do it with thy might."   At Quarter Sessions, on July 2, 1702, Oates's defence was that the lady had first plucked him by the sleeve, but this was held to be merely by way of admonition.   He got off finally with a severe reprimand and a fine of six marks.   Eleanor had petitioned for his cane to be burnt, writing to the House of Lords on the subject.   "Was it a crime?" she plaintively asks, " for me, who have taken kings, princes, and governors by the hands, to take him by the sleeve, Devil rather than Doctor that he is ? "

It must have been between this date and 1705 that Tom Brown—the Tom Hood of his period—having seen the famous brass monument in Westminster, went in the next place by a natural sequence (had not Dryden compared the liar to a brazen serpent ?) "to see Dr. Oats."   He found him in one of the coffee-houses overlooking the courts—" a most accomplished person in his way, that's certain."

In Axe Yard, Oates's career of infamy came to a final close on Thursday, July 12, 1705.

So lived and died Titus Oates, a human being, who, it is believed, has hitherto successfully repelled the advances of the most intrepid of biographers.   To have accomplished such a task, hardly and imperfectly indeed, is perhaps not a matter for unmixed self-satisfaction.   But the endeavour at least confers upon Oates's biographer the opportunity of placing upon record his unhesitating conviction that Titus has not been in the least degree maligned, and that he is, in all probability, rhythmically speaking, " the bloodiest villain since the world began."

THE BEAUTIFULL SIMONE

SIMON FRASER,

LORD LOVAT.

(1667-1747.)

" I. charges, for these rebels: they offend none but the

(Henry IV., Pt. I., Act III., sc. 3.)

I.

SIMON FRASER was of an ancient Norman family, to whom heralds had given, for coat-of-arms a . . . . The seat of Lord Lovat, ... castle Downie, otherwise . . . . was, called " of Beaufort " . . . . being only the fourth son of Hugh, ninth . . . . He possessed a small house at Lovfich . . . where Simon was born some . . . . mother was Sybilla, daughter of . . . .

. . . . . was educated at King's College, Aberdeen, took the M.A. degree, and acquired the happy . . . . ration from Virgil, Horace, and Ovid. His . . . . taken in it . , and soon after, being . . . . service of civil law," he preferred to accept a . . . . him in the regiment of Lord Murray, son . . . . of Athole. Thereby the world perhaps lost a . . . . In after life he often boasted that . . . . the wise . . offer was only considered toler . . . . ly an . . the part of the Murrays that the . . . . was . . . to betray its allegiance to William on . . . . con-

THE BEAUTIFULL SIMONE

SIMON FRASER,

LORD LOVAT.

(1667–1747.)

"God be thanked for these rebels: they offend none but the virtuous."

(*Henry IV.*, Pt. I., Act III., sc. iii.)

I.

SIMON FRASER was of an ancient Norman family to whom the heralds had given, for coat-of-arms, a field azure *semé de fraises*. The seat of Lord Lovat, head of the Fraser clan, was Castle Downie, otherwise called Beaufort. Simon's father, Thomas, called "of Beaufort," did not, however, reside there, being only the fourth son of Hugh, ninth Lord Lovat. He possessed a small house at Tannich in Ross-shire, and there Simon was born some time in the year 1667. His mother was Sybilla, daughter of Macleod of Macleod.

Young Simon was educated at King's College, Aberdeen, where he took the M.A. degree, and acquired the happy knack of apt quotation from Virgil, Horace, and Ovid. His degree was taken in 1683, and soon after, being about "to enter upon the science of civil law," he preferred to accept a commission offered him in the regiment of Lord Murray, son of the Marquis of Athole. Thereby the world perhaps lost a great lawyer. In after life Simon boasted that this otherwise contemptible offer was only rendered tolerable to him by an assurance on the part of the Murrays that the regiment was intended to betray its allegiance to William on the first con-

venient opportunity. It is not credible that an insignifican
cadet with hardly a hope of succession, in haste to make hi
way and with no other means of doing it than the " scienc
of civil law," should thus have despised the patronage of th
Murrays.

But promise, even of insignificance, is sometimes strangel
falsified. Death had already begun to clear Simon's patl
In 1672 the tenth Lord Lovat had died prematurely, leavin
one son only. Then, in 1692, came the death of Simon'
elder brother, Alexander. From that time the lordship (
Lovat was just within his reach. Hugh, eleventh lord, ha
married a Murray, and by her he had one daughter name
Amelia, like her mother. In 1692 he was still a young man
but if he died young and had no more children, then th
succession to the estates and chieftaincy would fall either t
the young Amelia or to Simon's father. Just before th
marriage of Lord Hugh the inheritance of Lovat had, b
a formal deed, been settled on the eldest daughter th
might be, in default of male children. But the question wa
serious—would this deed hold good? The chieftaincy (
a Highland clan was assuredly not a thing to be hande
over to a little girl in virtue of scribbled paper. It ha
never been held in the Highlands that such chieftainc
was strictly hereditary, any more than mediæval kingshi
Marriage settlements, from the clansman's point of view, ha
little to do with the matter. The will of the late chief migl
go for something, but, in the last resort, it was for the cla
itself to decide which of a chief's near relatives was h
fitting successor. And the clan was likely to object to th
chieftaincy of a girl, and still more to that of a girl chil
who would be rather more of a Murray than a Frase
Edinburgh law recognised no rights of election in th
clansmen; but need that matter? If only Lord Hug
would die speedily, and, before dying, would nomina
Simon's father as his heir, there might be a good chanc
despite all the Murrays in Perthshire and all the lawye
in Edinburgh.

And this is precisely what happened. Simon, as a po
and patronised cousin, had abundant opportunities of makir

himself useful and agreeable to Lord Hugh. Lord Hugh, on his side, as Simon himself assures us, was of "contracted understanding." So it came about that the young lord fell greatly under the influence of the strong mind of his cousin and constant companion. In the year 1696 Simon at length emerges from his obscurity. In that year Lord Hugh and he went to London together, and Lord Hugh seems to have lost, in the dissipations of the town, what little head he possessed, and to have plunged into excesses which had serious effects upon his constitution. He certainly became very ill, and finally died, on his homeward journey, at Perth, and in the arms of his loving cousin. This event, with which Simon's career fairly commences, took place on September 4, 1696. It is perhaps noteworthy that none of Simon's most virulent biographers have done him the honour of suggesting that Lord Hugh died from other than "natural causes." Neither do we make any such suggestion: but the event was certainly opportune. Now was seen the fruit of the friendly intercourse of the cousins. A will of the late lord, dated March 26th of that year, was promptly produced. It was drawn in faultless form, and set forth that whereas Lord Hugh's marriage settlement had been obtained by pressure amounting to fraud, and was contrary to the ancient custom of his family, he now settled the whole inheritance on Thomas of Beaufort, with a considerable sum in ready money as a legacy to Simon.

The first great crisis in Simon's life had now arrived. He had struck a bold stroke, for failure now might mean final and hopeless failure. If he had only had to contest the claims of the little girl, Amelia Fraser, he would have been safe enough; but behind the child of nine or ten years old were the Murrays, and the Murrays were more than powerful in the Highlands.

The eldest son of the Marquis of Athole, the newly-created Earl of Tullibardine, was now Lord High Commissioner of Scotland, and at the head of that exceedingly arbitrary body, the Scottish Privy Council. It was only too likely that Simon's claim would bring him into conflict, not merely with Edinburgh law, but with the actual Govern-

ment and Crown of Scotland.   The struggle that now opens
is represented by Simon, in the memoirs he wrote long after,
as the result of an impudent and tyrannical attempt on the
part of the Murrays to extend their authority over the Clan
Fraser and annex the estates of Lovat.   At the remembrance
his virtuous indignation knows no bounds.   He tells us how,
for a month before his death, which occurred in 1703, the
Marquis of Athole "was in the most deplorable condition,
blaspheming God and crying that he was already in hell
and surrounded with devils"; and that he died "in this
infernal kind of madness."   He adds, with edifying piety,
that this horrid death was "an exemplary judgment of God,
which ought to make those tremble who oppress the just
and destroy the innocent; for sooner or later their punishment is certain, and if they are spared in this world it is only
to aggravate their torments in the world to come."   But,
putting aside Simon's characteristic piety, there seems to be
a good deal of truth in his representation of the affair.   That
the Murrays designed to marry the little heiress to a member
or a close connection of the family, is probable; that Tullibardine used his political position as a means to attain
private ends is certain.   If Simon was greedy and unscrupulous, so also were his enemies.   Moreover, since
from the outset the great majority of the Clan Fraser
were in favour of Simon and his father, Simon had some
real claim, according to Highland law, to consider himself
ill-used.

It was, indeed, a goodly inheritance, well worth the
fighting for, that Simon fought to win.   The country of the
Frasers lay round Loch Ness, north and south, broken at
the north-eastern extremity of the lake by the township of
Inverness.   The Fraser district south of the lake is that
known as Stratheric, the wildest part of the domain, high
and sterile, full of morasses and heather and mountain mist.
Here it was that Simon was to organise his raids and find
sure refuge.   To the north of the lake lay the larger district
of the Aird, which stretches from near Inverness along the
flat and fertile shores of Loch Beauly, and then up the river
and through the wild regions westwards till its extremities

nearly reach the coast. Within these districts lay Beaufort,
or Castle Downie, and the estates of Lovat proper; but it was
for far more than the estates that Simon had made his bid.
For all the people of this country were Frasers, loyal and
uncomplaining subjects of any rightful chief, whose authority
they owned or no man's. It was a little kingdom that Simon
had set himself to win. The struggle opened promptly with
the death of Lord Hugh. Thomas of Beaufort assumed the
title of Lord Lovat, while, on the other side, the child,
Amelia Fraser, was proclaimed Baroness of Lovat. Then
follows nearly a year of intrigue and chicanery, accompanied
by confused turmoil in the Fraser country. During this
period Simon, of course, is active: now in Edinburgh
bearding, according to his own account, the "knave and
coward" Lord Tullibardine, to his face; now in Stratheric,
taking strong measures to quell dissension in the clan. The
clan was somewhat dubious and divided; but from the first
Simon and his father had completely the upper hand in the
Fraser country, though the Dowager Lady Lovat, the
Murray, remained in possession of Castle Downie, the family
headquarters. The inconvenience of having a child and
a girl for chief, jealousy of the Murray influence, and the
energy of Simon, carried the day with the clansmen. Dis-
sentients were roughly handled. Simon is said to have
attempted to get the little heiress into his clutches, but the
attempt failed, and the child was carried to safe keeping at
Dunkeld, a stronghold of the Murrays in Perthshire.

For nearly a year the Murrays seem to have been losing
ground, and the supremacy of Simon and his father in the
Fraser country getting more and more fully established. This
was, partially at least, due to the comparative inaction of the
Murrays. Legal proceedings, of an interminable character, at
Edinburgh did not in any way affect the situation; and the
Murrays seem to have been uncertain what course to take.
To force the child, Amelia, on the recalcitrant clan would,
clearly, be a very difficult piece of work.

But, in the course of the year 1697, the Murrays at length
decided on a plausible combination. There existed in the
Lowlands of Aberdeenshire a branch of the Fraser clan, long

ago separated from the main body, at the head of which was Lord Saltoun, a rich man and indubitably a Fraser. To this gentleman the Murrays appealed, first sending to the refractory clansmen to say that, since they persisted in requiring a Fraser for chief, one should be forthcoming. An arrangement of, apparently, a very indefinite kind was come to with Lord Saltoun, who seems to have been tempted to interfere by the prospect of a marriage between his son and the heiress. Such a marriage, or the prospect of it, might conceivably dispose of the objections of the clan to Amelia Fraser.

The news that Lord Saltoun was on his way from Edinburgh created some ferment in the wilds of the Fraser country, but the bulk of the clansmen held by Simon. Lord Saltoun was a stranger, a Lowlander, and he came to Castle Downie as a tool of the Murrays. He had, as Simon says, "little knowledge of the manners of those regions"; otherwise it is probable that he would have stayed at home. Soon after his arrival in the Fraser country he received a letter, signed by Thomas of Beaufort, Lord Lovat, and by twenty of the chief men of the clan, warning him that he had no right to interfere and that consequences might be serious if he persisted. Simon himself did not sign this letter, but he probably wrote it.

Of this warning Lord Saltoun took no notice, and it is evident that Simon regarded the position as dangerous. The dissensions in the clan must now, it would seem, have been serious, and Simon judged it necessary to nip in the bud the development of the Saltoun marriage project, and to convince his lordship that he had better go home again. The measures he took were prompt and strong. Setting out from Stratheric on the 6th of October with a band of trusty men—"pretty fellows" all, no doubt—he intercepted Lord Saltoun and his party near the wood of Bunchrew, between Inverness and Castle Downie, and made all prisoners. Along with Lord Saltoun was thus captured Lord Mungo Murray, a brother of Tullibardine. The prisoners were promptly shut up in the tower of Finellan, near at hand, and then Lord Saltoun was further dealt with. "A gallows was erected before the windows of my Lord Saltoun's room," says Major Fraser of the Manuscript, whose narrative is among the best authorities for Simon's life, "and a gentleman sent in to him with a message to prepare himself for another world, that he had but two days to live, and those gentlemen of the name of Fraser who gave him the call to their country was to cast the dyce to know whose fate it was to hang with him." This formidable announcement reduced the unlucky nobleman to beg his life, and finally sign a declaration that he would have no more to do with the matter—a promise which he was careful faithfully to keep after his subsequent liberation and safe return home, let us hope with gratitude.

The immediate object was gained, and if Simon had only stopped here all might have been well. His violence had indeed brought him within the purview of the criminal law, and there was no saying what action the Privy Council, under the influence of Lord Tullibardine, might take. Simon seems to have believed that he was hopelessly compromiséd, and the idea, perhaps, made him reckless. "There happened," he wrote, immediately after the "accident" referred to, to the governor of Fort William, "an unlucky accident that is like, if God and good friends do not prevent it, utterly to extirpate not only my father's family, but the whole name of Fraser." The hot blood was up, and Simon did not hesitate. Immediately after the capture of Lord Saltoun he sent the "fiery cross"—the burnt cross of wood, dipped in blood, that summoned to arms the vassals of a Highland chief—through Stratheric.

> "Both field and forest, dingle, cliff, and dell,
> And solitary heath the signal knew."

And there gathered at it fully five hundred armed men, or more.

The next step was to seize Castle Downie itself and make prisoners of all therein, including the Dowager Lady Lovat. For her daughter, the child heiress, she was safe in Perthshire. The seizure of Castle Downie was but the

natural sequel to the seizure of Lord Saltoun; what followed
cannot be so regarded. Deliberately, and almost in cold
blood, Simon proceeded to outrage the helpless and hapless
lady, after passing her through the forms of a marriage by
force. One Mr. Robert Monro, of Abertarf, "a poor sordid
fellow, a minister," officiated, but his part in the matter
appears to have been very subordinate. The service was
run through in the lady's bedroom, in the presence not only
of Simon, but of several of his ruffians. In the next room
the bagpipes were blown up lustily—whether to drown the
lady's hysterical cries or in ironic merriment is not clear.
After the "ceremony" the lady's stays were cut with a dirk,
and the rest must be left to imagination. Amelia Rioch, a
young girl and servant to the lady, swore at the subsequent
trial, "that next morning she went into the lady's chamber
and . . . did see all her face swollen and she spoke nothing,
but gave her a broad look." And further, "the deponent
thought that my lady was not sensible for a day or two
thereafter, for she did not know Lord Mungo, her brother,
the next morning when he came to see her." Also that she
said, piteously, to the girl, "Call me not madam, but the
most miserable wretch alive." In such piteous and pathetic
condition, shortly after the outrage, the lady was conveyed,
by Simon's orders, to the island of Aigas in the torrents of
the Beauly.

That the facts are as thus stated admits of no reasonable
doubt. In his memoirs, of course, Simon gives the whole
story a haughty denial. He states that he never went to
Castle Downie on this occasion at all, and that as for the
"chimerical monster of a rape," created by Lord Athole and
his son, the imposture was manifest. What interest had he
to do such a thing? The widow, he asserts, was "old
enough to be his mother, dwarfish in her person and deformed
in her shape," and, besides, a mere dependent on his bounty.
Unfortunately these statements will not bear criticism, and
are totally inconsistent with the defence actually set up by
Simon at the time of the occurrence. The lady, to begin
with, was apparently not more than thirty-four or thirty-five
years of age—only four or five years older than Simon himself.

It is certain, moreover, that at the actual time Simon, far from denying the allegations altogether, tried, on the contrary, to make out that the marriage was a genuine one, and that the lady, whom in letters he speaks of as "my dear wife," was highly enamoured of her suddenly acquired husband. There is good reason to believe that the lady did, at Aigas, demand and obtain that a proper marriage ceremony should be gone through. This is conceivable enough, without supposing that she had grown fond of Simon in the interval.

To explain Simon's exact motives in this affair is the reverse of easy. He can hardly have hoped that the Murrays would recognise the "marriage." Had they done so, indeed, such recognition would have formed a basis for compromise to the advantage of Simon, and it is quite possible that an audacious hope of this did spring up in Simon's mind. On the other hand the risk was great and the hope cannot have been strong. How was it that Simon's calculating faculty did not on this occasion bid him pause? "A man of my stamp," the first Napoleon is said to have remarked, "does not commit crimes." But Simon was not so cold-blooded. For him gratuitous crime—crime, that is, which is its own reward—had its natural attractions. We must remember, too, that he already hated the Murrays with a purity of hatred rarely developed, and that the lady was the daughter of the chief of his foes and the sister of the still loathlier Tullibardine. Finally, perhaps, he calculated that so long as the clan stood by him no decision of law courts in Edinburgh could make his position worse than it was already.

But if this was his idea he appears to have been mistaken. An atrocious outrage had been committed against the honour of one of the greatest of Scottish families. At Edinburgh the Lord High Commissioner became active. Citations were issued against Simon and his father and other persons concerned to appear for trial at Edinburgh. Their non-appearance was a matter of course; the difficulty was to serve the summonses. One gallant servitor of the Edinburgh courts contented himself with blowing a trumpet and reading the summons in the market-place of Elgin; and this appears

to have been lawful service under an act of the Scottish
Parliament.   Another, more enterprising, actually penetrated
to the shore of the Beauly, opposite Aigas itself, and there
left, by night, his piece of official paper stuck in the fork of a
cleft stick, and thereupon made the best of his way back
again.   On his side, Simon, finding that his marriage could
not be got recognised, released the lady, who returned to her
relatives.   And the war, as it was now becoming, went on.
In November, 1697, the Privy Council issued " Letters of
Intercommuning" against Simon and his father, commanding every one to boycott and otherwise damage the offenders,
and offering 2,000 marks to any one who should " bring in "
either of them, dead or alive.

This sort of excommunication was frequently issued at
that time against refractory Highlanders.   In this case it
had no more effect on the Clan Fraser than the piece of
paper left sticking by the Beauly.   More serious measures
were to come.   In February, 1698, the Government, having
decided that the " Beauforts " were " rebels," followed up
its letters of intercommuning with " letters of fire and
sword."   Under these, military officers were commissioned
to seize Thomas and Simon Fraser, and empowered to
summon the Sheriffs of Perth, Moray, and Inverness, to call
out their men to assist in doing so.   In the following June
proceedings were taken in the Court of Justiciary against
Simon and his father " for high treason in forming unlawful
associations, collecting an armed force, occupying and forti-
fying houses and garrisons, imprisoning and ravishing persons of distinguished rank, and continuing in arms after
being charged by a herald to lay them down."   On this
somewhat preposterous indictment they were condemned in
September, sentence of death and forfeiture being pronounced
against both of them.   Of course the trial was conducted in
the absence of the accused, and, of course, it was grossly
unfair.   Much ink and paper had been consumed in discussing the question whether and in what cases the trial of
persons for treason in their absence was lawful by Scotch
law.   Such a mode of trial must certainly have been convenient in that age for two good reasons.   In the first place

it was difficult to secure the presence of the accused ; and, secondly, if you did happen to lay hands on him after the trial you could hang him on the spot before he had a chance of escape or rescue.

It was now not merely the Murrays but the very Crown of Scotland itself with which Simon had to fight as best he could. Troops were sent out against the "rebels," and Stratheric itself was invaded. Simon sent his father, who was now over sixty, and seems all through to have followed the lead of his son, to the keeping of the Macleods of Skye. His late wife, Simon's mother, had been a Macleod ; and, in the safeguard of this friendly clan, Thomas of Beaufort and Lovat died in 1699. Simon himself, for some two years, lived the life of a rebel outlaw in the wilds of the Fraser country, indefatigably maintaining an unequal struggle. The troops found it hard work in Fraser country, what with the mountains and bogs, to say nothing of Simon's bands of pretty fellows. For Simon, though he can hardly have found it easy to live, was by no means a mere fugitive. The great majority of the Frasers indubitably regarded him as their rightful laird ; and Simon never lacked help or good company, even though the clansmen did not turn out for him *en masse.* In the course of 1699 Simon seems actually to have made prisoners a considerable body of troops, along with Lord James and Lord Mungo Murray, sons of Athole. In his memoirs he gives a detailed account of this brilliant action, which, however, is probably chiefly imaginary. He tells us, further, that he was strongly inclined to massacre the whole of his prisoners, and was only prevented from so doing by the entreaties of the chief men that were with him. Being thus baulked, instead of killing them he made them devote themselves "to the devil and all the torments of hell," if ever they came there again !

But what chance had Simon in the long run if the Government persisted ? As time went on his position of necessity grew weaker. He was reduced, in Major Fraser's phrase to "lurking up and down the country, the troops always in search of him." It was a hard life and a hopeless prospect. It could not be expected that the clan would remain, year after year, even partially faithful. Sooner or later he would find himself deserted and at the end of his resources. Extraneous aid must be obtained somehow.

In the year 1700 Simon appealed for assistance to Archibald Campbell, then Earl, afterwards first Duke, of Argyll. This great nobleman had been a zealous promoter of the revolution of 1688, and was, consequently, high in favour at the Court of King William. He could, certainly, be useful if he would, and that he would was probable. He had watched the affair of the Lovat inheritance from the beginning, with keen jealousy of his rivals, the Murrays. It was on the score of the balance of power in Scotland that Simon made his successful appeal to this potentate. In the autumn of the year 1700 Argyll made intercession with King William, and, apparently, secured for Simon his promise of an interview. Thereupon Simon left his mountains and hastened with due secrecy to London. On his arrival he found that the King was in the Netherlands. There was no time to be lost, but he was safe enough for the moment, and he kept his head admirably cool. After all the interview with King William might produce nothing; in that case the best thing that was to be done was to fall back on King James of St. Germains. As he had to go to the Continent in any case it would be as well, or better, to pay his respects at St. Germains before troubling King William. So Simon went from London to St. Germains. There was some risk attached to such a visit, of course—but how should King William hear of it? What passed at the little Stuart Court is not recorded with certainty; but Simon merely went to pave the way for a not improbable visit in the future.

From St. Germains he went on to see King William at Loo. The visit was only a partial success. Simon obtained a pardon, but a pardon not sufficient for his purposes. According to his own account, indeed, the King gave orders that there should be drawn up for his benefit "an ample and complete pardon for every imaginable crime," but that through the malice and treachery of his enemies, the pardon drawn in Holland was suppressed and another substituted. This story appears to be merely one of Simon's modifications of the truth. Anyhow, the actual pardon concerned only the alleged treasons. Simon's claim to the Lovat inheritance, now sorely prejudiced, was, of course, left entirely untouched, while he still remained liable to prosecution for his outrage on the Dowager.

Simon, nevertheless, having made tolerably quick work of it, was back in Scotland early in 1701 and appeared in Edinburgh, under Argyll's protection, to confront his accusers, bringing with him a large number of witnesses. It appears that it was he himself who took action to bring the whole matter before a law court, either, as he asserts, to prove his entire innocence, or, as Major Fraser declares, to prove the genuineness of his marriage with the Dowager. In any case his action was of a merely forestalling character; nor did he abide the issue. He declares that the case was predetermined against him; that all his judges were creatures of Tullibardine, and that Argyll himself said that were he "as innocent as Jesus Christ" these rascally judges would still condemn him. He thought it wiser, therefore, hastily to quit the field and return to Stratheric. On the 17th of February following he was cited before the court and outlawed for not appearing. Meanwhile he had gone back to his old way of life, and was preparing for a renewal of the struggle that had closed, for a moment, in the autumn of 1700. New letters of intercommuning were issued against him.

Simon's position was now practically the same as it had been before Argyll's intervention. Indeed, if anything, it was worse than ever, for the much-enduring clan was growing very impatient. Simon was reduced to bribing many of the principal clansmen with bonds for the future payment of considerable sums on condition that they stood by him. These bonds he afterwards, in the days of prosperity, refused to pay.

But the days of prosperity were still far off. For another year Simon maintained himself in Stratheric; then the death of William III. made it useless for him to remain there longer. For, under the new Government, the Murrays were more powerful than ever, while, on the other hand, Argyll's influence waned or disappeared. Simon had no choice but to give up the game altogether and make his peace, if that were possible, or leave Scotland and turn Jacobite for a time.

Jacobitism was, truly, a blessed refuge for the destitute in those days; and its value, in this respect, has not perhaps been fully appreciated. If a man had a good position and lost it, by fault or misfortune, let him go to St. Germains. There one could, with help of a little dexterity, at worst live passably on the bounty of the French King. And if ever a second blessed Restoration should take place—a by no means improbable event, as all men knew—would not one be a made man again? Many an unfortunate ambition, for which otherwise there had been no hope any more, found hope here. This way was always open and might lead to any-thing. As a Jacobite every rogue had a chance. And what man of spirit gives up while there is hope anywhere?

Certainly not Simon. Not for a moment, and never through the long years of misfortune that followed, did he lose heart or waver from his purpose of becoming in reality the Lord Lovat, and chief of the Clan Fraser. He did not abandon the field; he merely changed his base of operations. Stratheric and Argyll had become useless; henceforth, to conquer his inheritance, he must operate from St. Germains. For him there was no alternative. It would be ludicrous to impute to Simon any suspicion of conviction on behalf of the exiled family. Simon's most extraordinary mental charac-teristic appears to have been an entire absence of convictions except in personal relations. There, on the contrary, his beliefs were strong and lasting; and strongest of all was his conviction that the chieftaincy of the Clan Fraser was the most desirable of all earthly possessions. It is not difficult to understand the indomitable devotion with which he clung to this idea of the chieftaincy. Born and bred in the High-lands, he remained always, at heart, in spite of his tags of Horace and his later acquired French polish, a semi-bar-barian Highlander.

In his new line of life Simon was to have need of new weapons. So far he had displayed mere energy, dash, and boldness, a dominating power, which had made him some-thing of a hero in Stratheric, and a resolution a thought too sudden. Now his enormous talent for mendacity was to come into full play.

It was in the summer of 1702 that Simon left Scotland for St. Germains, with a considerable sum of money which he had levied on the estates at parting. He left behind him his younger brother, John, and the bonds with the principal clansmen to safeguard his interests, as far as possible, John proving a not unworthy lieutenant. Simon reached Paris in August or September. Before starting he asserts that he " visited the chiefs of the clans and a great number of the lords of the Lowlands, with William Earl Marishal and the Earl of Errol . . . at their head," and finally " engaged them to grant him a general commission on their part, and on the part of all the loyal Scots whom they represented," to the King of St. Germains. This was the falsehood upon which he proposed to set up in business at the Court of exile.

Simon, then, came to St. Germains in the character of an accredited agent of the chief lords of Scotland, provided with plans for the speedy restoration of his Sacred Majesty, King James III. His credentials were the weak point, and perhaps a hint of his reputation and real position in Scotland had reached the little Court. He was regarded from the first with some suspicion, and, in particular, Lord Middleton, " Secretary of State," thought proper to make difficulties ; for which he is duly rewarded in Simon's memoirs by every kind of abuse and calumny. It is not necessary to discuss Middleton's motives ; but there is reasonable suspicion that his opposition was not altogether disinterested. This ludi- crous-pathetic little Court of St. Germains was as full of puny jealousies and intrigues as the Court of the Grand Monarque himself. Simon appears to have allied himself from the first with the Duke of Perth, Lord Middleton's chief rival.

His energy and ingenuity silenced opposition for a time and gained him a partial success. He gained over Mary of Modena, the " Regent," more or less completely to his views ; and, apparently, also the French ministers, Torcy and Cal- lières. In order the more easily to push his schemes at the two Courts, he became a convert to Roman Catholicism—a proceeding which was promptly capped by Lord Middleton,

in spite of the latter's previous apophthegm, to the effect that
new light in the human edifice was generally let in through
a hole in the roofing.   His conversion procured him the
overwhelming honour of a special audience of the great King
himself.

It was not merely by force of audacity and plausibility
that Simon obtained his small victory.   The project propounded by him was indubitably a good one.   The proposal
was that King Louis should land five thousand French
soldiers at Dundee, and five hundred more near Fort
William, which, says Simon, "served as a curb upon the
Highlanders."   Then the Scottish Jacobites would raise full
ten thousand men in a short time.   Simon urged strongly
that the base of all Jacobite operations must be in the Highlands, and that Lord Middleton would get no good of his
friends in England.   In partially convincing the Court of St.
Germains and the French ministers that their chief hope lay
in the Highlands, Simon may be said to have done good
service for the Jacobite cause.   If he could only have communicated a portion of his own spirit to the futile Court and
its puny monarch, the Pretender would finally have become
a Protestant, and the second Restoration, in all probability,
an accomplished fact.

As a result of his negotiations, Simon, in May, 1703, was
commissioned to return to the Highlands and gather further
and precise information as to the intentions and proposals of
the heads of clans.   With him was sent one Captain John
Murray, by birth a Scotsman, but now a naturalised
Frenchman, bearing arms in the French King's service.
But, apparently even before they started on their dangerous
mission, the suspicious and hostile Lord Middleton, on his
own behalf, but presumably with the Queen's knowledge,
sent a certain James Murray as a spy on Simon's motions.

The precaution was far from being a mere formality.   As
Simon knew, there was no immediate chance of a Jacobite
rising.   At St. Germains he had posed as the trusted emissary of the chief Jacobite lords of Scotland, who would, on
his return, quicken his numerous and confiding allies to a
sense of the desirability of immediate action.   How on earth

was he to substantiate his statements upon his return to Scotland? Almost every statement he had made at St. Germains was false, as Middleton, the best informed of James's advisers, probably knew. Far from being the confidential ally of the chief Jacobite lords, he was by most of them either ignored or viewed with the utmost suspicion. He could hardly expect, master of duplicity as he was, to continue to hoodwink the zealous and observant Jacobite agents by whom he was shadowed. The situation was in reality horribly awkward. But Simon had a card up his sleeve. If the worst came to the worst, would it not be possible to buy possession of the Lovat inheritance, or, at least, some other good thing, by selling his new Jacobite friends?

He had first to get to Scotland, and this was no easy matter; but as we have only his own account of his adventures by the way, it will be prudent, in the interests of veracity, to pass them over. He sailed from Calais, it appears, and passed through England, of course in disguise. Soon after reaching the country he had an interview with his old ally, Argyll. Argyll was out of favour, and in no mood to betray him to his enemies, the Murrays, while on the other hand he could be useful in facilitating Simon's tour of discovery or in opening up communications with the Government; later on Simon was in no great hurry to play the betrayer; he would probably have remained, for the time, a mere Jacobite agent if things had gone well with him in that capacity. It is certain that he made actual use of his Jacobite commission, and confabulated with various Highland chieftains as to a rising—with Lord Drummond, Cameron of Lochiel, the Laird of Macgregor, Stuart of Appin, and others. Nothing, however, was definitely arranged, or could be, though protestations of zeal in the cause of his absent Majesty seem to have been plentiful enough. Simon doubtless came quickly to the conclusion that there was no present chance of conquering his inheritance by way of a Jacobite rising. This being so he was bound to endeavour to sell his Jacobite friends for what they were worth. He therefore proceeded to procure from the accomodating Argyll an introduction to the Duke of Queensberry,

High Commissioner in Scotland. With this representative of Queen Anne, Simon had an interview in Edinburgh in September, 1703. Not content with betraying mere Jacobites, Simon, with the Lovat inheritance constantly in view, took the opportunity to strike a blow at the chief of his enemies, Lord Athole. Among other documents he gave Queensberry a letter signed " M," for Mary of Modena, purporting to be addressed to this nobleman. " You may be sure," the ex-Queen had written, " that when my concerns require the help of my friends, you are one of the first I have in my view." The letter was genuine, but it was Simon, and not the Queen, who had added the address to Lord Athole. In his memoirs Simon admits having attempted to compromise Athole and declares that in so doing he was doing good service as a loyal and zealous Jacobite. For was not Lord Athole " notoriously the incorrigible enemy of King James"? and had not " his accumulated treasons rendered his person odious to all his Majesty's faithful servants " ? " God knows," he piously remarks, " what rewards these services have procured him."

As a result of his negotiations with Queensberry, Simon obtained, first a pass to London, and thence a pass to Holland, *en route* for St. Germains. He had offered, says Queensberry, to return there, and " do great service for the Government " as a spy. But he had gained nothing so far by his treachery, and his situation was very delicate. He had, indeed, succeeded in convincing his companion to Scotland, John Murray, that it had been necessary, in the Jacobite interest, for him to see Queensberry, and the apparent failure of their joint mission might possibly be explained to the satisfaction of St. Germains. On the other hand was the danger that the full story of his negotiations with Queensberry might prematurely be made public. But, convinced as he was that there would be no immediate rising in the Highlands great enough to serve his turn, he had no alternative but to pursue his risky policy or submit to sit down and wait.

In the November and December of 1703 Simon was at Rotterdam conducting a varied correspondence. To St.

Germains he sent a vainglorious "memorial of all that my Lord Lovat did in his voyage to England and Scotland by her Majesty's orders." He declares therein that Queensberry had made him magnificent offers, the account of which he must have written with a pang of regret that no such offers had been made—which, of course, he had magnanimously refused. This memorial seems to have been handed in at St. Germains in January, 1704, and it was unfortunate for Simon that he should have sent it so soon, for as yet he did not know that he was himself betrayed. In these same months he was corresponding also with Queensberry, and with the Jacobites in Scotland through the agency of Colin Campbell, of Glenderule, and the famous Robert Ferguson, "the plotter." Both these latter personages were, in fact, betraying him, and in December the whole story of his relations with Queensberry was made public. To Queensberry, who was now charged with plotting against his rival and colleague, Lord Athole, by help of forgeries, these revelations were a serious blow; to Simon they meant ruin, at least for the time. In February, 1704, Simon knew that he was betrayed. To brazen it out was his only chance. On February 24th he wrote to Campbell, whose treachery he had not yet discovered, with lofty sorrow and indignation. "My comfort is," he wrote, "that I neither betrayed my trust nor my friends, nor would not for the universe," and added, with holy horror, "For my part, I believe the day of judgment is at hand."

What was there now left for him but to go to St. Germains and meet his fate? He had ceased to be safe in Holland, and to return to Scotland or England would have been suicide. Was he to flee to Germany, or some outlandish region, abandon his career, and live a nameless outcast? At St. Germains he might, even yet, by dint of ingenuity and audacity, make out some sort of case. In any case he would keep his life and his pretensions, and who could tell what revenges time might bring? Even now Simon's heart did not fail him. "I thank God," he wrote long afterwards, "I was born with very little fear."

With hardship and difficulty, now disguised as an officer

in the Dutch service, now as a peasant, he reached Antwerp, and was passed on thence by the French authorities to Paris. His expedition had, to some extent, forestalled his enemies. Simon hastened to give his own version of what had occurred, and apparently with some effect. But his position became untenable as news came in from England and Scotland. It seems, however, that the French ministers were somewhat hard to convince, and it was apparently only in August that Simon was, at length, actually arrested under a *lettre de cachet* granted by the French King.

Simon had now reached the very lowest point of his fortunes, if we except, at least, his great, final fall. According to his own account he was conducted with ignominy to the Castle of Angoulême, and there "thrust into a horrible dungeon, which had been from time immemorial the unviolated habitation of coiners and murderers. It was a gentleman of this last class," he adds, "whom the consideration of Lord Lovat's friends obliged to give way to him in the present instance." In this dungeon he remained "shut up for thirty-five days in perfect darkness," tended the while by a "grim jailoress, who came every day to throw him something to eat, in the same silent and cautious manner in which you would feed a mad dog." How far this story is true is quite uncertain, but that some such severity was used seems rather probable. In any case, however, the French Government seems soon to have repented of its harshness, and Simon was released from his dungeon.

But for the next ten years Simon remained a prisoner in France, first at Angoulême, and afterwards on parole at Saumur. There is little to say concerning this long period of eclipse. It appears that after the first he was treated rather handsomely by the French Government. He himself asserts that at Angoulême he had the free run of the castle and park, and free intercourse with "the most considerable persons in the city and neighbourhood," and that he found it a "beautiful and enchanting prison." At Saumur, though a prisoner, he was not in prison at all; he simply resided there, not altogether uncomfortably, at the French King's expense. Major Fraser says that when he reached Saumur in 1714 " Lord Simon was then but very low in his person," but, on the other hand, his personal liberty seems to have been practically almost unrestricted. He made friends, too, among the gentle families of the neighbourhood, and in particular with that of the Marquis de La Frezelière, who seems to have recognised in him a kinsman. He also struck up a close alliance with the Jesuits of Saumur. It is tolerably clear that he could have left France long before he did had he chosen, but where could he have gone ? All through this period of disgrace he corresponded, as he found occasion, with the Whigs in England ; but this led to nothing, and the Court of St. Germains remained inexorable. On both sides the way was barred against him, and he could only wait. Nor was his position ever free of actual danger. Some fresh discovery might well lead to a renewal of the severe measures of 1704, and it is said that on the days when the post came in to Saumur from Paris he used to betake himself to some hiding-place, lest there should be fresh orders of an objectionable kind.

Many extravagant and some incredible tales were afterwards circulated concerning Simon's life and adventures in France. It was said that he took orders, that he became a Jesuit, and, in the character of father confessor, sadly abused the confidence of some of his fair penitents ; and even that he obtained a *curé* and became a popular preacher! There seems to be no tittle of evidence for any of these stories.

That Simon was not crushed by his misfortunes is certain, though the forced inaction to a man of his acutely restless temperament must have been a severe penalty. He emerged at length from his long eclipse with unmitigated zest for the good things of life, with the old unconquerable and never-to-be-satisfied avidity for power, pleasure, honours, and triumphs.

He emerged in this manner. In the year 1702 the young girl, Amelia Fraser, heiress of the Lovat inheritance according to the Murrays, was married to Alexander Mackenzie, son of Roderick Mackenzie, Lord Preston-

hall, a judge of the Court of Session at Edinburgh.
In December of the same year Alexander had obtained,
under a judgment delivered by his father, the estate of
Lovat, and therewith the chieftaincy for himself and the
long-disputed title for his wife. The estate was forthwith
settled upon the issue of the marriage, any heir under the
settlement being thereby bound to assume the name of
Fraser. After John Fraser, Simon's brother and representative, had been put down, the clan submitted, though
sullenly, to the new arrangement. In 1706 Mackenzie
foolishly had a deed executed whereby his heirs were empowered to retain the name of Mackenzie. This insult to
the clan pride was duly resented, and would probably have
led to immediate disturbance had the clansmen known
whether their true chief, Simon, was dead or alive. But,
as the Major says, " the most part of the name of Fraser
knew nothing of their natural chief's being in life " ; and
consequently, though there was unquiet fermentation,
nothing was done. In 1713, however, John Fraser, who
had taken refuge in France, ventured to return to his native
country, and the news spread that the " natural chief " was
actually living. The consequence was that a number of the
principal men of the clan arranged that one of them should
go off to France to find Simon and bring him back if
possible. The personage selected for this undertaking was
Major James Fraser, of Castle Leathers, the writer of the
" Manuscript " already referred to.

The Major set out on his arduous journey in May, 1714,
and with considerable difficulty reached Saumur. St.
Germains remained obdurate. On the other hand escape
from Saumur was tolerably easy, and escape was accordingly resolved upon. Simon himself seems to have doubted
whether the risk were worth taking, but he took it nevertheless. The two left Saumur together, Simon giving out that
he was going to pay a visit at Rouen. Suspicion was only
aroused later, and orders issued for their arrest; but too late.
Having spent a day in hiding at Rouen they started off in
the night and reached Dieppe, Simon riding and the Major
running beside him. There being no ships about to start

for England at Dieppe, they hurried on in the same fashion to Boulogne, and there, also, could find no ship to take them. The danger was now great, but they succeeded in hiring an open boat, in which they triumphantly crossed to Dover on the night of the 14th of November, though the storm was " so great " that "they all despaired of their lives."

From Dover they went on to Gravesend, where Simon remained some time in hiding, negotiating through the faithful Major, of whom he was strangely and most unjustly suspicious, with Lord Islay, brother of the Duke of Argyll, and other Scottish Whigs then in London. There was little or no use in attempting to reach the Highlands at once; but, meanwhile, Simon was far from being safe. Queen Anne, indeed, his most powerful enemy, was dead; but as soon as his other foes should get wind of his whereabouts they would assuredly bestir themselves. There was no time to be lost. As a result of Simon's negotiating, Lord Islay drew up a petition to be sent to the Highlands for signature by the leading men of those regions and then presented to the English ministers, asking for a pardon for Simon, and setting forth that " in case there was anything adoe, that he would be very useful at the head of his clan at home." With this paper the Major was sent north in December, and went round the Highlands in company with his brother-in-law, Alexander Fraser of Phopachy. When they had to deal with a Jacobite they told him that the petition really originated at St. Germains: to King George's friends they told the truth. In this manner they "travelled the five northern counties in the winter storm, and got the subscriptions of every leading man in that country," says the worthy Major. Their success is, indeed, very remarkable, but can be accounted for by the concurrent operation of opposed forces—the influence of Argyll, widespread dislike of the Murrays and Jacobitism. In February, 1715, the Major returned to London with his petition, now bearing the signatures of between sixty and seventy of the most important men of the Highlands, including the Earl of Sutherland and the members of Parliament and sheriffs of the northern counties. But the petition had no immediate effect; and just about this time Lord Athole had become suspicious that Simon was in England, and had written to the Duke of Montrose, in London, to hunt him out. Simon was now actually in London, and his position was very critical. If he were arrested now there was great danger that he would remain a prisoner till the troubles brewing in the north had passed over, and then his chance would be gone. "The Major and his chief was (*sic*) forced then to make many a moonlight flitting from one part of London to another," and in this manner eluded search till June. On June 11th, however, they were found and arrested in Soho Square, and thrust into a sponging-house. And just at this time outbroke the expected rebellion of the Highland Jacobites. The crisis had come.

When Major Fraser had been sent from Stratheric to France in 1714 it had been justly thought by the clansmen he represented that "if Simon could be stolen out of France he might come to fish in drumly waters." Now the waters at length were in commotion, and poor Simon in a sponging-house! If only his enemies could have kept him there for the next few months he would never have been Lord of the Frasers. But his Whig friends were convinced that he could and would be of use in this juncture, and they saved him. Several Highland gentlemen, with Lord Sutherland at their head, came forward and offered bail for him to the amount of £5,000.

In consequence Simon found himself free again, but, unhappily, whereas King George's Highland friends were now all ordered north, there was no pardon, and therefore, of course, no pass for Simon. If he went north, nevertheless, he must do so at the risk of arrest everywhere on the road.

But go north he must. A chance had come to him far too good to be thrown away for want of a little daring, and though Simon hesitated it was not for long. His course was clear before him if only, by the good help of his powerful friends, he could reach his own country. For Alexander Mackenzie, the usurper of the chieftaincy of the Frasers, had been foolish enough to declare for the rebels. Herein lay

Simon's luck, for if now he could induce his clansmen to desert their alien chief and throw them, in the nick of time, on the side of King George, he would thereby render service which could not but be handsomely rewarded if King George prevailed. At a blow he might gain the inheritance for which he had so long endeavoured. One may make bold to say that, in July, 1715, King George had no more zealous and devoted adherent than Simon Fraser.

Simon, therefore, set out for the north in the character of Major Fraser's servant, the Major himself having obtained a pass as acting under a lawful commission. At Newcastle they were arrested and detained by an obstinate mayor, and got free with difficulty; passing on into Scotland, they were helped by Brigadier Grant, one of Simon's bails, and by the Duke of Argyll, and reached Stirling without mishap. The difficulty of proceeding was now great, with, as the Major says, "the Highland army guarding all the roads." Simon resolved to go to Edinburgh, and thence by sea. "I was not two hours at Edinburgh," he wrote to Lord Islay afterwards, "when I was made prisoner by order of the Justice Clerk, and was designed to be sent to the castle that night, and, I believe, to be scaffolded the next day, if I had not been delivered and relieved from that danger by Provost John Campbell," who acted, in this matter, on behalf of his chief, the Duke of Argyll.

In company with John Forbes of Culloden, one of the gentlemen who had stood bail for him, Simon finally succeeded in embarking at Leith by night and reaching Fraserburgh on the coast of Aberdeen, though pursued and fired at by rebel boats on the way. From Fraserburgh they managed, at length, to get to Culloden Castle, the seat of the Forbeses, near the verge of the Fraser country.

The game, as it proved, was won as soon as Simon reached Stratheric. The whole Fraser clan rapidly gathered to him at his summons, leaving the unfortunate Mackenzie in the lurch. "Lovat is the life and soul of the party here," wrote the Earl of Mar, in February, 1716; "the whole country and his name dote on him; all the Frasers have left us since his appearing in the country." But

Simon's most important exploit was the capture of Inverness
from the rebels, concerted and carried out between himself,
the Forbeses and the Grants, in November, 1715.   In his
own account of this affair Simon appears both as the prime
mover and the chief actor in it; and, however this may be,
it was most certainly the withdrawal of the Frasers from
the Jacobite cause and their prompt engagement on the
other side that rendered it possible.   "This," wrote Simon
to Lord Islay, when he was engaged in enforcing gratitude
on the Government afterwards, "was the greatest piece of
service that was done in this country to any King, at several
ages; for as I took possession of Inverness the Saturday
before Sheriff Muir was fought.   If it had been delayed
three days, there had been about two thousand of the rebels
of my Lord Mar's army in the town of Inverness, so that it
would have been impracticable for the King's friends to have
attempted the reducing of it.   Then the Pretender would
have come there, and against the next spring would have
had a greater army than ever appeared for him in Scotland;
and having all the Highlands and isles behind his back to
retire to if he was beat, it would at least have cost several
thousand men and some millions to the Government before
he would be chased out of Scotland."   And in these too
emphatic phrases there is more than a little truth.

The final collapse of the rebellion, to which Simon's
action had not a little contributed, practically secured him
in the position he had won at the head of the Clan Fraser.
It only remained for a grateful Government to legalise that
position; and if there were still difficulties in the way of
Simon's complete establishment as Lord Lovat, they were
only of a legal complexion.

On March 10, 1716, Simon at last secured his "ample
and complete pardon for every imaginable crime," and in
the June following he was honoured with a special audience
of His Majesty, King George.   In August he received a
special royal grant of all the escheatable property of the
unlucky Mackenzie.

Alexander Mackenzie had escaped and been outlawed,
but he was not indicted for treason and there could be no

complete forfeiture. He only lost his personal property and his life-interest in the estates. The Crown could not defraud his heir under the settlement. Hence the estates would only belong to Simon so long as Alexander lived; after his death it would pass to his son, unless legal means could be found to prevent that issue. And the right to the Lovat peerage was still in dispute. But, meanwhile, Simon was in actual possession, and, if not yet recognised as Lord Lovat, was indubitably the MacShimi, chief of the Clan Fraser. Practically he had conquered his heritage. His unrelaxing and remorseless energy had carried him from the dungeon of Angoulême to a throne in the Highlands. He had known hard times and was nearing his fiftieth year, but his hand was as strong to grasp as ever, and his heart as strong to enjoy. Little now remained to be done to make him all he had ever dreamed of being, and that little it was in his power to do.

II.

No sooner was Simon seated on his hard-won throne than he plunged into litigation. To the MacShimi the peerage might well have seemed a trifle, and, in fact, Simon does not seem to have disputed it at law till after the death of Amelia, the whilome heiress. But the claim on the estates held by the Mackenzies he was utterly resolved to be rid of. There ensued a long and complicated lawsuit, which, with its risks and delays and chicanery would have been to most men a weariness and anxiety almost intolerable; but to Simon it was a joy like any other kind of fighting. Finally the harassed Mackenzies were induced to compound; in 1733 Hugh Mackenzie, the heir, gave up all his claims, including that to the peerage, for a consideration.

It was a magnificent position which Simon had achieved. The Fraser territories had, under letters patent of 1704, been made into what was termed a " regality," probably by way of assisting the Mackenzies against Simon's own adherents in the clan. This means that, in addition to the powers

ordinarily exercised with or without legal right by a Highland chief, Simon was in possession of extraordinary legal
powers. He had his own courts and his own police; he
could grant charters, build prisons, and even coin money.
The King's courts had no ordinary jurisdiction over his
subjects, the Frasers. He could claim them from the King's
courts, and hang or behead, drown, dismember, brand, whip,
fine, imprison, or banish them—not, of course, at his own
will and pleasure precisely, but as sovereign judge according
to Scottish law. He was, in fact, a miniature king, and with
more actual power than the generality of crowned kings;
for he had, on the whole, wonderfully submissive subjects,
and the superior powers were far off. Moreover, to the
honours and authority he had acquired the Government
added more: making him Sheriff of Inverness and, as such,
a judge with power of life and death, in case of murder,
throughout the whole county, and allowing him to maintain an "independent company," or private regiment, of
Highlanders.

For nearly thirty years Simon held his position as a Highland chieftain and lord of regality. Concerning this long
period of his prosperity it is difficult to gather many trustworthy details. Simon's aim, as chief, was to maintain and
strengthen the clan feeling, and, therewith, his own hold on
the clan, against the adverse English and Lowland influences
of the time. For the old Highland system was beginning to
break up under alien pressure. The Union with England
had come about in 1707, and, in 1726, General Wade and
his troops had come to the Highlands to make roads and
enforce order. It was the conquest of the Highlands that
was beginning—that painful though salutary process against
which the Highlands revolted in 1745. By all means in his
power Simon strove to keep up the old usages and the clan
spirit, on which the power of the chiefs depended; by all
means in his power he strove to acquire and preserve the
affection, as well as the obedience, of his clan.

He was, he represented, the father of his people; stern
doubtless, and despotic, as a father should be, but loving
withal. A very remarkable letter or manifesto which he

addressed, in 1718, "to the honourable the Gentlemen of the Clan Fraser" finely illustrates this. At that time he was ill and in London, and his position still unsettled. The letter is quite grand in its paternal and religious dignity. "My dear Friends," it begins—"Since, by all appearances, this is the last time of my life I shall have occasion to write to you, I being now very ill of a dangerous fever, I do declare to you before God, before whom I must appear and all of us at the great day of judgment, that I loved you all." Then, after solemn reiteration and expansion, and a dignified reference, in a spirit of Christian forgiveness, to poor Major Fraser and others, whom he was then treating with gross ingratitude, he goes on to conjure his people to stand by his family after he is gone. He warns them that if they fail in this their duty they will be driven from their country by the Mackenzies. "And you will be like the miserable, unnatural Jews, scattered and vagabond throughout the unhappy kingdom of Scotland, and the poor wives and children that remains of the name, without a head or protection, when they are told the traditions of their family, will be cursing from their hearts the persons and memory of those unnatural, cowardly, knavish men, who sold and abandoned their chief, their name, their birthright, and their country for a false and foolish present gain; even as the most of Scots people curse this day those who sold them and their country to the English, by the fatal Union, which I hope will not last long." Then follows the peroration, a fine display of lofty religious sentiment and mouth-filling orthodoxy. "I make my earnest and dying prayers to God Almighty, that He may in His mercy, through the merits of Christ Jesus, save you and all my poor people, whom I always found honest and zealous to me and their duty, from that blindness of heart that will inevitably bring those ruins and disgraces upon you and your posterity; and I pray that Almighty and merciful God, who has so often miraculously saved my family and name from utter ruin, may give you the spirit of courage, of zeal, and of fidelity, that you owe to your chief, to your name, to yourselves, to your children, and to your country; and may the most merciful and adorable Trinity, Father, Son and Holy Spirit, three persons, one God, save all your souls eternally, through the blood of Christ Jesus, our blessed Lord Saviour, to whom I heartily recommend you."

Let it not be imagined that there was nothing genuine in the sentiments thus blasphemously and eloquently expressed; Simon had assuredly a certain clan patriotism; and the thought that after his death a Mackenzie might possess the chieftaincy, and the name of Fraser cease to be, was altogether intolerable to him.

Simon, however, did not die, but lived and enjoyed the fruits of his labours. At Castle Downie, we are told, on the authority of James Ferguson, the astronomer, who at one time lived there several months, "he kept a sort of Court, and several public tables, and had a very numerous body of retainers always attending. His own constant residence, and the place where he received company, and even dined constantly with them, was in just one room only, and that the very room wherein he lodged. And his lady's sole apartment was also her own bedchamber; and the only provision made for lodging, either of the domestic servants or of the numerous herd of retainers, was a quantity of straw, which was spread overnight on the floors of the four lower rooms of this sort of tower-like structure. Sometimes about four hundred persons, attending this petty Court, were kennelled here, and I have heard the same worthy man, from whose lips the exact account of what is here related has been taken, declare that of those wretched dependants he has seen . . . three or four, and sometimes half a dozen, hung up by the heels for hours, on the few trees outside the mansion."

Simon kept open house, and even the raggedest ruffian of the clan could dine at Castle Downie. The ranks and orders of men, however, were strictly observed, and with due regard to economy. At the head of the long table sat Simon, and, near him, distinguished guests. For them there was claret and French cookery. Lower down came the more important class of vassals, enjoying solid beef and mutton, and some inferior wine. At the lower end were crowded the inferior vassals, with sheep's heads and ale or whiskey before them. And on the castle green in summer, and in the winter, in the outhouses, were the lowest class of clansmen, mere ne'er-do-weels, landless men and beggars, gnawing the bones and enjoying the offal. What was left over from the lord's table went to the domestic servants, who seem to have got little, if anything, else. Simon is said to have shown much dexterity in soothing feelings ruffled by these rather invidious arrangements. "Cousin!" he would call out from the head of the table to some dis-satisfied Fraser at the lower end, "I told my lads to bring you claret, but I see you like ale better: here's to your roof-tree!"

In this picturesque and mediæval fashion lived Simon, Lord Lovat, near the middle of the last century; uncomfort-ably enough, according to modern notions, but despotically and after his own heart. With his clansmen he affected a coarsely genial manner, without forgetting dignity. That he was a harsh and grasping and even a cruel master is certain. We have noticed already men "hung up by the heels"; we hear, also, of men and women thrust into peculiarly un-comfortable dungeons, and kept there, without law, till they had made sufficiently abject submission. A subject who dared to cross or molest Simon was in danger of having his barns burned some night, and his cattle driven off or injured, and his wife and children pulled out of their beds. Yet, in spite of all this, Simon had to go through a great deal of litigation with certain of his clansmen, in consequence of his refusal to pay the old bonds of 1702, and other just debts. Brave Major Fraser, Simon's partner in the escape from France, was one of those who suffered from the chief's ingratitude. In any case, however, it seems certain that Simon retained his power over the clan undiminished to the close. Highlanders, of course, expected to be roughly handled, and it was no use treating them otherwise. And, though Simon was doubtless grasping and somewhat tyrannical, he was, probably, a just ruler when not per-sonally crossed; and he certainly kept good order, not only in the Fraser country but as Sheriff of Inverness.

Simon was twice married in the days of his glory; first to Margaret Grant, daughter of the Laird of Grant, in 1717, and, in 1733, a year after her death, to Primrose Campbell, daughter of John Campbell of Mamore, who was brother to the first Duke of Argyll.   About the marriage with the former lady some difficulty seems to have arisen in connection with that old affair of the Dowager Lady Lovat, who was still living, and lived down to 1743; but this was speedily set aside.   His second marriage marks the highest point of Simon's fortunes.   He had then won all his points, and the marriage allied him with one of the very greatest of Scottish families.   The Duke of Argyll and his brother, the Earl of Islay, the Countess of Mar and Lord Elphinstone, the bride's uncle, attended the wedding, and Duncan Forbes was one of the witnesses.   According to tradition Simon treated his second wife with shameful brutality; but, considering who she was, this is probably either totally untrue, or, at least, a gross exaggeration.   Simon had several sons and daughters, but with all but one of them we have nothing to do.   There seems to be no trace of any natural affection in Simon, unless his expressions of regret for the death of his brother, John, can be so taken.   John Fraser died in 1715, apparently as the result of drinking and debauchery.

We now come to the story of the great blunder of Simon's life and his consequent fall.   Even in the early years of his reign at Castle Downie Simon had turned again towards St. Germains.   It is certain that he was implicated in the Jacobite and Spanish conspiracies, which led to an abortive and hopeless Jacobite landing in 1719.   At that time he actually fell under suspicion of the Government, and had to go to London to clear himself, which he did so successfully that King George consented to stand godfather, by proxy, to his first-born.   But from that time onwards he engaged himself continually and more and more deeply with the Court of St. Germains.   Gradually the Government became again suspicious, and first his independent company, then his post of sheriff, was taken from him, in 1741.   As his favour waned in London his interest in the Court of St. Germains waxed.   Thus Simon's divergence into Jacobite courses after

1715 led to action on the part of the Government which sorely irritated him and increased his inclination to stake something on the restoration of the Stuart. But how are we to explain that divergence? He may well have thought that the restoration of the Stuart would mean the complete restoration of the old, now threatened, Highland system and the practical independence of the Highland chiefs. The rising of 1745 appears to have been rather a rising against the English and the Union than a rising on behalf of the Stuart—at least to most Highlanders the two things were the same. Simon may have actually shared in the sentiments that gave its strength to the rising. Moreover, the restoration of the Stuart, even so late as 1745, must, at least in the Highlands, have seemed no very improbable an event. It was not easy for any one there to tell how much or how little effective Jacobitism there might be in England. And, if such a restoration should come about without Simon having had a part in it, he would assuredly be ruined. All this, however, does not appear sufficient by itself to explain Simon's conduct. The fact is that he was not content with what he had won in 1716. And why should we expect him to have been so?

To be content is the note of a nature far less stirring and daring. What such a man as Simon enjoys is not so much possession as the struggle for possession, not so much the triumph as the battle. To him ends are but pretexts for action. In 1716, already, he had conquered; but was there no more to conquer? Lawsuits could not satisfy his soul. The exact object—a dukedom, the extension of his estates, a dominant position among the lords of the Highlands— was comparatively unimportant. But all these things might be attained through Jacobitism, and being far from easy of attainment were proportionately attractive.

Thus, in 1745, Simon had many intelligible reasons for risking his head. If the rebellion succeeded he would become Duke of Fraser—that had been arranged for already. His "independent company" would be restored, and he might reasonably expect to further enrich himself out of the spoils of his Whig neighbours so as to become dominant in the central Highlands. Finally, and in any case, his independence as a Highland chief would become more absolute and secure by the establishment of the Stuart. And on the other hand he ran the risk of utter ruin by taking the Government side. But all this involved the assumption that the Pretender had a reasonable chance of success. Simon ought, it seems to us now, to have known better. He did know that the risk was great; perhaps he even understood that the chances were against the Jacobites. When the news of the Pretender's landing, which took place in July, was brought to Castle Downie, he remarked that he did not land like a prince, having no army with him, but a few servants only. Doubtless Simon had hoped for the landing of a French army; and he must have known that without French troops success was at least exceedingly doubtful.

He did know it, and he made his plans accordingly. Openly to declare for and join the Pretender he did not dare—the risk was not worth taking. He must hedge, and, if possible, stand not to lose, whatever happened. Study of his remarkable letters of this time reveals the fact that from the beginning of the uproar his plans were formed. He was now an old man, verging on his eightieth year, and might reasonably be supposed to be infirm and even decrepit. His age and his assumed infirmities formed the base of his project. So old and decrepit a personage could not be expected to turn out himself on either side; and was it to be expected that he would be able to control his wild Highlanders at such a moment of excitement? Besides, had not the Government taken away his regiment? If he was to join in suppressing the rebellion he would have first to arm his men—and where were the arms to come from? These considerations duly urged in the proper quarters would certainly enable him to temporise, and meanwhile he could be, without inconsistency, preparing for action. If things went badly for the Pretender at the outset then his loyalty would triumphantly reassert itself; and if, on the other hand, the Pretender looked like winning, would it not be possible to give him all the help he could reasonably expect while remaining, in appearance, loyal to the Government? It was delicate dealing, but it might be possible. Simon had a son, a boy of nineteen only, but old enough to head the clan to war if authorised to do so. Him he could send to the Pretender with a sufficiency of men, taking no refusal on his part. On the other hand, would it not be possible to make out that his clan had rebelled, that his son had gone out against the will, in defiance of the positive orders, of the poor, infirm, despised old chief? If this could be done he would be safe on both sides. If the Pretender should prove victorious he would have done enough. If King George should triumph, his son might be hanged but not he.

Such was Simon's combination; subtle certainly, and all the more fascinating to him because requiring the most delicate handling. But one can hardly say that, in the event of a Jacobite failure, it had any real chance of success. Had Simon been a man "above suspicion" he might perhaps have safely indulged in such tricks in his old age; but the Government was suspicious of him from the start, and was sure to look sharply into his proceedings. And, whatever might be his infirmities, it was notorious that he was one of the most despotic chiefs in the Highlands. His plea of incapacity was simply incredible. At the time it was thought by some that age had affected Simon's wits. Sir John Clerk, who knew him personally, was of this opinion: "He was all his life a cunning, double man, but this dexterity left him a year or two before the Rebellion, for in drawing on to his age of seventy-eight, seventy-nine, and eighty, he began to dream and dote, so that in his conduct he committed many great absurdities." Yet he carried out his plans with astonishing dexterity, and never was his wondrous power of lying so superbly manifested as in this last struggle of his life.

Soon after the Pretender's landing Simon commenced operations by having lists drawn out of the number of his clansmen capable of bearing arms, and began to look out for arms for them. On August 23rd he wrote to the Lord Advocate Craigie of Glendoick. "I am as ready this day," he wrote, "to serve the King and Government as I was in the year 1715. . . . But my clan and I have been so

neglected these many years past, that I have not twelve
stand of arms in my country. . . . Therefore, my good lord,
I earnestly entreat that, as you wish I would do good service
to the Government on this critical occasion, you may order
immediately a thousand stand of arms to be delivered to me
and to my clan at Inverness, and then your lordship shall
see that I will exert myself for the King's service." This
audacious attempt to get arms out of the Government for
use according to circumstances failed, and its failure ought
to have been a warning to Simon. But this is not all. Simon
was careful to add that he had been "entirely infirm these
three or four months past," and further to hint at serious
disaffection in his clan. "My people," he wrote, "cry out
horridly."

But it was not the Lord Advocate whom Simon was most
concerned to convince of the purity of his intentions, but
Duncan Forbes of Culloden, Lord President of the Court
of Session. Forbes was an old ally of his, had been counsel
for him in the earlier litigation with the Mackenzies, but
was, nevertheless, a thoroughly honest as well as a very
able man ; and of all men in high official position in
Scotland at that time, was probably the most entirely
trusted by the Government. It was essential to the
successful carrying through of his plans that he should
absolutely convince the Lord President ; and the more so
as Forbes's house at Culloden lay close to the edge of the
Fraser territories.

On August 24th he writes to Forbes to much the same effect
as he wrote to the Lord Advocate. His clan is unarmed and
unprotected ; the rebels threaten to harry the lands of those
who will not join them ; some of his people are thereby
affrighted and others eager to join the rising ; he himself
is very ill. "However, if I be able to ride in my chariot the
length of Inverness, I am resolved to go to Stratheric next
week and endeavour to keep my people in order." It was
most important for the success of his combination to represent his clan as unruly and infected with Jacobitism from the
very outset. But so far was this from actually being the
case that Simon seems to have been obliged to employ con-

siderable pressure to get his men to turn out at all. He was probably already in August in actual correspondence with Jacobite chiefs; and in September we find him writing to Cameron of Lochiel in a warning and regretful tone. " I fear," he wrote, "you have been over-rash in going ere affairs were ripe. . . . I'll aid when I can, but my prayers are all I can give at present. My service to the prince, but I wish he had not come here so empty-handed. Siller would go far in the Highlands."

On September 21st was fought the Battle of Prestonpans— for Simon, as it proved, a most unlucky victory. If only the Highlanders had been beaten we may be sure that Simon's loyalty would have shone forth as conspicuously as in 1715. But the result of the battle determined Simon on putting into execution the ruinous combination already explained. Up to this time he had damaged the cause of the Government by his inaction, but he had not precisely compromised himself. Now he proceeded to compromise himself hopelessly.

He began at once to actively gather and distribute arms, tents, and other munitions of war, to hold rendezvous of the men of the clan, and to apply the necessary pressure. During the next three months he threw off the mask—at least so far as his own clansmen were concerned; entertained the Earl of Cromarty and other Jacobite chiefs passing through to the front, and drank at his own table "Confusion to the White Horse." All this was doubtless necessary if he was to do anything for the Pretender at all, but it was none the less ruinous. In November he wrote to the Pretender's secretary, John Murray of Broughton, to excuse himself for not having joined sooner, and to promise immediate aid. " I solemnly protest, dear sir, that it was the greatest grief of my life that my indisposition and severe sickness kept me from going south to my dear, brave Prince, and never parting with him while I was able to stand, but venture my old bones with pleasure in his service." But being unable to go myself, "I send my eldest son, the hopes of my family and the darling of my life. . . . I have sent him to venture the last drop of his blood in the glorious Prince's service," and

with him all the best men of the clan. Along with this
letter he sent another in exactly the same strain, and much
in the same words, to the Pretender himself. And to
Lochiel he wrote, " I am resolved to live and die with
courage and resolution in my King and royal Prince's
service ; . . . no death that they can invent can lessen
my zeal or fright me from my duty."

All this was emphatic and as it should have been; but
it was in the letters written in these same months to
Duncan Forbes that Simon exhibited the art of lying in
its perfection. All through September, October, and
November, he wrote to Forbes letter after letter giving
his version of the occurrences in the Fraser country. The
way in which he gradually insinuates the increasing unruliness of his clan is masterly. On October 11th " the
contagion " has become " so universal " that he knows not
what to do. On the 17th his son is resolved to join the
Pretender. On the 20th, " I cannot help it. I must submit
to the will of God, and there I must leave it." His son
is past all control. " And, as God Almighty has at many
times wonderfully delivered me out of many dangers and
difficulties by land and sea, I throw myself on His Divine
Providence, and trust myself entirely to it ; for if God in
His Providence save my estate, I do not give three half-
pence for my life, for it is but wearisome to me and full
of troubles." On October 27th he is so ill that he can
hardly walk !

On his side Forbes was doing his best, by argument,
exhortation, and, later, by menace, to show Simon the error
of his ways, and clearly hinting at his absolute incredulity
concerning the alleged rebelliousness of the Clan Fraser.
But Simon was infatuated and held on his course. His
letter of October 30th, in answer to one in which Forbes
warned him in the clearest manner, is a masterpiece in its
way. " I give your lordship," Simon wrote, " a thousand
thanks for the kind freedom you use with me, . . . for I see
by it that, for my misfortune in having an obstinate, stubborn
son and an ungrateful kindred, my family must go to destruction, and I must lose my life in my old age. . . . Am I, my

lord, the first father that has had an undutiful and unnatural
son? Or am I the first man that has made a good estate
and saw it destroyed in his own time by the mad, foolish
actings of an unnatural son, who prefers his own extravagant
fancies to the solid advice of an affectionate old father? I
have seen instances of this in my own time, but I never
heard till now that the foolishness of a son would take away
the liberty and life of a father that lived peaceably, that was
an honest man, and well inclined to the rest of mankind.
But I find the longer a man lives the more wonders and
extraordinary things he sees." All through November he
continues in this strain, speaking of himself, on November
6th, as " left a contemptible old fellow in my house, and no
more notice taken of me than if I was a child." But meanwhile the Government had determined to take strong action,
and late in November Simon was informed that a strong
body of troops was about to enter his country.

But it was too late. On the 1st of December Simon
wrote to Forbes to announce that his son had, at last, fairly
started for the Pretender's army. The letter is a masterpiece, and must be quoted in its entirety. " My dear Lord,"
wrote Simon, " I have had many proofs of your lordship's
sincere friendship for my person and family, but there was
never a period of my life that made me so much the object of
compassion as I am at writing this letter. My very enemies,
if they knew the unsupportable griefs of my soul this morning,
must sympathise with a man so disconsolate and void of
comfort. I dare not descend to particulars. My son has
left me under silence of last night, contrary to my advice,
contrary to my expectations and to my earnest request ;
and the consequences of his doing so are to me terrible
beyond expression ; though, I declare, I could not have done
more to save my own life and the lives of my clan, as well
as the estate of Lovat, as I have done, by smooth and rough
usage, to detain him at home. This is a subject so melancholy that I can neither write nor talk upon it ; and therefore I have sent the bearer, who has the honour to be known
to your lordship, to make a faithful report of the uprightness
of my conduct in this matter ; and I hope your lordship will

give credit to what he says.   I pray God your lordship may
meet with no event in life so disastrous and afflicting as this
is to me; and that you may live long in perfect health, as
the honour of your country, the support of your friends, and
the comforter of the afflicted, and, whatever happen to me in
life, I shall always continue with unalterable zeal, gratitude,
and respect," &c.

Clever as his letters of this period are they made no
impression upon Duncan Forbes.   Simon was lost from the
moment he allowed his son to set out southwards.   It must
here be distinctly stated that, so far from it being true that
the young man had insisted on joining the rebels against
his father's will, it appears, on the contrary, that Simon had
put considerable pressure upon him to induce him to go at
all.   We have now only to sketch the final collapse.   On
the 11th of December Lord Loudoun, commanding for the
Government in those regions, came to Castle Downie with
eight hundred men, arrested Simon, and took him to Inverness, less as a prisoner than as a hostage for the future.
Very shortly after, however, Simon made his escape and got
to Stratheric.   Probably nothing could now have saved him;
but it would have been better to stay quiet at Inverness.
Immediately after his escape he received a letter from the
Pretender, strongly urging him to declare openly for the
rebellion, " in which case we are certain that there is not a
man beyond the Forth, however timorous or cautious (except
some few who have already destined themselves to perdition)
but will appear with the greatest alacrity and cheerfulness."
To this high compliment to his reputation in the Highlands
Simon returned, through his son, a characteristic reply.   He
declares that he never spoke " so much as a fair word " to
Lord Loudoun or Duncan Forbes except to save himself
from arrest, and describes himself as a fugitive wanderer
" in hills and woods and inaccessible places."   As for
declaring openly, that he certainly cannot do unless, at all
events, the patent for his dukedom is immediately drawn
out.   Hard upon this came the news of the fatal retreat
from Derby, and Simon began to perceive that the game
was played out.   He sent a hasty message to his son,

bidding him return home at once, on the pretext of raising
more men for the Pretender's service, but really, of course,
to obtain the credit of his recall, and strengthen his own
case with the Government. Unfortunately the young man,
whose life had been so foully played with, absolutely declined
to listen to this suggestion. Steadily the rebel army was
driven northwards, and Simon must have seen with terror,
if he ever felt fear at all, the soldiers of Cumberland drawing
nearer and nearer to his own domain. On April 16, 1746,
the wreck of the Highland army was destroyed at Culloden,
and the game was over.

The Pretender, in despair, fled into the neighbouring
Fraser country, and visited Simon at Gortuleg, where he
was then living in the house of a vassal. The old man's
spirit was as high as ever. He is said to have sternly
rebuked 'the young Prince for his declared intention of
abandoning the struggle. " Remember," said he, fiercely,
"your great ancestor, Robert Bruce, who lost eleven battles
and won Scotland by the twelfth." But there was no longer
hope nor courage in the councils of the Prince, save only in
Simon himself, and the fugitives dispersed in haste. Simon
betook himself to an island on the Lake of Muily and, behind
him, Cumberland's soldiers were burning Castle Downie to the
ground. Near Loch Muily Simon had a last interview with
some of the Jacobite chiefs, and made a last effort to procure
the adoption of his desperate counsels. He proposed that
they should raise, between them, three thousand men, and
make a last, fierce stand in the mountains ; so as, if possible,
to wrest their pardons from a harassed Government. But
there was, in fact, nothing to be done, and the conspirators
went each his own way to save his own head, if possible.
Simon's way led him, after obscure wanderings, to an island
on Loch Morar, not to be reached except by a boat which
was in his own possession. There, nevertheless, he was
discovered and captured, hidden in a hollow tree, early in
June, 1746 ; a boat having been dragged to the lake shore
over the strip of land separating Loch Morar from the
western sea. The " old fox of the mountains," to use an expression belonging to Mr. R. L. Stevenson, was snared at last.

Simon was now conveyed, a prisoner, through his own country, amid the lamentations of his people and the wail of the women following his litter, to Edinburgh, and thence by easy stages through Berwick to London. One incident only of the journey deserves mention. At the White Hart Inn at St. Albans he was met and interviewed by Hogarth, who utilised the opportunity to make a likeness of him—the famous portrait which forms the frontispiece to this volume. He was lodged in the Tower, and, in December, 1746, articles of impeachment were voted against him.

The trial commenced on March 9, 1747, and sentence was pronounced on March 19th, five days having been occupied in the hearing of evidence. In accordance with the unfair custom of an impeachment Simon was not allowed the assistance of counsel except upon points of law, and all cross-examination of the adverse witnesses had to be done by himself. But however unjust this might be in many cases one is not sure that it was not an actual advantage to Simon. For he had, in fact, no defence ; and the denial of counsel's assistance in cross-examination enabled him to strengthen the plea for mercy which was his only chance. On being informed that he must cross-examine himself or not at all, he replied, with pathetic dignity, " My lords, it is impossible for me then to make any defence, by reason of my infirmities. I do not see; I do not hear; I came up to your lordships' bar at the hazard of my life. I fainted away several times, I got up so early. I was up by four o'clock this morning ; and I am so weak that, if I am deprived of the assistance I ask for, your lordships may do as you please; and it is impossible for me to make any defence at all, if you do not allow my counsel or solicitors to examine the witnesses. I therefore submit myself to your lordships." And thereafter he almost entirely declined to cross-examine. It must be added that the eloquent phrases, " I do not see— I do not hear," conveyed an entire untruth. Simon's sight, at least, seems to have been remarkably good to the last.

Nothing could have saved him ; there was no manner of doubt about his guilt. His own secretary, as well as the secretary of the Pretender, John Murray of Broughton,

THE INTERIOR OF WESTMINSTER HALL DURING THE TRIAL OF LORD LOVAT.

appeared as witnesses against him. His Jacobite letters already referred to were produced. The flimsy plea of rebellion on his son's part hopelessly broke down; indeed Simon practically abandoned it. He did not call a solitary witness for the defence. He tried, indeed, to make out that he was prevented from doing so by the force and fraud of his enemies—that his witnesses were detained in Scotland or intimidated. But he offered absolutely no evidence for these assertions. Practically his defence was a simple plea for mercy on the ground of his age and infirmities. In urging these upon the court, with due exaggeration, he displayed much dexterity, and it does not seem as if there were anything else to have been done. His bearing throughout was dignified and pathetic. But his doom was assured. On March 19th he was sentenced to death with the usual barbarous and antiquated formula, having been unanimously declared guilty. He made a dignified and last appeal for mercy, on the ground of his age and past services, ending with the words, "God bless you all, and I bid you an everlasting farewell. We shall not meet all in the same place again; I am sure of that." And, with this last piece of ironic defiance on his lips, he was removed from the bar and taken back to the Tower to await execution.

Concerning his behaviour in the last days between his trial and execution there are many stories, more or less untrustworthy, but forming, no doubt, a tolerably accurate representation of the fact. He was cheerful, even gay, to the end, except when he fell into his religious vein. He declared that he was a Roman Catholic and "would die in that faith," and added, strangely enough, that he was a Jansenist. On the Sunday before his execution he wrote a remarkable letter to the son whose life he had been ready to give away for his own. "You are always present with me," he wrote, "and I offer my prayers to Heaven for you. You see now, by experience, that this world is but vanity of vanities, and that there is no trust to be put in the arm of flesh; you see that God's providence rules the world, and that no man or family but must yield to it, whether he will or not. Happy is the man that, in all the cross accidents of this life submits himself to the will and providence of God with sincere humility and patience. . . . I do sincerely thank God for these troubles, because they have brought me from the way of sin that I lived many years in, to a way of repentance and humiliation, and instructed me to follow my dear Saviour, the Lord Jesus Christ, as I ought to do." From this he goes on to urge his son to repentance and good living, "with the sincere heart of a tender and affectionate father," and concludes thus, "So, my dear child, do not be in the least concerned for me, for I bless God I have strong reasons to hope that when it is God's will to call me out of this world, it will be, by His mercy and the suffering of my Saviour, Jesus Christ, to enjoy everlasting happiness in the other world. I wish this may be yours."

The day before his execution his thoughts reverted to the Highlands that he had, in his fashion, loved. He said that he wished to be buried in the church of Kirk Hill, a few miles from where Castle Downie had stood, and that he had once intended that all the pipers from John o' Groats to Edinburgh should pipe at his funeral, and that, even now, he hoped the coronach would be heard over his grave. " And then," said he, " there will be crying and clapping of hands ; for I am one of the greatest chiefs in the Highlands." He expressed, further, grave concern about the bill then before Parliament for abolishing the jurisdictions of the Highland chiefs. " Do you think I am afraid of an axe ? " he replied to some officious person who took on himself to be " sorry that the morrow was to be such a bad day with him." He was beheaded on Thursday the 9th of April, 1747. A great crowd had assembled to see the execution. Simon remarked on it as he went up the scaffold steps. " God save us ! " says he, " why should there be such a bustle about taking off an old grey head that cannot get up three steps without two men to support it ? " It was about this time, also, that a scaffolding, erected for the convenience of spectators, fell, several persons being killed. " The more damage," said Simon, sardonically, "the better sport." Having mounted the scaffold he went up to the executioner and handed him a purse. " Here, sir, is ten guineas for you ;

pray do your work well, for if you should cut and hack my shoulders and I should be able to rise again, I should be very angry with you." Then he felt the edge of the axe and remarked that he thought it would do. After that he went over to his coffin and read the inscription thereon: "Simon, Dominus Fraser de Lovat, decollat. April 9, 1747. Aetat. suae, 80." Then, sitting down, he said, doubtless with due solemnity: "Dulce et decorum est pro Patriâ mori," and after a pause added, from Ovid :—

> "Nam genus et proavos, et quae non fecimus ipsi,
>   Vix ea nostra voco."

What was he thinking of, this old man who had seen and done so many strange things? His last words of import were addressed to one James Fraser, who was in attendance. "My dear James," he said, "I am going to heaven, but you must continue to crawl a little longer in this evil world." And with that he made himself over to the executioner.

In such manner died Lord Simon of Lovat, crowning his audacious life with a defiant close. Some there were who considered this execution of a man of eighty an uncalled-for and unjustifiable severity. But we cannot wish that it had been otherwise. Simon died as he had lived. And there was no coronach over his grave, for they buried him in the Tower. But there was lamentation in Stratheric; and long after there survived, as a living monument to Simon in his own country, a man of great age who had let his beard grow uncut from that fatal day onward.

COLONEL FRANCIS CHARTERIS.

(1675-1732.)

" Il avoit tresmauvaise opinion des femmes et ne les croyoit toutes chastes."—Brantôme.

THE connoisseur in heredity and predestination must search in vain the records of the Charteris stock for any suggestion of the inborn infamy which rendered famous the last male representative of the line. The family was ancient and honourable, and Captain Charteris, who was captured, tried, and executed by the Covenanters, redeemed its history from insignificance. His brother, Sir John Charteris, was also a decided Royalist, who stood fast by Montrose, and lived to see the two sons borne him by Lady Catherine Crichton grow up to manhood. Of these sons the elder, Thomas, inherited the family estate of Amisfield, which passed to his daughters and their descendants, while John married the daughter of Sir Francis Kinloch, and became, in 1676, the father of Francis Charteris.

Young Francis received the usual liberal education of his day, and thus enabled Pope to assert that he " scarce could read or write." He was, however, a lad of sharp wits, and on being sent to Belgium as an ensign of a foot regiment, from which he soon exchanged to become a cornet of dragoons, he was not slow to discover that he possessed certain advantages over his brother officers. He exhibited unexampled proficiency at games of chance, and in no long time he had stripped all who would play with him of such money as they possessed, and had lent it them back at one hundred per cent. The losers did not bear their misfortune quietly, and Charteris's

COLONEL CHARTERS

COLONEL FRANCIS CHARTERIS.

(1675-1732.)

... qu'a opinion des femmes et ne les cr yoit ... ...

... connoisseur in heredity and predestination ...
... such in vain the records of the Charteris stock
... gestion of the inborn infamy which rendered fam
last male representative of the line. The family ... a
... cient and honourable, and Captain Charteris, who ...
... tured, tried, and executed by the Covenanters, ... lcer ...
... ... ry from insignificance. His brother, S... j ...
C... ... ris, was also a decided Royalist, who stood fast ...
... ... and lived to see the two sons borne him by ...
... ... Crichton grow up to manhood. Of these s... ...
... ... Thomas inherited the family estate of Amisfi...,
which passed to his daughters and their descendants, while
... married the daughter of Sir Francis Kinloch ... and
... ... father of Francis Charteris.

... received the usual liberal education of his
... ... abled Pope to assert that he " scarce could
... He was, however, a lad of sharp wits, and
on... ... to Belgium as an ensign of a foot regiment
... ... exchanged to become a cornet of dragoons.
... ... slow to discover that he possessed certain advan-
t ... es over his brother officers. He exhibited unexamp!...
proficiency at games of chance, and in no long time he h...
stripped all who would play with him of such money as t... y
possessed, and had lent it them back at one hundred per cent.
The losers did not bear their misfortune quietly, and Charteris

COLONEL CHARTERIS.

skill at cards and dice was brought to the notice of Marlborough, who ordered him to be put under arrest and tried
by a court-martial, composed of English and Scottish officers
in equal number. By this impartial tribunal Charteris was
sentenced to return all sums received by him as interest, to
be deprived of his commission, and drummed out of the regiment with his sword broken. Francis returned to his home
in Edinburgh with his military ardour undamped, and induced
his father to buy him a commission in the Guards; but his
reputation went before him, and the officers refused to allow
his enrolment. He was more fortunate in being received
into a marching regiment bound for Flanders, where he
succeeded in winning not merely money but the good graces
of his seniors, who imprudently entrusted him with three
months' pay and a considerable sum of money wherewith to
raise recruits in England. Setting out with the best of intentions, Charteris found time on board ship hang heavily on
his hands, and proposed a game of cards to another officer
who was a fellow-passenger. Either his fortune or his skill
failed him, for he lost all his own money, and that which did
not belong to him followed. Landing at Harwich penniless,
he put up at the best inn and ordered a good fire to be
lighted in his bedroom. He dined sumptuously in the best
of spirits, condescendingly inviting the landlord to share in
his potations. In the morning, when Charteris wished to
rise, the landlord was loudly summoned to his room and was
made acquainted with the fact that his guest's breeches had
disappeared in the night. Moreover, in the pockets of the
missing garment were sixty guineas and a valuable gold
watch. A tailor was promptly summoned, and enabled
Charteris to face the world again, and publicly threaten the
direst vengeance on the landlord. His house was evidently
a den of thieves, and would be henceforth ruined, and he
must forthwith accompany Charteris before a magistrate.
The terrified innkeeper, anxious only to save the reputation
of his house, was finally allowed to make good the loss, and
Charteris, somewhat mollified by restitution, paid his bill
like a gentleman and proceeded on his way. He had burnt
his breeches in the night.

After taking the necessary steps to safeguard his honour by representing in the proper quarter how he had been robbed of the money entrusted to his charge, he once more made his way home to his parents. He would seem to have stayed with them for some time, and it was doubtless at this period of his life that he began to acquire the unsavoury reputation as a foe to honest women, which he maintained throughout his life, and which made him loathed wherever he was known. He was now about two-and-twenty years old, a well-grown man, six feet in height, and proportioned in every way. If he had to pay for his amusements, he took care to make his friends and acquaintances provide him with the necessary means. Whether because his family was held in esteem or because he himself possessed graces of manner not suggested by his recorded history, young Charteris was received into decent society, and allowed to justify his claim of being a cleverer man than the fools he met. When the Duke of Queensberry was in Edinburgh as Commissioner to the Scottish Parliament the Duchess invited Charteris to play cards with her. He could scarcely have designed that his hostess should sit down to the game with a large mirror behind her, which enabled him to see her cards; but he was not the man to lose the opportunity thus presented to him, and won from her Grace as much as £3,000. On another occasion he was less fortunate. He was invited to play with some gentlemen, who discovered loaded dice in his possession. It was not necessarily the fashion of the time to visit such maladroit persons with social ostracism, and the party determined that a fitting punishment for the cheat would be to strip him forcibly of his clothes and make him stand in the corner with his back towards the company for the remainder of the sitting. The ignominy of the situation weighed less on Charteris than the desire to regain his liberty, and he did not shrink from further shame in behaving in so bestial and unrestrained a manner as to drive his companions from the room, and thus enable himself to get access to his clothing and the door.

Incidents of this kind must have relieved the monotony of a bachelor's life in Edinburgh, but the time had come for

Charteris to settle down, and his father having died and left him a modest inheritance, he married, in 1702, Helen, the daughter of Sir Alexander Swinton, Master of the College of Justice. Any novelty that wedded life may have possessed for him quickly wore off, and he made the discovery that Edinburgh did not offer scope enough to his ambitions. Accordingly he brought his wife up to London and took a house in Poland Street, where he set up an establishment in the first style. Respectability became the order of the day, and though tradesmen's bills for the entertainments lavishly given to friends were heavy, they were punctually paid. If the friends provided the money by losing at cards it was not ostensibly the fault of their host, who spared no pains to make them otherwise happy. But Charteris had not come up to London to live the tame life of a civilian. He still believed in the army as the first among profitable careers for a gentleman, and by the efforts of influential persons whose acquaintance he carefully and successfully cultivated, he became an exempt in the Fourth, or Scotch, Troop of Guards. The position was socially excellent, but did not satisfy Charteris. To appear at Court was a good thing, but there was not necessarily money in it, and money, both as an end and means to his amusement, was the goal of his ambition. Fortune, however, continued to smile on him, and in February, 1710, he was able to expend three thousand guineas on the purchase of a company in the Foot Guards. The step was justified by the opportunities afforded by the position to get back what it had cost to obtain, and Charteris lost no time in seizing them. He kept his company at half strength or less, and drew pay for the whole; he perfected a system of protecting creditors by the pretence of enlisting them, and he extorted large sums from his soldiers before he would grant them a discharge. Things went smoothly and lucratively in this way for nearly a year, when, owing to a disagreement with a ruffian whom Charteris employed as assistant in his illegitimate proceedings, attention was called to what was going on. Patrick Hurley, the man in question, took upon himself the office of informer, and by dint of perseverance succeeded in a petition being presented to Parliament. As a result a committee, of which Sir Roger Mostyn was chairman, was appointed to inquire into the matter. A large number of witnesses was heard on both sides, and chiefly owing to the bad character of Hurley Charteris had a fair chance of acquittal, but he was indiscreet enough to threaten and beat a sergeant who had given evidence against him. For this offence he was taken into custody by the Sergeant-at-Arms and brought before the House. His humble apology was accepted, and instead of being cashiered as was expected he was let off with the Speaker's reprimand, which he received kneeling. The committee, however, reported strongly against him, and the report being adopted four months later by the House, he was voted incapable of serving further in the army, and was dismissed without liberty to dispose of his commission.

The untimely end of his military career did not interfere with Charteris's promotion, for, if the story may be believed, he obtained the rank or title of " Colonel " by winning it at cards from a Colonel Holmes. And if he obtained his rank when no longer a soldier, it was then, too, that for the only time in his life, he saw anything like active service. This was in the rebellion of 1715. He was at the time deputy-lieutenant and a magistrate, and happened to be in Lancaster when the Pretender's forces were marching on the town. It being expected that he should take the lead in devising measures of defence, he insisted that the bridge over which the army must pass should be blown up, and only gave way when it was pointed out that the river was fordable at low water. He then ordered the powder to be thrown into a well in the market-place, and led the retreat to Preston. Meanwhile a detachment of insurgents had been told off to visit Hornby Castle, which belonged to Charteris, in search of provisions for man and horse. The commanding officers considerately refrained from sending any Scotsmen on this expedition, as being certain to burn all the possessions of their little-loved countryman, and selected Colonel Oxburgh to lead a select party of English troops to the house. They took only a meal for themselves and their beasts, but the steward, a worthy servant of his master, presented a bill for

£3 6s. 8d., and took Oxburgh's note of hand for the amount. When the struggle was over Charteris pressed for payment, but whether successfully or not is not known. He also brought in a bill against the Government for the value of thirty horses which he alleged he had lost during the rising, and was allowed to pick a like number out of those belonging to the vanquished Jacobites. By force of contrast this episode came to be regarded by Charteris as the bright glory of his life, and many years afterwards, when he was lying under sentence of death, the staple argument in his petition for the King's mercy was his behaviour at the Preston rebellion. His enemies said at the time that he had made his arrangements to be found fighting for whichever side might get the upper hand.

But if Charteris was spared much experience of warfare on the grand scale, his private life was not always peaceful. The lesson he had received as a young man at Edinburgh did not altogether reform his methods of play, which frequently gave rise to suspicion, and were seldom such as to lead to nothing but quiet enjoyment. Quarrels, in fact, between him and those whose luck or choice it was to be pitted against him, were not infrequent, but it was not Charteris who sought them. He was not the man to endanger his life without particularly good cause, and, though not a coward, knew when valour should give way to discretion. Thus once when he had won a large sum from a young nobleman, who took his revenge by thrashing Charteris and promised to continue doing so till the money was repaid, he refused either to retaliate or refund, and afterwards explained that he would take twice as much before he would lose the handsome profit he had made. But another adversary who had nothing to lose and tried similar tactics received a sound beating, and was given to understand by Charteris that though he could take, on occasion, a cuff or a kick from a fool of quality or substance, he was not obliged to do so for every scoundrel. Another quarrel was to have resulted in a duel in Marylebone Fields, and the combatants met on the scene of action. Charteris, however, succeeded in persuading his opponent that it was much wiser not to fight, but that they ought, for the sake of appearances, to give one another a friendly scratch. The practice of tossing not being in vogue, a long discussion arose as to who should scratch first, and it was only ended by Charteris seizing his sword and inflicting a terrible gash in the other's right arm. He declined on any terms to receive his own scratch, and loudly boasted everywhere of having spared his victim's life. Even the friendliest critics of Charteris must have owned that he was not over-scrupulous as to the choice of the weapons he employed. If nothing better offered he did not hesitate to use his teeth, and once he closed a dispute with a miller in the market-place at Edinburgh by biting off the man's nose. An action was brought, and Charteris was cast in £80 damages. Delighted at getting off so cheaply, he proffered £10 to the judges for their liquid refreshment, and was fined an additional £50 for contempt of court.

It is easy enough to believe that Charteris was well compensated for such occasional crosses by the very lucrative nature of the transactions which usually led up to them. His compulsory retirement from the army does not appear to have injured his social position, for he continued to amass riches at private gaming-tables and in the coffee-houses. How he succeeded in finding dupes enough to play with him is a question for wonderment, but find them he did ; and besides being, of necessity, men of substance, they were generally of high rank. His enormous winnings were not squandered, but invested in landed property or stocks. He speculated successfully in the South Sea Company, and the record of appeals to the House of Lords bears testimony to his shrewd observation of the market. When the price of South Sea stock was 320 he sold £5,000 worth to the Earl of Hyndford at 410 ; but payment was to be postponed for a year on the security of the Earl's estates. When at the end of the year neither the purchase-money nor the interest was forthcoming, Charteris sued for what was due to him, but a cross-action was brought to void the sale as coming under the statute of usury, and successive courts decided against Charteris. It was not in his nature to have refused to make so advantageous a bargain with a fool, but the evidence showed that he was by no means anxious to sell the stock, and even when the transfer was made he had offered to release Hyndford from the deal.

Charteris had a predilection for lending money on land, and he is supposed to have followed the practice ascribed to other successful gamesters of lending back the money he had won on the security of estates which also ultimately fell into his hands. He certainly became, within the course of a very few years, a large owner of land. Among his properties in Scotland were Cambo in Fifeshire, an old manor near Musselburgh called Stoney Hill, and Newmaine in Haddingtonshire, which he rechristened Amisfield, and thus justified the designation "Charteris of Amisfield," by which he was always known. Hornby Castle, already mentioned, he bought in 1713 from the Earl of Cardigan for £14,500, and he was also the possessor of two other Lancashire manors—Cockerham and Ormskirk. Some of these estates were no doubt purchased for the sake of the substantial revenues attached to them, but there would be some excuse for the casual critic who should conclude that the main purpose of Charteris's country seats was the various gratification of his inordinate concupiscence. His brilliant and enduring success at play would have been enough to make the name of any other man famous, but the notoriety Charteris acquired as a voluptuary altogether eclipsed the distinction he gained deservedly by his performances at the gaming-table. In the one case he victimised comparatively few; in the other a whole sex was his prey. His appetite was unbounded, and wherever he went he stopped at nothing which might help to satisfy it. The care he took that, on his arrival at one of his dreary country houses, his bodily comfort should be well looked after was almost worthy of a better cause. Hornby Castle, in particular, under his rule, became a standing scandal and its owner the object of execration by every father and husband in the county, so that when Charteris stood as Parliamentary candidate for Lancaster in 1715 he found it all but impossible to obtain a lodging in the town. Nor while Charteris attended to his own wants did he neglect

any opportunity of making pleasure step side by side with
business. The guest at Hornby who allowed himself to be
beguiled by cards till it was necessary to pass the night at
the castle would find his bedroom already tenanted, and,
should he bring an end to the negotiations that ensued by a
gift in money, he might learn, by questioning, that only a
tenth of the sum would be retained by the recipient, ninety
per cent. being claimed by his host. On his frequent
journeys to and from his Scottish estates Charteris usually
managed to make his name and presence unfavourably
remembered in the towns where he put up for the night.
On occasion his adventures would lead to a humorous
situation, as once when he had met with a trifling accident
while passing through Yorkshire and a kind-hearted rector
offered him the hospitality of his house till he should have
recovered. Charteris accepted the invitation, and lost no
time in endeavouring to abuse his position by making love
to the womankind. One of the rector's daughters was a
lady of the humour Charteris loved to meet with, and, since
the rectory afforded no possible place of assignation, it was
she who suggested that a room should be hired for the
purpose from a tradeswoman of her acquaintance in the
town. The lovers found their opportunity on a Whit
Sunday, when the world was supposed to be at church,
and chance only prevented their enterprise from being kept
as secret as they would have wished. It happened that the
ground-floor room under that in which they met was used as
a carpenter's shop, and some children, playing with matches
among the shavings, set fire to the house. The alarm was
raised, and Charteris and his companion rushed to the
window which, by this time, was the only means of escape.
Apparently they had already felt the power of the flames, for
when they leaped out on the mattresses spread to receive
them it was seen by the delighted crowd that they wore but
a single linen garment apiece. Charteris got well out of his
escapade, for the parson, who at first was all for bringing
an action against him, was finally persuaded to devote his
attention to taking better care of his other daughters.

It is possible that Charteris may have respected the

sanctity of his home, but the precincts of such sanctity were narrow, for while he lived in Poland Street he frequented an establishment in Golden Square where vice and he were equally at home. History, perhaps happily, is almost silent as to his purely domestic life. Mrs. Charteris was a good and affectionate woman, and to hope that she did not suffer would be mere audacity. Their only child was a daughter, Janet, who, in October, 1720, was married, with the assistance of a magnificent dowry, to the Earl of Wemyss. It appears probable that after the marriage Mrs. Charteris spent much of her time with her daughter, and for the rest lived in Scotland with her people. Charteris took full advantage of his liberty, and exchanged the house in Poland Street for another in George Street, Hanover Square, which soon acquired the worst possible reputation. He employed procuresses to watch systematically the arrivals of waggons from the provinces, and any likely-looking girl who alighted was at once engaged as domestic servant to Charteris.[1] A very few days sufficed to learn the kind of duties expected from her, and unless specially favoured the girl was, after seduction, turned loose upon the town. One young woman of the kind, Sarah Wilkins by name, was allowed to become the mother of three of his children. Extraordinary stories were current of the scenes which took place at the house in George Street—of damsels forced into compliance by a pistol at the head, of orgies that might have made envious Tiberius—and their dissemination bred an active dislike of the Colonel among the classes from whose ranks the frequent vacancies in his establishment were filled. On one occasion this unsympathetic feeling nearly led to disaster. A woman spread a rumour that her sister was being detained against her will, and at her eager bidding a furious mob soon surrounded the house clamouring for Charteris's blood and the girl's release. They broke all the windows and the leaders got through the doors; but luck was in the Colonel's way, for the alleged prisoner declared herself

[1] The notorious "Mother Needham," who is depicted interviewing Kate Hackabout on her arrival in London, in the first plate of the " Harlot's Progress," is said to have been thus employed by Charteris.

15

perfectly happy, and declined to be removed on any terms. The virtuous populace had no choice but to take itself off discomfited. Such moral triumphs, however, were of rare occurrence, and it more often happened that Charteris found he had the law to reckon with. Not once nor twice only did he have to rely on the power of his purse and the kindly offices of a magistrate to hush up a budding scandal. Sometimes the matter went a step further, as in the case of Sarah Selleto, who refused to be contented with anything less than security for the maintenance of the child she expected to bear. Even his purse proved useless to pay for a dangerous freak he indulged in while visiting Edinburgh in 1721. He was walking along a country lane when he was seized with a passing fancy for an honest housewife whom he overtook. The good woman suddenly found herself confronted by a dilemma presenting the choice of death or dishonour, and was not ready to die. She told her husband, and a warrant for Charteris's apprehension was issued, but he had crossed the border before it could be executed. The law took its course in his absence, and, despite the eloquence of Duncan Forbes, of Culloden, who defended him, he was convicted of rape and condemned to death. After some little anxiety Charteris obtained a pardon from the King and returned to Scotland to surrender to the court and flourish the precious document from the dock.

When life is made up of excitement and excess it is not surprising if the strongest constitutions feel the strain. Charteris was no more than human, and his manner of existence occasionally told upon his health. At one time his bodily vigour was so much reduced that it seemed as if death might be not far off, and instantly the mind of Charteris was filled with charitable thoughts. He proposed to erect a charity school for his natural children, who were to be convened by advertisement, and to build twenty-four almshouses for the accommodation of poor women to whose progress in life his conduct had proved detrimental. The notion so pleased its author that he had the necessary estimates prepared, and employed an architect to execute the plans, but meanwhile his health returned, and Charteris's creditable atonement reached no nearer perfection than any other good intention.

It would be agreeable to believe that at this period of his life Charteris was attracted to the society of men more spiritual than himself. There is some foundation for such belief in an account that was published of a dinner given by Charteris in George Street to the notorious bachelor in divinity, Thomas Woolston. Charteris had requested his guest to bring with him his "Discourses on the Miracles," and was so entertained by the reading and his share of the seven bottles of port consumed between them, that he desired nothing so much as to suitably reward the learned divine. Woolston could not becomingly accept the Colonel's bountiful offer to put a harem at his disposal, but Charteris promised to make his new friend his private chaplain when a vacancy should occur. When Charteris afterwards fell into disgrace, Woolston felt called upon to deny, by advertisements, that this interview had taken place, but it must be remembered that Woolston also denied the miracles.

Charteris resumed his old habits as soon as he was able, fleecing his dupes when occasion offered, and for the rest amusing himself with such unwary females as he could entrap into his house. This particular diversion became more difficult as time went on ; so notorious had he become that his quarry had grown very shy, and its successful pursuit required all the patience and subterfuge of the wild-duck hunter. That Charteris was equal to his self-imposed task cannot be reasonably doubted, but the state of his health warned him that unceasing activity was not advisable, and on the advice of his doctor he determined to try the fashionable cure at Aix-la-Chapelle. The news of his arrival at the watering-place created an immense sensation, and crowds of visitors flocked in to see, in the flesh, the great English gamester and rake. Charteris was not at all indisposed to exhibit his prowess in the first of these characters, and some too curious Continental players found to their cost that his reputation for playing to win was exceedingly well founded. It was said that he won enough to increase his income by £1,000 a year,

and when there was no money to be won he did not
disdain to be paid in kind, taking on one occasion a
berlin with a team of Flanders mares which he shipped to
England. He was less prudent in making a wager, or
agreement, with Lord Dalrymple that the survivor should
receive from the other £1,000 a year. Another venture was
equally and more immediately unsuccessful. He drew a
bill for £5,000 on Alderman Child, of London, and, on his
return, having, it is to be supposed, forgotten about it,
repudiated all knowledge of it, and declared the signature
a forgery. But the Alderman was made of sterner stuff than
Charteris had imagined, and, disregarding the Colonel's
bounce, caused him to be arrested, and before the case
came on for hearing obtained his money.

It would have been well for Charteris had not the yearning
for his old pursuits induced him to leave the pleasant and profitable society at Aix for his home in London. He had scarcely
settled down again in George Street when a girl named Ann
Bond entered his service. She had been procured by one of
his agents who, knowing by experience that the most abandoned of women showed fright at the name of Charteris,
had offered to find her a place at Colonel Harvey's. Ann
Bond's master at once began to show her attention, but she
modestly rejected all his advances, backed up though they
were with promises of riches. After three days' resistance
the girl became aware of the Colonel's identity, and applied
to the housekeeper for leave to go away, which was naturally
refused, while strict orders were given to the other servants
to prevent her escape. The next morning, November 10,
1729, Charteris sent for her, and without more ado effected
his purpose in a somewhat indelicate manner. Ann was
then turned out of the house on the pretence of having stolen
a purse of guineas, and in her distress informed a friend of
what had happened. On the advice of this person she exhibited articles against Charteris for an assault with intent
to ravish, and a warrant was issued. With customary fore-
thought Charteris had withdrawn to Brussels, and there he
sought the advice of his friends as to the course he should
pursue. The general opinion was that the case was one for

a settlement, but on the representation that if this were done Charteris would expose himself to continual blackmail, he resolved to return and stand his trial. Meanwhile the grand jury considered the matter, and at the instigation of one of their number who irrelevantly urged that Charteris had victimised his daughter, they found that the attempt mentioned in the indictment had been an accomplished fact, and brought in their bill accordingly.

When, therefore, on Thursday, February 26, 1730, Colonel Charteris surrendered at the Old Bailey, it was for rape he was on his trial. The prosecution told a straightforward tale, but the examination and cross-examination of the string of witnesses who appeared to give evidence to the discredit of Ann Bond, took some hours. Their efforts, however, were fruitless, for the jury brought in a verdict of guilty, and this, according to the harsh law of the period, could only lead to one sentence. He was taken to Newgate, and brought out on the Saturday evening to hear sentence of death passed on him in company with nine malefactors.

The excitement which had been aroused in London, and indeed throughout the country, at the news of the trial was trebled at the result. It was well kept up by the story of the siege of the Colonel's house and its brave defence by his faithful retinue when the sheriff came to seize the forfeited goods of the convicted felon. Everybody had his own scandalous tale about the unfortunate man, and the hawkers found a ready sale for inaccurate and exaggerated pamphlets which purported to tell the history of his life. It is to this period that we owe what is certainly the best, and probably the only authentic, portrait of Charteris. It is a good piece of mezzotinting, and represents a fine, though not a handsome, man standing in the dock of the Old Bailey with his thumbs tied. The face is powerful and intelligent, and its best feature, the nose, is well formed and notably prominent; but the eager, protruding eyes and thick, sensual lips are not beautiful. The portrait, the author of which is not known, is labelled "Colonel Francisco," and beneath it are engraved these lines :—

" Blood ! must a Colonel with a Lord's estate
  Be thus obnoxious to a scoundrel's fate?
  Brought to the bar and sentenc'd from the bench
  For only ravishing a country wench ?
  Shall Gentlemen receive no more respect?
  Shall their diversions thus by laws be check'd?
  Shall they b' accountable to saucy juries,—
  For this or t' other pleasure? *H—ll and Furies!*
  What man thro' villainy would run a course
  And ruin families without remorse
  To heap up riches—if when all is done
  An ignominious death he cannot shun ? "

While the town was thus amusing itself at Charteris's expense, he was lying in irons in Newgate, sick in body and heart, and almost without hope. It was not much in his favour that he had already once received a pardon for a similar offence, and still less so that a new King who did not know Charteris, and could not make allowance for his weakness, was on the throne. Yet his friends were hard at work, doing all that was possible to obtain his pardon, and it bears testimony to the good points in his character, that among these friends were such men as the Duke of Argyll, and James Bruce, both of whom had been in the Horse Guards when Charteris was an exempt in the same regiment, and Robert Walpole. His son-in-law, the Earl of Wemyss, took lodgings in Ludgate Hill, so as to be near him, and Mrs. Charteris, who had come up post haste from Edinburgh, found rooms in Warwick Lane hard by. During the whole time of his imprisonment Charteris was very ill, and at the beginning of April the doctors could hold out but small hope of his recovery, so painful was the asthma and so high the fever. But his cure was being effected in the chamber of the Privy Council to whom his case had been referred. Duncan Forbes, of Culloden, who rented a house near Edinburgh from Charteris, came to London to plead for him, and pleaded so successfully that the Council unanimously advised his pardon, which the King therefore granted. The good news found the Colonel still in bed, but he so soon recovered that the following day he was able to leave the gaol on bail to appear at the next sessions to plead his pardon. He was further required to settle a sum of eight hundred pounds on the girl who brought him into the undignified position he had recently occupied.

Once more a free man Charteris joined his wife at her lodgings, and lost no time in sending her back to Scotland. He then thought fit to retire, and caused it to be believed that he had gone to Bath for his health; but he went no further than Kensington, where he took rooms at the Gravel Pits. His misfortunes were not yet at an end, though it was only mischance that revealed his presence in the suburbs. On the Saturday night following his discharge from prison Charteris, rejoicing in his recovered health and freedom, called a coach and started with two friends to drive to Chelsea. On the road some loafers recognised the Colonel, and seeing that two women were his companions stopped the coach; a crowd collected, and, hauling Charteris out, beat him most barbarously. This practical evidence of the unpopularity of his hardly-earned pardon seems to have induced Charteris to give up London in disgust. He had not the heart to seek punishment for those who had inhumanly assaulted him, but sorrowfully made his arrangements for retreating to his country seats.

For the next eighteen months little is heard of him. In February, 1732, he was at Hornby Castle, and becoming very ill he insisted on being removed to Stoney Hill. Edinburgh was nearly reached when it was thought necessary to send for Dr. Clark, who thus wrote to Duncan Forbes, under date February 22nd:—

"But the terriblest patient I had in my life is your monster of a landlord. I was obliged to go sixteen miles out of town to meet him on his way from Hornby. I lived two days in hell on earth, and conveyed him with much difficulty to Stoney Hill, dying exactly as he lived, but swearing little or not at all. He can neither sleep nor eat—seems to be dying of decay of nature, his blood being exhausted. . . . As for his own honesty, the only sign he has shown of it was one day when he thought he was going off, he ordered, with a great roar, that all his just debts should be paid."

While he thus lay dying at Stoney Hill Charteris was
lovingly tended by his wife and daughter. He pondered
over the unknown future awaiting him, and repeatedly
offered to give £30,000 to anybody who would assure him
there was no such place as hell. The money was not
earned though Mr. Cumming, the minister, was unceasing
in ministrations of comfort. So attentive was he that
Charteris, who in death as in life liked to have money's
worth, became anxious as to the amount of the honorarium
that would be expected, and put the question to his
daughter. Lady Wemyss, who by reputation inherited the
" nearness " of her father, replied that it was unusual to
give anything on such occasions. " Well, then," said
Charteris, " let us have another flourish from him," alluding
to the good man's prayers. The end came on a night when
a terrific storm raged, and in it, as the people of the
neighbourhood assured themselves, the Colonel's soul
passed to the place from which his wealth could not save
him. These same good people were not willing that more
respect should be paid to Charteris's helpless body than they
expected would be dealt out to his helpless soul. When the
funeral procession started from Stoney Hill they were lining
the avenue leading to the house, and pelted the hearse as it
passed with filth and garbage. Their unseemly demonstra-
tions were continued by the open vault in the church of
Greyfriars in Edinburgh, where an attempt was made to
tear the body from the coffin. When at last it was safely
lowered the carcases of dead dogs and cats were flung in the
tomb to bear it company.

The disposition of Charteris's wealth had been determined
oy a settlement dated June 5, 1730, under which his estate
was left to Francis, the second son of his daughter and the
Earl of Wemyss, subject to the proviso that he and his heirs
should take the name of Charteris. Special legacies confirmed his daughter's marriage settlement, gave £1,000 and
the life-rent of a house worth £100 a year to his advocate,
Duncan Forbes ; £1,000 to Lord Milton ; £500 to an aunt ;
a pair of pistols to the Duke of Argyll, and his horses, which
were numerous and valuable, to Robert Walpole. At the

time the will was made Charteris was anxious to show his gratitude to those who helped him out of the awkward fix in which his experience of Ann Bond had placed him, and to this reason must be attributed his omission to mention the unfortunate women and children whom he had earlier intended to benefit.

Charteris's character was of no complex nature, and is best seen in the story of his life. His contemporaries were inclined to judge him harshly, and Pope, in particular, could forego no opportunity of gibbeting him in verse. Swift, though he deplored the man's vices, did not regard him as exceptional, and was able to inform Pope that in Dublin, in 1736, there was a number of "old villains and monsters, four-fifths of whom are more wicked and stupid than Chartris." Hogarth, according to Warton, introduced Charteris into the first plate of the "Harlot's Progress," but in making this statement the good doctor possibly showed himself overcredulous. The severest critic of all was found in Arbuthnot, who composed and published the celebrated epitaph which spares not one of Charteris's foibles. It runs as follows :—

> "Here continueth to rot the body of
> COLONEL DON FRANCISCO;
> Who with an inflexible constancy,
> And inimitable uniformity of life,
> Persisted in spite of age and infirmity
> In the practice of every human vice,
> Excepting prodigality and hypocrisy;
>   His insatiable avarice
>   Exempting him from the first,
>   And his matchless impudence
>   From the second.
>   Nor was he more singular
> In that undeviating viciousness of life
> Than successful in accumulating wealth;
>   Having
>   Without trust of public money, bribe,
>   Work, service, trade or profession,
>   Acquired or rather created
>   A ministerial estate.

Among the singularities of his life and fortune
　Be it likewise commemorated
　That he was the only person in his time
Who would cheat without the mask of honesty ;
　Who would retain his primeval meanness
After being possessed of 10,000 pounds a year :
And who having done, every day of his life,
　　Something worthy of a gibbet,
　　Was once condemned to one
　　For what he could not do.[1]
　　Think not, indignant reader,
　　His life useless to mankind ;
　　PROVIDENCE
Favoured or rather connived at
　　His execrable designs,
　　That he might remain
　　To this and future ages
A conspicuous proof and example
　　Of how small estimation
Exorbitant wealth is held in the sight
　　Of the ALMIGHTY,
　　By his bestowing it on
　　The most unworthy
　　Of all the descendants
　　Of Adam."

Charteris's career almost justified itself in giving occasion
for this fine piece of writing, which does not exaggerate the
generally received opinion of its subject.   But it is possible
that in some cases the public, which so keenly interested
itself in the doings of the unhappy man, exaggerated their
wickedness.   It were kinder to take leave of him here with
the charitable and truthful account given of him by courtly
Sir Robert Douglas: " He was a man of good parts and
great sagacity, and by his particular skill and knowledge of
men and manners of the time he lived in, acquired a vast
estate."

[1] There is no other evidence for this triple slur on the capacity of
Charteris, the veracity of Ann Bond and the sagacity of the grand
jury.

JONATHAN WILD.

JONATHAN WILD.

(1682–1725.)

"I am distressed for thee, my brother Jonathan."
2 SAMUEL i. 26.

HAD Henry Fielding, novelist and police magistrate elected to write an authentic history of Jonathan Wild, instead of merely using his name as a peg on which to hang a satire, the literature of biography would have been enriched by an addition which can now be given. The novelist's pen, assisted by the magistrate's personal knowledge of the curiously loose system of the harsh criminal law of his time, might have given a living portrait of the famous Thief-taker, whose materials are now in a great measure wanting, certain of those whose place in history can only be given after the lapse of many years, and a different writer, nearer his own day, could at once have taken the measure and put on record a veracious chronicle of his doings and misdoings. It is true that when his career came to its untimely end biographers were to be found in plenty but they were of the lightning kind, whose works were to be sold for twopence or sixpence in the streets, the matter being furnished according to the price. It was their duty to supply a want felt by the public, and, as often happens, gossip and invention best suited the popular fancy, there was no use for careful or minute research. The want, in fact, was supplied, but as years went on and interest subsided, the name of Jonathan Wild became a

JONATHAN WILD.

(1682–1725.)

"I am distressed for thee, my brother Jonathan."
2 SAM. i. 26.

HAD Henry Fielding, novelist and police magistrate elected to write an authentic history of Jonathan Wild, instead of merely using his name as a peg on which to hang a satire, the literature of biography would have stood enriched by an addition which can now be never made. The novelist's pen, assisted by the magistrate's personal knowledge of the curiously loose system of working the harsh criminal law of his time, might have presented a living portrait of the famous Thief-taker, for which the right materials are now in a great measure wanting. Wild was not of those whose place in history can only be determined after the lapse of many years, and a dispassioned writer, nearer his own day, could at once have taken his measure and put on record a veracious chronicle of his doings and misdoings. It is true that when his career came to its untimely end biographers were to be found in plenty, but they were of the lightning kind, whose works were to be sold for twopence or sixpence in the streets, the matter being furnished according to the price. It was their pleasant duty to supply a want felt by the public, and since, as sometimes happens, gossip and invention best served to tickle the popular fancy, there was no particular need to spend time in research. The want, in fact, was so adequately supplied that as years went on and interest was still sustained, the name of Jonathan Wild became as that of a very

Theseus and was identified with any sort of adventure, imaginary or otherwise, which might be reckoned on to make the hair stand on end. In later days the authors who labour to edify youth have seized upon Jonathan as a hero for their inexpensive romances, and with all the resources of fiction and of their art at hand have made him the centre-piece of well-nigh every deed of darkness it may have been convenient or salutary to depict. They have done no great wrong to the man's memory, but the embellishments of their narratives are calculated to discount any sober-sided sketch of the true man or such fragments of him as have been preserved. Yet there is no need to apologise for Jonathan Wild as a subject for the moralist who would point the right way of life by exemplifying the evil that is to be avoided. Enough of him is known to make it certain that there was little enough of what can be reckoned good in him.

He was born at Wolverhampton about 1682, and, in the absence of evidence to the contrary, it is fair to assume that his parentage was respectable. His father, indeed, was a peruke-maker whose circumstances were, perhaps, not over-prosperous, for instead of bringing up his eldest son Jonathan to his own trade, he apprenticed him to a buckle-maker. His time served, Jonathan set up as a journeyman in his native town, and soon found himself in a position to marry a wife and beget a son. Satiated for the moment with this mere taste of the fruit of wedded life he resolved to visit London, and, since the expedition was to be of a business character, he naturally elected to go alone. The story of his adventure with a lady doctor on the road is more than probably untrue. According to this legend, Jonathan possessed the power of dislocating his hip at will, and performed the feat in order to provoke the charity of a lady who was passing him in a carriage. The lady took pity on the lame fellow, and inviting him into her conveyance allowed him to accompany her as far as Warwick. Jonathan discovered the profession of his benefactress and disclosed his imposition, with a suggestion how his trick might be turned to their mutual advantage. He was in consequence provided

with the funds necessary to procure him the best hotel
accommodation and surgical advice afforded by the town.
The surgeons' efforts to restore his leg to the proper position
were all unavailing, but the lady, happening to hear of the
case, applied an ointment which seemed to effect a miraculously speedy cure. The faculty admitted a superior force,
and the lame, halt, and blind of Warwick and the neighbourhood hurried as quickly as they might to procure boxes of
the remedy. The same game was played in the chief towns
on the road with the same success until London was
reached. Whether the tale be true or not the result was
the same, for Jonathan arrived in London and found employment at his trade. But the remuneration to be gained by
buckle-making was insufficient to meet the expenses of
town life, and before Jonathan had time to achieve fame
or fortune by his proficiency he was arrested for debt and
placed in the Wood Street Compter. He remained there
four years, and was perforce thrown into the society of many
persons of both sexes whose life had been less respectable
than his own. Among them was a woman named Mary
Milliner, who had been unfavourably known as a night-
walker and pickpocket, and under her instruction especially
the young countryman was educated in some of the possibilities of life. In the absence of direct testimony it is
impossible either to confirm or deny the harsh and gratuitous
inference of Mr. William Jackson, that, "considering the
character of the parties, there will appear but little reason
to suppose that they adhered to the strict rules of chastity."

The pair seem to have managed to leave the prison
together and to have found the means to start a little
establishment in Lewkenor's Lane, of the kind for which
that street had been noted since the Roundheads first
sneaked into its retirement to practise the vices they more
openly denounced. The house prospered, and enough
capital was put by to enable Wild and his partner to
abandon their dirty traffic and engage in another business,
which in these days would be considered scarcely more
reputable. They took a little house in Cock Alley, opposite Cripplegate Church, and opened it as a public-house.

Patronage was assured by Mary Milliner's extensive acquaintance with the thieves of London, among whom she had been popular, both as one of themselves and the instrument of their pleasure, and no unworthy feeling of jealousy barred the admission of Jonathan to the circle. His long stay in prison had enabled him to know, at least by sight, a large number of thieves, and since fate still threw him into their society he was content to stay there, though with the ever-present idea of turning the connection to his own advantage. The popularity of the little house among its particular *clientèle* could not fail to attract the notice of Charles Hitchen, who filled the office of City Marshal—from which he was, however, at this time suspended for misconduct. He was still allowed to play the part of constable, and there was no figure better known in the lowest haunts of London or to its lowest characters than the huge, ungainly form of the marshal, clad in a silver-buttoned coat, wearing a knotted wig, and with a heavy sword jangling at his side. It were hardly rash to assert of Hitchen that, taken all in all, no more infamous scoundrel ever trod the earth. His allotted duties were to assist in keeping the peace of London, to arrest malefactors, to inform against the proprietors of houses where thieves and other bad characters congregated, and to bring offenders against the law within reach of its arm. These duties he well and faithfully carried out when it suited his purpose—when, that is, he could gratify his spite, avenge an injury to his self-esteem, or make more by earning a reward offered for a capture than he could extort from the wretched being for allowing him to go free a while longer. But a far easier and more profitable way of carrying on his business lay at his hand in the opportunities it afforded him of levying blackmail, and of these he availed himself to the fullest extent. Among the horde of evil-doers who infested the City of London there were but few—were they mere thieves, pickpockets, footpads, housebreakers, shoplifters, highwaymen, disorderly women, or keepers of houses of ill-fame —that were not known personally to Hitchen, and very small was the proportion of them who did not have to pay him handsomely for immunity. But the work of following up even a part of the multifarious crimes that daily disgraced London, and of getting a fair share of booty or hush-money was onerous for one man who, though he had underlings at his disposal, had none among them in whom he could place great confidence. It occurred to Hitchen that such a person might be found in Wild, who was well fitted for the post by reason of his already extensive acquaintance with habitual law-breakers. He accordingly offered Wild the post of assistant, and the proposal being accepted a partnership was commenced. We have Wild's account of the evening on which he was initiated into his duties. The two worthies met at Temple Bar " and called in at several brandy-shops and ale-houses between that and Fleet Ditch ; some of the masters of these houses complimented the marshal with punch, others with brandy, and some presented him with fine ale, offering their service to their worthy protector." The replies made to these people were curt and dignified ; they were told that all the service required of them was to give immediate information of the whereabouts of any stolen property that had come into the possession of their clients. Passing on, they came to a house frequented by women of the town, and those off duty were lectured by the marshal on the impropriety of handing over to anybody but himself pocket-books and other trifles which they might abstract from gentlemen who sought their society. They were given to understand that Jonathan was his man, and, unless all property was delivered up to one or other of them, every lady present might count on being sent to Bridewell. A little further the pair came suddenly on three well-known pick-pockets, who were called upon to explain why they did not bow down before their lord, and were ordered to give an account of themselves and of their plan of campaign for the night. They, too, were introduced to the new assistant, and, after promising to give up their booty to either master or man, were allowed to go—"making a low congee and promising obedience." In such congenial pursuits the evening passed away, and Jonathan was enabled to form some idea of his new friend's importance. He took a liking for the occupation, and, armed with a staff as a token of authority, went on nightly rambles through the City with Hitchen. They bullied unfortunate women to enforce the giving up of stolen property; they swindled honest men who appealed to them for assistance, and made the lives of thieves burdensome by their threats of the Compter if greater returns were not given. If occasion offered, they disdained no chance of extorting money. Thus on one of their walks they saw a clergyman standing against a wall with his back towards them, and a woman happening to pass by at the moment, they seized both, and charged the priest with assault. In vain the unfortunate man protested his innocence; he must either go to gaol for the night or give security for his appearance in the morning. It was only the fortunate appearance on the scene of some friends of the clergyman who had sense enough to give the expected fee to the marshal, that prevented the ruin of the good man and the record of his captors being stained with one more case of perjury. At another time they might see the wife of some honest citizen walking home unattended, and would seize her as a lewd woman. She would be forced to accompany the "constables" to a tavern, where a hot supper and the best wines would be ordered for the gentlemen while the lady was directed to sit apart, as being vermin unfit for the society of decent people. When the two had well drunk and spent some social hours, their victim—if she had behaved well—was allowed to pay the reckoning, to empty her purse and depart. Such incidents as those narrated are but the mildest examples of the shocking adventures which Hitchen and Wild sought out for themselves in their pursuit of gain and power over sinners. Many of their proceedings were merely low, brutal, and sordid, but others, besides sharing these qualities, were of a kind that cannot be related without the graphic fearlessness of an ancient Greek or Roman historian.

Wild, meanwhile, was not neglecting to turn the knowledge gained by his apprenticeship to his own account. His connection with the thieving brotherhood daily increased, and new acquaintances could not do less than patronise the house kept by the marshal's man. There the talk would be of daring exploits done and booty won; but after mutual congratulations were over there generally remained the question of dealing in a profitable manner with the spoils. Had Wild been scrupulously honest he would no doubt have insisted on all property, the disposal of which was thus discussed in his presence, being handed over to Hitchen; but he may have felt that there would be some impropriety as well as harm done to his business if he carried home with him the quasi-official duties he combined with the marshal. Whatever his motive, it was in his private capacity that he listened to the conversations of his guests, and if it was not pure good nature that led him to suggest that the stolen goods might with advantage be handed over to him, he at any rate relieved the thieves from a difficulty which continually weighed on them. Wild undertook to sell, on the best terms possible, any goods entrusted to him, and to hand the proceeds—less a commission, for his own trouble—to the thief. Beginning in a small way, he did so well at his business that before very long he had at his disposal the most valuable part of the stolen property of London. He, in fact, beat Hitchen at his own game, and the two friends became mortal foes: Wild always having the upper hand by reason of the soiled character borne by the other, and the further disgraces in which he embroiled himself. Wild, however, for his own purposes, maintained his official character, and kept himself before the notice of the magistrates by haling before them from time to time, when it suited him, some criminal or enemy. He prospered exceedingly, for not only was his business large but he had absolute control of it; if he said he had sold a given article for so much there was none to disprove his word, and the pickpocket or burglar had to be perforce content with what Jonathan chose to give him, knowing full well, moreover, as he did, that to cast any doubts on mine host's straightness of dealing was as much as his freedom or perhaps his life was worth. But if business conducted on these lines went well it could not fail to go better when Wild put into practice an idea which would

naturally present itself to a man of his commercial instincts.
Where was the use of selling goods to some trader who
bought them only to re-sell at a profit when, by direct
dealing, that extra profit, and perhaps more, might be
pocketed by Jonathan himself? Accordingly he began an
open traffic in stolen goods, and in the hope that the original
owner of any particular piece of property might give more
for it than anybody else, he would obtain the owner's name
from the thief, and politely let him know that something
which belonged to him had found its way to the house in
Cock Alley, and would be restored for a consideration.
Open dealing of this kind gave a great impetus to thieving,
and, as Wild found numerous imitators on a smaller scale
in other parts of London, it quickly became a scandal which
attracted the attention of the Legislature. The result was
an Act of Parliament putting the receiver on more or less
the same level as the thief, and rendering him liable, on
conviction, to transportation for fourteen years.

Directly the purport of this Act was realised by those immediately concerned, the profession, not only of receiving
but of thieving also, for the moment staggered. For a brief
space of time it seemed as if the law by one happy stroke
had brought security to property. So long as receiving had
remained a lawful practice it had not been necessary for
thieves to trouble themselves greatly about getting rid of
their gains, and the receivers, having had no occasion to
pursue their calling otherwise than openly, were now
marked men. There remained only the pawnbrokers for the
disposal of such goods as could not be melted down, and
the wretched prices offered by them were not good enough
to compensate for the risk run in robbery. The thieves
of London lost courage, and starvation or honesty seemed to
stare them in the face; but Jonathan Wild, with fertile mind,
came to the rescue. On the coming into force of the Act
he had been sent for, it was said, by the Recorder, to whom
he was known both as a police witness and a receiver, and
was strongly advised by him to give up his business and
friendly relation with thieves, and to confine his energies
to detecting rogues and earning the rewards offered for their

discovery. But Wild was not born to settle down to a hap-
hazard and poverty-stricken, if respectable, existence. He
knew that in the new conditions brought about by the
displacement of any great industry was the opportunity
for the man of invention and resource. The little men in
the receiving line might go to ruin, as doubtless most of
them did, but Wild was resolved to make use of the alteration in the law as a stepping-stone to higher things. It
occurred to him that he might still act as intermediary
between the thieves and their victims without actually
handling the goods stolen. He proposed his plan to his
leading supporters among the thieves, who were only too
glad to welcome any suggestion which might help them to
carry on their business profitably, and he forthwith commenced to busy himself with the organisation of his system.
In its main lines this system was that all stolen property
should be deposited in certain places little likely to be
suspected. Wild was to be informed of each several
robbery, with such particulars as could be supplied of the
person robbed ; and he was then to open up communications
with the owner and, if possible, bargain with him for the
return of his property. The plan answered admirably.
Soon after he had received information of a theft Wild would
visit or write to his prey, saying he had chanced to hear
of his misfortune and had also happened to hear of a similar
article to that which had been stolen having been stopped
as suspected by a honest broker of his acquaintance ; if
the articles should prove to be identical, he thought restitution could be made if the person he had the honour of
addressing would be good enough to make a small present
to the broker for his trouble, and would promise not to
endeavour to set the law in motion against the good man
who had been unfortunate enough to have come into possession of stolen goods. People anxious to regain their property
usually fell in with the terms offered, and though they opened
their eyes at the size of the small present required by the
honest broker, they had no choice between paying the money
or hearing no more of their property. Some there were who
wanted an explanation of the coincidence that Wild should

know of the robbery and also the whereabouts of the goods
stolen, but these over-curious persons were hardened indeed
if they were not put to shame by the virtuous indignation of
their informant : "he had come out of pure good nature,
thinking to do a service, but if his motives were called in
question, and he was suspected of being an accomplice of
thieves, he had no more to say, save that his name was
Jonathan Wild, and that he resided in Cock Alley, Cripplegate, where he was to be found every day." If any grateful
recipients of the information brought by Wild were to
suggest the propriety of a gift to him, the offer was disdained,
and rightly so, from the point of view of his own advantage,
for such high-minded conduct could only serve to enhance
his character of disinterested probity, and the presents made
to "the broker" afforded a very handsome profit on the
transaction. Yet Wild was generous enough in dividing the
spoils with the thieves, without whom he could do nothing,
though he devoted a good deal of time to the training of
young thieves, who were practically his servants. The ease
with which Wild's good fortune enabled him to learn where
stolen effects might be recovered soon earned him a widespread reputation, and people who had been relieved of their
property began to come to him in search of news of it without waiting to be approached by him. Increasing business,
too, made his time more valuable, and he now judged himself in a position to open his house as an office for the
recovery of stolen property. This move was attended with
great success, and the office was thronged by persons anxious
only to get back their goods and not caring overmuch to
inquire into the mode of their recovery. But they were not
allowed to regain possession without considerable circumstance. On entering the office they would find the presiding
genius gravely seated behind his registers, and would be
requested to pay the nominal preliminary fee of five shillings.
This done, their names and addresses were entered in a
book, together with a description of the articles lost and the
manner of the robbery, and the amount of reward that would
be given. They were then told to call again in a few days,
when it was hoped some information would have come to

hand. On the second visit it was the custom to announce that the goods had been traced and demanded, but that the thieves pretended that the pawnbrokers would give more for them than the owner, and that the only way to make sure of recovering them was to increase the reward. Wild was judge enough of character to know how far this squeezing process could be safely carried on, and when the limit was reached he would ask for the payment and the goods would be delivered. To his credit it must be recorded that in no instance that is known did he ever receive payment in this way without restoring the property. If trade flourished as it did, it was due to the untiring efforts of Wild, who forced people to seek his assistance by giving his particular attention to the theft of their property. The thieves were gradually organised, and their number was systematically increased, and they were taught the value of articles which to the mere independent thief are useless and worthless. Things " of no value nor interest except to the owner " were especially sought after and easily found, so that among those who thronged the little office were always to be found merchants and shopkeepers whose account-books had been abstracted, ladies who had lost some prized personal trinket, or ship-masters whose ships' documents had been filched from them at the docks.

Wild rose with his business, and as became a man of his influence and position, wore laced clothes and carried a sword. He is said to have tested the sword's temper by slicing off the ear of the faithful Mary Milliner, who still shared his roof, though remaining far beneath his new status. No doubt he wanted to get rid of her, and their quarrel effected his purpose. Still he treated her generously, for he set her up as mistress of a little house in Moorfields, and never failed to come to her assistance when business with her was slack. For himself he had loftier notions. He left Cock Alley, and established a new and grander office at 68, Old Bailey, where his clients failed not to come after him. He looked about him, too, for another lady to take the place of a wife, and succeeded in winning the affections of one as to whose name there is some doubt, it being according to some authorities Mary

Read and to others Judith Nun. During her short reign—in the nine years which passed before his premature death Wild " remarried " four times—she was well treated, but the union was unfruitful, and it is possible that Jonathan, in whom philoprogenitiveness was strongly developed, did not greatly regret the loss which her death inflicted on him. At any rate he very soon recovered his spirits, and again chose a widow for companion. The marriage ceremony took place at St. Pancras Church, and was performed by the Ordinary of Newgate, who had attended the bride's first husband at Tyburn where the good man had lost his life. On Wild's wedding morning the Ordinary's duties first took him to Tyburn in the company of three thieves who had to be executed, and who may, or may not, have been gratified at seeing their spiritual adviser wearing the marriage favour and white kid gloves with which he proposed to honour the union of the happy couple. They were hanged in good time, and the Ordinary was able to duly attend at the tying of a different kind of knot, amid less dispiriting surroundings. The festivities, indeed, were great, and were carried on lavishly, for some days at the house in Old Bailey. If there was no bounty to the poor, at least the poor prisoners in Newgate were not forgotten, but were entertained with such victuals as were not eaten by the invited guests.

But though Wild from time to time allowed himself these diversions of a bigamist (his wife at Wolverhampton still lived) his real heart was in his business, and all his best energies were devoted to its development. It gradually grew too big for his personal superintendence, but even in the difficult task of selecting responsible deputies he showed his remarkable judgment and insight into the character of men. It might be said of him, as it has been said of Archbishop Tait, that he had a genius for delegation, and though his assistants or colleagues were themselves thieves, or very little better, they faithfully rendered the services expected of them. His first branch office was opened in Newtonhouse Lane, Abraham Mendez being placed in charge of it as clerk of the Northern road, and shortly afterwards Quilt Arnold, who from the public point of view was a notorious rogue, was installed clerk of the Western road. Their principal duty was to keep a sharp eye on the thieves, some of whom would show signs of unruliness from time to time, and to keep themselves well informed of all important events which were likely to afford golden opportunities for the exploits of the children of Jonathan's gang, as it was called. The gang was admirably organised by Jonathan and his lieutenants. There was the swell mob division, or, as they were then called, "spruce prigs," who were well-dressed gentlemen, told off to present themselves at theatres, operatic performances, balls, race-meetings, entertainments at Court, or any other description of festivity patronised by the wealthy and well-to-do. No expense was spared in making the appearance of these pickpockets equal to that of those on whom they plied their craft, and in the hands of their special trainer, one Lunn by name, they successfully aped the manners of the gentry. Lunn met with an untimely end, for, employing his leisure at highway robbery, he was caught and hanged, and it was found difficult to replace him, till Jonathan conceived the happy notion of sending his most promising pupils to be instructed by a professional teacher of dancing and deportment. Some of the gentlemen thieves had places found for them as footmen or *valets-de-chambre*, and kept them as long as there was anything left to steal, or till they were discovered and turned out. Others took rooms in the more expensive parts of the town and ordered costly goods from shopkeepers which they removed as occasion offered. Valuables obtained by some of these methods could not, of course, be offered to their owners, and were transferred to a special department which was formed for the alteration or melting down of watches, rings, and other jewellery. The burglar division were supplied with the implements of their art from a store of such articles which were lent to those thieves who could put them to good use. A careful watch was necessarily kept by Wild and his lieutenants on the persons entrusted with their property, and at a fair or race-meeting Wild himself might often be seen looking after his interests, though, armed with a silver staff as a mark of assumed authority, he gave himself out as being on the watch for thieves and disorderly characters.

Wild, in fact, still continued to pose everywhere as an officer of justice, and while commiserating with the clients who came to him for the restoration of their property, he assured them of his earnest wish to catch the thief. And sometimes it suited his purpose very well to do so. Cases of insubordination or recalcitrancy among the members of his gang were always visited with swift and severe punishment, inasmuch as the rebels were straightway informed against and evidence to ensure their conviction was always adduced. Wild christened himself "the Thief-taker," and in his enterprising way anticipated more modern resources of publicity by paying newspapers to insert references to the Thief-catcher General, and by treating condemned prisoners at Newgate on the condition that they made a reference to his prowess in their dying speeches from the gallows-cart. If a suitable reward were offered for a capture and he had no personal interest in preventing it, he would really exert himself. Thus he gained great distinction in the case of the murder of Mrs. Knapp, who was shot by some thieves who were robbing her son at the time, in Gray's Inn Lane, on the 31st of March, 1716. It was suggested to him that a description of the supposed murderers would enable him to assist in their detection. He thought he could be of no use in the matter till a reward of fifty guineas was mentioned, when, touched to the quick, he exclaimed, " I never pardon murder," and set himself in good earnest to the task of discovering Mrs. Knapp's assailants. By the 8th of June three of the men concerned were hanged through Wild's good offices; a fourth would have been had he not, when caught, turned evidence and given information as to twenty-two of his former accomplices in crime, and a few months later Timothy Dun, the last of them, who had secreted himself in a cellar, was unearthed by Wild and driven to Tyburn.

A man who could make himself so useful was not one on whom the authorities responsible for law and order in the metropolis could afford to be too severe unless for very flagrant cause. It might well be that he was the cause of much disrespect of the law, but since it suited him sometimes to act as the law's minion, and the law was in constant need of examples to justify its existence, a man who could at will provide so much material was not to be lightly overthrown. To lay Wild by the heels was in a measure to kill the goose with the golden eggs. So it happened that, although frequently exposed, and still more frequently suspected, and on one occasion even ordered to Newgate, Wild escaped actual punishment, and was able to pursue his course practically unmolested. His efforts to bring about the arrest and conviction of criminals were as nothing compared with those required for securing their acquittal, and it was not seldom that these latter efforts had to be brought into play. If one of his gang was unfortunate enough to come within reach of justice it was Wild's interest to do what he could to get the man off, and that he should exercise his not inconsiderable influence in this way was part of the arrangement under which he and his men worked so amicably together. His methods of bringing about this object were various, and sometimes ingenious. The most obvious one was to suborn witnesses, or, if the witnesses were not of a kind to be tampered with, to devise a means of keeping them out of court. If the prosecutor could be prevented from appearing against the prisoner the matter was easier still, but the employment of this expedient was attended by a good deal of risk, as Jonathan once, at least, discovered. Arnold Powell, a particularly low thief, who to many other bad qualities added open defiance of Wild, was foolish enough, after having been once acquitted of a charge of robbery, to commit a burglary. News of it reached the wide ears of the Thief-taker, who promptly informed the victim of the identity of the burglar, and persuaded him to prosecute. But before the sessions Powell came to his senses and sent for Wild, who named his terms, which were eagerly accepted, and promised an acquittal. When the trial came on the prosecutor was absent, Wild having informed him that, in order to save his time, he would send word when the case should come on for hearing. Three separate times was the prosecutor called in vain, and then the case was dismissed, and the recognisances of the prosecutor were ordered to be estreated. This gentleman, when called upon to pay, was anxious to explain his absence, and did so with such success that Wild was severely reprimanded from the bench and ordered to Newgate, though the prosecution of him was afterwards allowed to drop. Powell was condemned to death at the next sessions on another indictment.

But Wild's favourite means of procuring the acquittal of his friends—a means which fulfilled a double end—was to furnish them with material for turning King's evidence. Prisoners who could give such information as to their accomplices and others as would ensure their conviction, could generally obtain their own release, and Wild, when the life of a valued colleague was at stake, would not hesitate to furnish him with certain particulars, with which he was sure to be well stocked, of some less-esteemed miscreant whose head would be put in the noose to afford the escape of the other. This, in fact, was the simplest method of revenge on the rebellious members of the profession who had refused to bow to Jonathan's authority. They were not always arrested on the first opportunity that offered, but allowed to continue in iniquity until some worthier disciple was in trouble and informed against them. If the charges made in evidence were not true, so much the worse for the scapegoat; hard swearing on the part of the informer gave them colour, and, if further evidence was called for, Wild could supply perjurers numerous enough to secure the conviction of an angel. Proceedings of this kind were frequent enough to exalt Wild to a very high position in the eyes of the thieves, who were morally obliged to endow him with omnipotence where they were concerned, and to pay him the respect that became such a quality. Many of his trustiest supporters were altogether in his power as being transported convicts who had returned home before the term of their expatriation had expired and it was from their ranks that he liked best to win recruits. Recruiting was a branch of his business to which Wild gave close attention, and when returned convicts ran short he would repair to the Mint in Southwark, a locality which, in Ball's Ginshop and the Music-house at Bankside could

boast two of the most infamous dens in London. Ball, of
the Ginshop, was one of Wild's staunchest adherents, and it
was but the irony of fate which led to his being shot, at a
later period, by Burnworth, who was one of the cleverest
thieves ever trained by Wild, and was considered in the
profession to be a better man than Sheppard. A man of
the Surrey side, who was cast down by ill-fortune, would
naturally go to Ball's in search of consolation, and if Wild
found him there he would cheer him with the assurance
that all was not lost, that if he had failed in one walk of life
there was at least one other career to be successfully followed by a brave heart. When he had gained a listener
Wild proceeded to instil a knowledge of thieving made easy,
and was ready with the necessary capital or outfit to give a
respectable start to the recruit. The only condition was
that the Samaritan who had rescued the man from the
gutter was to receive a handsome percentage on the profits
of the new undertaking. Nothing would probably be said
of any penalty for neglect to observe this condition, but the
fool who thought himself strong enough to disregard it
would not be long in discovering that in dealing with Wild
it paid best to be honest. A certain dissipated cheese-
monger, whose name has been forgotten, had been in his
distress thus befriended by Wild. He was provided with a
horse and commenced business on the highway, meeting,
in a very short time, with extraordinary success. Finding
his new calling both easy and profitable he began to doubt
the wisdom of sharing the proceeds with Wild, and failed
to report himself. Wild heard through his agents of the
highwayman's exploits on the Oxford road, and receiving
no account from the man himself determined to make an
example of him. He set out on the same road, and some
miles from Oxford met with a party who had just stood and
delivered. Wild rode on, and presently came up with his
man, who expected to find in the solitary rider a further
prey. Without waiting to parley or even reproach the
ex-cheesemonger for his ingratitude the Thief-taker shot
him dead and cantered on to Oxford to report the service
he had done the State.

But the State was beginning to think that, despite his
services, Wild was becoming a too prominent character. If
he can be charged with committing an error in judgment
it was in the too ostentatious use of his very considerable
wealth. He moved from his house in the Old Bailey to a
larger one on the other side of the road, next the Cooper's
Arms, and maintained the establishment of a man of means.
Mrs. Wild walked abroad attended by a footman in livery.
They dined every day from five courses, and the remains
were sent to the prisoners on the common-felon side of
Newgate gaol hard by. There was, indeed, no pretence
of mystery about Wild's principal business of middleman
between thieves and the rest of the public, and if his actual
complicity with the former party could not be actually proved
the large extent of his dealings must have bred suspicion.
Moreover, Wild's old friend Hitchen, inspired by frantic
jealousy, published a pamphlet which he called "The
Regulator; or a discovery of Thieves, Thief-takers," &c., and
in which he held Jonathan up to reprobation and charged
him with most known crimes. Wild replied with a counterblast in which he admitted the evil influences of Hitchen on
himself but disavowed the more serious charges, while he
brought others, far worse, against his tutor. Not much
notice was taken of this literary warfare which was not
needed to draw attention to Wild's proceedings. So again
the watchful Legislature made him the special object of an
attack by passing the Act which created it a capital offence
to take a reward for restoring stolen effects unless the thief
was apprehended or caused to be apprehended by the person
accepting the reward. Jonathan was for once almost down-
cast by this direct interference with his means of subsistence.
He talked vaguely at first of setting up an office for insurance
against burglary, but the limited facilities for advertising led
him to reconsider the idea, and he abandoned it when he
had thought out a project for circumventing the new law.
He decided that though he could no longer receive money
for goods he could still keep open his office for the benefits
of such people as cared to seek his advice. When his
advice was sought he made the usual preliminary inquiries,

and after two or three visits would inform an applicant that if a certain sum of money were deposited at a certain place the stolen goods would be restored. In these cases, as under the old system, justice was done and the property recovered, if the money was duly paid, but the victims of Wild's gang were more shy than they had been of coming to the office, and business did not flourish as it had. Stolen goods accumulated, and the gentlemen who had procured them required money in exchange. Face to face with this difficulty Wild reflected, as became a citizen of the world, that London was not the only place where honest trading might be done, and that in other countries no inconvenient questions would be asked as to the origin of merchandise or as to the person who wished to dispose of it. Accordingly he invested a part of his savings in the purchase of a sloop, and found a suitable master ready to his hand in that peerless blackguard, Roger Johnson. The new enterprise worked well. The good ship set out with her miscellaneous cargo and made for Ostend, as a rule, or sometimes Rotterdam, and after landing the goods returned to the port of London, or as near thereto as she might safely get without attracting the notice of the custom-house officers, laden with a new cargo of brandy, lace, and other articles of contraband. After two or three years' successful trading misfortune fell on the sloop owing to a quarrel between the skipper and his chief mate, who revenged himself by laying an information against Johnson for smuggling. The State seized the ship and its captain was called upon to pay fines to the extent of £700, the expense of which fell upon Wild.

Jonathan meantime was reverting to his old methods of business, being urged thereto by persons who had been robbed and were anxious only to get back what they had lost. But great caution was necessary, and Wild, whose necessities were greater even than his resources, was constrained to run great personal risks. He had a narrow escape from the persecution of a Mr. Jarvis, whose bulky trunk he had happened to notice in an inn-yard at Smithfield. He sent his man, Jerry Rann (an expert thief, but not to be confounded with the Rann of a later day, better known as Sixteen-string

Jack), to carry off the trunk, and when Jarvis applied to Wild for its recovery it was returned to him on payment of ten guineas. Rann, however, soon afterwards had a dispute with Wild, who ended it in his usual summary way by giving Rann into custody. Rann was tried and condemned to death, but on the day before his execution he sent for Jarvis and acquainted him with the adventures of the trunk. Jarvis resolved to prosecute Wild, and in all probability would have successfully done so had he not happened to die at this fortunate moment. Experience such as this, combined with growing insubordination among the thieves, who, now that his opportunities were restricted, regarded Wild with less respect, bred in him a feeling of insecurity. He put his position to the test in January, 1729, by a petition to the Corporation for the Freemanship of the City on the ground that he had assisted in the apprehension and conviction of several notorious thieves. To his disgust no notice was taken of the application. He began, too, to make frequent appearances in the police-court, and though he managed to wriggle out of the charges brought against him by his accusers, who were former supporters, he feared that he would not be able to escape always. A letter is extant in which he beseeches the Earl of Dartmouth to protect him from the violent persecution of some magistrates who had encouraged thieves to swear against him, and he promises in return to do public service by discovering, apprehending, and convicting numbers of notorious criminals. In a later letter he has heard that the Earl has lost some things "on the road," and asks for particulars of them in order that he may use his diligence to serve his lordship. But all was to no purpose, for the toils were gathering round him. His only chance of recovering his reputation was by activity in causing the arrest of thieves, and in consequence of their disaffection he was the more willing to undertake the work.

Few of Wild's gang were better known than Joseph Blake, or, to give him his more popular name, Blueskin, who was a clever pickpocket, but not so clever but that he frequently found himself in custody. At one time he had spent many months in the Wood Street Compter, being unable to find security for his good behaviour, and during this time Jonathan had allowed him sixpence a day. On his release he joined his friend, that " marvellous boy who perished in his pride," John Sheppard, and together they accomplished many robberies and burglaries. They broke loose altogether from Wild's authority, declining to give him a share in the proceeds of their exploits, and consequently when Mr. Kneebone, a former employer of Sheppard, sought Wild's assistance in the discovery of the thieves who had robbed him of a bale of valuable cloth, Jonathan was delighted to suggest and personally arrest Blake as the culprit. He affected sorrow at what he had been obliged to do, and though he could hold out no hope of getting his prisoner off he cheerfully promised that his body should not be dissected but decently buried in a coffin. The sensitive Blueskin, anxious as he was as to the disposal of his remains, was even more anxious that Wild should have no hand in the matter, and on receiving a visit from Wild before his trial, drew a knife and cut his captor's throat. Happily the knife was blunt, but Jonathan was so seriously hurt that he had to forego the pleasure he had promised himself of assisting at Blake's conviction by giving evidence against him in person. In his absence some hard words were said of him in open court, but, none the less, Blueskin was duly hanged on November 11, 1724. Sheppard had been condemned for the same offence, but his execution was delayed by his escape from prison.

Blake's was not the only sacrifice of a former friend made by Wild in his effort to retrieve reputation, and if he had confined himself to perfidy of this kind he might have lived to enjoy old age. But he could not afford to abandon his old mode of life nor to quarrel with all his best friends. He disliked quarrelling, and it was an endeavour on his part to act as peacemaker in his own peculiar way that commenced the last chapter of his busy life. His old ally, Roger Johnson, was at the bottom of it. Johnson frequented a house much patronised by thieves and kept by Thomas Edwards, and the two quarrelled over the partition of some stolen property.

Both were fired with indignation, and happening to meet in the street gave each other into custody for felony. Wild went bail for Johnson and persuaded him to drop his prosecution of Edwards, but this ungrateful innkeeper gave certain information to the authorities, as a result of which Wild's premises were searched and vast quantities of stolen property brought to light. This discovery was too much for the great friendship which Jonathan bore his friend, and swearing that the goods belonged to Johnson he caused Edwards to be arrested on Johnson's behalf. But Edwards, too, had friends who bailed him out, and he then devoted himself to the pursuit of Johnson, who prudently remained in hiding. At last he ventured out, and was met by his enemy, who straightway gave him into custody. Johnson enticed the officer into a beer-shop and sent word of what had happened to Wild, who promptly attended with his aide-de-camp, Quilt Arnold. The pair got up a miniature riot for the purpose of allowing Johnson to escape, which he failed not to do. For this friendly rescue an information was laid against Wild, who retired for observation till he thought the matter had blown over, when he returned with Arnold to the Old Bailey. No sooner were they back when Jones, the eminent high-constable of the Holborn division, appeared at the house, and after arresting them took them to Sir John Fryer, a magistrate, who sat up in his bed to examine them. They were committed to gaol the same evening, February 15, 1725, and remained there till February 24th, when Wild demanded to be discharged or put on his trial. The interval had been employed in getting up a case against Wild, and three days after his application he was ordered to be further detained on the strength of various articles of information filed against the Thief-taker. The articles, eleven in number, made some damaging charges, alleging amongst other things that he had been for many years the confederate of highwaymen and thieves of all sorts; that he had formed a corporation of thieves of which he was director-general; that he had been a receiver of stolen goods; that he concealed and supplied with clothes and money convicted felons; that he encouraged coiners; and that he had often sold human blood by swearing or procuring false evidence. When the information had been read the high-constable produced another, which charged the prisoner with capital offences to be proved by two convicts. These convicts received a free pardon as a condition of appearing against Wild. At the sessions on April 10th Wild applied by counsel for a postponement of his trial on the grounds that he did not know what was charged against him, and that two material witnesses were absent in the country. In spite of this inconsistency his request was granted and the trial postponed to the next sessions. The delay was disastrous to Wild as it enabled the authorities to get up against him another case supported by better evidence than that of convicted criminals.

On the 15th of May Wild appeared to his trial on two indictments: first, that on January 22, 1725, he had stolen in the house of Catherine Stetham fifty yards of lace, the property of the said Catherine; secondly, that on the 10th of March he had feloniously received of the said Catherine ten guineas on account, under pretence of restoring the said lace, without apprehending and prosecuting the felon who stole the property. It is to be observed that on the second of these dates Wild was in Newgate, and yet was able to carry on his usual profitable traffic. He had employed the days preceding the trial in literary composition, and distributed among jurymen and others a list of persons apprehended and convicted by his means, including thirty-five highwaymen, twenty-two housebreakers, and ten convicts who had returned too soon from transportation. Fortified by this defence in anticipation Wild duly appeared in the dock and asked that the witnesses might be heard apart from one another. The request was complied with, but the evidence was not to be shaken. The story was a simple one. On Wild's instructions Henry Kelley and Margaret Murphy had gone to Stetham's shop, and on the pretence of making a purchase had stolen a box of lace, which they handed over to Wild; he had examined its contents, and, telling them the lace was worth ten guineas, had given them five to divide between them. Kelley and Murphy both deposed to these facts, but Wild's counsel pointed out that he could not be legally convicted, as it had been shown he was not " in the house " as stated in the indictment, but had in fact waited outside. The judge, Lord Raymond, declared there could be no doubt as to the prisoner's guilt, but recommended him to the mercy of the jury, who, on the strength of the legal quibble, found him " Not guilty." Then followed the trial on the second indictment, and Catherine Stetham bore witness how after the theft of her lace she had advertised for it, but with no result, and had then sought the assistance of Wild. He had put her off two or three times, but pretended he knew the persons who had the lace, and she had expressed her willingness to give twenty-five guineas for its recovery. Meanwhile Wild had been put in Newgate, but on the 10th of March he had sent her word that if she would bring ten guineas her lace would be given up to her. She had gone to the prison and seen Wild, who instructed her to give the money to a porter; the porter had disappeared for a short time and had then brought back the lace, one piece of which was missing. She had asked Wild what satisfaction he expected, and he had replied, " Not one farthing : I have no interested views in matters of this kind, but act from a principle of serving people under misfortune. I hope I shall be soon able to recover the other piece of lace and to return you the ten guineas, and perhaps cause the thief to be apprehended. For the service I can render you I shall only expect your prayers. I have many enemies, and know not what will be the consequences of this imprisonment."

If this were a place to indulge in the pleasures of imagination it might be permitted to picture the triumphant look of innocence justified with which Wild turned to the jury at this repetition of his noble words; but Jonathan's triumph, if it existed, was short-lived, for the judge said the case was plain, and the jury, taking the same view, brought in a verdict of " Guilty." Sentence of death was passed.

Wild could not believe that there was any serious intention of cutting short his promising career. He might be quartered on the condemned side of Newgate, but he asserted his confidence that the King's pardon would be granted to one who had aided in the suppression of so many evil-doers, and had put so many people in possession of goods wrongfully taken away from them. He felt certain that members of the nobility whom he had thus benefited would combine to interest themselves on his behalf. But the days passed on and nothing was heard of a reprieve. It was observed that Wild's manner grew strange, and he being asked what ailed him replied that he thought his mind must have been affected by cracks on the skull received when capturing thieves, and by the cut which Blueskin made in his throat. But even this touching explanation availed nothing. Towards the close of the ten days which separated his trial from the day fixed for his execution Wild fasted, and though he refused to attend service in the chapel he gave a good deal of attention to the ministrations of Mr. Puyney, the Ordinary. If the accepted version of his last days be true he inquired of the good divine what was the meaning of the words "Cursed is every one that hangeth on a tree," and what was the state of the soul after its departure from the body ; but for answer he was oddly enough advised to turn his attention to matters of more importance. On the day before his execution he received the sacrament and spent the evening in a discussion with the Ordinary on suicide, making reference from his well-stocked mind to the cases of noble Greeks and Romans who had taken their own lives. In the end of the argument he allowed himself worsted, but in the early morning he administered to himself a large dose of laudanum. The quantity he took combined with his fast to prevent the poison from taking full effect, and while he lay stupefied two kindly-hearted fellow-prisoners raised him to his feet and walked him up and down. The exercise caused him to be very sick, and he again became nearly insensible ; but the day had broken, and in his piteous condition he was placed in the cart which was to take him to Tyburn. The ride from Newgate to the Marble Arch is not a long one, but Wild, aroused from his torpor by the mud and stones flung at him by the mob which lined the whole road, must have wished it shorter. Yet, having failed to kill himself, he was in no haste to die, for on his arrival at Tyburn he asked time for meditation, and continued to sit with folded arms in the cart stolidly staring at the multitude which stood around cursing him. So long did he sit that the crowd, thirsting for justice and its sport, yelled at the hangman to do his duty, and at length so seriously threatened that worthy, who had already hanged three persons that morning, that he was compelled to arouse Jonathan and perform the task appointed him. As Wild's body rose into the air the angry crowd ceased its cries, and his breath left him amid a profound and impressive silence.

On the evening of the same day, May 25, 1725, Wild's body was cut down, and it was buried in St. Pancras church-yard at two o'clock the next morning. His bones had no long peace, for shortly afterwards they were secretly disinterred and consigned, it was supposed, to the dissecting-room. A skull, said to be Jonathan Wild's, was exhibited in London in 1860, and up to about the same time a surgeon at Windsor boasted of the possession of the headless skeleton. Other relics of him are few, but at the Record Office and at the Guildhall there are papers in his handwriting, and there probably still exists the musketoon, originally presented by Wild to Blueskin, and afterwards by Sir John Fielding to his brother Henry, which was exhibited at the Society of Antiquaries in 1866.

Whatever be the judgment passed on Wild's character—and there is not much room for two opinions—it cannot be denied that he was a man of exceptional parts. His pre-eminence lay in his knowledge of how to use his fellow-men as tools, and it must be admitted that a history of Wild, to be complete, should properly include the history of his relations with the various members of his gang. Few things are more to be regretted than that tradition, which has brought down to us so much that is useless and unedify-ing, should have left us with no more than the mere names of many of the chosen band, men and women who helped both to support Wild and to lift him to greatness. Old Sue Belcher? What shall we ever know of her, save that she well and faithfully served her mistress, Sarah Hull? And what of Sarah Hull? Yet it has been given to few women to know the thrilling experiences of Sarah, who was married four times, and saw three of her husbands hanged and the fourth condemned four times, and yet preserved to his wife by a merciful Providence. Pre-eminence in any branch of industry is worthy of record, but we must be content to know that Mary Arnold was the most expert shoplifter ever known, and must remain in ignorance of the justification for the fame she won. These gentler spirits, together with others of the sterner make, Paul Groves, Richard Oakey, Matthew Flood, and Jonathan's brother Andrew, who kept a " case " at the " Black Boy " in Newtonhouse Lane, to mention no more—they are all but shadows on the stage where Jonathan Wild stalks ablaze, extinguishing all paler lights.

MR. JAMES MACLAINE,

THE GENTLEMAN HIGHWAYMAN.

(1724–1750.)

> " One that can
> Shew thee what 'tis to be a gentleman."
>
> I. C., *Art. Mag.*, 1649.

IF a man has any claim to the title of " Gentleman " his surest way to sustain it, is to leave no one any room to doubt that he thoroughly deserves that of " scoundrel." For if, when the time arrives for a public acknowledgment of his right to the latter, his friends hesitate to insist upon his honourable origin, he may be quite sure that it will be remembered—as an additional aggravation—by his enemies. Had Mr. James Maclaine been content to confine his energies to the dispensing of sand and small-coal in the neighbourhood of Welbeck Street, Cavendish Square, it is more than probable that no one would have suspected his connection with an honourable family in the north of Scotland. From such a stock, however, did he derive his descent. His father, Lauchlin Maclaine, after having been educated in the University of Glasgow, proceeded to Ireland to take charge of a Presbyterian congregation at Monaghan, and there married his wife, a lady of a family as reputable as his own. To them were born three children—Archibald, James, and Anne Jane. Mr. James Maclaine first saw light in 1724, and passed his early years under the eye of his father from whom he imbibed those Principles of Religion which, according to his own account, persisted in obtruding them-

JAMES MACLAINE.

MR. JAMES MACLAIN

THE GENTLEMAN HIGHWAYMAN

(1724-1750)

> "One that ...
> ... what 'tis to be a gentleman."
> I. C. ...

IF a man's one only claim to the title of "Gentleman," ... were to assist in it, is to leave no one an ... to doubt that he thoroughly deserves that of "scoundrel," ... the time arrives for a public acknowl ... of ... to the latter, his friends hesitate to ... his ... origin, he may be quite sure to ... receive ... ideas an addition of aggravation—by like ... Had Mr. James Maclain been content to con ... energies to the dispensing of sand and small-coal ... of Welbeck Street, Cavendish Square ... probable that no one would have so per ... ... an honourable family, in the north of ... ... stock, however, did he derive his de ... ... John Maclaine, after having been edu ... ... of Glasgow, proceeded to take a ... ... a Presbyterian congregation at Mon ... ... married his wife, a lady of a family as reputable as ... own. To them were born three children—Archibald, J ... and Anne J... Mr. James Maclaine first saw light in ... and passed his early years under the eye of h... ... from whom he imbibed those Principles of Rel... ... according to his own account, persisted in obtr... ...

JAMES MACLAINE.

selves upon him throughout his life. Of the evil effects of evil surroundings upon the youthful mind we have all been warned—less attention has been bestowed upon that tendency to violent revolt which is sometimes fostered by the precepts of the pious. When the cynic comes to multiply instances of this phenomenon Mr. James Maclaine must not be forgotten; meantime take this from the philosophy of Yuba Bill, " Ef that's the man, I've heerd he was the son of some big preacher in the States. . . . They're the wust kind to kick when they once get a foot over the traces. For stiddy, comf'ble kempany, give me the son of a man that was hanged ! "

Besides imparting to him religious instruction, Mr. Maclaine, who intended his son for a mercantile career, also "grounded him in Latin, writing, and accompts "—a system of education to which the ungrateful youth was afterwards rather inclined to attribute his many errors and even his untimely end. A scheme for the advancement of his son, which was being discussed between Mr. Maclaine on the one side and a Scottish merchant in Rotterdam on the other, was put an end to by the death of the minister, and, his mother having died some years previously, James was left an orphan at the age of eighteen. His brother, already established as English chaplain at the Hague, appears to have been absent from home at the time of his father's death, for James immediately took possession of all their little inheritance and applied it to his own purposes. His contempt for learning he displayed by selling his father's books, and his vanity by the purchase of a gay coat and a gelding. Thus furnished he began his career as a squire of dames, and for the next twelve months was constant in his attendance upon the daughters of the neighbouring farmers at all the fairs for ten miles round. This occupation Mr. Maclaine doubtless found more pleasant than profitable, and so the idea of establishing his fortunes by a rich marriage—an idea to which he clung throughout his short life—naturally occurred to him. Naturally, because, as one of his early biographers says, " He never could put it out of his head that the ladies, who are extreme good judges—at least of the natural parts—could look upon his charming person with indifference."

With these natural advantages and some assistance from a cheap tailor he set out for Dublin in pursuit of his design, but whether it was that the ladies of that city were not such " extreme good judges " as he supposed, or he was lost in a superfluity of handsome men, Mr. Maclaine's hopes were not realised. He advanced no further in his attempts upon the heiresses than to an acquaintance with their lacqueys, and having in a few months spent all his substance he was forced to sell his tawdry finery and to set out on foot for Monaghan. His relatives, who had been deaf to his requests for assistance while he was at Dublin, either received him coldly or refused to see him, and they who had been the companions of his former riots made him " the may-game of the town." His credit was gone, and only his sister remained faithful to him and assisted him with her pocket-money. In these straits he took service with a Mr. Howard, —to supply the place of a livery servant who had just then died—and accompanied his master to England. His insolence procured his dismissal from this situation, and once more he set his face towards Monaghan, where he heard his sister was on the point of being married to a man of wealth. He went ostensibly to lay before his relatives a plan of emigration to the West Indies, which only awaited their approval and support, but though this was an enterprise which they would no doubt have gladly sanctioned, it was not, he discovered, one in which they felt inclined to embark any capital. In addition to this disappointment, the gentleman who was engaged to his sister felt compelled to decline the honour of an alliance with him and broke off the match. Once again Mr. Maclaine was involved in difficulties, and however much his pride must have rebelled, his necessities again consented to service, and he became butler to a gentleman in the neighbourhood of Cork. In this situation he took such excessive care of his master's property that he was unable to distinguish it from his own, and was in consequence reduced to wander about the country, saved only from starvation by remittances from his brother at the Hague.

About this time it was proposed to Mr. Maclaine that he should take service in the French army, but here the Principles of Religion made their inconvenient appearance, and he found that his conscience would not allow him to ally himself with the professors of another faith. Upon which his biographer remarks with some simplicity, and probably more truth—"I am afraid, at least it would appear by his future conduct, that he must have had some other motive to decline that service than scruples of conscience." To the English army, however, there were no such objections to be made, and by the generous assistance of the master whom he had robbed he was put ·in the way to join Lord Albemarle's troop of Horse Guards ; his passage to London was paid, but upon his arrival he appears to have found the attractions of the metropolis too powerful, and Lord Albemarle, who was then in Flanders, never had the honour of numbering Mr. Maclaine among his troopers. Cast once more upon his own resources, he essayed the *rôle* wherein Mr. Thomas Jones runs so great a risk of forfeiting our esteem. A countrywoman of his, a lady whose eccentricities do not appear to have been sufficiently pronounced to have preserved her name, cast favourable glances upon him, and under her auspices he was for some time enabled to make a flaming figure at all places of public resort. At last, however, it was manifested to him that the part he played was surrounded by dangers as well as difficulties, for one day when he was engaged in expressing his sense of his obligations to his inamorata, he was interrupted by the unexpected entrance of a " noble peer," to whom he was an entirely unauthorised under-study. The peer made his acknowledgments by bestowing a sound thrashing upon Mr. Maclaine and offering to run him through the body—attentions which the latter, though he was quite as strong and as well armed as his assailant, received without any active objection. No man had greater natural courage than himself, so Mr. Maclaine said, if only the cause were good : unfortunately for his reputation it generally happened that when an occasion arose for its display, it was not such as a conscience imbued with the Principles of Religion could well approve.

As a result of this incident the lady was reduced to pursue
her calling in a humbler sphere and Mr. Maclaine suffered a
temporary eclipse.   From his retirement he was drawn by
another countrywoman of his, a lady of quality, from whom
he again accepted the position of a petticoat pensioner. Here
he seems to have been as much impressed by the difficulties
of the situation as he had lately been by its dangers, and
he quickly came to the conclusion that the comparative
freedom of a matrimonial connection with the daughter of his
patroness was much to be preferred to the irksome drudgery
of his present service.   Unfortunately he was betrayed by
the younger lady's waiting-woman, whom he had engaged to
assist him in the prosecution of his design, and once more
his occupation was gone.   His confidence in the fair sex
was not, however, altogether misplaced, for at this juncture
some ladies of his acquaintance came to his assistance and
provided him with means to emigrate to Jamaica—a project
with which he once more flattered the hopes of his relatives.
Once possessed of the money, however, his thoughts turned
in other directions, and having redeemed the fine clothes,
which his necessities had obliged him to pawn, he put on
with them a fresh resolution, and forgetting Jamaica betook
himself to a masquerade instead.   Here the gaming-table
quickly robbed him of what remained of these friendly contributions, but Fortune, faithful to the old adage, recompensed
him with the affections of a Miss MacGlegno, the daughter
of a respectable innkeeper and horse-dealer.   The charms
of this lady, or the more substantial attractions of five
hundred pounds, her portion, so prevailed upon Mr. Maclaine
that he married her and settled down to the commonplace
existence of a grocer in Welbeck Street, Cavendish Square.
Here he earned the reputation of being both industrious and
obliging, and but for a certain extravagance in dress would
hardly have invited the attention of his neighbours.

At the end of three years his wife died, and her loss proved
to Mr. Maclaine a calamity far greater than he could possibly
have imagined.   She had been attended during her last
illness by one Plunkett, an Irish apothecary, and though it
is suggested that she had not been killed by any excessive

kindness on the part of her husband, this worthy took upon himself the task of lightening the affliction of the widower. Addressing Mr. Maclaine familiarly as " Honey," he said, " though he had lost a good wife, yet, as she was gone, it was to no purpose to grieve much about the matter, since it might in the end turn out the most lucky incident of his life, for if he would allow him to go snips with him in the fortune, he would help him to a woman worth at least £10,000 in possession."

This proposition at once commended itself to Mr. Maclaine; it had been an early dream of his, and his faith in his own merits was always sufficient to keep such a project well within the limits of the practical. He sold up his stock in Welbeck Street (he afterwards explained this action by saying that he " found a decay in trade, arising from an unavoidable trust reposed in servants "), he consigned the child his wife had left him to the care of his mother-in-law, and took lodgings for himself in the neighbourhood of Soho Square, whence he, who a few weeks before " was not ashamed to carry a halfpenny-worth of sand or small-coal to his customers," emerged in all the glory of laced clothes, hat, and feather. Taking upon him the title of a peer, Mr. Maclaine, with Plunkett in attendance as his servant, set out upon his quest which led him eventually to the Wells; there, during an altercation in the public room, my Lord was recognised by a half-pay officer who had known him as a footman, and ignominiously kicked out of the company. Returning to London with but five guineas in his possession, Mr. Maclaine yet once more bethought him of Jamaica, and having been fortunate enough to meet with a sympathetic fellow-countryman upon 'Change, he was by his efforts put in possession of a sum of sixty guineas to fit himself out for the voyage. But it was not to be. Mr. Maclaine was not destined to leave his country for his country's good—at least not by way of Jamaica. He went to a masquerade to take one last farewell of the gaieties of London; he tempted Fortune, and though she smiled upon him at his entrance, she ended by entirely averting her countenance, and he left the place without a guinea in his pocket. In these straits the Spirit of Evil appeared in the guise of Mr. William Plunkett, who, upon hearing of Mr. Maclaine's desperate situation, delivered himself of the opinion that brave men had a right to live and not want the conveniences of life while dull, plodding, busy knaves carried cash in their pockets—upon such they must draw to supply their wants. Although this method of ministering to one's necessities was, according to Mr. Plunkett, the prerogative of the brave, he ended somewhat illogically by declaring that scarce any courage was needed for putting it into execution. Mr. Maclaine listened to the voice of the tempter, and failing upon this occasion to hear anything in reply from the Principles of Religion, he decided to commence highwayman. Two horses were hired, while the necessary pistols seem to have been directly provided by Mr. Plunkett, from which circumstance it has been surmised that this was not his first entrance upon this profession : possibly it was thought that he, being an Irish apothecary, was already sufficiently well armed with weapons of offence for all legitimate occasions.

On the evening following the taking of their resolution the companions met upon Hounslow Heath, intending to lie in wait for people going to and from Smithfield.

Their first victim was a grazier, whom they robbed of about seventy pounds. In this, and indeed in all their subsequent transactions, Mr. Maclaine was very far from displaying that light-hearted recklessness usually associated with gentlemen of his profession. He was, as a rule, content to view the proceedings from a distance, or at most to hold the horses' heads, while his companion took the risk of a bullet from any " dull, busy, plodding knave," who might object to hand over what he had about him. Mr. Maclaine has left us his own explanation of his diffidence, which is indeed fortunate, for were it not offensive to our reason to suppose that a gentleman would boast of that which he did not possess, we might almost have been inclined to suspect that he was an arrant coward. Nor did Mr. Maclaine easily recover his equanimity : upon this first occasion he was overwhelmed with apprehensions, and refused for some days to stir out of the room which he and

Plunkett had engaged at an inn some ten miles from the scene of their exploit. Nothing would satisfy him but to retire for a week or two into the country; and with this desire Mr. Plunkett appeared to comply. Accordingly they set out in the direction of St. Albans, but they had not proceeded more than three miles upon their way when the ex-apothecary informed his companion that it was not retirement he was seeking in the country, but more favourable opportunities for the exercise of the profession they had adopted. It was only with the greatest reluctance that Mr. Maclaine promised his co-operation, and when a stage-coach immediately came in sight, he was most urgent to be allowed to withdraw. But Mr. Plunkett reproving his want of confidence, he at length agreed to stand to his promise, saying (which was scarcely complimentary to his friend), " Needs must when the devil drives ; I am over shoes and must over boots." From the passengers in the coach they obtained two gold watches and about twenty pounds in money, with which they returned to London, after having lurked for several days in the neighbourhood of Richmond and Hampton Court.

Mr. Maclaine's face was now steadfastly set towards Jamaica, but he was so truly unfortunate in timing his arrival in London that he found that the ship, whose passengers he might probably have insured against any risk of drowning, had sailed two days before. Henceforth he appears to have resigned himself to his fate, and to have finally adopted the profession which he may be said hitherto to have followed only *en amateur*. He took up his residence at the house of one Dunn, in St. James's Street, opposite the Old Bagnio, in order that he might make himself acquainted with the movements of the gentlemen who frequented that establishment, and take occasion to follow them when they set out. Mr. Plunkett lodged in Jermyn Street, and the faces of the confederates were as well known, says Horace Walpole, as those of any gentlemen in the neighbourhood. For some time they confined their operations to the environs of London and reaped a rich harvest ; but it might be said of them, as of other gentlemen of similar pursuits, that what they collected with spoons they dissipated with shovels. Mr. Plunkett, like Captain Cottle, "was all for love, and a little for the bottle," while Mr. Maclaine, *bene natus* as he was, had a proper desire to appear *bene vestitus*, and endeavoured to find distraction in the society of "young people of figure and fortune." But the latter's "sickly conscience" allowed him no repose ; he was frequently observed to be under extreme agitation of mind, "even to the rolling about his room in great agony," and the ladies and gentlemen of his acquaintance were moved to inquire whether such conduct did not betoken some embarrassment of his affairs.

Besides his residence in St. James's Street, Mr. Maclaine found it convenient to have another place of resort, a country lodging at Chelsea. Here he appointed to repay a sum of twenty pounds which he had borrowed from a confiding citizen's wife with whom he had an intrigue—an indulgence in honesty which he was the better able to afford as he had arranged, without the lady's knowledge, that his friend Mr. Plunkett should meet her on her return to London. This was not the only trick Mr. Maclaine played upon those who had some reason to expect better treatment at his hands, for having, in company with Mr. Plunkett, taken to the Chester road, he robbed among others an intimate acquaintance by whom he had but two days before been most hospitably entertained in London. Immediately upon their return from this expedition the confederates learned that an officer of the East India Company's service was upon the point of setting out for Greenwich with a large sum of money in his possession. They succeeded in waylaying and robbing him, but certain circumstances connected with this exploit filled Mr. Maclaine with more than usual apprehension, and he judged it advisable to prescribe change of air both for himself and his companion. Accordingly, having previously divided their booty, early in the year 1749 they set out—Mr. Maclaine to visit his brother at the Hague, and Mr. Plunkett to confer a similar favour upon his own and his friend's relatives in Ireland. The chaplain, who had hitherto been accustomed only to his brother's claims upon his charity, expressed some surprise at his altered circumstances, but James explained that he had received a fortune with his late wife, and, in addition, her father had been good enough to leave him a considerable legacy. Mr. James Maclaine made himself extremely popular among the good people of the Hague by the lavish manner in which he entertained them, and if watches and other trifles were missed by his guests, it was only by the light of later information that they were able to date the disappearance of their property from their acceptance of his hospitality.

Mr. Maclaine appears to have left England before his friend, for after his departure a letter arrived for him from his sister, Anne Jane—"a very sensible and affectionate one," writes Mr. Plunkett, "but nothing in it that you may not hear soon enough at our meeting." For a time all went well with Mr. Plunkett; he spent several days, much to his satisfaction, in Chester and Liverpool, "these being places of spirit where they have assemblies," &c. In Ireland, possibly because there was nothing much to steal, he did not fare so well, and his letters to "Dear Jemmy" are, except in one particular, anything but reassuring. He had the misfortune to fall from his horse and dislocate his shoulder—an injury, which, aggravated by a tumble in getting over a stile, "very much obstructed his happiness"; the said horse went blind, he was unable to dispose of the watches he carried with him, he ran into debt, and altogether, as he expressed it with more force than elegance, he was "fretting his guts to fiddlestrings." He begged his friend to desist from an amour in which he was engaged, which could but result in the loss of time and money on his part and of reputation on the part of the lady, and to give his serious attention to the establishment of their fortunes by means of a wealthy marriage.

This brings one to the only bright spot in Mr. Plunkett's correspondence. Before leaving England he had "espyed a doe of £40,000 enclosed in a park:" true, she was "in some small measure despicable in person," and there was "a stern old fellow at the gate," but he thought "if a gentleman of figure and fortune were accidentally to meet her at church and would promise to bring her to her beloved London, he might have a chance of the prize." In the meantime he was anxiously awaiting a remittance which would enable him to rejoin his friend in England. Mr. Maclaine, either wearied of the Hague or trusting to the fame of his last exploit in this country having blown over, had already returned, and having met with some success at the gaming-tables, was able to supply his confederate with the necessary funds, and they were once more united and at liberty to start upon their matrimonial enterprise.

Having provided themselves with two horses and an appropriate wardrobe, they set out, Mr. Maclaine in quality of a peer—of his own creation—and his companion as his servant. They halted at an inn in the next village to that in which resided "the deer that they should strike." The father of the lady whom Mr. Maclaine intended to honour with his attentions happened to be lord of the manor, and the peer, having borrowed a gun, requested of him permission to shoot, and laid the spoils of the chase, in the shape of two woodcocks, at his feet. He also sought opportunity to make his acquaintance by a diligent attendance at the parish church, and one Sunday ventured to address him, but the "stern old fellow" was true to Mr. Plunkett's description of him, and received his advances in anything but a conciliatory mood. Meanwhile Mr. Plunkett on his side had not been idle; he had gradually contrived to worm himself into the confidence of the old gentleman's butler and the maids of the house, and from one of the latter he learned to his dismay that the father had discovered Mr. Maclaine's business in that neighbourhood and that he was no lord; he had even gone so far as to call him a sharping scoundrel and to threaten him with the stocks. This intelligence determined Mr. Maclaine to raise the siege, and so, after three months thus wasted, the confederates returned to London to resume their old occupation.

In the beginning of November, 1749, Mr. Maclaine performed his most famous exploit. In company with Mr. Plunkett he stopped and robbed Horace Walpole in Hyde

Park, at about ten o'clock, as he was returning from Holland House. Upon this occasion he discharged the only shot which he is recorded to have fired during the whole of his career as a Gentleman Highwayman; his pistol, owing no doubt to the agitation occasioned by his conscience, went off by accident, the ball passed through the top of the coach, and Walpole's face was scorched by the explosion. Mr. Maclaine afterwards protested that if his unlucky shot had taken effect nothing would have prevented him from using his remaining pistol upon himself—a declaration which moved Walpole to ask if, in a certain contingency, he could well do less than promise to be hanged. Upon his return to his lodgings the ingenuous Mr. Maclaine wrote two letters to his victim, apologising for having been compelled by disappointment in a matrimonial scheme to resort to this method of raising supplies, and offering him a chance of redeeming any trifles which he might happen to particularly value. To this end he appointed a meeting at Tyburn at twelve o'clock at night; Mr. Plunkett attended on behalf of the confederates, but Walpole, satisfied probably with one escape, failed to put in his appearance.

Details of the exploits of these gentlemen during the early months of 1750 are lacking, but one may safely assume that they were not idle. The end, however, was at hand. Upon the 26th of June they set out upon the road to Brentford, and between that place and Staines they stopped the Salisbury coach. Mr. Maclaine, though he was the instigator of this particular expedition, lagged behind as usual until the eloquent voice of his conscience was drowned by the reproofs of Mr. Plunkett. Once on the spot, and convinced that there was no chance of meeting with any resistance, he was loud in his threats as to what would most certainly befall the passengers if they presumed to conceal any of their property. There were five gentlemen and a lady travelling by the coach, whom the confederates obliged to dismount and deliver up all that they had, and then, having, with the assistance of the driver, put up before them on their horses two cloak-bags which were contained in the boot, they allowed their victims to continue their journey.

On the same morning they encountered and stopped Lord
Eglinton in the neighbourhood of Hounslow.   Mr. Maclaine
stood in front of the horses, taking care to shelter himself
behind the post-boy, while Mr. Plunkett, thrusting a pistol
through the glass at the back of the chaise, threatened to
blow his lordship's brains through his face if he did not
immediately throw to the ground a double-barrelled blunderbuss with which he was armed.   Lord Eglinton thought it
prudent to comply, and was robbed of his portmanteau and
forty guineas.

Among the passengers by the Salisbury coach was one
Mr. Josiah Higden, who immediately took steps to adver-
tise his loss and describe his property in the public papers.
Now either Mr. Maclaine had no time to read the papers,
or he was destined to be a more than ordinarily striking
example of the truth of the saying, " *Quem Deus vult
perdere, prius dementat,*" for on the 19th of July he went to
the shop of a Mr. Loader in Monmouth Street, and leaving
his address with him requested him to call and negotiate
for the purchase of some wearing apparel.

Mr. Loader came and took away with him certain articles
which Mr. Maclaine offered for sale, but when he reached
home he was struck by the similarity which the gold lace he
had just bought, bore to some which he had himself sold to
Mr. Josiah Higden.   His suspicions moved him to send for
that gentleman ; he came, and there followed a warrant for
the apprehension of Mr. Maclaine.   On the 27th of July the
constable succeeded in finding Mr. Maclaine at home : he
was taken before Mr. Lediard at his house in New Palace
Yard, and by him committed to the Gatehouse.   The
contents of Mr. Maclaine's lodgings were eloquent of his
profession and character.   The officers discovered there
clothes and other property, afterwards identified as
belonging to Mr. Higden and his fellow-passengers by the
Salisbury coach, and to Lord Eglinton, the latter's redoubtable double-barrelled blunderbuss, twenty-three purses
of various descriptions, besides pistols and a great many
rich suits which were allowed to be part of Mr. Maclaine's
own stock-in-trade—the whole in charge of a lady who
appears to have been better known than respected.

JAMES MACLAINE AT THE BAR.

... rang with talk of Mr. Macl...
... his ... dsome person, and Mr. ...
... appearance of a theatre ...
... m of the Gentleman His...
... upon a table were the ...
... Mr. Maclane's lodging...
... Lord Mountfort, Lord ...
... ons of distinction." ...
... ed the proceedings wi...
... our of the Gentleman H... was ...
... however edifying as an exhibition ...
... seful conscience, w... ...
... nt which is expected in a gentleman ...
... which is supposed to obtain ...
... d wept, offered to betray his friend Mr. ...
... own life, and when his offer was ...
... ofession (which he later on attempted ...
... of the crime with which he was ...
... robberies in which he had been ... And ...
... mination he was committed to take his tri...
... old Bailey, and was again removed to the Gatehouse ...
... ge of a sergeant's guard, for so great ...
was ... there might be some ...
... ladies who had accompanied him ...
... ring the hearing conveyed to him more ...
... their sympathy in the shape of a purse ...
... ace of his trial he was daily visited ...
... of fashion who contributed liberally to ...
... mine among his comforters were La...
... sham, afterwards Countess of Harrington, ...
... Whether these ladies had any belief in his ...
... er were of opinion that the fact ...
... was an additional attraction ...
... sible to say, but they earned for themselves ...
... of "Polly" and "Lucy" from Horace Walpole, wh...
... Lady Caroline if their *protégé* did not say wit...
... "Heath ...

"... I stand like the Turk, with his ...

JAMES MACLAINE AT THE BAR.

All London rang with talk of Mr. Maclaine, his exploits and his handsome person, and Mr. Lediard's house presented the appearance of a theatre upon the occasion of the examination of the Gentleman Highwayman before him.

Arranged upon a table were the various articles that had been found at Mr. Maclaine's lodgings, and the Earl of Chesterfield, Lord Mountford, Lord Duncannon, and many other "persons of distinction," including a number of ladies, watched the proceedings with breathless interest. The behaviour of the Gentleman Highwayman upon this occasion, however edifying as an exhibition of the working of a remorseful conscience, was scarcely consistent with the self-restraint which is expected in a gentleman, or even that honour which is supposed to obtain among thieves. He whined and wept, offered to betray his friend Mr. Plunkett to save his own life, and when his offer was refused made a full confession (which he later on attempted to disclaim) not only of the crime with which he was charged, but of all the other robberies in which he had been engaged. At the end of his examination he was committed to take his trial at the Old Bailey, and was again removed to the Gatehouse in charge of a sergeant's guard, for so great was his popularity it was feared there might be some attempt at a rescue. The ladies who had accompanied him with their tears during the hearing conveyed to him more substantial proof of their sympathy in the shape of a purse of gold, and up to the time of his trial he was daily visited by a crowd of persons of fashion who contributed liberally to his support. Prominent among his comforters were Lady Caroline Petersham, afterwards Countess of Harrington, and Miss Ashe. Whether these ladies had any belief in his innocence, or were of opinion that the fact that he was a highwayman was an additional attraction in his personality, it is impossible to say, but they earned for themselves the names of "Polly" and "Lucy" from Horace Walpole, who asked Lady Caroline if their *protégé* did not sing with Captain Macheath :—

"Thus I stand like the Turk, with his doxies around."

This question led to the publication of a print (one of many in which Mr. Maclaine was the principal figure) in which the ladies were represented supporting the " lovely thief " on either side. Lord Mountford too, with half the members of White's, prompted no doubt by curiosity as to one who had so lately been their neighbour, visited Mr. Maclaine in the Gatehouse. He was removed from this place of confinement to Newgate on the 7th of September, and on the 13th at twelve o'clock he was put upon his trial. He had the assistance of counsel, but his defence, such as it was, was read by himself. Mr. Loader proved the sale of the clothes, which Mr. Higden identified as his property, though he was unable to swear to the persons who had robbed him. Mr. Maclaine's account of the manner in which he became possessed of the said clothes was ingenious. It all arose from the generous manner in which he had behaved to one Mr. Plunkett, to whom, while he was engaged in the " grocery way," he had advanced sums amounting in all to £100. Pressed to discharge his obligation, Mr. Plunkett, who had induced him " to believe that he had travelled abroad, and was possessed of clothes and other things suitable thereto," prevailed upon him to accept payment partly in goods and partly in money. Among the goods were included these very clothes which Mr. Maclaine confessed that he did sell, " very unfortunately, as it now appears, little thinking they were come by in the manner Mr. Higden hath been pleased to express." The contracting of this debt and the manner of payment being matters of a private nature, it was hardly to be expected that he should be able to produce witnesses to the truth of his story. Unfortunately there remained his rash confession, and Mr. Maclaine's manner of dealing with this was hardly likely to appeal to the most sympathetic of juries, though in concluding his address he claimed to have accounted for it. It was very true, he said, that when he was first apprehended the " surprise confounded him, and gave him a most extraordinary shock : it caused a delirium and confusion in his brain which rendered him incapable of being himself, or knowing what he said or did :

he talked of robberies as another man would do in talking of stories; but after his friends had visited him in the Gate-house, and had given him some new spirits, and when he came to be re-examined before Justice Lediard, and was asked if he could make any discovery of the robbery, he then alleged that he had recovered his surprise, that what he had talked of before concerning robberies was false and wrong, and was entirely owing to a confused head and brain." Nine gentlemen—one " — Barlowe, Esq." is the only person named—were called to speak to the good cha-racter of the prisoner, but in spite of their evidence the jury found him guilty without leaving the box, and by half-past one it was all over. From this point the interest in Mr. Maclaine rather increased. On the Sunday following his conviction three thousand people are said to have visited him in Newgate, and he twice fainted owing to the heat of his cell. On the 20th of September he was brought up, with the other prisoners convicted at the sessions, to receive sentence; he came provided with an appeal for mercy, which had been written for him by one of his friends, but after repeating the first few words of it, he stopped—there was a profound silence for three or four minutes, broken at last by the cry, " My Lord, I can go no further I " and Mr. Maclaine received sentence of death.

> " But soon his rhetorick forsook him,
>   When he the solemn hall had seen,
>   A sudden fit of ague shook him,
>   He stood as mute as poor Macleane."

So writes Gray in his " Long Story," but though the Gentleman Highwayman could say so little for himself, petitions in his favour were started on all sides. One was forwarded to the King, who was then in Hanover, and was by him referred to the Lords of the Regency, and another was presented to the Duke of Bedford. Archibald Maclaine, who had written more than one letter expressive of his deep concern at his brother's disgrace, was reported to have arrived in London to intercede on his behalf; this does not appear to have been the fact, though no doubt he exercised, according to his promise, such influence as he possessed to preserve his life. But the Government was determined not to encourage Gentlemen Highwaymen, and the following extract from *The General Advertiser*, of September 24, 1750, is a very good indication of the attitude of the Press : " We hear that great interest is making for all the 16 male-factors condemned the last sessions at the Old Bailey. For some, because they are young, and for others because they are old : for some because they have good Friends, and for others because they are friendless: for some because they are hand-some, and the Objects of liking, and for others because they are so ugly that they are the objects of compassion : for some because they have kept good company and are well known, and for others because they were never heard of before. At the same time we are informed that the robberies committed within a week last past in and about this Town do at the highest computation amount to scarce 200."

With the remainder of Mr. Maclaine's career it is some-what difficult to deal. Professing himself a Presbyterian, he sent the day after his conviction for Dr. Allen, a minister of that persuasion, who attended him up to the night before his execution. Dr. Allen published the usual edifying account of the condemned man's behaviour, and seems to have been impressed with the sincerity of his repentance, so perhaps it is hardly for us at this date to cast any doubts upon it. His love of pleasure and of a gay appearance, Mr. Maclaine said, had undone him. He lamented that he had not been brought up to some employment which would have made industry necessary, instead of writing and accompts which as a genteeler business was chosen for him. "I have often thought," he continued, " when in my necessity and innocence that had I had a mechanic Trade in my hands that would have employed my *whole time*, altho' I could have earned by it but ten shillings a week, I had been an happy man." These and similar reflections he delivered in such a manner as to induce Dr. Allen to testify that " he was really a man of good natural sense, and had an handsome elocution." Early on the morning of the fatal day,

Wednesday, October 3rd, Mr. Maclaine wrote his last letter to the friend to whom he had entrusted the carrying out of his wishes with respect to the few trifling articles that remained to him. Two books, an inkhorn, and a seal he desired should be carried with his blessing to his good old landlady in Chelsea; a Bible, a leaf having been first torn out, was to be given to some member of Dr. Allen's family, and his sleeve-buttons to " poor N. B., with my last blessing to her "; his shoe-buckles his mother-in-law had begged for his child—he thought it unnecessary, but was willing to indulge her in it. He desired that a letter should be written to his sister, and that his " Life " should be done as soon as possible " in a modest, penitent manner," and that his child should share in the profits of it, if there were any. Then, with a prayer that his friend would take all necessary precautions to prevent his body from becoming a prey to the surgeons, Mr. Maclaine concluded his letter " within eleven hours of eternity."

It was expected that he would be allowed, in consideration of his quality, to take his last journey in a coach, but the authorities, as if to disappoint this very expectation, at the end of September issued an order that for the future criminals should not be allowed to go in coaches to Tyburn. Accordingly Mr. Maclaine made one in a party of three who occupied the last cart in the melancholy procession from Newgate, his immediate companions being William Smith (also the son of an Irish clergyman) convicted of forgery, and one Sanders, who had stolen a metal watch. Twelve criminals in all suffered upon this occasion, which was also signalised by the reappearance of Mr. John Thrift, the hangman, who, owing to his having unofficially put an end to the existence of one of his Majesty's subjects, had for some time past been living in seclusion. A greater concourse of people had never been seen at Tyburn, but if they came expecting any startling demonstration on the part of Mr. Maclaine they must have been disappointed, for he only spoke to pardon the constable who had arrested him, and to utter a prayer for the forgiveness of his enemies, of whom he was himself the chief, if not the only one. His body, having been first taken to the house of one Harrison, an undertaker in Clare Market, is said to have been buried at Uxbridge. Thus, in the twenty-sixth year of his age, died Mr. James Maclaine, who without, as far as one can see, a single quality which could appeal even to the most perverted imagination, has exceeded in interest all malefactors of his class. The Ordinary of Newgate who attended him at the place of execution puts the finishing touch to the task of stripping him of any attraction he might be supposed to possess. He was, says the Ordinary, "in person of the middle size, well-limbed, and a sandy complexion, a broad open countenance pitted with the small-pox, but though he was called the Gentleman Highwayman, and in his dress and equipage very much affected the fine gentleman, yet to a man acquainted with good breeding that can distinguish it from impudence and affectation there was very little in his address or behaviour that could entitle him to that character."

GEORGE ROBERT FITZGERALD.

GEORGE ROBERT ...

"FIGHTING F..."

(174. ...)

... we broad-sides? no ... the ...

What! shall we have ... ? shall w...
King H...y ...

IT would have been stran... ... had ...
Fitzgerald and a Hervey ... ...
... rum citizen—one who... ... ...
turbulent Norman-Irish G... ... ...
belonged to that family con... ... ...
Wortley Montagu remarked, "God made
and Herveys."

A scion of this stock, Georg... Robert F... ... ...
some time in the year 1748. The place ... ...
...oskfield House, in the fer... vale of ... ... County
Mayo, some two miles to the north of its ass... ... Castlebar. There the family had lived since the time of Cromwell,
having been transplanted thither from Kildare in the dist...
... th Their annals were not eventful. Mr. G... F...
... father of the subject of this memoir, ...
inherited a clear three thousand per annum as ... ...
of the Turlough property; but he very soon ... ...
his resources, and became, by the wretchless...
...cle... living, an object of detestation to ... ...
relatives.

The Lady Mary Fitzgerald, who had bee... ... ...

GEORGE ROBERT FITZGERALD.

GEORGE ROBERT FITZGERALD,

"FIGHTING FITZGERALD."

(1748–1786.)

"Fear we broadsides? no, let the fiend give fire.

· · · · · ·

What! shall we have incision? shall we imbrue?"
King Henry IV., Part II., Act II., Sc. iv.

I T would have been strange indeed had the offspring of a
Fitzgerald and a Hervey been an ordinary, harmless,
humdrum citizen—one whose sire was a descendant of the
turbulent Norman-Irish Geraldines, and whose mother
belonged to that family concerning whom Lady Mary
Wortley Montagu remarked, "God made men, women,
and Herveys."

A scion of this stock, George Robert Fitzgerald, was born
some time in the year 1748. The place of his nativity was
Rockfield House, in the fertile vale of Turlough, County
Mayo, some two miles to the north of its assize town, Castlebar. There the family had lived since the time of Cromwell,
having been transplanted thither from Kildare in the distant
south. Their annals were not eventful. Mr. George Fitzgerald, father of the subject of this memoir, is said to have
inherited a clear three thousand per annum as the produce
of the Turlough property; but he very soon made havoc of
his resources, and became, by the wretchlessness of his
unclean living, an object of detestation to his wife's noble
relatives.

The Lady Mary Fitzgerald, who had been maid of honour

to the Princess Amelia, was, one may well believe, "eccentric"; still, it was scarcely evidence of a defect of character that she was incapable of enduring throughout her life the ill-usage of her husband. In consequence of this, she, taking her elder son George with her, returned to her own family, and was immediately replaced in the Fitzgerald household by a Miss Norris, whose machinations had much to do with the dissensions which arose subsequently in that establishment. A younger son, Charles Lionel, was left behind with his father and this lady—these three forming a triple alliance against George Robert, the heir to the Turlough estates.

That individual was in due course sent to Eton, where he picked up a fair collection of classical crumbs, and thereafter received a commission in the army. He began the recorded exploits of his life in his quarters at Galway. One day, having vaulted over the counter and snatched a kiss from a milliner of gentle blood, he was challenged to his first duel, being then sixteen, by the keeper of a neighbouring shop. This plebeian the head of the Geraldines (for so he considered himself) disdained, but must needs fight with a Mr. French, who had brought the challenge. The parties retired to a lonely public-house and locked themselves into the parlour, but were interrupted before any harm had been done. Fitzgerald's next affair, though still showing signs of crudeness, marks a distinct advance in depravity. The young captain having provoked continuously and beyond endurance one of his subalterns, a quiet and very patient man named Thompson, succeeded at length in being called out by him. The meeting took place at five in the morning, when Thompson again tried to accommodate matters, and behaved in every respect like a brave man—but to no purpose. At the second discharge Fitzgerald was struck by a ball on the forehead, and was found by the neighbours stretched on the ground, lamented over by his unwilling antagonist, whom on coming to his senses Fitzgerald had the grace to exculpate by acknowledging the gross manner in which he had insulted him. The operation of trepanning, which saved the young duellist's life, was, to the patient's great comfort, performed without damage to his toupee. Mr. Fitzgerald senior showed his joy at the safety of his yet loved son by a tolerably determined attempt to run through the body a relative who had come to condole with him on his probable loss. This skull-wound may afford a plausible explanation of George Robert's subsequent career, although, as has been remarked, "the descendant of a Hervey needed not this physical aggravation."

It would appear that the young captain's appetite for fighting was temporarily quelled, for soon after he let slip a very promising chance of a duel. A certain Mr. Dillon, a great talker, having been baulked by him of the lion's share of the evening's conversation, addressed to him the following very plain speech: " I lay down my watch on the table, and if you attempt to say a word for one hour, I will make it a personal matter unto you; you understand me, young sir!" To the surprise of all present Fitzgerald waited until the hour was over, and then began to talk again without showing any sign of having been offended.

Fitzgerald, still in his teens, next went up to Dublin, where he was received into the best society, less, perhaps, on account of his fighting reputation than because of his being a nephew of the Bishop of Derry. The ladies thought him a most fascinating creature, and especially Miss Conolly, sister of the Right Hon. Thomas, then known in Ireland as "the Great Commoner." Though this personage opposed a marriage, Fitzgerald continued to make love fiercely, and ended by eloping with the lady. Her family were soon appeased, and her husband got both a fortune and a most tender and attached wife, who was able while she lived to keep him, to some extent at any rate, out of mischief. The newly-married pair went almost immediately on the Continent. They were received at the French Court, where our Hibernian made a great sensation by his splendid extravagance and audacious feats. The peaceful King Louis XVI. is said to have turned his face from " this fine, fighting, frolicsome Irishman "; but his brother, the Comte d'Artois, appears to have found it to his interest to do otherwise, and won three thousand louis from him at play. When, however, the latter, still owing him the money, proceeded to bet against his hand at picquet, the prince demanded payment, and being refused, literally kicked the defaulter from Court. To wipe out this disgrace Fitzgerald appeared some time after at the royal stag-hunt at Fontainebleau, where, amidst the shrieks of the ladies and the astonishment of the gentlemen, he leapt after the stag over a wall into the Seine, and brought it to bay on the opposite bank. At Paris he met Rowan, the future United Irishman, and tried, according to this person, to swindle him out of a horse. Soon after, nevertheless, Rowan acted as second to Fighting Fitzgerald in a duel which took place near Lille, between Fitzgerald and a certain Major Baggs. Rowan's account of the affair is curious. At the outset, each being suspected by the other of being *plastroné* (that is, of wearing mail underneath his clothes), had to submit to an examination, after which the duel proceeded. "Major Baggs sank on his quarters, something like the Scottish lion ; Fitzgerald stood as one who had made a lounge in fencing. They fired together, and were in the act of levelling their second pistols, when Major Baggs sank on his side, saying, 'Sir, I am wounded.' 'But you are not dead,' replied Fitzgerald, and at the same moment discharged his second pistol at his fallen enemy. Baggs immediately started on his legs, and advanced on Fitzgerald, who, throwing his pistol at him, quitted his station, and kept a zigzag course across the field, Baggs following him. I saw the flash of the major's second pistol," continues Rowan, "and at the same moment Fitzgerald lay stretched on the ground." The Irishman rose and wanted to begin again, but at this point Baggs was taken to his carriage. Rowan asked his principal how he came to discharge his second pistol, to which he replied somewhat tamely, "I should not have done so at any man but Baggs." What was the nature of Fitzgerald's duelling ethics we shall see later, both from his theory and in his practice. Sir Jonah Barrington was certainly mistaken in fancying him "too genteel to kill any man except with the broad-sword."

Fitzgerald was disabled for a time after this, and when he recovered went to London,[1] where his name soon became notorious in consequence of his general behaviour—his extravagant style of living, his gaming propensities, and, above all, his Hibernian swagger; and particularly on account of his connection with the Vauxhall affray.

This *fracas*, happening "in a period of the year (1773) most barren of consequential events" (Johnsonese for the silly season) helped to enliven the columns of *The Morning Post, The Morning Chronicle,* and other papers of the period.

On Friday night, July 23rd, Mrs. Hartley, an actress, was at Vauxhall in company with her husband (by whom she set little store), and several other gentlemen, one of whom was a clergyman named Bate. A party of Maccaronis, among them Fitzgerald, came up and stared very rudely in her face for some minutes, whereupon the parson took upon himself to resent the insult, and received a challenge from a certain Captain Crofts. Fitzgerald interrupted the arrangements by claiming prior satisfaction for a Captain Miles, described by him as his friend, but who was in reality a hired chairman.

The affair with Crofts having been patched up, "Captain Miles" now provokes Bate to a pugilistic encounter, to which the clergyman, nothing loth, consents. The party then adjourns to a room in a coffee-house, where "after a fair set-to for about twenty minutes," the parson, who was a powerful man, gains a decided victory. A few days later Bate is knocked up in the small hours of the morning at his chambers in Clifford's Inn, by Fitzgerald and a party of hired bravoes, and an unsuccessful attempt is made to entice him into the street, where no doubt he would not have met with very tender usage.

A controversy now began between Bate in *The Morning Post* (of which paper he soon after became editor) and Fitz-

---

[1] How long he stayed in France, and when precisely his first wife, who left a daughter, died, is not to be exactly ascertained from our authorities. One account says she died in France, but in the Walker controversy Fitzgerald writes as though she were still living.

gerald in *The Gazeteer*, with which Timothy Brecknock, in after-years so intimately mixed up in his affairs, was connected. Mr. Bate had much the best of the matter, in spite of the capital which his opponent made from the fact of his being a clergyman and yet willing to fight a duel. "Fighting Fitzgerald" himself refused to atone in any such manner for his own conduct, and kept very carefully out of Bate's way.

From the few important contributions which appeared in the course of the newspaper discussion it may be gathered that while the affair was discreditable to all concerned, Fitzgerald and his associates, the notorious Tom Lyttleton and Captain Crofts (whose courage in another case his colonel was obliged to stimulate by a threat of cashiering), came out by far the worst. Comments on the effeminate appearance of our little Fitz are frequent in *The London Packet*, where he is named "Miss Biddy F——d." In the same paper, however, there is just animadversion on the conduct of the "Rev. Bruiser," with his "newspaper sermons" and "artificially created public." Captain Miles, according to this paper, was to have received twenty guineas and to have been "raised to the military rank of butler" had he been victorious, whereas in the event he only got £10 and was in bed for a fortnight.

The Rev. Henry Bate became soon after this affair curate to James Townley, at Hendon. This exemplary clergyman is said to have been educated at Oxford, but of the degrees of M.A. and LL.D. which he claimed there is no record. He resigned the editorship of *The Morning Post* in 1780, when he started *The Morning Herald*. For a libel on the Duke of Richmond in the former paper he was imprisoned. In 1784 he assumed the name of Dudley. He was subsequently accused of simony. After holding several benefices in Ireland he finally became rector of Willingham, Cambridgeshire, and Prebendary of Ely, and in 1815 was created a baronet. He was a friend of Garrick, and wrote *libretti* for several of Shield's operas. Of him Dr. Johnson said to Boswell, "Sir, I will not allow this man to have merit. No, sir; what he has is rather the contrary: I will indeed allow him courage, and on this account we so far give him credit." He married a sister of Mrs. Hartley.

A curious appendix to the Vauxhall affray is the following from *The London Packet* of August 21, 1773 : " Mrs. Hartley was seen in Richmond Gardens last Sunday with another lady and gentleman, and Mr. Moody the player ; who wittily took and turned the lady about, when any person looked at her, laughing and saying, ' You sha'n't see her ' ; supposing to allude to the stale story of Captain Crofts' looking at the beautiful actress." The opinion that was held in England of Fighting Fitzgerald after the Vauxhall affray may be judged from the fact that when Captain Scarven of the Guards commented unkindly on his conduct and was challenged for so doing, he was placed under arrest by the officers of his regiment in order that he " should not stoop so low as to go out with his antagonist." His Majesty was left " to decide on the propriety of their separate conduct in a military capacity."

The next episode in Fitzgerald's career was a pitiful quarrel he had with a ruined *habitué* of the turf familiarly known as " Daisey Walker." This individual was twitted by his opponent with having been the son of a glazier, but at this time he is described as " Thomas Walker, Esq., Ci-devant Cornet in Burgoyne's Light Dragoons." Before coming of age, he had, on his own admission, run through a large fortune, and had been obliged " to avoid the horrors of impending confinement " by retiring for a while to the Continent. During his absence from England Fitzgerald had been sold for a small sum a note for £3,000 which Daisey had left undischarged, and on the return of the latter payment was requested. As, however, he represented himself as a ruined man, the fighting Hibernian agreed to cancel the note on receiving the sum of £500. The money was paid, and the transaction seemed complete ; but some time after, Fitzgerald, apparently in want of ready money, attempted to raise some by demanding from Walker the balance of £2,500, which he evidently thought that worthy capable of paying. The latter denied the obligation, and meeting Fitzgerald at the Ascot races received the blow provocative

from his riding-whip.   In due course a duel took place.
The Irishman received without injury his adversary's fire; his
own pistol flashed in the pan, but on its being fired the second
time (seemingly an unusual practice, but not uncommon
with Fitzgerald), Walker was wounded in the shoulder, and,
declaring that he could not raise his arm, was borne off the
scene of combat.   Before having his shot Fitzgerald offered
an apology for the blow he had given, and proposed not to
proceed with the matter, provided Walker could give undeniable proof that his finances did not allow of his settling
the bill.   At the same time, to temper generosity with
bravery, he offered to bet one thousand guineas he could kill
his man.   Fitzgerald also wished for a second meeting, but
a paper war in the shape of an appeal to the Jockey Club by
both parties was all that followed.   In this encounter also
the Irishman came off considerably the better.   The facts
in dispute are hardly worth considering, but some examples
of the style of literary warfare indulged in by Fighting
Fitzgerald may be of interest.

In the course of the controversy he quotes the Laws of the
Twelve Tables and Publius Syrus, and writes confidentially
of "the Socratic tenet of trusting one's own Good Genius,"
instructed by which "internal monitor," he declares he
"called Mr. Walker very seriously to account."   Then he
gives the Jockey Club a short discourse on the nature of True
Courage, "upon the great outline of which" Fitzgerald tells
them it has been his constant study to form his character.
He concludes that it consists in *moderation* alone; and he
himself, though confessing that "in the ebullition of youth,
when the passions are indomitable and the judgment not
ripened with full maturity," he had found this theory—"so
easy and beautiful"—almost impossible to carry into
practice, is yet proud to own that he has formed his
character "upon the line of manly, not of brutal courage."

But the brightest gem of the whole collection of this
moral bravo is the scientific exposition he gives of the art of
duelling, which we will venture to present *in extenso*.   Reply-
ing to Daisey's charge of unfair manœuvres during the late
encounter, the hero of eleven past combats writes naïvely:

"Of what benefit is theoretic knowledge if it is not to be carried into practice at the only time it can be of effectual service to us? Accustomed to study arms not superficially but *scientifically*, the moment you levelled your pistol at me, at that very instant I made as outstretched an *élongé* as it was possible for me to make, and by thus throwing myself into a sideway position, I not only presented as little surface of body as could be, but also lost full sixteen inches of my natural height. Besides, by throwing myself into this attitude, and by keeping my eye in a direct level with the muzzle of your pistol, I was enabled to cover both my head and heart from your fire, for the bullet must first have penetrated the palm of my hand before it could have reached the lobes of my brain, and it must have perforated the whole horizontal length of my right arm, which is almost impossible, before it could have made its passage to my heart. This, sir," he triumphantly adds, " is properly understanding the *science* of arms as a Science ; and even when you shall have advanced thus far there are a thousand other fair advantages an Adept hath over a novice, which no mercenary artist either will or can teach you, and which are only to be acquired by intense study and private practice, which, like a masked battery, should never be made known to our adversary but by its sudden, unexpected effect."

This master of the duello also relates how he proved that Walker had been padded in the late meeting, by firing from twelve paces at a thick stick covered with a lined coat, two lined waistcoats, and one double-milled surtout; with the result that the bullet penetrated an inch deep into the stick. " There is nothing like experimental philosophy for a fair proof," he concludes; "it beats your *ipse-dixits* all hollow. You see, sir, how ingeniously I pass away my private hours —I am always hard at study—

'*Nunquam minus solus, quam cum solus.*' "

In whose favour the august arbiters of this important dispute decided we do not gather. One authority tells us that Fitzgerald fought a duel with one of them at Lille.

As, however, this person's name was Scarven we are inclined to the view that both the individual and the quarrel
have already found their true place in this sketch. Be these
things as they may, the exploits of our Hibernian outside
his native isle have been recorded, and it is now necessary
to follow his fortunes in Ireland, whither he betook himself
early in the year of grace 1775.[1] And, as he was now in the
heyday of life with some promise of a career before him, this
opportunity may be taken of seeing what kind of man he
appeared to his contemporaries.

Sir Jonah Barrington says of Fitzgerald : " A more
polished and elegant gentleman was not to be met with ;
his person was very slight and juvenile, his countenance
extremely mild and insinuating." Dr. Richard Martin, a
more hostile critic, gives a somewhat similar description :
" The elegant and gentlemanly appearance of this man as
contrasted with the savage treachery of his actions, was
extremely curious, and without any parallel of which I am
aware." From another source we learn that Mr. Fitzgerald
possessed a fund of legal knowledge and was a very good
orator. When his house at Turlough was looted by the
Castlebar mob, books to the value of over £400 were claimed
in the inventory of damages. The articles of jewellery
which also appear, including a complete set of diamond vest
buttons, a diamond loop and button for a hat, and a hat-band
ornamented with five or six rows of pearls, show that he
did not neglect the adornment of the outer man.

Fitzgerald spent the next four or five years between his
house in Merrion Square, Dublin, and the family estates in
County Mayo. He was ambitious of taking part in public
affairs, and was doubtless encouraged in this ambition by

---

[1] When referring to this controversy, which raised the question of
the private character of Fitzgerald, we must do that gentleman the
justice to remark that although his courage in the field, his honour
on the turf, and his credit on the Royal Exchange might not have
been altogether unimpeachable, yet that his conduct towards the
fair sex, which he claims to have been equally spotless, seems never,
at this time or afterwards, to have been brought up against him.

his brother-in-law, Conolly, and his uncle, the Earl of Bristol and Bishop of Derry.

The last-named personage, who was the last of the martial bishops, lodged at his nephew's house, and made him the handsome present of a thousand pounds in return for his hospitality, during the volunteer convention at Dublin. The prelate rode up to the meeting in semi-warlike attire and attended by a mounted bodyguard of young parsons. In after-years the earl-bishop lived in Italy, and when summoned to his see by the primate and two of his colleagues, vouchsafed for answer the following only :—

" MY LORDS,
   Three huge blue bottle flies sat upon three blown bladders ;
   Blow, bottle flies, blow—burst, blown bladders, burst."

Such were the Herveys.

To return to the nephew. How Fitzgerald spent his time in Dublin history sayeth not. It cannot, however, be considered improbable that he fought many duels there. According to Sir Jonah the year 1777 saw an epidemic of duels in Ireland. One of the first questions asked of the suitor for a young lady's hand was " Did he ever blaze ? " Tipperary and Galway were, he informs us, the ablest schools of the duelling science, the former being " most scientific at the sword," the latter " most practical and prized at the pistol "; but Mayo, be it noted, was held " not amiss at either." This, his native county, George Robert Fitzgerald wished to represent in Parliament. His father had come forward at the vacancy in 1775; and " the Wilkes of Ireland," as he is fondly termed by the author of " The Case," though defeated, ran the Castle candidate very hard. George Robert then determined to enter the lists on his own account, and at the Lent assizes of 1778 commenced his campaign by a state entry into Castlebar. As a volunteer he was all for legislative independence, but, on the other hand, as a narrow Protestant, was against concessions to the Catholics. He began his candidature magnificently: " A string of cars

from the city of Dublin, of an amazing length, preceded the
company several days, loaded with the choicest articles the
metropolis could furnish necessary for the occasion—to them
succeeded in proper order cooks and confectioners of different
nations, sexes, and colours; sempstresses, taylors, mantua
makers, milliners, perfumers, hairdressers, musicians, fire-
workers, players, shoeblacks, and—five times the numbers
of beggars."

High holiday was kept in Castlebar for three days. Fitzgerald himself appeared " covered with a profusion of jewels."
The seat of his carriage was filled with guineas sealed up in
parcels of fifty each—" for he played nothing under." All
this no doubt was so much to the good; but Catholic Mayo
was grievously offended when, for the purpose of creating
freeholders, Fitzgerald proceeded to invite a colony of
Presbyterians from Ulster to settle on his estate, promising
at the same time to build a chapel and endow a minister
for them. He also made himself unpopular by assisting in
enforcing the measures necessary for regulating the Connaught linen trade, and when Castlebar, as a place, had
become his fixed enemy, by attempting to injure its market
to the advantage of that of Turlough. For other reasons
also he became odious to the bulk of his neighbours; but
apart from these Fitzgerald's hopes of a public career were
speedily doomed by the embroilment of his domestic affairs,
the causes of which must now be unfolded.

Let it be remarked, *en passant*, that George Robert had no
idea of letting his own chances of election for Mayo be prejudiced by his father's failure, which he attributed in a
speech to the electors, to " his parsimony *and many bad
qualities.*" The " parsimony " is easily explicable; and the
reference to the bad qualities, if somewhat unfilial, was true
enough. For Fitzgerald *père* was a typical example of the
dissolute, spendthrift, utterly worthless Irish squire of the
day, always in debt and always in mischief. On his eldest
son's first marriage an agreement had been entered into
between father and son that the latter, on whom and his
heirs male the Turlough estate was entailed, should receive
an annual charge on the rents in consideration of a sum paid

down for the relief of the former's immediate necessities. But when George Robert arrived from England not only were there large arrears owing to him, but his interests as heir had also been severely injured by the granting of long leases on scandalously low terms, among others, to his brother Charles Lionel, for whom his father now also seems to have demanded a share in the inheritance of the property. That the heir had no notion of yielding up any of his rights is made clear by the reply of the servant girl who found his superstitious old father praying (without his wig) that his sons might be united in affection. Though "the loaf" might, as the old reprobate said, be "sufficiently ample" for both, if divided between them, in her opinion such division was not practicable, and she told her master to put on his wig and clothes and take his breakfast, for "the prayers of the whole world would not prevail on her young master to give up his birthright, or any part of it, to Master Charles." In reality the father and younger son were in league together against the heir; and harshly as the old man was afterwards treated, he had to thank George Robert about this time for saving him from lifelong imprisonment by paying a large sum in discharge of his debts. Circumstances and Fighting Fitzgerald's own diabolical temper contributed to make of this family quarrel a source of disturbance to the whole county of Mayo.

The death of his first wife was a heavy blow to George Robert. He mourned for her extravagantly, and nearly murdered an innkeeper who objected to having a *foreign* corpse in one of his rooms which was occupied by Fitzgerald when journeying with the body to the family vault in Kildare. His habits became gloomy and his behaviour savage. He alarmed the neighbourhood by hunting at night, and acquired a fondness for strange pets : of which latter circumstance more anon. His arrogance was something extraordinary. He would send a man off the hunting-field solely on account of a capricious objection to his person ; and on one occasion refused to sit at table with a relative of his host, because he, being a fat man, must needs, he averred, be a gross feeder. Fitzgerald did, indeed, console himself by a second marriage, the lady being a Miss Vaughan. It is probable enough that the match did not commend itself to her family; but the story of her hand having been won only by her lover's pretended conversion to Catholicism is somewhat discredited by the fact that the Vaughans were Protestants. Fitzgerald's affection for this lady and her attachment to him seem indubitable; but the statement that his desire to effect a settlement on her was the chief cause of quarrel with his father and brother may fairly be doubted.

Besides numerous other general enmities, Fitzgerald had a personal and political feud with the Browne family of Mayo, of which Lord Altamont was the head. Not only did Fighting Fitzgerald trespass on the property of that nobleman, beat his keepers, and drive his kinsman off the ground, but he even went up to his house and shot a large mastiff of Lord Altamont's which was nicknamed "The Prime Sergeant." Now the real Prime Sergeant was his lordship's brother, Denis Browne. When, therefore, Fitzgerald announces in the market-place of Westport that he had shot the Prime Sergeant, the people supposed Browne to have been his victim. Whereupon Fitzgerald explains to them his grim joke: "Gentlemen, don't be alarmed for your big counsellor. I have shot a much worthier animal— the big watchdog." After committing this outrage, he left behind him at Westport House a considerate note to the effect that "as he always felt for the ladies, he would allow Lady Anne, Lady Elizabeth, and Lady Charlotte Browne to have each one lap-dog."

All this was done to draw Browne into a duel; and after being called a coward before his servants, Denis consented to a meeting. On his proposition, broadswords were agreed upon as the weapon; but as he was going forth to fetch a second, Fitzgerald discharged a pistol-bullet in his face. This put an end to all prospects of a fair fight, and the matter was brought into the courts, where Fitzgerald only escaped a heavy sentence by a mistake in the indictment.

Nor did Fitzgerald behave much better towards a certain Mr. Cæsar Ffrench, a Galway gentleman, who had entered into the league against him, engaging in a sort of predatory warfare with him by carrying off his cattle and opposing to his armed followers a similar band of desperadoes. After much provocation a duel took place between them. Ffrench was wounded on the hip by Fitzgerald's sword, and the latter claimed the honour of the day: but the fact was that he only saved his own life by falling to the ground when he was getting too hardly pressed by the superior weight of his opponent, who thereupon quitted the field. Once again the old charge is made against our little duellist, one of the spectators declaring that he saw Ffrench's sword bend on his waistcoat.

To return to the more immediate affairs of the Fitzgerald family. George Robert, unable to obtain any satisfaction from his father, obtained an order from the Court of Chancery giving him possession of the family estate until his claim should be met. He seized upon Rockfield House, and put it into a state of defence, but found it difficult to collect any rent from the tenants. Constant frays now ensued between the party of the father and of the reversionary in possession. Advantage was taken of one of these by George Robert's opponents to indict him for riot. He was acquitted, but when bound over to keep the peace was unable to find bail, and had to avoid arrest by escaping from the jury room by the roof. These proceedings, and the danger of the reversion of the estate going to his brother, on account of his not himself having a male heir, aroused the light slumbers of the devil in Fitzgerald. He determined to separate Charles Lionel and his father by taking possession of the latter's person. He therefore had his affectionate old parent waylaid when on a journey from Ballinrobe to Dublin, carried him off to Turlough, and there kept him prisoner. Charles Lionel now indicted his elder brother at the Mayo Assizes of 1782 for illegal imprisonment, and by order of the Court arrested him in person, when sitting in the jury room as one of the grand jurors.

It appeared at the trial which immediately took place at Castlebar, and lasted from 9 a.m. till 12 at night, that in order to induce his father to make a will in his favour,

George Robert had kept him chained to a block of wood and had had three of his teeth knocked out. A sentence of three years' imprisonment and a fine of £1,000 were passed, and in spite of Fitzgerald's subsequent complaints of the unfairness of the trial, the decision was upheld on appeal. But " the idea of any kind of restraint was perfectly ungrateful to the mind of Mr. Fitzgerald," who managed, after only four days' captivity, to escape from Castlebar gaol by means of the combined agency of a brace of pistols and a bag of silver. As soon as he was outside the walls he leapt upon a horse and rode to Turlough House, where old Fitzgerald was still confined. Near here the Turlough volunteers had mounted a small fort with cannon obtained from a foreign ship which had been wrecked in Clew Bay, and Rockfield House was speedily got ready to stand a siege.

Mr. Cæsar Ffrench and his party not being quite equal to the emergency, the Viceroy was appealed to, and a military force was despatched from Dublin, while the volunteers of all the neighbouring counties received orders to join in hunting down the outlaw. Fitzgerald, finding the odds now too heavy for him, having spiked his guns and dismantled his fort, flew northwards to Killala, taking his father with him. The story goes that, pressed thus on all sides by the emissaries of the law, he now crossed over into Sligo, and embarked with the old man in a boat on the open sea ; and that under stress of dire peril, the father once more consented to terms, which, however, finding himself soon after at liberty in Dublin, he immediately repudiated. In another version George Robert gives up his father to Sir Maltby Crofton, in order to save himself. How this could be the result (for his own life, according to Irish law, was forfeit for prison breaking) is not easy to see ; and how Fitzgerald found himself in Dublin, when both the sea and the land passes had been guarded to prevent his escape is not a little mysterious. Nevertheless it is certain that the little desperado (for whose apprehension a reward of £300 was offered), was easily arrested while walking about, "in a careless and indifferent manner," in College Green. Once more we find Fighting Fitzgerald wielding the pen ; for

during the hours of his imprisonment was produced his
" Appeal to the Public "—an able manifesto filled with in-
numerable charges against his enemies, and particularly
Charles Lionel, his brother, whom he loaded with every
conceivable crime.[1] He remained some months in the New
Prison, but eventually received, probably through the efforts
of the Herveys, a free pardon.

The sole condition of the pardon seems to have been that
Lord Temple exacted a promise from Fitzgerald that he
should abstain from duelling. Nevertheless he was no
sooner free than he found it incumbent upon him to fight
a Galway lawyer, Mr. Richard Martin, who had insulted the
Fitzgeralds in general, and George Robert in particular, in
the course of the trial at Castlebar.

This worthy was a friend of the Brownes, and seems to
have been incited by them to take up the case of the younger
Fitzgerald and his father against George Robert. Barrington
received from the counsel a MS. account of the doings of the
family at this period.   Martin was not unduly complimentary
to his clients ; for, in answer to the plea of " a battered old
counseller on the other side," to the effect that " it would be
unjust to censure any son for confining such a public nuisance " as Fitzgerald *père*, he remarked that " though be-
lieving that in the course of a long life this wretched father
had committed many crimes, yet the greatest crime against
society and the greatest sin against Heaven that he ever
perpetrated, was the having begotten the traverser ! " George
Robert smilingly replied, " Martin, you look very healthy,
you take good care of your *constitution ;* but I tell you that
you have this day taken very bad care of your *life.*"

This last recorded fight of Fighting Fitzgerald was a truly
typical one. The affair began in the streets of Castlebar
(Martin having previously been insulted in a Dublin theatre),

---

[1] Many of the accusations were undoubtedly true ; but though in
the lifetime of his elder brother Charles Lionel seems to have been
fully his equal in lawless behaviour, yet when he had entered into his
inheritance he appears to have become quite an orderly member of
society.

where Fitzgerald " enthused " the mob by declaring the duel a county match—the Mayo Cock against the Galway Cock. The duellists, amid shouts of " Mayo for ever ! " retire to a barrack-yard ; and in the combat which follows Fitzgerald illustrates his principles of duelling. Colonel Dick having just shot a man *quite fairly*, extraordinary precautions seemed necessary. Accordingly, when pistols were levelled at a distance of nine yards, Fitz suddenly proposes, " for quick work sake," that they should both advance two paces. His experience taught him that a pistol loaded for one distance will not be so sure for another. Then, again, knowing the value of disconcerting a first aim, he interrupts action a second time with a " Stop, I am not prepared ! " Nor was this all. The first shots were fired without effect : by Martin's second Fitz is hit in the breast. His opponent now considered that he had seriously, if not mortally, wounded his man, when suddenly up springs Fitzgerald, takes elaborate aim, and exclaiming, " Hit for a thousand," shoots Martin also in the body. Neither wound appears to have been fatal, though, according to one account, horse pistols were used ! [1]

Fitzgerald took down with him from Dublin, as law adviser, a notorious person named Timothy Brecknock, who waged his wars against Patrick McDonnell, the legal champion of Charles Lionel and his faction. A would-be predecessor of Mr. Brecknock, a certain Mr. T., had parted company with his client after a very short experience of that gentleman's amusing qualities. This person, on getting into the chaise at the gate of Phœnix Park, was astonished to find not only Fitzgerald, but also a strange bulky gentleman. This gentleman he could by no means get to move, so that he was sorely pressed for room. On arriving at Kilcock Fitzgerald asked for some *raw meat* for the *foreign gentleman*, whom the lawyer now saw to be

---

[1] Can this be the same duel (the preceding circumstances are the same) of which another authority writes : " Mr. Fitzgerald and Mr. Martin afterwards met, and fought a duel, in which neither party received any hurt " ? The plating hypothesis would here afford an easy explanation.

wrapped in a blue travelling cloak with a great white cloth tied over his head. When the solicitor saw his companion's face he was so much alarmed that he screamed and awoke him; whereupon their faces touched. The stranger was a Russian bear which had been brought up by Fitzgerald! When after this the animal obeyed his master by giving the lawyer a kiss, accompanied by a roar, Mr. T. struggled from the grasp of his client, broke open the carriage door, and made his way across country, as best he could, to Dublin.

Mr. Timothy Brecknock, Fitzgerald's present legal adviser, had had a chequered career. The son of a Welsh bishop, he was educated at Jesus College, Oxford, with a view to the Church. In consequence of certain speculative doubts he had, however, adopted the profession of the law, which he combined with the pursuits of a man of pleasure. In his early days this gentleman is said to have "obtained great credit with the people in general" at the expense of the judges by coming into the Court of King's Bench and making use of an obsolete statute to extort a fine from Lord Mansfield and his brethren for wearing cambric. A greater exploit was the successful defence he set up of a highwayman, whose acquittal after a full confession to himself of his guilt he obtained by the following trick. At the trial the testimony as to identity was based chiefly on the recognition of both the prisoner and his horse by the light of the moon, the crape mask worn by the former having fallen off while he was forcing open the door of the coach he was about to rob. This, in connection with the rest of the evidence, seemed to make a clear case, when counsel for the prisoner produced a copy of Ryder's Almanack, according to which the moon did not rise till more than three hours after the time when it was sworn the robbery had been committed. Some time afterwards it was discovered that in this copy the lunations had been tampered with, and that, to make the imposition complete, several other copies, containing similar alterations had been distributed in the Court.

Brecknock had also been employed as a political pamphleteer, and had had a book advocating Divine Right burned by the hangman. But at that point in his career at which we have now arrived he was a religious enthusiast, who let his beard grow, lived on bread and vegetables only, and preached the millenium. Among his peculiar doctrines one was the nobleness of revenge; and, as he believed that he was now for ever freed from sin, no matter what his actions might be, and was withal a man of undoubted ability, he seemed marked out by Heaven (or hell) as the adviser of Fighting Fitzgerald. It is an instance of the cruel irony of fate that this regenerated creature, as he journeyed by coach from London to Holyhead on his way to Ireland, was objected to on account of his *mischievous beard* by a maiden lady of mature age, and had to ride outside the vehicle.

Another ally of Fitzgerald's was the son of a Carrick-fergus turnkey, Andrew Craig, or Creagh, by name, but called in Mayo " Scots Andrew." Before becoming gentleman's servant he had been blacksmith and horseboy, and had seen much of Irish life. Many are the stories told of him : how, before being dismissed by one of his masters, he had one night lured the old gentleman into a bog by imitating the lowing of a favourite cow; how, by raising the cry of fire, and thus calling away master and guest from the festive board, he had managed to partake of the deserted wines; and how, having by means of a bolster evaded the chastise-ment merited by his roguery, he had yet pretended to die from the effects thereof, and spread consternation at the wake by rising at midnight from the dead. Scots Andrew and Brecknock played equally prominent though very different *rôles* in the tragedy of Fitzgerald's end, which was now approaching. The great protagonist of the adverse party was a Mayo attorney, Patrick Randell McDonnell. One great cause of the bitter enmity borne him by George Robert Fitzgerald was the fact that he, an obscure civi-lian, had been a successful candidate against himself, an ex-captain in his Majesty's service, and, moreover, the head of the Geraldine family, for the colonelcy of the Mayo legion of volunteers. But there were other springs of mutual ill-feeling, arising to a great extent from the similarity of their characters and circumstances. Mr.

Alexander McDonnell was an even worse father than Mr. George Fitzgerald. He hated his son Patrick, because his estate was entailed on him, and drove him to the protection of a maternal uncle who educated his nephew as an attorney. Patrick soon showed appreciation of his training, when on coming of age he learned that a property of £300 a year left him by an uncle had been fraudulently disposed of by his own father. Learning that the will had been placed in the hands of the purchaser of the estate, the young lawyer entered the house of that person in his absence, broke open the black box in which it was hid, and carried off his title-deeds. McDonnell senior prosecuted his son for burglary, but was defeated with contumely, and Patrick, by subsequent process, proved his title and obtained possession of the estate, which he dubbed, in memory of his prowess, Chancery Hall. Now this property almost adjoined the Fitzgerald estate at Turlough. The neighbours were also cousins ; and Mr. Patrick Fitzgerald, who brought up the young McDonnell, had entertained George Robert when houseless. The latter, in return, had been expected to renew a profitable lease held by his host from him, but had refused. This grudge was cherished by the nephew, who had also obtained from old Fitzgerald an easy lease. He took his revenge by successfully pushing the claims of two ladies named Dillon on George Robert's estate, and by acting as adviser to the league of Charles Lionel and the tenantry against him. The rivals were alike fierce and revengeful. Fitzgerald was a Protestant, McDonnell "but one remove from a Papist," since his father had only read his recantation in order to obtain some property. In view of the rancorous hatred borne by these men to one another, it appears strange that they never came to a duel. The only explanation of this fact is that Fitzgerald was deterred by family pride from meeting one who, though he happened by marriage to be his cousin, he yet deemed infinitely his inferior in birth. Assassination, aided by Connaught law, was the method of revenge contemplated by both. Who was the actual aggressor may be doubted : for each had been heard to express a wish to shoot the other. However, McDonnell was first wounded in the leg (or pretended to be so), and retired to Castlebar for safety. On the other hand, a man whom he imprisoned in a private house (he was a Connaught magistrate), as an alleged assassin employed by Fitzgerald, swore afterwards that he had been offered £300 to make that identical charge.

It is probable that Fitzgerald designed his enemy's death by some manner of law, as that term was understood by Brecknock and practised in Connaught. Warrants were procured against McDonnell and two of his friends from a magistrate named O'Mealey (whose judicial character was seemingly not worthy of great respect), for imprisoning the man Murphy, who has been mentioned, and for shooting some of Fitzgerald's dogs. The head constable and his party were backed in the execution of their office by a gang of Fitzgerald's boys, and an opportunity for the arrest was seized upon when, on February 20th, McDonnell, Andrew Gallagher, a Castlebar apothecary, and Hipson (against whom the Squire of Turlough had an old grudge), were making an expedition from Castlebar to Chancery Hall. The three friends took refuge in a house on the way, but were taken and carried off to Turlough for the night, McDonnell, scarcely yet recovered from his recent wound, being dragged forth from a heap of malt in which he had hidden himself.

Andrew Gallagher alleged at the trial that during that night he overheard orders given to Craig and the rest, " that if they saw any rescue, or chance of a rescue, to be sure and shoot the prisoners and take care of them "; that Fitzgerald said, " Ha ! we shall soon be rid of them now," and Brecknock replied, " Oh, then we shall be easy indeed."

The evidence that this conversation could have been overheard was somewhat weak; but circumstances made the existence of such a plan appear probable.[1] For, early next morning, when the prisoners were being conducted, as Fitzgerald said, to a magistrate, the rear of the procession was fired at, either by McDonnell's friends or, as the informer asserted, by men hired for the purpose by the

[1] Brecknock appears to have fished up an old law by which, if a rescue were attempted, it was lawful to shoot prisoners.

Squire of Turlough. Hipson and Gallagher, who were tied together, were immediately shot by their captors, and the former killed; and McDonnell, as he fled with both arms broken over the bridge of Kilnecarra, was pursued and despatched by Scots Andrew. Gallagher was re-captured and brought back to Turlough, but not further injured.

And now the country was up against Fitzgerald. The Castlebar mob, accompanied by a troop of horse and some volunteers, with a magistrate, arrived at Turlough House, and speedily arrested Brecknock and the subordinate actors in the affair. It was some time before Fitzgerald himself, who had before their arrival made several attempts to mount his horse and ride away (Brecknock had been for remaining, to show a *mens conscia recti*), was discovered hidden amidst a heap of blankets in a chest. He was with difficulty protected from violence, but was at length brought off and lodged in a room in Castlebar gaol. The crowd lingered behind and ransacked his house, and one man is said to have wrapped round him a hundred yards of fine linen. Andrew Craig, the actual murderer of McDonnell, was taken near Dublin, but saved his neck by turning King's evidence at the trial, an attempt to poison him by mixing arsenic in his food having first failed. Before the trial took place another outrage was perpetrated. Just before midnight on February 21st, the day on which he had been arrested, the room where Fitzgerald was confined was broken into by a party of men, who knocked down the sentinel and attacked the unarmed prisoner with pistols and swords.

He fought desperately, but was only left by the assailants when he was thought to be dead. Several persons accused by Fitzgerald, among them being Gallagher, his brother the coroner who had headed the Castlebar mob, and Dr. Martin, brother of the "Galway Cock," were prosecuted by the Crown as perpetrators of the outrage; but witnesses were unable or unwilling to swear to their identity with the assailants, and they were acquitted. Truly might it be said that in this part of Ireland there was neither law nor police in 1786.

On April 10, 1786, Chief Baron Yelverton and Mr.

Baron Power arrived at Castlebar to try George Robert Fitzgerald and his associates. Two days later, that individual, disabled by the forty-six wounds ' he is said to have survived, was brought into court on his bed, and laid on the witnesses' table. A true bill was found by the grand jury against him together with Brecknock, Craig, and six others " for traitorously murdering " McDonnell and Hipson. The actual trials were put off to allow time for Fitzgerald's further recovery. At length, on Friday, June 9th, this once splendid person appeared in court in an old threadbare greatcoat, and with his head shaved and tied up in a clean pocket-handkerchief.

It was observed, too, that " he smiled at every one, as if he was in no way apprehensive of danger." The crowd of people in court was so great that proceedings were delayed by an alarm that the floor was falling, which proved to be false, and looks as if it had been raised to give a chance of escape to the prisoners. However, after a discreditable scene, in which " judge, jury, and counsellors ran promiscuously here and there," the trial began.

An attempt seems to have been made to keep out the rabble, but failed; and the people, " having prevailed by bribes, entreaties, &c., the crowd was such that they were sitting on each other's shoulders." Fitzgibbon as attorney-general "seemed to be very intent for the prosecution." It is said he had been struck two or three years before by the little duellist in the streets of Dublin; but it does not appear that he was actuated by personal motives. The charge he brought forward against Fitzgerald was that of " provoking, stirring up, and procuring ' certain persons ' to kill and murder Patrick Randell McDonnell and James Hipson." He supported it by three witnesses, but one of these was the infamous Scots Andrew, who had really done the deed on McDonnell. The evidence was certainly not conclusive; but though Fitzgerald is said to have spoken for three hours and to have made a most able defence, calling witnesses to swear that he was not present at the murder and did not assist it in any way, he was found guilty by the jury after but seven minutes' deliberation.

He did not on that day receive sentence. On being taken out of court he demanded, and was accorded, a private conference with the high sheriff, who was his old enemy, Denis Browne: but what was its nature did not transpire. The result must, however, have been unsatisfactory, for the convict, when he returned to his room, "threw himself on his bed, and continued lying on his face above three hours and a half without uttering a sound." His mother, Lady Mary, had sent a sum of money to be used for his defence, but at the same time declared that she had no desire for her son's escape if he were guilty. It is clear, however, that Fitzgerald himself expected to get a pardon through the Hervey influence.

On the Monday following his trial Brecknock was convicted as an accessory before the fact, and the other members of the Turlough gang for their several parts in it.

Sentence of death was now passed on Fitzgerald and Brecknock, and ordered to be carried out that same day. This haste seems to have been due to a fear that the first would commit suicide. By some it was also said that his enemies feared that respect for the law was not so great in the assize town of County Mayo as to obviate any danger to the carrying out of its decrees. Sentence, then, having been delivered, Fitzgerald said a few words in which, after protesting his innocence, he affirmed that he was not afraid to meet death in any shape, and added, that he would not accept of pardon, after having been found guilty " by such a jury," because he knew he could not face the world after it. He also denied having entertained any thought of suicide, and declared that he forgave every one.

Brecknock was recommended to mercy on account of his age—he was nearly seventy—but the presiding judge sent him to execution, together with Fulton, the chief of the subordinate assassins. These two suffered before their patron.

Brecknock, with his long, white beard and firm bearing, and " his hair neatly curled on his neck," must have been a dignified criminal. He had made his peace with God, and was not conscious of having committed a sin for fifteen years; and he repeated the Lord's Prayer in Greek before standing up in the cart and drawing the woollen cap over his face.

George Robert himself, preceded by a masked executioner, walked out at six o'clock by a by-lane to the place of execution. He was arrayed in an old uniform of the Castlebar Hunt, and had on dirty shoes and stockings and a hat tied with a hempen cord. This was the man who, a few short years before, had been accustomed to dress in the newest and most elegant Parisian modes. On arriving at the scaffold, he asked eagerly, " Is this the place ? " When answered that it was he shook hands with several of the bystanders, mounted the cart, and having made the usual preparations, adjusted the rope himself. He then called for and joined in a brief prayer, and having again shaken hands with Mr. Henry, the clergyman, and made the customary request to the executioner, very suddenly flung himself off. But the rope snapped, and Fitzgerald fell to the ground, exclaiming, " Is it possible the grand jury of Mayo will not afford me a rope sufficiently strong ? " The high sheriff replied cheerily, " Never fear, you shall have one strong enough, and speedily," and sent for another, adding to the hangman, " Do you hear ? No more botching ! " Before the arrival of a fresh rope Fitzgerald's courage apparently grew fainter, and he implored that he might have longer time for prayer. The request was reluctantly granted by the high sheriff, who it was reported by some had a reprieve in his pocket the whole time. At last the repentant duellist mounted the ladder; but the bungling executioner managed the rope badly, and his victim was only put out of his misery by a compassionate enemy, who shortened it. All was over in half an hour, and the body was taken to be buried at midnight in the family tomb in the chapel attached to Turlough House. His wife had been active in collecting evidence, and was faithful to her husband to the last; but Fitzgerald's fate was concealed from his daughter, who only learnt it years afterwards from a chance news sheet which she came upon when reading in a library.

Yelverton would seem to have been no better satisfied with the actual verdict than a lawyer of to-day might be ; for the judge's comment in the case is reported to have been : " George Robert *was* a murderer, and he *was* murdered." There can, however, be little doubt but that Fighting Fitzgerald would have come to a violent end of one kind or another. It is a thing to be wondered at that he should ever have reached the mature age of thirty-eight. Yet, as the compiler of the " Memoirs of George Robert Fitzgerald, Esquire," pathetically reflects, " Who that has sensibility can survey the ruin and ignominy of this fallen gentleman without regretting the imperfections of our species ! "

THOMAS GRIFFITHS WAINEWRIGHT.

(1794–1852.)

" Thoughts black, hands apt, drugs fit, and time agreeing."
Hamlet, Act III., Sc. ii.

THOMAS GRIFFITHS WAINEWRIGHT was born at Chiswick in October, 1794. His father was a solicitor, his paternal grandfather being a somewhat distinguished member of the same profession. His mother, whose maiden name was Ann Griffiths, was the daughter of Ralph Griffiths, LL.D., publisher and proprietor of *The Monthly Review*, now best known perhaps from the abuse showered on him by the various biographers of Oliver Goldsmith. Mrs. Wainewright appears to have been a woman of considerable accomplishments, and according to the obituary notice in *The Gentleman's Magazine*, was " supposed to have understood the writings of Mr. Locke as well as perhaps any person, of either sex, now living."

Wainewright could never have known either of his parents, as his mother died in the effort of presenting him to the world and his father did not survive more than a few years. He went to live with his grandfather, Dr. Griffiths, at Linden House, Turnham Green. Linden House was a fine mansion, standing in well-timbered gardens, which covered four acres of ground. An idea of its importance may be gathered from the fact that the rent was estimated at four hundred pounds a year and the purchase-money at twelve thousand pounds.

Dr. Griffiths' household at this time consisted of himself, his second wife, and his son by his first marriage, George Edward Griffiths.

In September, 1803, Dr. Griffiths, having attained the respectable age of eighty-three, departed this life, and George Edward reigned in his stead. He had not, however, the ability of his father, and in his hands *The Monthly Review* lost a good deal of its importance. A curious point arises in connection with the Doctor's will. He recites that on the marriage of his late daughter with Thomas Wainewright he advanced a certain sum of money, and covenanted that after his death a further sum should be paid by his personal representatives as a marriage portion, and goes on to will that his grandson shall have this sum, and this sum only. Except as regarded his grandson he wished his property to be divided as though he had died intestate. This provision was tantamount to a disinheriting of Thomas Griffiths, as the portion left had already been covenanted for, and could, no doubt, have been recovered by legal process. The explanation must probably be sought in the theory that he had been opposed to the marriage and had never altogether forgiven it. The money that thus became the property of the subject of this biography was £5,200 New Four per Cent. Annuities, invested in the names of Robert Wainewright, Edward Smith, Henry Foss, and Edward Foss as trustees.

Thomas Griffiths went to school at Charles Burney's academy at Hammersmith, and there evinced for the first time his love of art. As a draughtsman he even then attained considerable skill, and his drawing-book is stated to display "great talent and natural feeling." His schoolmaster was a cousin of his own, having married the niece of the second Mrs. Griffiths. Wainewright in later life spoke in terms of warm praise of his kinsman and pedagogue, as "a philosopher, an antiquarian, and an admirable teacher."

After leaving school, while still a mere boy, he was "placed frequently in literary society," and for a short time devoted as much attention as his "giddy, flighty disposition" allowed him to bestow on any one subject—to painting, or "rather to an admiration for it." But he was restless, and before long, but exactly when is uncertain, entered on a military career. According to his own accounts he was successively an orderly officer in the Guards and a cornet in a yeomanry regiment. He appears to have partaken rather freely of spirituous liquors at this time, if his own statement that he was in the habit of taking ten tumblers of whisky punch every evening, which had the not unnatural effect of "obscuring his recollections of Michael Angelo as in a dun fog" is to be credited.

His military fervour did not last very long. "My blessed art touched her renegade ; by her pure and high influences the noisome mists were purged : my feelings, parched, hot, and tarnished, were renovated with a cool, fresh bloom, childly simple, beautiful to the simple-hearted." Wordsworth's poems touched him deeply; he wept over them "tears of happiness and gratitude." And naturally he left the army.

About this time he had a severe illness, followed by hypochondria in which he was "ever shuddering on the horrible abyss of mere insanity," and, though he at length recovered, he was left in a more or less broken state, unable to accomplish steady work.

This illness preceded January, 1820, when the first number of *The London Magazine* appeared. It had a brilliant staff of contributors, including within the first few years Charles Lamb, Hood, Hartley Coleridge, Hamilton Reynolds, Allan Cunningham, Hazlitt, De Quincey, Procter, and others, besides Wainewright. The latter wrote pretty constantly between January, 1820, when his first article ("A Modest Offer of Service from Mr. Bonmot to the Editor of *The London Magazine* ") appeared, and January, 1823, when his last (" Janus Weatherbound ; or the Weathercock Steadfast for Lack of Oil ") came out. Between these dates he was responsible for about fifteen essays, though he was in no sense a regular contributor. Thus between January and June, 1820, he wrote no fewer than seven articles, while he was altogether silent between September, 1820, and April, 1821.

He wrote under the pseudonyms, " Egomet Bonmot," " Janus Weathercock," and " Cornelius Van Vinkbooms," and generally affected somewhat fantastic titles, such as " Sentimentalities on the Fine Arts," "Dogmas for Dilettanti," and "The Academy of Taste for Grown Gentlemen; or, The Infant Connoisseur's Go-cart." Procter suggests that Scott willingly accepted his clever but eccentric essays as a relief from the more serious papers of his other friends. The subjects he discoursed of were principally art in its wider sense, including music, the stage, the collecting of engravings and ornaments, and so on, and himself.

Of pictures he wrote fluently and frequently. He is primarily an impressionist, describing his sensations on beholding works of art, often with considerable ability, always with conviction, sometimes even with power. At times, however, he is somewhat technical, as when in his estimate of Polidoro di Caldara he says : " His lines are flowing and sweepy; and in their emanation from and connection with each other uniformly harmonious. His chiaroscuro is forcible and well conducted, giving to single figures and groups prodigious roundness; and his composition compact." It is characteristic of him that he always spoke of Paul Veronese as Cagliari and of Titian as Vecelli. He believed largely in the virtues of conception, had but a poor opinion of commonplace subjects faithfully delineated, and speaks with contempt of "the painters of bitten apples, cut fingers, and all the long list of the results of mere diligent observation and patient imitation of objects intrinsically worthless and devoid of the genuine elements of either humour or pathos." While admiring Sir David Wilkie, he says : " It offends me to the soul to see a parcel of chuckleheaded Papas, doting Mammas, and chalk-and-charcoal-faced Misses, neglecting that beautiful eccentricity of Turner's yonder in the mahogany frame, and crowding, and squeezing, and riding upon one another's backs to get a sight—not of the faces of the folks hearing the Will, but of the brass clasps of the strong box wherein was deposited the Will." He is never quite comfortable when discussing contemporary work, feeling acutely that want of perspective to which none but the most self-satisfied of critics can be a stranger. "Things," he says, "that spring

up under my nose dazzle me. I must look at them through
Time's telescope. Elia complains that to him the merit of
a MS. poem is uncertain—'print,' as he excellently says,
'settles it.' Fifty years' toning does the same thing for a
picture. It is very possible that Sir Thomas Laurence and
Phillips and Owen are as good in their way as Vandyke (and
they have certainly less affectation). Wilkie may be better
than Teniers, and Westall be as much the originator of a
style as Coreggio. I really believe our posterity will think
so; but in the meantime I am dubious and uncomfortable.
I have not the most distant notion of the relative merits of
Claude and Turner, and am truly mystified by Stothard and
Fuseli." Wainewright was also for a brief period a painter
and exhibitor, himself, taking refuge from his own criticism
in the comparatively secure province of cattle pieces.
Between 1821 and 1825 he exhibited six pictures at the
Royal Academy and one at the British Institution, the
subjects of all being similar to those of Cuyp.

But besides art there is one other subject on which he
is never weary of speaking—himself. He feels himself a
"gentleman," and he takes care that his reader shall know
it. He despises "*Tatnam* Court Road"; he has "heard
of" Sadler's Wells; he finds "by reference to the picture
of London" that the Royal Cobourg Theatre is in South-
wark—"faugh"; but he wants to be reminded of more
elegant life—"something that would suit better with the
diamond rings on our fingers, the antique cameos in our
breast-pins, our cambric pocket-handkerchief breathing forth
attargul, our pale lemon-coloured kid gloves." He describes
to us his horse, his drives to town, and his room—the last
with great minuteness. We have a catalogue describing
the pattern of the Brussels carpet, the "water-tabby-silk
linings" of his "choice volumes," the piano, the hothouse
plants, the lamp, and so on, down to the Newfoundland dog
and the cat. "We immersed a well-seasoned, prime pen
into our silver inkstand three times, shaking off the loose
ink lingeringly, while, holding the print fast in our left hand,
we perused it with half-shut eyes, dallying awhile with our
delight."

That Wainewright's prose has considerable merit is undeniable. Charles Lamb thought it "capital." Writing to Bernard Barton in 1823, he says: "*The London*, I fear, falls off: . . . it will topple down if they don't get some buttresses. They have pulled down three—Hazlitt, Procter, and their best stay, kind, light-hearted Wainewright, their Janus." His sympathy with art was genuine, his knowledge of it considerable. An occasional aphorism such as "I hold that no work of art can be tried otherwise than by laws deduced from itself" strikes home by the lucidity and elegance of the expression; an occasional simile like "The polyanthus glowed in its cold bed of earth, like a solitary picture of Giorgione, on the dark oaken panels of an ancient dreary Gothic gallery," is full of pretty imagery, but, neutralising his knowledge and his merit, is an all-pervading affectation of a peculiarly irritating character, and a sense of individual importance almost boundless. His cleverness does not avert a sense of tediousness and annoyance, and he is difficult to read except in homeopathic doses.

Literature, however, did not during these years absorb the whole of his artistic energies. His sketches were bold and graphic, and he exhibited to his friends a portfolio of drawings of the female form divine in which "the voluptuous trembled on the borders of the indelicate."

Of Wainewright's personal appearance the accounts are somewhat conflicting. He is stated to have had a large and massive head, with eyes deeply set, and a square, solid jaw. His hair was curly, and parted down the middle, but its colour is variously given. Mr. Hazlitt says that it was dark, he himself that it was black, but Mr. Forster, who knew him personally, calls it sandy. He wore moustaches. His hands were exquisitely white, and covered with "regal rings." He was a dandy: used to dress in the height of fashion, and affected a blue undress military coat, perhaps as a compliment to his late profession. A writer in *The North British Review*, who met him at a literary dinner given by Messrs. Taylor and Hessey in 1821, describes his appearance as "commonplace," which seems hardly consistent with the other evidence; but it must be remembered that all the accounts we have were written after he had become criminally notorious, and are coloured by subsequent impressions. Later in life he developed a stoop, and, in the eyes at least of some who knew him, a " snake-like expression at once repulsive and fascinating." His conversation was smart and lively without being deep. He would talk on the subjects most familiar to his acquaintances,[1] showing sufficient knowledge to make himself agreeable to them, while allowing them the satisfaction of imparting information. But the most circumstantial account of his manner and appearance is that given by B. W. Procter. "In person Wainewright was short and rather fat, with a fidgety, nervous manner, and sparkling, twinkling eyes, that did not readily disclose their meaning. These, however, had no positive hardness or cruelty. His voice was like a whisper, wanting in firmness and distinctness. A spectator would at first sight have pronounced him thoroughly effeminate had not his thick and sensual lips counterbalanced the other features and announced that something of a different nature might disclose itself hereafter. . . . He was not entirely cruel. I imagine that he was perfectly *indifferent* to human life, and that he sacrificed his victims without any emotion and for the purpose simply of obtaining money to gratify his luxury. Sometimes I have suspected him of gambling. . . . He was like one of those creatures, seemingly smooth and innocuous, whose natural secretions, when once excited, become fatal to those against whom they are accidentally directed."

In 1821 Wainewright married Miss Frances Ward, a remarkably handsome woman, the daughter by her first husband of a Mrs. Abercromby, of Mortlake. The latter had in all four children—a son by her first husband, Mr. Ward, as well as the daughter who became Mrs. Waine-

---

[1] At any rate if (as Mr. Hazlitt considers) Dickens's account of Julius Slinkton in "Hunted Down" can be considered biographical.

wright, and two daughters by her second husband, Lieutenant Abercromby—Helen Frances Phœbe, born in 1809,
and Madeleine, born in 1810—both of whom developed
into very good-looking girls. Abercromby died in 1812,
penniless, and his widow, to supplement a small income of
about £100 a year left her by her first husband, was reduced
to taking in lodgers at her house in Mortlake. The two
younger girls were granted small pensions of ten pounds
each by the Board of Ordnance during their mother's
life.

The Wainewrights' regular income seems to have been
limited to the interest on the £5,200 left by Dr. Griffiths,
and cannot greatly have exceeded £200 per annum. This,
though insufficient for more than very moderate comfort,
might have proved enough if Wainewright's tastes had been
simple and not extravagant. But this is exactly what they
were not. He was, in Mr. Oscar Wilde's words, " an
amateur of beautiful things and a dilettante of things de-
lightful." He collected proof engravings freely ; he loved
good wines, hothouse plants, majolica, and other extremely
pleasing but expensive luxuries. Moreover, he had a
good deal of entertaining to do. He moved in very good
literary society ; he knew personally most of the leading
artists of the day. We have records of many dinners at
which he met distinguished company. No doubt he had
to entertain in turn, and we may be sure that when he was
the host the guests had no reason to complain. We know
of Macready, Sir David Wilkie, Richard Westall, Barry
Cornwall, and Lamb dining at his house. At one time he
lived some thirteen or fourteen miles from London, so a
horse and trap were necessary for his existence. He
speaks several times with obvious pride of his horse "Contributor."

Procter relates how he dined once at Turnham Green
(this was a little later, during Wainewright's residence at
Linden House, about 1830), when Westall, Wainewright's
wife, her son (a little boy), and her sister, Madeleine Abercromby, a fair, innocent-looking girl, about nineteen years
old, were present. "Although," he says, "I had known

Wainewright for two or three previous years, I was not aware till then that he had a child. Indeed, he seemed to have little affection for the boy, who (scandal whispered) was the son of a dissipated and extravagant peer. Mrs. W. was a sharp-eyed, self-possessed woman, dressing in showy flimsy finery. She seemed to obey Wainewright's humours and to assist his needs; but much affection did not apparently exist between them."

Wainewright's private collection of books, if small, was *recherché* and curious. Rare old Herbals with heavy leather panels shouldered curiously bound works on astrology and the occult sciences on the shelves of a massive antique book-press. In a secluded corner, we are assured, he had two or three old books on poisons; these latter were richly bound by Roger Payne, and it is to be hoped still gladden the heart of a collector. They were doubtless sold to make up the insurance expenses of 1830. The presence of the books on Hermeneutics suggests that he may have gone through an unremunerative course of alchemy before he sought to fathom the dangerously fascinating secrets of toxicology.

As a connoisseur he found opportunities from time to time of "raising the wind" which do credit to his ingenuity. Thus he bought a number of very costly engravings after Marc Antonio and Bonasone from Dominic Colnaghi; these he removed from their cardboards and sold at prices sufficient to compensate him for his outlay of time and trouble. He then purchased very cheap copies of the same prints and placed these on the cardboards to which the high prices of the genuine engravings were affixed in Colnaghi's hand. He parted with these to particular friends (not art-amateurs) at prices slightly reduced, as an especial favour, from those quoted on the mounts.

Besides occasional deals of this nature he had constant recourse to loans, and among others applied to Procter for a sum of two hundred pounds, "which," says the party appealed to, "it was not convenient for me at that time to advance." By methods such as these Wainewright managed for a time to keep his head fairly well above water. But his feline nature had a horror of these hazardous expedients. Money in abundance was necessary to the proper development of his exotic character.

There were certain expectations, it is true, from his uncle, George Griffiths (his grandmother had died in 1812), who was already an old man, as he might reasonably anticipate the reversion to Linden House and whatever money his uncle had; but George Griffiths remained provokingly well and hearty, and expectations are not cash. A profound and growing sense of dissatisfaction at the delicate and unsettled state of his finances led an exquisite and enthusiastic egotist such as Wainewright, by the most natural stages, to resolve upon the commission of his first crime. It was not a very serious one perhaps; indeed it sinks into absolute insignificance when compared with his later proceedings—only forgery—but it was unfortunately one for which at that period the penalty was death. Certain money was held in trust for him by four gentlemen; the interest was paid him regularly by the Bank of England; the money was *bona fide* his own. But by the stupid arrangement of the trust he could not touch the capital— and the capital was what he wanted very badly. It was clear that the arrangement must be set aside, and as neither his trustees nor the Bank were likely to see it in quite the same light as he did himself, it must be set aside without their consent. All he had to do was to present an order to the Bank, signed by the trustees, transferring some of the capital to himself, and all would be arranged. What harm would be done to any one? No one would lose a penny, and he would be a distinct gainer. Accordingly he forged the order for £2,259 (among his many accomplishments must have been a delicate skill in penmanship), the money was paid, and the pecuniary difficulties were temporarily overcome. It seems almost incredible, but is nevertheless true, that it was at least six or seven years before the forgery was discovered.

In the following year Wainewright made another and, as it proved, a final excursion into the realms of literature. He published a small duodecimo volume of forty-five pages,

of which the characteristic title page is here reproduced :—

> "Some Passages
> in the life, etc.,
> of
> EGOMET BONMOT, ESQ.
> Edited by
> Mr. Mwaughaim
> and now first published by
> ME."

It consists chiefly of a poem in heroic metre purporting to
be the dying confessions of Egomet Bonmot, with a few
pages of prose as an introduction, and a postscript.　It is
a satirical account of a great writer, whose works failed
entirely, and who was reduced to elaborate schemes of
puffing his own works and, by means of trenchant criticisms,
depreciating other people's.　Almost everything in current
literature—particularly Byronism, pessimistic poetry, and
the magazines, in which he claims to have himself written
pseudonymously everything worth reading (including incidentally, De Quincey's "Opium Eater")—comes under
the lash.　The poem is written with great spirit, some
facility in verse, and without too much bitterness, and
contains some of his best writing.　No apology is needed
for transcribing a few passages, more particularly as previous biographers appear to have rather curiously overlooked the book.

After describing how in his unsuccessful period the Muses
oppressed his days, he goes on :—

> "Again at night, if you'll believe me,
> They harassed me with dreams from which I learnt
> That rhymes like mine were written to be burnt.
> Night followed night, and still in vain I sought
> Relief in slumber from the monster—Thought.
> Spellbound by day, I strove my sense of pain
> To shake like dewdrops from the lion's mane ;
> But no, day's struggling efforts were in vain—

And every night in vision's dread array
Repictured the realities of day.
No change came o'er my dreams—my mind's eye sees
Shapes even yet which bid life's current freeze—
Octavo wrappers for two pounds of cheese.
Yea, worse than that—oh pain ! oh grief ! oh scandal !—
Quarto protection for a farthing candle.
Mine were those wrappers, that protection mine ;
Those quartos : those octavos—all the fine
Abstractions that united sense and sound
Hot pressed and beautifully published, found
Waste paper's ready sale—at fourpence odd per pound."

He satirises effectively, if superfluously, the Lytton-Bulwigian weakness for intellectual villainy :—

"In short, what's easier than that thing in vogue,
An honest rascal, or a noble rogue ?
What's easier than by help of lurking hint
To show a villain virtuous in print ?
And by a second hint's ingenious fetch
To nourish pity for this *misused* wretch."

On the subject of the contemporary magazines he is good enough to say :—

"On the whole Baldwin's ' London ' was the best."

But almost immediately impudently adds:—

"But Baldwin, when I left him, ceased to thrive—
He lost the honey-maker of his hive."

We are informed that Mr. Bonmot's last words were "I, I," and are given a picture of the tombstone which, when absolutely dying, he designed for himself :—

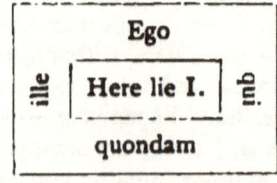

The numerous other volumes (the collected works of

Egomet), promised in this work· never appeared, and it does not seem likely that this last literary effort added much to the monetary resources of the Wainewrights. What these resources (so far as is known) were, has already been detailed, but, even with the windfall secured by the successful forgery, which, moreover, had the necessary but unfortunate effect of diminishing the settled income, they were quite inadequate to meet the expenses of the establishment. A second deviation from the path of mere collective morality became requisite in the year 1829, when the Wainewrights were on a long visit at Linden House. They had previously been occupying (1827–8) luxurious furnished apartments in Great Marlborough Street, and entertaining such distinguished guests as Mr. Serjeant Talfourd, Mr. John Forster, Mr. Macready, and others at dinner. Debts must have been accumulating fast, and it could only have been by extreme cleverness and address that the debtor could have prevented them becoming overwhelming.

A fortunate invitation had opened Linden House to the married couple, who were still childless, about the year 1828, and they accordingly took up their residence with their bachelor uncle, George Edward. This must have been, pecuniarily speaking, a great relief, and such a handsome mansion as Linden House, with its magnificent grounds, must have been particularly grateful to Wainewright. But the debts remained, and no amount of skill in delay is sufficient to keep creditors permanently at bay. Presumably Wainewright's did not differ materially from other specimens of the same tribe, and at last there came a time when their importunity was such as to render it necessary for something to be done. The head of the house was an old man, in the best of health it is true, but there is nothing so very remarkable in old men dying suddenly, and certainly no ground for suspicion. Could not his demise be arranged to occur rather earlier than Nature insisted upon—almost immediately, in fact? The advantages that would accrue were obvious: not only would the fine house and all it contained pass by natural descent to the nephew, but also—and more important—there was certainly a fair sum of money which would pass with it, though Uncle George had not been, like his father, a remarkably successful man. Wainewright had a considerable knowledge of the effects of certain poisons—far in advance, indeed, of the average medical man of the time —and he thought this a good opportunity for testing his knowledge in a practical way.[1] So George Edward Griffiths died, and was buried, and peace for a short time reigned at Linden House. The poison employed is usually stated to have been strychnine, but no record of the symptoms remains. Probably the murderer pursued the same course as in his later murders, when relating the last and greatest of which it will be necessary to discuss shortly the means employed.

In the same year there was an addition to his household, Mrs. Wainewright being confined of her only child—a son, who was christened Griffiths, after his grandfather—and in the next a still larger addition, for it became necessary, owing to their having become so poor as to be almost destitute, to find a home for Mrs. Abercromby and her two daughters, Helen and Madeleine.

The relief that was brought by the death of the late owner of Linden House appears to have been of a transitory nature. The ready money was probably quite absorbed by immediate needs, and only the house remained. But the house by itself was more of an encumbrance than a relief, as to keep it up properly—and of course the Wainewrights would wish to do it properly—required a large income. Mr. Hazlitt, from his personal knowledge of it, estimates it at least a thousand pounds a year. It therefore followed that very shortly after the Abercrombys took up their residence with the Wainewrights it became the duty of the head of the house to find means to again pacify creditors, and this time, if possible, to secure sufficient surplus to be able to defy them permanently. Naturally his thoughts turned to his last successful operation ; but there were difficulties. There

---

[1] The evidence connecting Wainewright with this murder is not conclusive, nor, indeed, very strong, but in the face of his subsequent actions there can be little doubt of his guilt.

were no expectations now; no one existed whose death
would be of any benefit. But had he not heard that the
object of life insurance offices was to provide large pay-
ments in the event of premature death in return for a
small premium down? That was just what he wanted.

In searching for a victim his attention was directed to
Helen Abercromby. She was almost ideally situated for
his purpose. She had implicit confidence in him, knew
nothing of business, and could easily be persuaded to do
anything he wished. It was essential that he should not
appear in the matter in view of possible complications.
Moreover, the English law does not allow any one to insure
any other person's life unless he has a pecuniary interest in
it. But it does not prevent the assured from making over
a policy to a friend for a real, or even a nominal consideration. So she must make the proposals in her own name,
and as life offices inquire more carefully into the objects
of a proposed assurance when the proposal is for a large
amount than when it is for a small one, it was advisable
that the risk should be spread over as many offices as
possible. But in case they should show unseemly curiosity,
it was as well that she should be provided with some statement to make. So a cock-and-bull story was invented
about a pending chancery suit which would probably soon
terminate in her favour, but if she were to die in the next
year or two the property would go elsewhere. This tale
had the advantage of accounting for the proposals being
for short periods (one or two years), and not for the whole
of life, and this method of assurance has the advantage of
reducing the premium by more than one-third.

Miss Abercromby suspected nothing, and apparently
having no objection to the innocent fictions which, if not
necessary, would at any rate tend to smooth over the
preliminaries, put herself in Wainewright's hands. In
March, 1830, accordingly, she made two proposals—one for
£3,000 for a period of three years to the Palladium, at an
annual premium of £39, and one for the same sum at the
Eagle for a period of two years. Mrs. Wainewright accompanied her to the offices, as she did subsequently to other

offices. The object of the assurances was stated to be to get possession of property which would fall in within three years.

A pause of some months followed. This may have been due to Wainewright's sense that the longer the interval between the proposal and the death, the less suspicious the offices would be likely to be, but it is more probable that Mrs. Abercromby objected to the proceedings. What, she may reasonably have asked, could be the good of insuring for short periods the life of a practically penniless girl who was very healthy and almost certain to outlive the policies? It was throwing money away. Helen, in all probability, while willing to gratify her brother-in-law, if that were possible without offending her mother, may have been of the same opinion. So, as £5,000 was clearly an inadequate sum for which to dispose of the girl, especially as it might be largely increased, a delay was inevitable.

Meanwhile, financially speaking, things were getting worse every day. In July a money-lender, Mr. Sharpus, held two of Wainewright's securities, a warrant of attorney, the consideration for which was £610, which became due in the next month, and a bill of sale for the whole furniture and effects of Linden House. Moreover, money was due for such prosaic necessaries as bread, groceries, meat, and coals. The tradesmen had great confidence in the possessors of old Griffiths' mansion, but their complaisance could not be relied on for ever, and it was already being sorely tested. Something' must be done, and that right quickly. Mrs. Abercromby stood in the way. She must be removed. So in August, just as Mr. Sharpus's bill fell due, she died.

It has usually been assumed that Mrs. Wainewright was the partner of her husband's crimes, but in the absence of direct evidence, and in the face of the fact that her own mother was one of the victims, we incline to believe that the idealist's astuteness was sufficient to deceive her as it did every one else.

The bill was arranged for—that is, Wainewright made an affidavit that he had given no other security to any one, and payment was postponed to the 21st of December.

A decent interval was necessary for mourning, but the

exigencies of the situation demanded that it should be as short as possible. Miss Abercromby, who had now attained the age of twenty-one, wrote to the Ordnance Office stating that she was "totally unprovided for," and requesting the continuance of the £10 pension. She also made an affidavit to the same effect. The assurance scheme was also revived, and during the months of September and October she made proposals to seven offices for an aggregate amount of over £20,000, of which £12,000 was accepted — the Alliance declining on the ground that two years ago a young lady had come to take out a short period policy and had died very soon afterwards from foul play, and the Eagle not wishing to increase their risk. At other offices some of the necessary questions were answered falsely — at the Imperial she stated that she was not insured elsewhere but intended to make a £2,000 proposal. The officials of the Company discovered that she actually had a policy for £5,000 and had also made an unsuccessful proposal. Nevertheless the assurance was granted. She also stated that she wished to secure a sum of money for her sister in case she died within two years, after which other sources would be available. At the Globe she was declined owing to statements which were known by the Company to be false. Here, when asked the reason, she said she didn't exactly know : some money matters had to be arranged— ladies did not know much about these things. At the Provident the case, though accepted, was never completed. This can only be attributed to lack of funds to pay the premium with. Indeed it is remarkable that Wainewright was able to raise as much as he did, over two hundred pounds, considering his straitened condition.

On the 12th of December, 1830, the family, consisting of Mr. and Mrs. Wainewright, the Abercrombys, the baby, Harriet Grattan the old family nurse, and another servant, removed to furnished lodgings over a tailor's shop at 12, Conduit Street. The ostensible reason was to allow the young ladies to see something of the sights of London, and there was still some business to be transacted. So on the following day Helen went to the office of a Mr. Leest, and there made a will in favour of her sister Madeleine. This was one of Waine-wright's cleverest ideas, as it removed the appearance of the numerous policies being for his own benefit, and he would have no difficulty in getting the control of the money after-wards, even if he did not again take refuge in poison. There is no evidence that he had any designs on Madeleine's life, but it certainly does not seem improbable. But as ready money was urgently needed for his immediate needs it was as well that some of the assurance money should be available at once. Accordingly he got his sister-in-law to assign the policies in the Hope and the Palladium to him—the first assignment being prepared by Mr. James Bird, an attorney, on the 13th, the second by Mr. Thomas Kirk, also a lawyer, on the 14th. In each case there was a nominal consideration of £19 19s. which was, almost certainly, never paid.

All these business transactions must have been annoying to the poor girl, but as a compensation there were the joys of the theatre. On the 13th, and again on the 14th, the party went to the play. On the night of the 14th they walked home, and, it being wet, Miss Abercromby—ladies are so incautious—having thin shoes on, got her feet damp. Nevertheless she was able to partake heartily of the supper of lobsters and porter. During the supper she began to feel very unwell, and in the night had a bad, restless headache and was very sick. In the morning she was still ill, but got up to dinner.

As she seemed gradually to get worse Dr. Locock, whom Mr. Forster describes as a distinguished physician, was called in. He found the patient sitting in her bedroom, with bad headache, a weight over her eyes, and partial blindness. He prescribed simple remedies—a black dose, calomel, and senna—which did not appear to do much good. Accordingly, to abate feverish symptoms, which began to develop, he ordered tartar emetic, which produced violent vomiting. Still the disease increased, and by the 20th sedatives were necessary. The next morning she was decidedly better, so much so that Wainewright, who had been greatly worried of late, went with his wife up the Thames sketching. His wife administered a last dose before starting. When they were gone the patient became hysterical and complained of a little boy coming along the room. This was followed, after a burst of tears, by violent convulsions. The servant who was in the room, being alarmed, sent for Messrs. King and Nicholson, apothecaries, and a Mr. Hanks came and saw her. Dr. Locock also called and found her better and sensible. She said, " Doctor, I am dying; I feel I am; I am sure so." He said, " You will be better by and by." The family nurse said that Mrs. Abercromby had died in the same way, and Helen cried out, " Yes, my mother! oh, my poor mother! " The doctor left, but the convulsions returned, and an hour or so later she died. A grim figure in the sick chamber was the old nurse who from the first expected a fatal result, and who uttered gloomy and despairing cries to the effect that Helen's mother and Dr. Griffiths had died in exactly the same manner.

Dr. Locock thought that the death was due to brain mischief, and proposed to make an examination, which Wainewright at once assented to. Accordingly, next day the brain was opened by Hanks and a considerable quantity of water was found on the lower part, pressing upon the upper part of the spinal marrow. Two days afterwards the stomach was given to a surgeon—Mr. Graham—for examination, but beyond a few points in which the blood vessels were much more injected with blood than usual, and a few specks under the coat of the stomach it appeared to be normal.

Some doubt exists as to the poison employed. It is always given as strychnine, the evidence being the specks on the stomach, the convulsions, and the fact that Wainewright was afterwards found with it in his possession. Dr. Locock himself subsequently believed in this theory, and accounted for his failing to detect it on the ground that at that time the action of the drug was very imperfectly known. That strychnine was the immediate cause of death is likely enough, but that it was the only poison used is at least doubtful. In the first place the convulsions did not commence until the 20th, whereas the illness first developed on the 14th; in the next, strychnine is not an easy drug to administer to a healthy person, as, so far from being "almost tasteless," as one of the biographers says, it has an exceedingly bitter taste, which it is practically impossible to conceal. If, therefore, a dose of it had been put into Helen Abercromby's beer she would very likely have declined to drink it altogether on account of its nastiness. Again, vomiting, with which the illness commenced, is not a symptom of strychnine poisoning. On the whole evidence seems to point to the belief that Wainewright first prepared her with some other drug, possibly antimony, and then finished the business with nux vomica. If this is so it is worth noticing that one of the first remedies applied was tartar emetic, which is itself a preparation of antimony. It may also be noted that the suggested double poisoning is the method attributed to the notorious William Palmer, the Rugeley murderer.[1]

The way seemed now clear to affluence, but an unexpected difficulty arose. The offices declined to pay, alleging that the assurance was not *bond fide* for Miss Abercromby's benefit, and that, even if it were, sufficient false statements had been made to them to invalidate the policies. Wainewright consulted yet another solicitor—Mr. Acheson—who advised him that his claim was a just one, and suggested legal proceedings. Accordingly steps were taken to commence proceedings in Chancery against the directors of the Imperial, it being understood that the decision of the case would govern the others. Wainewright's usual acumen did not desert him in the choice of the office to fight, as the contention of the offices that the assurances were really for his benefit would have been much strengthened if either of the offices whose policies had been actually assigned to him had been selected.

Financially speaking things were as bad as ever. The bills were coming due, and to meet them there was only the prospect of money which could not be paid before the action

---

[1] Palmer's case presents several points of resemblance to that under consideration. For an interesting and elaborate account of the Rugeley case (especially from the medical aspect) see G. L. Browne and C. G. Stewart's "Reports of Trials for Murder by Poisoning." 1883.

came off, and proceedings in Chancery were very much more deliberate then even than they are now. Still, as the prospects of ultimate success were considered hopeful, it might be possible to raise a loan, and in January of the following year a gentleman was found willing to advance £1,000, with which Sharpus was paid off, and certain other creditors.

Wainewright's spirits seem to have remained high. We have a record of his serenading a young lady, the daughter of a friend of his—a Norfolk gentleman who had been in the army—at Caroline Place, Mecklenburgh Square, when writs were abroad for his arrest, and when a friend of Mr. Thornbury, who was staying in the same house, was actually arrested in mistake for him. This sort of life could not last long; a prolonged visit to the Continent was deemed advisable, and the Norfolk friend expressed his willingness to go with " kind, light-hearted " Wainewright to Boulogne. So about May, 1831, Wainewright left his wife, whom he never saw again, and put the sea between himself and his creditors.

A story is told of yet another murder which is supposed to have occurred about this period. The story is this: the Norfolk gentleman was suffering from that common disease, lack of funds, and was anxious to raise a loan on personal security. Wainewright suggested that this could best be managed through an insurance office; many such transact this class of business. A bond is prepared stipulating for repayment—usually by instalments—within a certain period of time—say five years—and interest and instalments have to be guaranteed by two substantial sureties. An assurance is effected on the borrower's life for about twice the amount of the advance, out of which the Company repays itself should death take place before the loan is finally paid off. The policy is assigned to the Company, and the loan, less the first year's premium and legal expenses, is paid over. The method is simplicity itself provided the sureties are forthcoming, and advantageous to all parties—except, perhaps, to the sureties. The scheme was adopted; Wainewright thought the Pelican a good office for the purpose; the life was considered a good one, a policy was issued for £3,000, and the advance was carried through. Wainewright's motive is represented as being one of simple revenge, he being enraged at the resistance offered by the offices to his just claims. So one evening when coffee was brought in after dinner he squeezed poison from one of his numerous rings into the cup of his friend, who died shortly afterwards in convulsions. Wainewright, of course, could not stop long alone with his deceased friend's daughter, so he shortly left Boulogne for St. Omer, in Brittany, his journey being consoled by the thought that he had got £3,000 out of the Pelican.

The whole tale would appear to be of the most doubtful authenticity. The motive is preposterously inadequate. In all the previous murders the object was immediate or deferred benefit of a very substantial character. Here it was either a feeble piece of spite—feeble because it was directed not against an individual, but against a Company which would hardly feel it—or a wanton enjoyment of crime for its own sake contrary to the whole nature of the man. But there are more positive objections. The absence of details is so marked as to be alone almost conclusive. No name is given—a Norfolk gentleman is vagueness itself; no date is given; no single detail is given except that the policy was for £3,000 and effected with the Pelican. But on inquiry at that office the writer was informed that after careful search no trace of any such assurance could be found. The evidence points clearly to the theory that the whole narrative is mythical.

Madeleine Abercromby married, in the May of the next year (1832), Mr. Wheatley, auctioneer, of Piccadilly. If Wainewright had ever any criminal intentions with regard to his second sister-in-law they probably had disappeared before this, but this must have been a final blow to any hopes he might still have indulged in of keeping the insurance money in the family.

Of Wainewright's Continental wanderings during the next few years we know extremely little. In the early part of 1833, however, he was in Paris, where he fell into extreme destitution. Procter received a letter from him in 1833

asking for a very small loan or gift in money, which was
sent. " The letter was in his usual fantastic style, referring to some pictures which I then had, particularly to my
'Dusk Giorgione,' as he termed it. But when he had to
tell of his wretched state, his tone deepened. 'Sir, I
starve,' he said, adding that he had been obliged to pawn
his only shirt in order to enable him to pay the postage
of the letter." He had, it must be presumed, long discarded
"our pale lemon-coloured kid gloves and the antique
cameos in our breast-pins."

He is said to have resided for a time at Calais, where we
are gravely assured he became personally intimate with a
married female, whom fear of detection " or some other
strong motive " induced him to poison. But here it is
obviously necessary to be on one's guard against the
insidious growth of a Wainewright legend. He may have
committed another murder at Calais, or he may not ; the
evidence seems confined to a vague, bald, and most unconvincing assertion. The reputation of an established poisoner
is evidently of the most elastic kind, and people credit him
with a mysterious disappearance as glibly as they father a
belated joke upon Douglas Jerrold. But such attributions
are often merely decorative hypotheses, in regard to which
it is necessary, even in the case of the Borgias, to maintain
an attitude of critical, if not incredulous reserve.

A period of six months, between 1833 and 1836, was spent
by Wainewright in a Parisian prison as a suspect, his
account of himself being inconsistent with known facts.
Moreover, strychnine was found on his person ; but to this
little importance was attached, as it was only considered
evidence of eccentricity natural to an Englishman. It was
not until June, 1837, that he again returned to England, but
in the meantime events had occurred which demand a little
attention.

Legal proceedings are proverbially slow, and at most
periods of history complaints on this score arise. Helen
Abercromby died in December, 1830, and proceedings were
commenced almost immediately, yet it was not until the end
of June, 1835, that the trial came on. Mr. Serjeant Tal-

fourd, who certainly should know, airily attributes the length of the interval to "proceedings in Equity." Distinguished counsel were engaged. Mr. Erle, Sir William Follett, and Mr. Henderson, for the plaintiff. The Attorney-General, Sir John Campbell (afterwards Lord Chancellor), Sir F. Pollock, and others for the defendants. The evidence need not be dealt with in much detail as most of the facts have already been set out. The actuary to the Imperial, called by the plaintiff, proved the policy, and in cross-examination repeated the misinformation given him by the assured and Mrs. Wainewright. The servants gave evidence as to the nature of the symptoms. In cross-examination the nurse told of the similar death of Mrs. Abercromby, and both said that their wages had not been paid. Dr. Locock detailed the symptoms and remedies tried at length. He had no doubt death was due to natural causes, and attributed the illness to the oysters and wet feet. Effusion on the brain was the immediate cause of death, and this was caused by oysters (as seen above, he afterwards modified his opinion). In cross-examination he admitted that most vegetable poisons leave no trace. This was all the evidence offered. The defence did not call witnesses, but contented itself with pointing out the suspicious features of the case, the poverty of Miss Abercromby, the indebtedness of Wainewright, the astonishing amount of assurance money at stake, and so on. It contended that the nominal proposer was a mere tool in her brother-in-law's hands, and that in any case the misrepresentation was vital. Lord Abinger, who tried the case, pointed out that murder was no defence, and practically censured the defence for the course it had pursued. The only points for the jury were the importance of the misrepresentation and the *bonâ fide* character of the assurance. The jury deliberated for two hours, and then being six and six, with no prospect of agreement, was discharged.

The case was retried early in December. The evidence offered for the plaintiff was substantially the same as in the previous trial, the chief exception being that Hanks was called to strengthen the medical evidence. He said that there was nothing in the state of the stomach to cause suspicion. The defence, however, changed its tactics. Without dwelling so much on the possible criminal acts of Wainewright, it called a variety of witnesses to prove the statements of counsel. Representatives of many of the other offices involved proved the other insurances. A clerk in the Ordnance Office proved that at the time they were effected Miss Abercromby described herself as being totally unprovided for. The solicitors, Kirk, Leest, and Bird, spoke to the assignments and the preparation of the will ; tradesmen and others showed that the Wainewrights were at the time unable to pay their debts. Lord Abinger, who was again the judge, changed his position somewhat, and was much more favourable to the defence. " The case," he said, " was pregnant with suspicion," and moreover " not a tittle of proof had been adduced to substantiate the reasons given " for the assurance. The jury almost immediately found for the defendants on the ground of misrepresentation, and of Miss Abercromby having no real interest in the insurance.[1]

In June, 1837, Wainewright returned to his native country —why is uncertain, but according to one tale there was a woman in the case. Great precaution was necessary, as warrants were now out for the forgery, which had at length been discovered. He put up *incognito* at a hotel in Covent Garden. One morning when in a sitting-room on the ground floor, he happened to push aside the blind to discover the cause of a noise in the street, when, by a curious coincidence, one Forrester, a Bow Street runner, was passing. Forrester recognised him. " That's Wainewright, the bank-forger!" he exclaimed, and at once proceeded to arrest him. His trial took place early in the next month. At this time, though forgery was still punishable by death, a serious agitation had set in in favour of milder treatment. The Bank expressed their willingness not to proceed with the charge of forgery if the prisoner would plead guilty to uttering the forged cheque, which was not a capital offence. Wainewright con-

---

[1] The trial settled the not altogether unimportant point in insurance law, that verbal misrepresentations might be sufficient to annul a policy.

sented, and was sentenced by the Recorder to transportation for life.

Many tales are told of Wainewright's conversation during the few days that elapsed before he was transported. It was then that he was recognised by Macready, who was going over Newgate with Dickens, Hablot Browne, and Forster. To quote Mr. Forster's account, they "were startled by a sudden tragic cry of ' My God! there's Wainewright.' In the shabby genteel creature, with sandy, disordered hair, and dirty moustache, who had turned quickly round with a defiant stare at our entrance, looking at once mean and fierce, and quite capable of the cowardly murders he had committed, Macready had been horrified to recognise a man familiarly known to him in former years, and at whose table he had dined." He seems to have talked freely of his crimes, though, if the murders were so well known, it is extraordinary that he was never put on trial. To one who asked him how he could kill such a beautiful girl as Helen Abercromby, he replied, " I don't know. She had very thick ankles," or something to that effect. The following story is better authenticated, and is vouched for by a friend of the other speaker.[1] The conversation was as follows :—

Visitor : " I do not intend to preach to you—that would be idle ; but I ask you, Mr. Wainewright, as a man of sense, whether you do not think your courses have been, to say the least, very absurd ? "

Wainewright : " No. I played for a fortune and I lost. They pay me great respect here, I assure you. They think I am here for £10,000, and that always creates respect."

Visitor : " Well, but if you look back upon your life, and see to what it has brought you, does it not demonstrate to you the folly of your proceedings ? "

Wainewright : " Not a bit. I have always been a gentleman, always lived like a gentleman, and I am a gentleman still. Yes, sir, even in Newgate I am a gentleman. The prison regulations are that we should each in turn sweep the yard. There are a baker and a sweep here besides myself. They sweep the yard ; but, Sir, they have never offered me the broom."

[1] *British Quarterly Review* (1848).

There is a tale of Wainewright's having left at St. Omer a diary, which was secured by the representative of the insurance offices, in which full details of his criminal pro- ceedings were recorded with cold-blooded exactness. This tale is probably false. Had such a diary been in existence, is it credible that the author would never have been charged with the murders ? Moreover Mr. Hazlitt found, on inquiry at the offices, that they knew nothing about it. The positive and negative evidence combined appear conclusive.

Within a few years of his arrival in Tasmania he was admitted to the hospital at Hobart Town, where he stayed some years, though sufficiently well to make a number of water-colour sketches, many of which are now—or were until recently—in the possession of Dr. G. H. F. Nuttall, of Baltimore, the son of the doctor at the hospital, and are described as remarkably fine. They include an excellent portrait of Dr. Nuttall, and a pencil sketch of his own head, with the inscription, ' Head of a convict : very charac- teristic of low cunning and revenge.'

In 1844 he made an application for a ticket-of-leave, which is given in full. It shows all the old impudence, rising at times almost to sublimity, and demonstrates that Janus Weathercock's adventures in real life had not materially affected his literary style.

" To His Excellency, Sir John Eardly Wilmot, Bart., Lieut.-Governor of Van Dieman's Land, etc., etc.

" The humble petition of T. Griffiths Wainewright, pray- ing for the indulgence of a ticket-of-leave.

" To palliate the boldness of this application he offers the statement ensuing. That *seven* years past he was arrested on a charge of forging, and acting on a power of attorney to sell stock *thirteen years previous*. Of which (though looking for little credence) he avers his entire innocence. He admits a knowledge of the actual committer, gained though some years after the fact. Such, however, were their relative positions, that to have disclosed it would have made him infamous where any human feeling is manifest. Neverthe- less, by his counsel's direction, he entered the plea Not

Guilty, to allow him to adduce the '*circonstance attenuante*,' viz., that the money (£5,200) appropriated was, without quibble, *his own*, derived from his parents. An hour before his appearing to plead he was trepanned (through the just but deluded Governor of Newgate) into withdrawing his plea, by a promise, in such case, of a punishment merely nominal· The same *purporting* to issue from the *Bank Parlour*, but in fact from the agents of certain *Insurance Companies* interested to a heavy amount (£16,000) in compassing his legal non-existence. He pleaded guilty, and was forthwith hurried, stunned with such ruthless perfidy, to the hulks at Portsmouth, and thence in *five days* aboard the *Susan*, sentenced to Life in a land (to him) a moral sepulchre. As a ground for your mercy he submits with great deference his foregone condition of life during 43 years of freedom. A *descent* deduced, through family tradition and *Edmondson's Heraldry*, from a stock not the least honoured in Cambria, nurtured with all appliances of ease and comfort, schooled by his relative, the well-known philologer and bibliomaniac, Chas. Burney, D.D., brother to Mdme. D'Arblay, and the companion of Cooke. Lastly, such a modest competence as afforded the *mental* necessaries of Literature, Archæology, Music and the Plastic Arts ; while his pen and brush introduced him to the notice and friendship of men whose fame is European. The Catalogues of Somerset House Exhibitions, the *Literary Pocket Book*, indicate his earlier pursuits, and the MS. left behind in Paris, attest at least his industry. Their titles imply the objects to which he has, *to this date*, directed all his energies : 'A Philosophical Theory of Design, as concerned with the Loftier Emotions, showing its deep action on Society, drawn from the Phidean-Greek, and early Florentine Schools' (the result of seventeen years study), illustrated with numerous plates, executed with conscientious accuracy, in one vol., atlas folio. 'An Aesthetic and Psychological Treatise on the Beautiful ; or the Analogies of Imagination and Fancy, as exerted in Poesy, whether Verse, Painting, Sculpture, Music, or Architecture,' to form four vols., folio, with a profusion of engravings by the first artists of Paris, Munich, Berlin, Dresden, and Wien, ' An

Art Novel,' in three vols., and a collection of ' Fantasie, Critical Sketches, etc., selected partly from *Blackwood*, the *Foreign Review*, and the *London Magazine*.' All these were nearly ready for, *one* actually at, *press*. Deign, your Excellency ! to figure to yourself my *actual* condition during seven years ; without *friends, good name* (the breath of life), or art (the fuel to it with *me*), tormented at once by memory and ideas struggling for outward form and realisation, barred up from increase of knowledge, and deprived of the exercise of profitable or even of *decorous* speech.   Take pity, your Excellency ! and grant me the power to shelter my eyes from Vice in her most revolting and sordid phase, and my ears from a jargon of filth and blasphemy that would outrage the cynicism of Parny himself. Perhaps this clinging to the lees of a vapid life may seem as *base, unmanly*, arguing rather a plebeian, than a liberal and gentle descent. But, your Excellency ! the wretched *Exile* has a child ! and *Vanity* (sprung from the praise of Flaxman, *Charles Lamb*, Stothard, Rd. Westall, *Delaroche, Cornelius*, Laurence, and the god of his worship, Fuseli) whispers that the *follower of the Ideal might* even yet achieve another reputation than that of a *Faussaire.* Seven years of steady demeanour may in *some* degree promise that no indulgence shall ever be abused by your Excellency's miserable petitioner.

"T. G. WAINEWRIGHT."

On this remarkable and most unveracious production the Governor laconically endorsed " A. T. L.[1] would be contrary to Act of Parlt. T. L. refused. 3rd class wages received (?)."

When discharged from the hospital Wainewright continued to paint portraits. Of one of these, a small oil painting of a girl's face, which was shown at a party at Gore House in 1847 by Lady Blessington, Mr. Forster says that Wainewright " had contrived somehow to put the expression of his own wickedness into the portrait of a nice kindhearted girl," but as he does not appear to have known the original, the statement may be accepted *cum grano.* No

<hr>

[1] Ticket-of-leave.

such criticism, at any rate, has been passed on any other of his pictures made at this time. The sketches shown by Lady Blessington to Bulwer Lytton are described as very clever, and showing considerable delicacy of taste.

It is stated that Wainewright's criminal propensities did not desert him in Hobart Town, that he became a confirmed opium-eater, was of grossly sensual habits, took pleasure in traducing persons who had befriended him, conversed indelicately with lady sitters, and twice attempted to murder his sitters. A gruesome story is told of his hissing in the ear of a dying convict whom he disliked : " You are a dead man, you ——. In four-and-twenty hours your soul will be in hell, and my arms will be up to that (the elbow) in your body dissecting you." Some of these tales may be true, but we can hardly believe that, after he had attempted to murder one sitter, he would have been allowed to continue his occupation ; and many of the other details are possibly fictions.

What is more certain is, that he was very unpopular, having practically only one friend, a cat (throughout life he entertained an affectionate regard for this animal) and died very miserably of apoplexy in the hospital about 1852.

The words of Barry Cornwall are sufficiently suitable for an epitaph :—

" Who would have supposed that from a man who was absolutely a fop, finikin in dress, with mincing steps and tremulous words, with his hair curled and full of unguents, and his cheeks painted like those of a frivolous demirep, would flame out ultimately the depravity of a poisoner and a murderer ? "

EDWARD KELLY.

(1855–1880.)

"O for a fine thief of the age of two-and-twenty, or thereabouts ! "
(*Henry IV.*, Pt. I., Act III., sc. ii.)

AUSTRALIA, with its marsupials, echidna, and platypi, its cockatoos, its lyre-birds, brush-turkeys, and bush-rangers, is pre-eminently the home of strange and archaic types of life. The Australian bushranger, recently extinct, was a bandit of very ancient type. We cannot call him a highwayman, for he rejoiced in the scarcity of highways. He lived in the scrub and the waste hills, whence he operated against the little oases of civilisation that dotted the far-spreading wilderness. The bushrangers who preceded the Kellys, however, had more in common than they with our highwaymen of the last century. They did business, it seems, chiefly with travellers and mail-coaches. The last of this old-fashioned school was a man named Power, who was extinguished eight years before the Kellys went to work. The scene of his exploits was the same that was afterwards dignified by the labours of his successors—in the north of the colony of Victoria about Benalla. But after his extinction several years elapsed before any other bushranger took the field against society. Times had changed, and the risks of the business were increasing. To Ned Kelly and his comrades belongs the credit of attempting the revival of this declining branch of industry. And not only did they revive it, but they introduced improvements on the older methods ; operating on a much larger scale than their comparatively commonplace predecessors. Instead of coaches they robbed

NED KELLY IN HIS ARMOUR.

EDWARD KELLY.

(........)

"O....... of the age of ....
(Henry ... Pt. I ....)

...... A, with its .... e... ....,
.... its lyre-birds, brush-tu...
....ently the home of stran...
.... the Australian bushranger, re...
....very ancient type. We can...
....to be register...l in the scarcity ...
....to and ... he waste hill...
.... the ...tle ...es of civilisation
....g wilderness. The bushran..
...... Kelly, however ...d more in com...
.... en of the ... century. The...
It S...... ...... with trav .... and mail-coa...
of tra .... and ... d was a man named ...
was .... d ..h't years before the Kellys w...
The s...... ......xploits was the same that w.s
...... by .... of his successors—...r. the ...
...... of Vi...... about Benalla. But after he
...... d y .... before any other bushran..e
.... s...... Things had changed, and the
.... s were ...erensing To N...t Kelly and h...
...... the ...... empts the revival
...... g ...... which ...... And not only did ...
it, but ...... introdu...d ...... ments on the ol'ea n...
oper...... on a much larger s..le t an their ...mp...
...... predecessors. Instead of coa hes they r...

NED KELLY IN HIS ARMOUR.

banks; they terrorised whole towns instead of a few travellers; they aspired to wreck trains, and clear the countryside altogether of that objectionable institution, the police.

By parentage Ned Kelly was an Irishman. His father,
John Kelly, had been sent out to do fifteen years' penal
servitude for killing a man in a faction fight at Belfast.
After his release he had married a certain Ellen Quin, an
Irish-Australian, whose family, says Superintendent Hare,
who ought to know, "were all thieves." This hopeful
couple had six children, of whom Ned, born probably in
1855, was the eldest. There were two brothers, James and
Daniel, and three sisters, Bridget, Mary and Kate. Dan
Kelly, who is almost as much the subject of this sketch as
Ned himself, was about five years younger than his elder
brother.

Ned's early childhood was passed on a farm near Avenel
in Victoria. He was, we may fairly say, born and bred to
robbery. His father, indeed, died while Ned was yet a little
boy, but the paternal teachings were not lost, and the mother
remained to enforce them. After the death of Mr. John
Kelly the family removed to another farm on Eleven Gun
Creek, four miles from the township of Greta, which itself is
about fifteen from Benalla, in the Murray district of northern
Victoria.

The Kelly boys grew up strong and hardy, with plenty of
early practice in riding their own horses and in stealing
those of other people. Their mother may well have chosen
her place of residence with reference to the predatory habits
of her family. Behind the farm was a wide stretch of
wilderness, with abundance of scrub and low hills—a
difficult country to travel in and an easy country to hide
in. At the age of fourteen Ned was already engaged in
the profitable and tolerably safe business of horse-stealing.
Horses straying in the bush were captured and sold; others,
purloined after a more enterprising fashion, were hidden in
the bush and produced on the offer of a reward. In this way
Ned became an apt and precocious student of bush-lore.
Before long he knew every yard of the country round Greta;
he had learned how to track through the waste and how to

conceal his own tracks. Police tracks in especial he studied
with care. At the age of fifteen Ned must already have
recognised the possibility that he might be forced to take
to living in the bush altogether.

But there was not enough in mere horse-stealing to satisfy
Ned's boyish ardour. When about fourteen years old he
engaged himself as assistant to the bushranger Power,
already referred to. With Power he served a short
apprenticeship. His part of the work was to hold horses
in readiness at a distance while Power went into action.
After a connection of less than a year's duration the two
separated, luckily for Ned, for Power was captured immediately afterwards. After the dissolution of their
partnership they spoke evil of each other. Power accused
Ned of cowardice, declaring that he turned pale under fire.
Ned complained of the bushranger's bad temper, and said
he would have been murdered had he stayed with him.

Ned now again devoted himself with great energy to the
stealing of horses and cattle, aided henceforth by his brother
Dan. In the following years the two brothers became the
terror of the farmers and drovers of the country about Greta.
Their doings were soon notorious, and were sadly interfered
with by the police. Several times they were convicted, and
in 1871 Ned was sent to prison for three years. But the
business was too exciting, and probably too profitable, to be
abandoned, and the brothers held to it till, in the April of
1878, the crisis came.

At that time Dan Kelly happened to be wanted by the
police, though, for some reason, Ned was not. Constable
Fitzpatrick accordingly went to the lonely farmhouse on
Eleven Gun Creek to arrest him. It was a very rash
proceeding, especially as the constable seems to have been
unarmed. In the house he found, apparently, the man he
wanted, along with Mrs. Kelly and Ned and two friends
of the family, men named Williamson and Skillian.
Skillian had married Ned's sister Bridget. The parley
grew hot, and the Kellys were overpowered by their indignation at being thus interfered with. Mrs. Kelly seized the
fire-shovel and knocked the intruder down, and, in the

scuffle that ensued, a pistol was fired, probably by Dan, and the policeman hit in the wrist. The disabled officer of the law was then graciously permitted to depart, first swearing that he would reveal nothing of what had happened. This promise he, naturally, did not keep.

It was a very serious affair for the brothers. Ned, as an old offender, could hope for no mercy from the defied authorities. Dan, who was of an even more reckless spirit, was by no means inclined tamely to submit to imprisonment. The bush or the prison was the alternative before the two young men, and they were off to the bush at once. The police, a little too late, arrested their valiant mother and Messrs. Skillian and Williamson, and shortly after a reward of £100 was offered for the apprehension of the brothers.

Shortly after this retreat into the desert, whereby the Kellys first cut themselves loose altogether from society, they were joined by two other young men, by name Joe Byrne and Stephen Hart. Byrne was twenty-one years old, a tall and powerful man, whose native place was Woolshed. Later on he became invaluable, having a good head and being able to read and write. He was even a poet, and wrote songs which the four outlaws used to sing in the wilderness. His subjects were the delights of bushranging and the iniquities of the police. Steve Hart, twenty-four years old, came from Wangaratta. He and Dan Kelly seem to have been the most brutal and reckless members of the gang.

To apprehend them was by no means easy. The four young men were of the hardiest breed, inured to cold and privation, able to sleep an abnormal number of hours at a stretch, and hence to bear the lack of sleep if necessary; and they knew the country and its ways thoroughly. Imagine a far more extensive Dartmoor, thickly overgrown with trees and shrubs, with farms and small hamlets dotted about, and no roads to speak of; in such a country it would not be easy to arrest four well-armed and mounted men, who knew every track and covert and cleft in the hills. Roughly speaking, and allowing for the difference of vegetation and the comparative scarcity of water, such was the country in which the Kellys maintained themselves for over two years in defiance of the resources of civilisation. They had plenty of room besides. Their range extended from the Wombat Hills in the south, beyond Greta, for more than a hundred miles to the north, over the New South Wales frontier.

Nevertheless it would have been impossible from the first for them to have held out but for the co-operation of their respective families and the general disinclination to assist the police. Among the rude and rather primitive settlers of this wild and extensive tract of country the police seem to have been unpopular. At all events none of them were inclined, even for £100, to risk interference with desperate men on behalf of the public good. And on the other hand, the comparatively law-abiding members of the families of Kelly, Byrne, and Hart, were active and even zealous on behalf of the outlaws. Mrs. Kelly, indeed, was in prison, and remained there till the end of the story, but Ned's sisters, especially Bridget Skillian and Kate, were of immense service. A system of "bush telegraphs" was soon concerted, and by means of such signalling from hill to hill, as well as by more direct means of communication, the four men were kept well informed of the movements of the parties of police in search of them. When the Greta district was too thickly beset with men of the law they could move off to Wangaratta, and be in touch with the Harts, or to Woolshed, where the Byrnes came to their aid.

But a collision with the police was sure to occur sooner or later. After six months of bush life the whereabouts of the fugitives was betrayed to the police in October, 1878. The betrayer repented himself immediately afterwards, for he thereupon proceeded to betray the plans of the police to the fugitives. They were then ensconced in the Wombat Hills; and thither Sergeant Kennedy with three constables, all mounted and fully armed, were sent to take them. To send only four men to arrest four others equally well armed, seems somewhat rash, but doubtless the authorities had no more men available and the opportunity seemed too good to let slip.

On this occasion, forewarned and aware of the weakness of their enemy, the bushrangers resolved to teach the police a lesson. It seems clear that they would have had no difficulty in avoiding the police party if they had chosen to do so, but they chose to do the contrary. Ned, as commander-in-chief, was responsible for this decision, but no more than that can be said. What exactly was the design of the bushrangers there is nothing to show, but the result of their action compromised them hopelessly.

The small police party camped in the scrub among the hills, unwitting of the fact that the men they had come for were actually watching them. In the afternoon two of them, Sergeant Kennedy and a man named Scanlan, rode off to reconnoitre ; the others, Lonergan and McIntyre, remaining at the camp. The two men sat outside the tent without thought of danger, and McIntyre unarmed. Suddenly, with a cry of "Bail up and throw up your hands !" there were four rifles levelled at them from close quarters. McIntyre obeyed ; Lonergan made an attempt to draw his revolver and was shot dead on the spot by one of the Kellys.

All four of the bushrangers were on the scene. They possessed themselves of all the arms in the tent, and bade McIntyre keep where he was. He was to warn the other policemen on their return that resistance was useless, and tell them that they would be shot if they did not surrender. The bushrangers concealed themselves in the scrub close at hand, and all five men were quiet, waiting. At last Kennedy and Scanlan appeared. When they were close to the tent McIntyre rose to meet them, calling out, "The bushrangers are in possession. You had better surrender." Both the men addressed, acting on the first impulse of brave men, sprang from their horses with intent to fight. Scanlan was shot dead on the instant ; Kennedy got behind his horse as cover, but the horse, misliking the situation, bolted. As the horse plunged past him Constable McIntyre sprang on it and managed to scramble into the saddle. The terrified beast carried him headlong away through the scrub, and Kennedy was left alone to face the four ruffians. Even now he would not surrender, but ran for his life from tree to tree, turning and firing back as he went. At last, a quarter of a mile from the camp, he lay in the scrub, badly wounded and his revolver empty. For the sake of his wife and children he begged his life. If Hart and Byrne had done their part in the previous murders his life, it seems, might have been spared. But the prudent Ned, as he told Aaron Sherrit, of whom we shall hear later, feared that they "might round upon him, as they had not killed a man yet." He therefore ordered the two of them to discharge their rifles into Kennedy's body, and the order was obeyed. Having compromised his comrades by this piece of brutality, Ned, with curious inconsistency, proceeded to show his respect for the dead man's courage by fetching a coat from the camp to cover his body. "He was the bravest man I ever heard of," said Ned.

Meanwhile Constable McIntyre, sole survivor of the expedition, reached a place of safety and told his story. Another party of police was forthwith despatched to the scene of the encounter. The bushrangers had of course decamped. We obtain an idea of the difficulties against which the police had to contend in the bush when we learn that, after arriving at the desolate camp, it took them three days to find Kennedy's body lying in the scrub a quarter of a mile distant. Ned and his comrades were now formally outlawed, and the reward for their capture was increased to £1,000.

The position of the outlaws was now becoming desperate. If they were taken it would be a hanging matter for all of them; and the police, active before, were certain to be far more active than ever. Moreover, the reward of £1,000 might reasonably be expected to induce many persons hitherto neutral to take sides with the police. Even their own relatives could not be supposed to be above temptation. Under these circumstances it is somewhat strange that the outlaws should have made no attempt to get clear of the districts in which they were known, altogether. But the dangers and difficulties of a northerly march into the unsettled wilderness of central New South Wales, through which they might have hoped to reach a new country and start life afresh, would doubtless have been great. They preferred to remain at bay. But in order to do so with any prospect of ultimate escape, it was absolutely imperative to have money. They did not want money for themselves—it could be of little or no use in the bush; but the Government had set a heavy price on their heads, and it was necessary to meet the Government with its own weapons. Money, in fact, was necessary to enable them to maintain the zeal of their relatives, and to purchase assistance or connivance on all sides outside their own families. Hitherto, during their outing in the bush, they had abstained from robbery, obtaining their food supply partly from their relatives and partly living on what they could pick up in the bush, where rabbits and other small game were to be had for the shooting. Hitherto they had lived merely as fugitive outlaws, now circumstances compelled them to take to brigandage. And it would be, moreover, of no use to rob mere travellers, or to raid isolated farms; petty gains would not serve their turn. If they were to maintain their position they were bound to operate on a large scale.

After some two months of devious and uncertain wanderings they resolved on a grand *coup*: nothing less than the robbery of the bank at Euroa, a little town lying on the railway between Melbourne and Sydney, and not far from the Wombat Hills. Whose the idea was we cannot say; but it was Joe Byrne who worked out the details of the plan of action, wrote them out fair on paper, and read them over to his comrades till each man knew his part perfectly.

On the southern side of Euroa, about three miles from the little town and close to the railway, was a station farm called Faithful Creek. This place was fixed on as their base of operations against the bank. The plan of the bushrangers was simplicity itself, but required caution, no less than audacity, to carry into successful execution. They were to go to Euroa and obtain admission to the bank after the closing hour, to overpower any one who might still be within, and secure the booty. But, this done, it would never do to simply ride off with the plunder, leaving their prisoners to

raise the hue and cry. Neither would bonds and gagging
afford sufficiently complete security. They must have a safe
place wherein to bestow their prisoners, while they made
good their escape to the bush. Faithful Creek was to serve
as a temporary prison.

In the morning of the 10th of December, 1878, the four
men appeared, on horseback, at Faithful Creek. Only an
old man and an old woman were in the house when they
arrived, the rest of the population of the station being out
at work. The bushrangers stabled and fed their horses,
which had probably been ridden far and were in need of rest.
The two old people naturally offered no sort of resistance.
As the men working about the farm dropped in to dinner by
ones, twos, and threes, they were seized by the bushrangers,
who had their revolvers cocked, and thrust into a large
store-room, a wooden structure about six paces from the
main building. Mr. McAulay, the master, was served like
the rest. Since the bushrangers had resolved on making
Faithful Creek their base of operations, it was manifestly
necessary to secure every one about the place, lest the alarm
should be given in Euroa. The women of the station were
not, however, imprisoned with the men, but remained free
in the house to attend on their captors, who, when every one
was secure, proceeded to rest and refresh themselves, making
their prisoners preliminarily taste everything they chose
to eat, in fear of poison. The arrival of a hawker, with a
cart full of miscellaneous wares, produced momentary disturbance. The hawker, finding bushrangers in possession
and seeing little chance of doing any profitable trade, desired
to move on. This, of course, could not be allowed ; but,
in spite of an intimation to that effect, the man obstinately
endeavoured to get back into his cart. Dan Kelly would
have shot him on the spot, without a moment's grace or
parley, had not Ned interfered to prevent the useless murder.
Mr. McAulay was then brought out from the store-room
to reason with the recalcitrant hawker, who was at length
persuaded to go and take his place in the store-room with
the rest. Then the bushrangers rifled his cart, dressed
themselves in new clothes from it, and used his scent-
bottles plentifully.

They were in no hurry, and intended to spend the night at the station. The delay appears somewhat risky, but it was perhaps necessary for the sake of the horses. The afternoon hours dragged somewhat under the circumstances; and Dan Kelly was inclined to pass away the time by insulting the women prisoners. Ned, however, having doubtless sense to perceive the danger of such practices, put a stop to this amusement. The night passed with two of the bushrangers on guard while the others slept.

On the following morning there was still nothing to do but wait. It was no use getting to Euroa till the bank was closed. Two gentlemen who came by on horseback, with their servants, were seized and thrust into the store-room; but no other incident of note occurred. Before the time of starting, however, the outlaws took the precaution to cut the telegraph wires on each side of Euroa. The break in the communications having been noticed, a man sent to see about it arrived at Faithful Creek and was promptly conducted to the store-room. At last the time came for a move, and soon after two p.m., Ned and Dan and Steve Hart started for Euroa, leaving the horses and the prisoners in charge of Joe Byrne. Hart rode; the other two went in the hawker's cart, taking the hawker's boy to drive and make himself useful generally. They took with them, also, a cheque on the bank, kindly written for them by Mr. McAulay. They timed themselves precisely, arriving at the bank a few minutes after it had closed for the day, Hart having meanwhile put up his horse at the hotel. Ned presented himself at the front door, cheque in hand and revolver hidden. On being informed that he was too late, Ned was voluble concerning the inconvenience of not getting his cheque cashed that day, with the result that the clerk good-naturedly let him in. Ned closed the door behind him, and a second later had his pistol at the man's head. Meanwhile Hart had managed to force an entrance at the back, and he too now appeared on the scene. Under these circumstances the clerk surrendered without noise or fuss, and was securely tied up and deposited on the floor. The marauders then went to the private room of the bank manager, a Mr. Scott. They found him sitting at a table on which, close to his hand, lay a loaded revolver. He turned half round. " Bail up ! " said Ned, quietly, with levelled pistol. Mr. Scott instinctively reached towards his revolver; then, only just in time, recognised that his adversaries were beforehand with him and meant business. He stayed his hand and submitted to be bound like his clerk. Masters of the situation, the bushrangers proceeded to ransack the bank, securing about £2,000 in notes and cash. But there was more to be done. Mr. Scott lived on the premises and had a wife and family. Ned therefore introduced himself to Mrs. Scott, and, with his Irish courtesy, explained the situation. The lady at first was incredulous and declined to believe that he could really be a bushranger: his manners were too good. Ned, however, succeeded in convincing her that the fact was so. He informed her, politely but firmly, that she must immediately order her carriage and drive out to Faithful Creek with her children and servants. He himself would accompany them in his cart along with Mr. Scott and the clerk. Any attempt to draw the attention of passers-by on the road to the peculiar circumstances of this country drive would, he intimated, infallibly bring instant death to whomsoever made it.

The lady cheerily accepted the situation, and the queer party set out. On the way Ned conversed pleasantly with Mr. Scott, and told him the story of the encounter in the Wombat Hills. Faithful Creek was reached without mishap. There Joe Byrne, heavily armed, had been walking round and round the store-room in which were the prisoners. When the party from Euroa appeared in sight he thought proper to bring them all out and range them in a row. They found him walking up and down the line of prisoners, with his belt stuck full of revolvers and two guns in his hands. All the men, however, along with the new arrivals, were now sent back into the store-room, and the women, children, and bushrangers had tea. The bushrangers were naturally elated, and laughed and chatted gaily. After tea they got out their horses and prepared to start for the bush again. Before leaving, however, Ned thoughtfully went to the store-room to give some parting directions. " If any one

of you," he said to the prisoners, " leave this place within
three hours, I will shoot that man dead. You cannot escape
me in this country, and I assure you I will keep my word."
He then asked one of the gentlemen captured that morning
to hand over his watch as a memento of the occasion. The
gentleman in question objecting that the watch was a keep-
sake from his dead mother, " I will never take that," said
Ned; and he took Mr. McAulay's instead. With this little
episode the stay of Ned's party at Faithful Creek ended.
They went off, leaving all the men prisoners locked up
except Mr. McAulay, who was made specially responsible
for their not leaving the place till eleven o'clock that night.
When Mr. Scott reached Euroa again, at midnight, he found
the town still wholly unconscious of what had happened.

The business had been very neatly managed; and it is
clear that Ned's mates understood the necessity of a strict
obedience to orders. Careful investment of the money now
in hand might enable them to defy all the efforts of the
police for some time to come. Round about Euroa there
was regular panic, and many wild reports were afloat. The
Melbourne Argus was highly indignant, and the Government
increased its activity. All the banks round Euroa were
specially guarded. But the bushrangers were flushed with
success and bolder than ever. Two months had not passed
before they made a still more daring *coup* in another
quarter.

This was at Jerilderie, a small township or village of
between two and three hundred inhabitants in New South
Wales, sixty miles north of the Murray River, and at least
one hundred and twenty miles from Euroa. In going so far
north the bushrangers broke new ground altogether, and had
the advantage of operating in a district where they could
hardly be expected. Jerilderie, in spite of its petty population, boasted four hotels, a police-station half a mile from
the town, with two mounted constables, and the essential
feature—a bank.

At midnight on Saturday, the 9th of February, 1879, after
what was probably a very hard ride, Ned and his mates were
outside the Jerilderie police-station. They shouted the police-

men awake, and when the sleepy men put their heads out to
inquire the cause of the disturbance they were informed
that a drunken man had done murder in the town. Thereupon the constables, by name Devine and Richards, hastily
dressed and came forth, when they were promptly seized
and reduced to silence and submission with threatening
revolvers. The keys of the lock-up were then taken from
them and they were run in. There they might yell for
assistance to their heart's content; nobody would suppose
that they were other than riotous drunkards justly incarcerated. The police of the town thus disposed of, Ned and
his friends proceeded to make prisoners the wife and children
of Devine, and shut them up in one of the rooms, where
Hart stood sentry over them. They informed Mrs. Devine
that if she made a noise the two constables would be killed
first and she and the children afterwards. They then
collected all the arms in the station, stabled their horses
in the police stables, and waited quietly for the morning.
Probably none of them had ever been in the place before,
and it was therefore impossible to go at once to the bank.
Moreover, the next day was Sunday; the bank would be
closed all day, and there might be difficulty in getting in
or in doing much when they got in. They had probably
resolved to stay over the Sunday and do their business on
the following day.

To act thus required caution no less than boldness. Mrs.
Devine was accustomed on Sunday morning to prepare the
church for service. Her absence would be remarked; so
when the morning came she was bidden to get about her
business as usual, Joe Byrne attending her to the church to
ensure her good behaviour. Later on in the day Ned and
Steve Hart, having donned policemen's uniforms, took Constable Richards out of the lock-up and made him walk about
the town with them in friendly fashion as brother officers
of the law. He was compelled to point out the principal
buildings to them, including, of course, the bank, and to
explain to any one who was curious that the strangers were
fresh policemen just sent in for the better security of life and
property at Jerilderie. It was death to disobey, and he sub-

mitted to his part. Let us hope that he was not altogether unconsoled by a sense of the humour of the situation.

In this manner the Sunday was safely passed, and on the following morning the bushrangers, having completed their plans, set to work in earnest. To begin with, one of them, in the guise of one of Jerilderie's new protectors, took two horses to be shod and brought them back to the police stables. At eleven in the morning the whole four went in a body to the Royal Hotel, which stood only a few steps from the bank, leaving the constables, and, presumably, Mrs. Devine and the children, safe in the lock-up. Ned politely explained matters to the hotel manager, and promised that no one should be hurt who did not make himself unpleasant. The manager, no doubt, was duly deferential; and the bushrangers now made the hotel their headquarters. The bank clerks at least had to be incarcerated somewhere before the adventurers could safely leave Jerilderie with their spoils, and it appears that the lock-up was full. But in the hotel there was a large dining-room which would excellently serve the purpose.

All persons in the hotel were now conducted to this room and shut up; and it was necessary to deal similarly with every one who came to the hotel in the course of the day. After securing the hotel Ned and his brother went down to the bank, leaving the other two on guard. At the bank they had no difficulty. Mr. Tarleton, the manager, a powerful man who had just returned from a forty miles' ride, was surprised by Dan in his bath. He could make no resistance, and was marched off to the hotel. The two accountants also surrendered without giving trouble. One of them was taken straightway to the hotel, the other remained with Ned to open the safes for him. Ned took all the cash and notes he could find, and burned four of the bank books. Then he returned to the hotel with his prisoner.

The deed was now done, and only the final preparations for a retreat remained to be made. Two of the bushrangers went to the telegraph office, overhauled the messages sent during the day, cut the wires, and brought the clerks back, prisoners, to the hotel.

By this time, it may well be supposed, a good many persons in the little town, besides those in the hotel, knew that bushrangers were in possession. Some of these, however, were "sympathisers," and the rest prudently held their peace. Public spirit, strong enough to make a man risk his life for the protection of things in general, is not a commonly diffused quality; and few people have won the right to complain of its absence. On their side the bushrangers were fully conscious of the moral strength of their position. They did not hurry themselves to be off. Ned is even related to have sauntered into another hotel and had a chat with the landlord. "Any one can shoot me," he cheerily remarked, "but they would have to take the consequences: every man in the town would be shot." As he happened to want a new horse, he selected a blood mare from the stable of McDougall's hotel, and sent Dan out for a canter to try it.

At length it was really time to be off. The horses were brought round, and Ned paid a farewell visit to his prisoners. Steve Hart, who had been guarding them, had taken several watches. These Ned now made him return, remarking that he did not want to take private property; all he wanted was bank-money. Nevertheless, he thought proper to take the watch of Mr. Tarleton himself. Presumably the property of the bank manager was in the same category as "bank-money" in Ned's mind. Before leaving he delivered a short oration. He had never, he said, committed a crime till that encounter in the Wombat Hills; he had stolen 280 horses, but that was all. He was an unfortunate, persecuted fellow. How would they, he asked the prisoners, like to have constables coming to their houses and threatening their mothers and sisters with revolvers? After that he rode off with his comrades, taking one of the police horses to carry the booty. Ned and Hart seem to have gone off in the police uniforms they had worn all through. As a last piece of bravado, and to finish the exploit with a noble flourish, Hart and Dan rode wildly up and down the principal street, singing, shouting, and waving their revolvers, before they galloped after the others. Three days later a correspondent of *The Melbourne Argus* significantly writes : " The last of the known confederates of the Kellys cleared out this afternoon."

After this feat the Governments of Victoria and New South Wales joined in offering a reward of £8,000 for the apprehension of the " Kelly gang "—the largest reward, we may add, that has ever been offered for the capture of bushrangers in Australia. Yet, in spite of the reward, and in spite of the great exertions now made by the police, under the energetic direction of Superintendent Hare, Ned and his companions defied all the efforts of the authorities for more than a year to come. It is a remarkable fact that, from October, 1878, when the encounter in the Wombat Hills had taken place, to June, 1880, not one of the numerous search parties of police seems ever to have set eyes on the bushrangers. All that time they were riding up and down the country, making occasional raids ; and all that time they eluded the police absolutely. After the robbery at Jerilderie, indeed, the activity of the police prevented the outlaws from making any more raids on a grand scale ; from that time onwards they had to be content with comparatively petty freebooting. But that, after the Jerilderie robbery and the offer of £8,000 reward, the outlaws should have continued at liberty for more than a year is, perhaps, the most notable fact in the whole story.

It is clear that they owed their liberty primarily to the money obtained at Euroa and Jerilderie. It is to be remarked that even the notes seized at the latter place were practically available, inasmuch as the numbers of them were quite unknown to the Jerilderie authorities. And the money was well and generously invested. Superintendent Hare found that the countryside was full of " sympathisers "—persons, that is, who had shared or hoped to share in the profits of the bushrangers. It appears very unlikely that, outside the families of Kelly, Hart, and Byrne, there can have been many " sympathisers " of any other kind. But, in return for the stolen goods, the friends of the bushrangers were active to supply them with necessaries and, above all, with intelligence concerning police move-

ments. " It was wonderful," says Mr. Hare, " how all the
trains were watched by Kelly sympathisers." As for the
families of the outlaws, they became more than ever active
in the cause as the danger increased, their zeal being
doubtless stimulated by a large share of the profits. Ned's
sisters, Bridget and Katie, in particular, were constantly to
be seen riding about the hills on errands, the nature of
which was indubitable ; and Joe Byrne's mother was a no
less valuable ally. The two young women spent money
freely, and Katie, says Mr. Hare, " rode a good horse, and
wore lots of jewellery ; the latter, however," he adds,
" disappeared if there was a long interval between the
robberies." And, besides all these interested allies, there
was doubtless a large number of people far too fearful of
possible consequences to venture to give any aid to the
police. On their side, too, the outlaws did what they could
to avoid arousing more hostility than was needful. They
never robbed a poor man or insulted a woman.

The police worked indefatigably. They spent days and
nights camping out in the unfamiliar bush, suffering
tortures from cold, weariness, and hunger. They employed
natives, " black trackers " as they were called, to track the
outlaws through the wilderness. They kept assiduous watch
on the doings of the families of the bushrangers. But they
were heavily handicapped, and the vigilance of their enemies
proved too much for them.

On one occasion the police suffered a repulse, both humili-
ating and painful. This time it was Mrs. Byrne who played
the part of heroine. Superintendent Hare had secured the
services of an old friend of the Kellys, who had been a
partner with them in their horse-stealing days—a strange
being named Aaron Sherrit. Aaron was still in the confidence of the bushrangers when he sold himself to the
police, Mr. Hare promising him the £8,000 reward if the
gang should be caught through his agency. His special
knowledge and the fact that he was a good and hardy
bushman made him a very valuable ally. He was an
oddity, too, of the first-class: a born thief, and candid and
treacherous as a child. " Whatever number of horses I

had," he told Hare, " I could not help stealing my neighbours' ! "

It was Aaron's opinion that, sooner or later, the outlaws
were sure to pay a visit to old Mrs. Byrne at Woolshed.
His plan was simple. The police were to camp out in an
admirably concealed hollow in the bush and wait for the
bushrangers. During the day they were to lie close in their
hiding-place, and each night to creep down close to
the house. The scheme was put into execution, and for
twenty-three days and nights Superintendent Hare and his
men camped out accordingly. Aaron himself spent his
days and nights with the police and his evenings with Mrs.
Byrne and her daughter, to whom he was engaged to be
married. Every day Mrs. Byrne was in the habit of walking
about looking for police tracks ; and she very soon found
them. A whittled stick in her stockyard first caught her
attention; and the same evening she informed Aaron,
positively, that the police were about the place. Aaron
spent the next day in an assiduous mock search for police
tracks, and told Mrs. Byrne in the evening that she had
been mistaken, and there were none. The old lady knew
better, and the only result of Aaron's asseverations was to
draw her shrewd suspicions upon himself.

Honest Aaron was greatly offended by the unreasonable
suspicions of his intended mother-in-law, and he took
characteristic revenge by stealing a horse of hers and
selling it. The theft was traced to him, and Mrs. Byrne
obtained a warrant. When reproached for introducing this
awkward complication, Aaron's reply was sublimely ingenuous. " I could not help it," said he. " I did not want
the horse, but Mrs. Byrne has not behaved well to me
lately ; she has been so cool that I felt I must do something
to her."

On the other hand Mrs. Byrne, who prowled about day
after day in order to make certain of the whereabouts of the
police, at length discovered their hiding-place. In consequence it became palpably useless to remain there any
longer, and the camp was broken up. The police had
suffered severely from cold and exposure, not having once

dared to light a fire the whole twenty-three days. The whole party was more or less knocked up, and Mr. Hare himself was forced to obtain sick leave for a time. It is clear that the police, who did not know the bush and were no hardier than ordinary civilised men, were at a great disadvantage. The four bushrangers seem to have cared nothing for cold and exposure, and to have been able to sleep under any circumstances and for any required length of time. They had only one greatcoat among them, and this afforded them amply sufficient covering at night, while the police were encumbered with the rugs and wraps under which they shivered. The outlaws, according to Aaron Sherrit, slept as he did himself, curled up like a dog, their heads between their knees. Aaron himself could sleep in this wild-beast fashion on the coldest night, with no covering but his ordinary clothes, and he declared himself to be far less hardy than the four outlaws.

After the defeat at Woolshed the police tried the effect of arresting the whole of the near relations of the bush-rangers. About twenty persons were arrested at a swoop, on the charge of aiding and abetting the Kelly gang. But absolutely no positive evidence could be obtained against them. The magistrates did what they could, and kept remanding the prisoners from week to week, till it became absolutely necessary to discharge them. The manœuvre had no other result than to increase the unpopularity under which the police laboured.

It almost seems as if the outlaws might have continued at large for an indefinitely long period had they not run their own necks into the noose. But that they did so resulted from the very nature of the situation in which they were placed. Their safety depended, ultimately, on their power to purchase support, and such purchase was expensive. The proceeds of the robberies at Euroa and Jerilderie became exhausted, and petty thefts were quite insufficient to supply their needs. By June, 1880, the outlaws found themselves under the necessity of attempting another grand *coup*. In face of the vigilance and activity of the police the risk was enormous; but they could not help themselves. "Their sisters," says Mr. Hare, "were in debt everywhere," and probably even their sisters were likely to be seriously influenced by such considerations. Without fresh capital for investment the concern must collapse.

Under pressure of these circumstances the outlaws adopted a scheme more daringly ambitious than any they had yet undertaken. Their objective was the bank at Benalla; but they were well aware that the raid could not be made successfully in the casual fashion of the raid on Jerilderie. It was absolutely necessary, at least, to draw off the police at Benalla in a wrong direction. But they aspired to do more than that. On the line between Benalla and a little place called Beechworth, lay a small station, at Glenrowan. At Beechworth lived Aaron Sherrit, now married, though not to Miss Byrne. Mrs. Byrne had, doubtless, ere this, let the outlaws know her suspicions of Aaron, and it is even probable that she knew more of the matter than the police supposed. If Aaron should be murdered at Beechworth on a Saturday night a party of police would be made up at Benalla and sent by special train to Beechworth as soon as possible. There were no ordinary trains on the Sunday, and the special would not stop at Glenrowan. Meanwhile the outlaws would have taken up the rails at a certain convenient spot just beyond Glenrowan station. The special would be wrecked, and the outlaws near at hand to finish off any chance survivors. Rid of the police they could then ride on the fourteen miles to Benalla and loot the bank there at leisure.

It was an excellent, if desperate, device. Its failure would not necessitate the capture or death of the contrivers. Its success would mean not merely the acquisition of fresh capital, but an immense increase of prestige, a terrible blow to the ardour of the police and revenge on a traitor into the bargain. It was extremely difficult of execution; but, if the worst came and the outlaws had to fight for their lives, they were by no means ill-prepared. Not only were they tolerably well armed; they were armoured also. Each man had by him a complete "suit" of body armour, rudely forged out of old plough-shares, and weighing 97 lbs. The iron plates were a quarter of an inch thick, and, as was proved, would keep out bullets very effectually. When this armour was first adopted by the outlaws is uncertain, but it does not appear that they wore it either at Euroa or Jerilderie. It had probably been made after the latter exploit, and was doubtless the work of some skilled local artisan.

Late in the evening of Saturday, the 26th of June, 1880, Aaron Sherrit was called upon by an acquaintance of his, knocking at his door and asking information about the way to somewhere. Aaron came out to give it, and as soon as he appeared at the open door he was shot dead by Dan Kelly and Byrne, who were in attendance. There were four constables actually in the house at the time. Some hours later, at about half-past two on the Sunday morning, two platelayers at Glenrowan were roused from sleep by Ned Kelly and Hart. They were forced to dress hastily and proceed to the point on the line that had been fixed upon. A mile and a half beyond Glenrowan station, on the way to Beechworth, the line ran down a rather steep incline and then took a sharp curve. On one side of the curve was a deep gully. Ned made the platelayers take up the rails just beyond the incline. From above, the break in the line would be invisible till it was too late, and the train, with its gathered momentum, would be hurled sheer down the gully. Decidedly, when this had happened, there would not be much trouble with survivors.

It was, of course, absolutely necessary to confine the platelayers and the station-master till the smash had taken place. The station-master, his wife and family, with the platelayers, were locked up most of the Sunday in the railway official's own house under guard of Steve Hart; but Glenrowan itself was fixed on as the headquarters. Early on the Sunday morning the outlaws arrived at Jones's Hotel, Glenrowan. They took possession, and selected a large room as a temporary lock-up, thrusting into it at once all persons found in the hotel. Then they quietly awaited the arrival of the doomed special, making prisoners meanwhile of as many people as they caught about the hotel, and bringing over the station-master and platelayers in the course of the day. By nightfall there were no less than sixty-two persons under guard in the hotel; but it is clear that many of these were of the sympathetic class. Among them was the solitary Glenrowan policeman, an efficient officer named Bracken, who had been lured out of the police-station and marched off to the hotel under the usual threats.

Ned made no secret of the horrible catastrophe he was waiting for. On the contrary, he was frankly jubilant; forcibly, if not elegantly, remarking that he meant to "fill all the ruts round with the fat carcases of the —— police." In spite of his candour the great majority of the prisoners kept up their spirits wonderfully. They had long to wait: the special train did not leave Melbourne till 10.15 on Sunday night. In the evening the bushrangers and, apparently, some of the prisoners commenced dancing to while away the time. But there were some, at least, among the prisoners who did their duty. Among these was a Mr. Thomas Curnon, the Glenrowan schoolmaster, whose name ought always to be honourably mentioned in connection with this affair. He, with his wife and sister, had been stopped as they drove home past the hotel and imprisoned with the rest. Forcible escape was out of the question. All Mr. Curnon could do was to endeavour, in the first place, to gain the confidence of the outlaws. He loudly professed his sympathy with them and his hatred of the police; he assured Ned that he was with him heart and soul, and flattered and fooled the desperado to the top of his bent. Ned became quite genial. This result obtained, Mr. Curnon insinuated that it would be only charitable to allow him to take his wife, who was ill, home. There was some demur, but eventually Ned foolishly consented to allow it. Mr. Curnon, with his wife and sister, were allowed to go home under the escort of a member of the gang. On their arrival they were told that if one of them dared to leave the house all three would be killed; and, with this warning, their guard left them, remarking further, however, that he would return in half an hour to see that they were all safe. But Mr. Curnon was not to be deterred either by these threats or by the terror and entreaties of his wife, whom he left fainting.

The police special was late; and it was lucky that it was so, for had it not been nothing could have prevented the disaster. As it was Mr. Curnon, driving along the line towards Benalla, was only just in time. When the pilot engine, which preceded the police train, arrived within a mile of Glenrowan station a breathless man was standing on the line in front, desperately holding up a red scarf before a lighted candle. The pilot stopped. The man in front shouted hurriedly that the rails were torn up beyond Glenrowan and the bushrangers in possession of the place. Then he fled, without waiting to give details, crying that his wife and children would be murdered if he were not back in time. He had saved the train. Superintendent Hare expressly states that under the circumstances the pilot engine would have been useless.

Meanwhile, at the hotel where the dancing was going on, Constable Bracken had, also, been doing his duty as he best could. He, of course, was far too suspect a person to hope to obtain release by a pretence of sympathy. But the carelessness of Dan Kelly gave him a chance. When the dancing began, Dan, who had the front door key, found it cumbersome and casually laid it on the mantelpiece. Bracken, dancing with the rest, took opportunity as he waltzed or polka'd past the mantelpiece to whip off the key, turned up his trousers and thrust it into the fold. He was too closely watched, however, to be able to escape at once, and it was not till the police train was heard to stop—the hotel being quite close to the line—that his chance came. As soon as the train was heard approaching the outlaws had proceeded to don their armour. Already Steve Hart had been sent to the station with the station-master, who was to be forced to signal the line clear. When the train was heard to stop intense excitement and much confusion naturally prevailed in the hotel. Bracken slipped away, reached the front door unnoticed, let himself out, and ran for the station. He was the only man on the platform, which was in total darkness, when the train moved slowly in.

Guided by him the police forthwith set out for the hotel—only one hundred yards off. It was about three o'clock on the Monday morning.

It must have been a trying moment for the bushrangers when they heard the train stop. The game had become desperate and their own capture far from improbable. Probably the best they could have done would have been to take horse at once for the bush. But in that case the "black trackers," who accompanied the police, would have had a hot scent, and it is certainly doubtful if they could have escaped. Even if they had done so, their position would then have been worse than ever, inasmuch as the police would now be more than ever wary. They came to the fatal decision to stand their ground in the hotel. They must, as Superintendent Hare thinks, have calculated on killing every one of the policemen before fresh forces could arrive, for to attempt to stand a siege without such a hope would have been mere insanity.

Superintendent Hare seems to have had considerable difficulty in getting together the party of police and "black trackers" with which he had set out from Benalla, since it was past midnight when his special train reached Glenrowan. He has unfortunately omitted to give the numerical strength of his party, but it is clear that the bushrangers were heavily outnumbered.

Jones's Hotel was a long, low, wooden building with a verandah running the whole length of the front. All lights had been put out inside when the police arrived. Behind the hotel the moon shone brilliantly, throwing the advancing police into full light and the hotel front into deep shadow. From the darkness of the verandah they were fired on as they approached; and a voice, supposed to be Ned's, shouted: "Fire away, you (language) beggars; you can do us no harm." For a quarter of an hour the firing was hotly kept up, and a fearful shrieking arose from the crowd of unlucky captives within. Then the outlaws retreated into the house.

The police now surrounded the hotel. Telegrams were sent in all directions asking for reinforcements, and Constable Bracken, having caught a horse, rode off to Wangaratta, seven miles distant, to bring men from there. Superintendent Hare had been wounded in the first volleying, and, after making a gallant attempt to continue on the scene of action, was forced to return, fainting, to the station, and thence to Benalla. At intervals thoughout the anxious night the police fired into the hotel, shouting to the captives to lie down or come out. Come out they would not, for fear of being shot. During the night nine fresh policemen arrived on an engine from Benalla, and eight more came in from Wangaratta. Before the dawn came the position of the outlaws was hopeless. "I have no hesitation in saying," writes Superintendent Hare, "that, had the men been without armour when we first attacked the hotel, and could have taken proper aim, not one of us would have escaped being shot. They were obliged to hold the rifle at arm's length to get anything of a sight." This necessity seems to have arisen from the fact that each man, when in full armour, wore a great head-piece—a sort of iron pot coming down on to the chest and back, so as to completely cover the throat. In this rude and monstrous style of helmet it must have been almost impossible for them to move their heads at all. But, if this were really the case, the fact argues considerable folly and a somewhat astonishing indisposition to risk their lives on the part of the outlaws. Granting that, in their armour, they were almost safe under fire, they ought to have known that, nevertheless, death or capture was certain unless they could disable their besiegers within the first few hours.

Early on the Monday morning, at about eight o'clock, a tall figure suddenly appeared in the rear of the police line. The police seem to have taken it for one of the black trackers, and held their fire. Suddenly the stranger drew a revolver and fired at one of them. It was Ned Kelly, with a long grey overcoat over his armour. Nine policemen closed in upon him, and a strange fight began. The soft Martini-Henry bullets dinted his armour but did not penetrate. Each time he was struck he staggered but instantly recovered himself "and tapped his breast, laughing derisively," and coolly returning the fire. "It appeared as if he were a fiend with a charmed life." For half an hour this strange combat lasted; then Sergeant Steele rushed in and shot Ned in the leg, bringing him down, then sprang on him and caught the hand that held his revolver. "He roared," we are told, "with savage ferocity," as he lay struggling on the ground, pouring out curses. He had two bullet wounds in his left arm, one in his right leg, and one in his right foot. The police managed to get his armour off, and he at once became quiet. He was taken from the scene of action, a prisoner at last. It seems certain that Ned had contrived to leave the hotel, and had spent the night outside in the skirts of the bush. The marks of his feet were found under a fallen tree, together with a quantity of blood, and, not far off, was found a rifle with more blood near it. It appears that, after the first brush at the hotel front, Ned had suggested that he and Byrne should slip out and make an attack on the police from the rear which the other two should second. But Byrne had refused to follow him, and he had gone alone. Why he came back is not so clear. But if, as is probable, he had been badly hurt before he got clear it must have seemed to him impossible to escape alone through the bush, and he made his attack, trusting to a sally from within and to his armour. But there was no such sally. Byrne had been shot dead at about 5.30 that morning while drinking in the bar, and Hart and Dan, deprived of their leaders, were cowed and helpless.

The siege continued. To rush the place would have entailed a quite unnecessary loss of life. The outlaws had hardly a chance of escape. The women and children prisoners in the hotel came out at daybreak, and, at about ten o'clock, the rest of the prisoners rushed out in a body, terrified out of their wits. Some ran frantically about, screaming to the police for mercy. Others flung themselves down on their faces in their agony of fear. Their exeunt was dramatically appropriate to the parts they had most of them played.

All the morning, reinforcements of police were arriving on

the scene, but the outlaws made no sign of surrender. After one o'clock they ceased to return the fire of the police, but still kept sullenly at bay. It was presumed that they were waiting for nightfall to make a desperate attempt to force their way out.

Their besiegers grew anxious and impatient. The difficulty with which Ned had been forced to succumb to enormous odds gave good grounds for fear. Various rather queer suggestions were made. A telegram was sent to Melbourne asking for a field-gun. "We must get gun before night or rush the place." An ingenious Queensland official, with reminiscences perhaps of the Roman "tortoise," telegraphed a suggestion that a dray should be furnished with a large wooden bullet-proof shield, behind which a body of men might reach the hotel walls in safety. Another ingenious person advised the adoption of the electric light. Finally it was settled that, when evening came, bonfires should be lighted all round the hotel. This plan, however, was abandoned before the afternoon closed. The field-gun did not arrive, and the police decided to fire the hotel. One objection to this plan was the fact that there was still in the hotel an unfortunate old man, who had been wounded during the firing and had been unable to escape with the rest of the outlaws' prisoners. The plan was persisted in, nevertheless. While the preparations went forward Bridget Skillian rode up smartly attired. She was appealed to to enter the hotel and beg the two remaining outlaws to surrender. She replied that she would rather see them burned. The firing of the hotel was accomplished without any resistance being met with, and the outlaws did not come forth. Father Gibney, a priest, and some of the police rushed into the rapidly burning house and succeeded in rescuing the unlucky old man still within, who, however, died of his wounds afterwards. It is uncertain whether he had been shot by the police or by Dan Kelly. A glimpse was caught of Dan and Hart lying on the floor of one of the rooms, but it was impossible to reach them. There can be little doubt that they had shot themselves. They died at bay, and worthily after their fashion; and they had a worthy burial. Their bodies were taken to the Skillians' place at Seven Mile Creek, and an uproarious wake held over them by friends and relatives of the families. Seven Mile Creek would have been an unsafe place to visit that day. "Kelly sympathisers," it is reported, "who had made themselves drunk at the wake, were bouncing about, armed and threatening to attack the police." One man solemnly and drunkenly swore to avenge the death of the outlaws, but nothing came of it.

Ned only remained; and, it must be confessed that, shorn of his armour wherein he had trusted too much, Ned afforded a sorry spectacle. His condemnation was, of course, as certain as well-deserved. In his prison at Melbourne his mother had an interview with him, and exhorted him to "die like a Kelly." Whether he died "like a Kelly" or not, he certainly died miserably, so broken down with terror that he had to be supported to the gallows. The coroner stated that he had never seen a man show so little pluck under the circumstances. But it is one thing, after all, to die fighting, and another to face the gallows in cold blood. To the end he persisted, as far as his courage went, in the part of the heroic outlaw. This is the best that can be said of his last moments. He asserted that he had only been captured at Glenrowan through an heroic refusal to leave his comrades in the lurch. "If I liked," he declared, "I could have got away. I had a good chance, but I wanted to see the thing end. Perhaps I would have done better if I had cleared away with my grey mare." It is conceivable that this version of the story was true—that Ned returned simply to "see the thing end," and aid his comrades. It is far more probable that he returned because he could not have got away alone.

Thus wretchedly ended the career of the last of the bushrangers; and with what shall we dismiss him? Certainly he has no claim to rank among heroic brigands. Perhaps, after all, his best epitaph was furnished, in act, by his own family. On the evening of the very day of Ned's execution his sister Kate and his brother Jim—the latter known merely as a horse-stealer—appeared on the boards of a Melbourne music-hall. For an entrance fee of one shilling the pair exhibited themselves to an admiring public. Kate held a bouquet of flowers, and bowed and smiled in the approved fashion. Thus were Ned's manes propitiated, not inappropriately.

APPENDIX OF AUTHORITIES.

A.—NOTE ON BOTHWELL.

Of the hundred best books on Bothwell we may mention but a few. First, of course, his own memoir, "Les Affaires du Conte de Boduel," printed by the Bannatyne Club in 1829, by Labanoff in 1856, and by Teulet in 1859. It is at best a studied lie ; but, when its perversions have been corrected and its omissions filled in from the "Register of the Privy Council of Scotland" and all the other handsome Treasury tomes which are at the elbow of every serious student of History, its psychological value is fully established. Facts we can get in these fat books, nay a few in the partisan historians of Mary's Scotland, contemporary and modern (See *Scotland*, British Museum Catalogue), but we cannot get such a direct glimpse of the wicked Hepburn as in his own narrative from Malmoe. Of modern monographs the largest and best is by Professor Schiern, accessible in English since 1880, which is especially valuable for the Danish episodes of the Life. At St. Petersburg in 1873 Dr. Petrick published a volume on the never-ending topic of the Casket Letters, and in 1874 a book devoted to Bothwell, entitled "Zur Geschichte des Grafen Bothwell." See also Wiesener's "Marie Stuart et Bothwell," and, if variety be a care, the books of the American, J. Watts de Peyster. The latter's "Vindication of James Hepburn, 4th Earl of Bothwell, 3rd husband of Mary, Queen of Scots" (Philadelphia, 1882), and "An Inquiry into the Career and Character of Mary Stuart ('Crux Criticorum') and a justification of Bothwell ('audire est operæ pretium ')," (New York, 1883), are fantastic attempts to prove our dear villain little better than an angel ; but the volumes will prove of more value to an American biographical dictionary than to the seeker after Bothwell. In contrast with this high-falutin stands the accurate digest of facts in the "Dictionary of National Biography."

For other works, of a poetic or romantic character, but "founded on fact," there are the poor verses of Aytoun, Swinburne's long but powerful twin drama to "Chastelard," and those passages of Byron's "Corsair" which had their inspiration from the story of the Scottish freebooter. And once upon a time James Grant wrote a Bothwellian romance, which must have delighted those boys who encountered it during their Sunday reading.

No portrait is extant. In 1858 some antiquaries opened the traditional coffin of Bothwell in Faareveile Church; but Professor Schiern, with some show of common sense, refuses to believe that the grave-worn face on which they gazed was that of the Earl. A photograph of this head is preserved in the National Museum of Antiquities, Edinburgh. Perhaps some day in some dirty packet of broad-sheets may be found one of those placards, with the portrait in rough, which raised the hue and cry for the "murtherer of the King."

B.—NOTE ON SIR EDWARD KELLEY.

The materials for a biography of Sir Edward Kelley are for the most part meagre or mythical; authentic information is meagre, and more detailed accounts are mythical. There are, however, a few exceptions to this rule, and first among them comes "A True and Faithfull Relation of what passed between Dr. Dee and some Spirits," a solid folio published in 1659, with an introduction by Meric Casaubon, son of the famous scholar; it is one of the most curious and diverting books in the language, and the first edition was bought up with unexampled rapidity; a selection from it was published a few years back in the *Journal of the Psychical Research Society*. Next comes Dee's private Diary printed by the Camden Society, and no less important are the letters and reports from various persons residing in Germany and others, containing an account of Kelley's plot against Parkins, his dealings with Rudolf and Burleigh, and his last days in Bohemia; these are printed in Strype's Works but have been hitherto unaccountably neglected by Kelley's biographers. Occasional references to Kelley occur in the State Papers, Spedding's "Bacon," Lilly's "Autobiography," and Pierce's "Supererogation." This practically exhausts contemporary authorities, but the next century produced more or less trustworthy accounts in Wood's "Athenæ Oxonienses," Ashmole's "Theatrum Chemicum," Weever's "Funeral Monuments," Dr. Thomas Smith's "Vitæ Quorundam," and various MSS. in the British Museum, *e.g.*, Sloane 3645, Harleian 6485, and others in the Cotton and Lansdowne Collections. Of modern accounts the best is in Dr. Wright's "Narratives of Sorcery and Magic," (pp. 226-253); others are contained in Godwin's "Lives of the

Necromancers," Mackay's "Memoirs of Popular Delusions," Davenport Adams's "Witch, Warlock, and Magician," Cooke Taylor's "Romantic Biography," Lenglet du Fresnoy's "Histoire de la Philosophie Hermetique," Niceron's "Memoires," and Waite's "Alchemical Philosophers": the last author has also published a translation of Kelley's works with a biographical introduction. More fragmentary notices will be found in Baines's "Lancashire," Hibbert and Ware's "Manchester," Chambers's "Worcestershire Worthies," Green's "Worcester," Nash's "Worcester," Cooper's "Athenæ Cantabrigienses," and last, but not least, concise biographies of Dee, Kelley, and others connected with them, are given in the "Dictionary of National Biography."

Kelley's career probably suggested the idea of Ben Jonson's "Alchemist," and certainly inspired many passages in that play. More recently Harrison Ainsworth by a "poetic license" of anachronism has made Kelley a prominent actor in his "Guy Fawkes." References to Dee and Kelley abound in books of, and on, Elizabeth's reign, when opinions about him were as various as they are now.

C.—NOTE ON MATTHEW HOPKINS.

In addition to the contemporary accounts of the witch trials between 1645 and 1647, several of which have been quoted in footnotes, the chief authorities for Hopkins are the pamphlets of the Witch-finder himself and his confederate Stern, and Gaule's "Select Cases of Conscience touching Witchcraft," all of which are alluded to in the text. The remaining sources are those for the study of witchcraft generally, during the seventeenth century, and in England. Among these may be specified—Glanvil's "Sadducismus Triumphatus," Richard Baxter's "Certainty of the Worlds of Spirits, fully evinced by unquestionable Histories of Apparitions and Witchcrafts . . . written for the conviction of Sadduces and Infidels," Francis Hutchinson's "Historical Essay concerning Witchcraft," Lecky's "History of Rationalism," Thomas Wright's "Narratives of Sorcery and Magic," Scott's "Letters on Demonology and Witchcraft," Mackay's "History of Popular Delusions," Davenport Adams's "Witch, Warlock, and Magician," Maury's "La Magie et l'Astrologie," and some scattered notes in Buckle's Posthumous Works. A good brief notice of Hopkins is supplied by the "Dictionary of National Biography." Another appears in Gifford's edition of Ford —his "Witch of Edmonton." A well-supported Note on Witchcraft in volume i. of "Phantasms of the Living" demonstrates the total absence of respectable evidence for all those alleged phenomena of witchcraft which cannot be accounted for as the results of diseased imagination, hysteria, hypnotism, and possibly of telepathy.

D.—NOTE ON JUDGE JEFFREYS.

The authorities for the life of Jeffreys correspond very nearly with those that are cited in Appendix *E*, in connection with the Judge's illustrious congener, Titus Oates. In addition to these must be mentioned Woolrych's "Memoirs of the Life of Judge Jeffreys," 1827, the Lives in Campbell's "Lord Chancellors," and Fosse's "Judges of England," and a number of contemporary Lives and accounts of Jeffreys' death, which have been largely utilised by Macaulay. The excellent memoir by Mr. G. F. R. Barker in the "Dictionary of National Biography," contains much that is supplementary to the more elaborate Lives in a very small space. "The Western Martyrology," Dr. Jessop's "Lives of the Norths," Sir John Bramston's "Autobiography," Inderwick's "Side Lights on the Stuarts," Mr. Ewald's "Studies Restudied," and "Magdalen College and James II.," published by the Oxford Historical Society, have also been freely consulted.

E.—NOTE ON TITUS OATES.

Of the four historical characters who figure in these memoirs, Oates alone has hitherto been spared the misfortune of meeting with a biographer. The facts of his earlier and later career are only to be found scattered hither and thither among contemporary records, and certain portions of his life will probably always remain shrouded in partial obscurity. Enough, at any rate, is known of his life to certify the inference that, at any given moment of his life, Titus, if not engaged in nameless abominations, was up to his eyes in mischief. For Oates's early history, Isaac Milles's Life, Wilson's "Memorabilia Cantabrigiana," Mayor's St. John's College Register, Wood's "Life and Times," and certain collectanea in the sixth series of *Notes and Queries* and in the *Gentleman's Magazine* for 1849 have proved of special value. For the central portion of his life there is certainly no lack of materials, the State Trials being supplemented by Roger North's "Examen," and the histories of Eachard, Ralph, and Rapin. The same period is illustrated by numberless pamphlets by Oates and his crew on one side and Sir Roger l'Estrange and his appren-

tices on the other. The "Western Martyrology," of which the best
edition is that of 1705, contains an account of the flogging and also
an eulogy of Oates's learning, generosity and services to the Protestant
religion. The House of Lords' MSS. now being published by the
Historical MSS. Commission, throw considerable light on the proceedings in regard to the reversal of his sentence, while scattered notes
in Evelyn's Diary, Reresby's Memoirs, Dryden's Works, Burnet's
"History of his own Time," "The Lives of the Norths," and
Tuke's Memoirs contribute information which is often of considerable value. Among more recent writers certain of the more salient
features in Oates's career are touched upon by Macaulay in his most
vivacious manner. A valuable "Selection from the State Trials"
has recently been published by Mr. Willis Bund, and the outlines of
the plot have been briefly and well narrated in an article by Mr. R.
K. Douglas in *Blackwood's Magazine* (February, 1889). The most
valuable authority for the whole of Oates's career is probably the
series of newspaper and other jottings supplied in Luttrell's "Brief
Historical Relation of State Affairs." For some particulars the
histories of Ranke and Klopp ("Der Fall des Hauses Stuart"),
and Groen Van Prinsterer's "Archives de la Maison d'Orange
Nassau" must be consulted, while side-lights of widely varying
interest and value are thrown by the "Lives" of Calamy and
Baxter, Aubrey's "Lives," the autobiography of Sir John Bramston,
the Hatton Correspondence, Sidney's Diary, Tom Brown's Works,
Ackerman's "Moneys Received and Paid for Secret Services
under Charles II. and James II." The Roxburghe Ballads, the
Bagford Ballads, the Luttrell Collection of Ballads and Broadsides, Lemon's Catalogue of Broadsides, and Stephens's invaluable Catalogue of Satirical Prints and Drawings in the British
Museum, the medallic histories of Pinkerton and Grueber, Stough-
ton's "History of Religion in England," Pike's "History of
Crime," and Lord Campbell's "Lord Chancellors," have all proved
useful in their several departments. Crosby's "History of the
Baptists" supplies some information respecting the closing years
of Oates's career, but for this portion, and indeed for the whole
of his life, the chief source of authority is naturally the enormous
mass of pamphlet literature which is to be found catalogued according
to Panizzi's "91 rules" in the British Museum Catalogue (under O., T. :
Oates Titus : popish plot : plot, popish : History : L'Estrange, Roger,
and many other headings), but which cannot be fully enumerated
here. Many of the most valuable are to be found in the two collections of "Somers' Tracts," and in the "Harleian Miscellany." The
Catholic view of certain phases of the "Conjuratio Oatiana" is fairly

put forth in the "Florus Anglo-Bavaricus," in Challoner's "Memoirs of Missionary Priests," in various articles in Gillow's Catholic Dictionary, and Foley's "Records of the English Province of the Society of Jesus," and, last but not least, in Lingard's "History of England."

It is perhaps worth noting here, that ridiculous (apart from its tragic consequences) as is Oates's so-called "plot" from its palpable improbabilities and inconsistencies, its association with the then Pope, Innocent XI., is equally grotesque on account of its singular ineptitude. Benedetto Odescalchi, who became Pope as Innocent XI., was born at Como in 1611. He had entered Rome in his twenty-fifth year, provided only with his sword and pistols, with a view of entering some secular office or the military service. By the advice of a cardinal he was induced to enter into the employment of the Court, and conducted himself with such ability and rectitude that he became popular among all classes, and was after a time created cardinal. During the sitting of the conclave on the death of Clement X., the people shouted his name within the hearing of the cardinals, and when his election become known the feeling of satisfaction was general. He aimed at a reduction of the pomp and luxury of the Court, and the suppression of abuses; he was also free from the failing of nepotism, which had led to so many evils, his own nephew living at Rome during his pontificate in a private condition. But his austerity, and his dislike of the Jesuits, then very powerful, made him many enemies. The chief events of his reign were the grave quarrel with Louis XIV. about the asyla in precincts in Rome —his cold reception of Castlemaine, envoy of James II., whose extreme courses the Pope strongly deprecated, as being certain in the end to militate against the true interests of Catholicism in this country—and the great affair of the Gallican articles of 1682, in which Bossuet took part against the Pope. Macaulay speaks of Innocent as a "pontiff of primitive austerity." His pontificate covered the whole period of the "*Popish* plot."

For this concise account of Innocent XI., and also for a most careful revision of the memoir on Oates, the writer is indebted to J. T. Seccombe, Esq., M.D.

F.—NOTE ON LORD LOVAT.

Among many scattered notices and documents of value the most important authorities for the life of Simon Fraser are four. The place of honour may be assigned to his own autobiography—a work that must be used cautiously, since comparatively few of the statements in it are wholly true. But though difficult of interpretation and often of no evidential value as to events, it is essential for the understanding of the man. As a really remarkable piece of lying it is almost comparable in ingenuity of suppression, exaggeration, and half-truths to the memoirs of Retz himself. Nor is it always wholly untrustworthy as a narrative; thus the narrative of the events of 1714–15 may be taken as substantially accurate.

In the Culloden Papers we have Simon's correspondence during 1745. Here his mendacity is seen at its best, and these letters are essential to the understanding of the part he played that year.

In Vol. xviii. of the "State Trials" we have the important depositions made at the trial, and an interesting glimpse of Simon at bay. The speeches of the lawyers throw little light on the matter. Appended is contemporary gossip concerning Simon's behaviour in the last hours: tolerably trustworthy.

Fourthly is "Major Fraser's Manuscript," of which quaint work there is a recent edition by Lieutenant-Colonel Fergusson. The Major is a shrewd and trustworthy man, now and then, perhaps, misled by vanity. His evidence is specially important on the events between the departure from Saumur and the triumphal installation in Stratheric.

Apart from these authorities there is much scattered evidence. All Simon's letters are valuable, and many are partly or wholly given in Burton's "Life." Some very curious information respecting the rape and other matters may be found in vol. xii. of the "Somers' Tracts," and in King's "Munimenta Antiqua." A fairly full list of references is appended to the very accurate article in the "Dictionary of National Biography." The contemporary "Lives," three of them dating 1746–7, are worthless, being written with much animus and little knowledge.

Of modern work far the most important is Dr. T. Hill Burton's "Life"—the result of careful industry. Dr. Burton, if he has not entered very fully into Simon's mind, has collated the evidence with much accuracy and judgment. A good essay on Simon's career appeared in the *Scottish Review* for January, 1893. Of other modern works none is worth mention. Mrs. Thomson in "Memoirs of the Jacobites" fails to rise to the subject, and is not accurate.

G.—NOTE ON COLONEL CHARTERIS.

Materials for the life of Charteris are to be found broadcast by such as care to search for them, while for others there is a plenty of monographs with the Colonel as subject, which were widely published about the times of his last trial. The aim of the compilers of the last-named works would seem to have been to offer "spicy" reading, and small attention was paid by them to fact, or even probability, if an opportunity presented itself of applying some old story with a dirty fellow as its hero to the subject in hand. Less care was given to style, and these productions are long-winded; but they afford valuable material. Among them may be named "Some Authentic Memoirs of the Life of Colonel Ch——s, Rapemaster-General of Great Britain," 1730; "Scotch Gallantry Displayed, or the Life and Adventures of Colonel Fr—nc—s Ch—rt—s," 1730; "Life of Colonel Don Francisco" (n.d.); "History of Col. Francis Ch—rtr—s." Besides such fugitive works as those mentioned there are numerous histories which could not well pass over the name of Charteris. Most of these are concerned only with his command at Preston, the story of which is set out at length in Patten's "History of the Rebellion," 1715, and side-lights on which as well on other of his appearances before the world are thrown by some of the Chetham Society's publications; and in the same connection may be mentioned Rapin's "History of England." Burton, in his "Life of Duncan Forbes," is the chief trustworthy authority for Charteris's last moments, while for his trial and the incidents which followed it there is almost a superabundance of matter to be found in the newspapers of the day, and such faithful registers of events as the "Political State of Great Britain" and "Angliæ Notitia." The British Museum owns a number of pamphlets and leaflets relating to the cashiering of the Colonel, and Douglas's "Peerage of Scotland" is supreme in genealogical information. Pope and Swift make frequent use of Charteris's name as a type of most forms of immorality, and the industrious editors of these authors have not failed to give brief notices of him in their notes. Walpole in one of his letters relates that he once, when a small boy, saw Charteris himself. The *Gentleman's Magazine* would scarcely be complete if it did not contain his name, and no doubt some interesting second-hand information might be produced by a diligent search in the back volumes of *Notes and Queries*.

H.—NOTE ON JONATHAN WILD.

The scarcity of trustworthy information on the career of Jonathan Wild is touched upon at the commencement of the foregoing biography. Little reliance can be placed in the details with which the popular histories of Wild abound. The best of them are, perhaps, " The Life of Jonathan Wild," by H. D., 1725; "An Authentic History of the Parentage, Birth, Education, Marriages, Issue and Practices of the famous Jonathan Wild" (would that this comprehensive title were a true one!); Hitchin's "Regulator," and Wild's reply are useful for the insight they give into thieves' and tavern life in London, and many solid facts may be gleaned from the newspapers. The account of Wild published by the Ordinary of Newgate is meagre and unconvincing, and the hero's Dying Speech and Confession are more than probably unauthentic. The best and most truthful accounts of Wild are to be found in some of the Newgate Calendars, the most satisfactory in this respect being Jackson's, which has been drawn on largely by the present writer. Incidental references of more or less interest are in Thornbury's "London"; the "Chronicles of Newgate"; and various MS. records preserved at the Record Office, the Guildhall, and elsewhere. Fielding's "History of Jonathan the Wild, the Great," is, with the exception of the account of his last days, purely imaginary, and the admixture of fact to fiction in Ainsworth's "Jack Sheppard" is scarcely sufficient to satisfy a pedant's canons. Wild has not infrequently done duty in the British Drama, but of later years he has found a more congenial home on the burlesque stage than on the legitimate boards. His character was one to which no form of literature could easily do justice.

I.—NOTE ON JAMES MACLAINE.

The chief sources for the history of James Maclaine are—" An Account of the Behaviour of Mr. James Maclaine, From the Time of his Condemnation to the Day of his Execution . . . By the Reverend Dr. Allen . . . London: 1750," "A Complete History of James Maclean, The Gentleman Highwayman . . .", " The Ordinary of Newgate's Account of the Behaviour . . . Of the Twelve Malefactors who were Executed at Tyburn on Wednesday the 3rd of October, 1750," "The Proceedings on the King's Commission of the Peace . . . for the City of London . . . held at the Justice Hall in the Old Bailey on Wednesday the 12th, &c., of September . . . 1750," "A Letter to the Honourable House of Commons . . . To which is added an Address occasioned by the Execution of Mr. James Maclaine, &c." Of more general sources of authority the most worthy of notice are Cunningham's edition of Walpole's Correspondence, Nichols's "Literary Anecdotes," ii. 452, Wheatley and Cunningham's "London Past and Present," and Caulfield's

"Remarkable Characters," iv. 87. Among numerous accounts in contemporary newspapers the least unsatisfactory are to be found in *The World*, No. 3, for the 19th of December, 1754, the *Whitehall Evening Post*, *General Advertiser*, and *London Evening Post*.

J.—NOTE ON "FIGHTING FITZGERALD."

The compiler of the articles on George Robert Fitzgerald in the *Dublin University Magazine*, whose account, although chiefly founded n Fitzgerald's own " Appeal to the Public," is discriminating and ess favourable to him than the anonymous " Memoirs of George Robert Fitzgerald." The author of " The Case of G. R. Fitzgerald impartially considered, and his Character and Conduct Vindicated," calls himself " an uninterested spectator,' but is manifestly a strong political, if not personal partisan, and we agree with the *Gentleman's Magazine* in thinking the vindication scarcely complete. He was a friend of Brecknock, whose account he accepts as veracious, and was probably a bookseller named Bingley.

Sir Jonah Barrington, pre-eminent among Irish romancers, seems for once, in the case of Fitzgerald, to have lost faith in himself as a faithful biographer, and lest he " might mistake and be called a ' bouncer' " actually has recourse to his friend Martin " to give me a circumstantial detail." He considers this statement as so perspicuous and fair as almost to amount to " perfect impartiality." He does not name the other friend from whom he had learned " a few facts "; and declines himself to become Fitzgerald's " general biographer," adding " in truth, he has never, to my knowledge, had any true one."

From his tone here an inexperienced reader might be led to view Sir Jonah himself in the light of a critical biographer, a kind of model editor of a " Dictionary of Irish Biography." Mr. Sylvanus Urban appears to have had a special correspondent at Castlebar who wrote for him " an authentic account of one of the most shocking murders ever committed," and also of the trial of the murderers. The *Gentleman's Magazine* for June, 1786, also in its Review and Catalogue of New Publications mentions " the Case " in order to say that " THIS is the original, whence a compilation under the title of ' Authentic Memoirs,' hath been very unhandsomely compiled." A short review appears in the next number. It is hostile in tone, but has appended to it a note saying that accounts recently received from Castlebar had created some suspicion that the prosecution of the criminals had been rather too precipitate.

K.—NOTE ON THOMAS GRIFFITHS WAINEWRIGHT.

The biographer of Wainewright is not overwhelmed by the mass of materials that has to be consulted. Mr. W. Carew Hazlitt, when editing the collected "Essays and Criticisms," focussed to a point most of the scattered references in contemporary Letters and Diaries, and supplemented the result with a good deal of carefully compiled fresh matter. Previous short accounts are given by Mr. Thornbury in his "Old Stories Retold," and by Sir T. N. Talfourd in his "Memoirs of Charles Lamb." B. W. Procter throws some curious side-lights on the picture; and the student of *Notes and Queries* will find most of the known details about the Tasmanian portion of Wainewright's career. Mr. Oscar Wilde has contributed an Artistic Appreciation to vol. xlv. of *The Fortnightly Review*; and there does not appear to be anything else worthy of particular mention.

Wainewright's life has inspired some well-known fiction. In Lytton's "Lucretia" he appears as Varney, while Lucretia Clavering is supposed to be Mrs. Wainewright. Dickens founded his unsatisfactory and melodramatic novelette, "Hunted Down," on the same subject.

L.—NOTE ON "NED" KELLY.

Practically the whole of our information concerning the career of the Kelly brothers is derived from the book of Mr. F. A. Hare, Superintendent in the Victorian police, entitled "The Last of the Bushrangers," and from the files of *The Melbourne Argus*. Mr. Hare's book is an unvarnished and praiseworthy tale written by the man who, perhaps, knew more than any one else of the matter, and without it our knowledge would be very incomplete. He records his personal experience as one of the heroes of the story. In the columns of *The Melbourne Argus* for February, 1879, and June and July, 1880, we have not only reports by special correspondents but also statements by actual actors or sufferers in the events, as by Mr. Scott of Euroa, Mr. Tarleton of Jerilderie, Constable Bracken of Glenrowan, and others.

We have been unable to obtain files of other Australian papers than *The Melbourne Argus* for the required dates, but it is unlikely that any other would contain first-hand information.

A little book entitled "History of the Kelly Gang of Bushrangers," by D. Kinnear, published at Melbourne in 1880, appears to be compiled from gossip, and, so far as it contains any information not contained in *The Melbourne Argus* or in Mr. Hare's book, is quite untrustworthy.

A very brief notice of the Kellys occurs in Mr. J. Henniker-Heaton's " Australian Dictionary of Dates," and a more adequate sketch in the " Dictionary of National Biography."

INDEX.

The Gresham Press,
UNWIN BROTHERS,
CHILWORTH AND LONDON.

www.ingramcontent.com/pod-product-compliance
Lightning Source LLC
Chambersburg PA
CBHW030956110726
47900CB00004B/1292